HELP! MY WIZARD MENTOR HAD A HEART ATTACK AND NOW I'M BEING CHASED BY A HORDE OF GIANT SPIDERS!

A LITRPG ADVENTURE FANTASY

AARON HODGES

Edited by Genevieve Lerner
Proofread by Sara Houston
Cover illustration by Eva Urbanikova
Typography by Nikko Marie

ABOUT THE AUTHOR

Aaron Hodges was born in 1989 in the small town of Whakatane, New Zealand. He studied for five years at the University of Auckland, completing a Bachelors of Science in Biology and Geography, and a Masters of Environmental Engineering. After working as an environmental consultant for two years, he grew tired of office work and decided to quit his job in 2014 and see the world. One year later, he published his first novel - Stormwielder.

FOLLOW AARON HODGES...

And receive TWO FREE novels and a short story!

https://aaronhodgesauthor.com/newsletter

ALSO BY AARON HODGES

The Sword of Light

Book 1: Stormwielder

Book 2: Firestorm

Book 3: Soul Blade

The Legend of the Gods

Book 1: Oathbreaker

Book 2: Shield of Winter

Book 3: Dawn of War

The Knights of Alana

Book 1: Daughter of Fate

Book 2: Queen of Vengeance

Book 3: Crown of Chaos

The Evolution Gene

Book 1: Reborn

Book 2: Havoc

Book 3: Carnage

Descendants of the Fall

Book 1: Warbringer

Book 2: Wrath of the Forgotten

Book 3: Age of Gods

Book 4: Dreams of Fury

The Alfurian Chronicles

Book 1: Defiant

Book 2: Guardian

Book 3: Conquest

**The Swords of Heaven and Hell**

Book 1: Darkstrider

**The Four Circles**

Book 1: Help! My Wizard Mentor Had A Heart Attack And Now I'm
Being Chased By A Horde Of Giant Spiders!

**The Untamed Isles**

The Path Awakens

THE FIRST CIRCLE

PROLOGUE

HEAVY FORESHADOWING

<u>WARNING:</u>

This is not a serious novel. In fact, it's quite the opposite. It's a satirical take on a LITRPG fantasy novel. It will make fun of everyone and everything you have ever held dear. No one will be spared. Consider yourselves warned!

TENSER SHIVERED AS THE BREEZE WHISTLED THROUGH THE RING of standing stones. Branches stirred in the canopy overheard, whispering the secret songs of the Enchanted Forest. From beyond the light of his fire came the stirrings of movement, of creatures come to investigate the stranger in the darkness.

They soon returned to their nests and burrows. They could sense his power. Not even the most desperate of creatures in these parts would risk such a confrontation. Though given the import of this night, Tenser had taken no chances. His Circle of Power shimmered overhead, its threads of silver, white and sapphire lightning crackling with imbued energies. The first of his safeguards. It would protect the ancient wizard for as long as mana flowed in his veins.

The fire crackled and spat, dragging Tenser back to the present. Absently, he bent and tossed another stick to the hungry flames, his mind absorbed in the words of the spell he meant to cast. A *whoosh* came as the wood took light, followed by a billowing of smoke. The wizard choked as a wayward gust swept the harsh fumes into his face.

Choking turned into a full bout of coughing, until Tenser was left bent over and clinging to his ivory staff for support. Eyes watering, he sucked in great lungfuls of air until the attack passed. Even then, his chest still ached as though he'd been half-drowned by the denizens of the Mermaid Isles.

"So much for the mighty wizard," he muttered to himself. "Defeated by a bloody campfire."

He managed a half smile. Much as he might deny it publicly, truth lurked beneath those words. Tenser had been mighty once, had stood alongside the greats that had first united the Four Circles. He had survived through war and peace, had joyed in great victories, and suffered the despairs of betrayal and defeat.

But now…

"This wizard still has one trick left up his sleeve," he muttered.

The words seemed to stir the very world to violence. A wild wind came howling through the trees and branches clashed. Somewhere above, lightning flashed. Seconds ticked by, but no thunder followed. There was only the whispering of the autumn leaves in the darkness. Amidst the shadows, those whispers seemed to Tenser the mirth of a thousand tiny voices.

Folly, folly, folly!

"Begone foul demons!" He bellowed to the dark, though he knew there were no demons. Not here on the outskirts of the Four Circles—as far from the Tower of the Dark Lord as one could get.

Which was just as well, for this night he would sow the seeds of the Dark Lord's destruction.

Beyond the soft glow of his flames, beyond the silent standing stones, the trees of the Enchanted Forest loomed, pale ghosts in the dark. A silent audience to his desperate gambit. He shivered. He had not wanted to do this alone. What had become of the elven princess, that Warrior of the Light who had battled so long against the enemy? He had called her to join him. But…long months and years he had passed in isolation, preparing for this day. Perhaps she had already departed, advanced beyond the limitations of the First Circle.

Or perhaps the Dark Lord had found her.

A tremor ran down Tenser's spine. If that were true, and the Dark Lord had somehow learned of his plan…

He shook his head. The time for doubt had passed. This day, he would change the Fate of the Four Circles forever—

"*Ahem…*"

Tenser flinched as a voice spoke from behind him. He spun, raising his wizard's staff to bring the full destructive power of his mana to bear—and froze as his gaze settled on the intruder.

A young girl leaned against one of the standing stones. She appeared no older than twelve years of age, but this was no stranger to Tenser. He recognised the ancient soul peering from those emerald eyes. Despite all of his power—and that the girl stood no taller than his navel—Tenser found himself retreating a step.

"Fate." He whispered her title like a talisman, though names held no power over this creature. "Why are you here?"

The goddess's laughter rang like a bell. She righted herself and stepped away from the standing stone. "Tenser," she *tsked*, raising a finger and wagging it in front of her face. "Did you truly think that I would not know?"

A lump lodged in the wizard's throat. Rage was quick to follow. A wave of fiery heat washed away his fears.

"You cannot stop me," he growled. "You cannot interfere."

Again the laughter. The sound was soft, almost gentle. To a lesser mortal, its might have been mistaken for the joyous mirth of a child at play. But Tenser heard its iron edge.

"You are right, of course," came Fate's reply. "But know this: interfere with my providence, and you invite Chaos into the Four Circles."

"I would rather Chaos than see my people suffer centuries more beneath the Dark Lord's yoke."

Fate spread her hands. "So be it, Tenser the Great. You have been warned."

With those words, the goddess stepped from the circle of stones. As she crossed the threshold of his magic, she took on a translucent glow, before fading away.

Alone again in the night, Tenser drew a steadying breath. He had come too far to turn back now…and yet a worm of doubt gnawed at him. Damned Fate. She served not Good or Evil, but her own immutable plans. She could not be trusted.

And so Tenser raised his arms, and began to chant the words of the spell.

Weariness came upon the wizard as mana rushed from him in a surge of transcendent energy. Darkness fled the forest then, cast back by a burning brightness. For a moment, the standing stones were revealed in stark relief, as though the sun itself had risen amongst them. Inscriptions upon the granite flickered, then began to glow as the powers within woke.

Tenser slumped to his knees as stars danced before his eyes. Energy crackled, heavy upon the air as the primordial magics of the stones took life. Crouched amidst it all, the wizard felt the pressure of that power upon him, and knew his spell had succeeded.

The energies continued to swell, forming into a knot of burning light. Such a working would send ripples through the Four Circles. Those with the talent to sense it would know something had changed, that the fabric of the world itself had been altered. They would seek to discover those changes, to prevent them. But they would be too late.

The die had been cast. Not even Fate could foresee now how it would land.

The Dark Lord would know, of course. He would send out his minions to seek the source of the disturbance. By the time they arrived, Tenser would be long gone.

The energies of the circle built to a crescendo. It was time.

Blood thrummed in Tenser's ears as he raised his arms and spoke words long forgotten by mankind. This magic, these stones, predated even the elves. It had taken him years to collect the torn and scattered shards of the tablet. Such a spell had not been seen in nigh ten thousand years.

A *crack* shook the forest. What remained of the creatures hidden in the nearby undergrowth went skittering for their burrows. A soft sizzling filled the air as reality itself warped. A thousand colours rippled on suddenly visible air currents, shifting from red to blue to yellow and back in the space of heartbeats. Heat washed across the clearing, only to become the icy breath of the dead.

Tenser cried out in pain and ecstasy, in joy and despair. Clinging to his knobbed staff, he could feel the spell slipping, the magic of the ancients stuttering. Something had gone wrong. Despite his meticulous calculations, the portal was unstable. If it failed, he was done. All his careful planning, all his preparations, they would come to naught.

But he was Tenser the Great. He would not fail. With a mighty cry, he gripped the ebony staff in two hands and brought it down.

Boom!

Tenser stumbled as mana flooded from him. Darkness crept upon the edges of his vision as the Circle of Power failed. But he clung to consciousness—and the spell stabilised. Slowly, almost tentatively, a portal formed in the air before the wizard. And for the first time in ten thousand years, a mortal of the Four Circles looked upon the mystical realm of Earth.

The wizard's eyes drifted closed. He could feel the warmth of the second sun upon his face. Its light cast back the darkness, filling him with wonder—and hope. Fate be damned, the spell had succeeded. The gateway was complete. Now all he needed to do was speak the final words of the spell. The words that would seek out the unknown soul long prophesised to rid the Four Circles of the Dark Lord.

The words to summon a hero.

CHAPTER 1
THROUGH THE LOOKING GLASS

When Tenser's portal first opened onto Earth, it appeared without purpose or temporal association. So it was that across the globe—and throughout the twenty-first century—humans of every writ and creed witnessed a series of strange and inexplicable phenomena. Wars erupted, halfwits briefly became popular electoral choices, and a double rainbow was witnessed somewhere over the Yosemite National Park.

Then Tenser's Words of Power passed down the infinite stack of turtles that separate all worlds, and the portal finally went in search of its true target.

A target whose precise coordinates in time and space were at 3:33pm on the 31st of May 2022, in the Portland Community College, Oregon. More precisely, in the communal restrooms where a thirty-year-old human male by the name of Patrik Conroy was presently in the midst of defecating…

Boom!

The moment the portal opened in front of him, Patrik knew his life would be changed forever. This foresight could partly be ascribed to witnessing the very fabric of reality torn open before his eyes. It could also partly have been due to the decidedly uncomfortable sensation of finding himself unable to move, breathe, or even scream.

But mostly, it was because in that same moment, Patrik was dragged bodily from the toilet upon which he sat and hurled into another world with all the dignity of a tiger cub stolen from its mother by Joe Exotic.

Thankfully, all of this lasted only a moment, a flicker of time in which Patrik witnessed a kaleidoscope of colours flashing before his eyes, glimpsed a monstrous face of untold proportions, and felt the whispered breath of the universe against his cheek.

Then the moment passed, at which point he slammed face first into the very hard ground.

A much longer moment passed as Patrik lay still, his mortal mind struggling to comprehend what had just happened. His body ached like he'd been beaten black and blue, and there was a ringing in his ears so loud he could barely think for the racket. He tried to open his eyes, but found stars dancing haphazardly across his vision. Even his sense of smell seemed off. When he inhaled air into his bruised lungs, instead of choking on the reek of the freshly utilised toilet, he instead encountered the pleasant scent of earth and ash. That was definitely wrong.

Or…am I somehow outside?

As the thought trickled through Patrik's awakening mind, he became aware of the dirt pressed against his face. He was definitely outdoors.

And his pants were somewhere around his ankles.

A bolt of adrenaline lifted Patrik into a sitting position. He still had a square of toilet paper in hand, torn from the roll as…whatever had happened, had happened. He made do with what he had. It then took several attempts and a lot of scrambling in the dirt to get his jeans back around his waist. By then his mind was fully alert. And it had become aware of three extremely pertinent facts.

First: it was now somehow nighttime. Darkness loomed around him, thick as cafeteria soup. There were no streetlights to pierce the gloom, no apartment buildings glowing in the distance—not even a glimpse of the stars or moon for guidance. The only source of light was the nearby crackling of flames, which at least allowed Patrik to come to his second realisation.

He was not just outside, but in some kind of forest. By the flickering glow of the fire, he made out the swaying of branches above and the pale trunks of nearby trees. Old leaves crunched amidst the dirt as he shifted, struggling to get his feet beneath him.

At least the forest explained the lack of modern lights. But it definitely did *not* make the last of Patrik's realisations any more comforting.

He was not alone.

As the ringing in his ears faded, Patrik became aware of the sounds around him. The soft hooting of an owl in the dark. The flapping of leather wings on night air. The rustling of a creature as it moved through the undergrowth. Whispers of a breeze through the trees.

And the harsh rasping of a man drawing breath.

Heart hammering in his chest, Patrik came to his feet. The pain of his crash landing had begun to fade. He tensed, gathering his strength in preparation to flee. He had already settled on two possible scenarios for his current predicament—either this was a terrible practical joke by his fellow students, or he was about to come face-to-face with a serial killer.

Movement shifted amongst the shadows. Footsteps approached. They lacked the steady thump of an adult man, but rather came as a strange scuffing, as though their owner was dragging his feet. Squinting in the gloom, Patrik strained for a glimpse of whoever had brought him to this place.

Whoosh!

He stumbled back as the campfire flared into a waist-high column of flame. It was as though someone had just poured gasoline onto the embers. Heat washed across his face and he had to turn away to keep from being blinded by the brilliance.

As the heat passed, he whipped his head back towards the

fire, half expecting an axe-wielding maniac to leap from the shadows.

The truth was stranger than either of his hypotheses.

By the glow of the now-blazing-fire, a man stumbled towards Patrik. But this was no serial killer—and definitely not a student at the Portland Community College. This man was so old he appeared to already have one foot in the grave. Time had carved deep ravines across the pale flesh of his face and age spots covered his withered arms. What little remained of his grey hair was revealed as he tripped on a loose rock, dislodging the pointed hat from his head. The only thing that kept the man from keeling over then and there was the old staff to which he clung.

Patrik's next thought was that this must be one of the professors. Some of them were wacky enough—one actually rode around campus on a unicycle. But not even a college professor was mad enough to wear full-length, bright blue bathrobes covered in shiny yellow stars in public. The hat he had lost even matched the robes.

"Ahhh," Patrik started, then trailed off as he found himself at a loss for words.

Seriously, how often did you wake up lost in the middle of the woods, only to stumble upon someone dressed as bloody Dumbledore? A very *sick* looking Dumbledore, for that matter. The man's laboured breaths rattled through the clearing as he took another step. Face haggard, he stretched out a hand towards Patrik, fingers like claws.

"Patrick…Conroy of…Portland?" The words grated from the old man's throat, more statement than question. Bloodshot eyes shone with desperation.

"I…yes?" Patrik stammered.

Just a few minutes ago, he'd been sitting peacefully on the toilet reading the news on his iPhone. Now he was…actually, he had no idea where he was. But apparently this old man did. At least, he knew Patrik's name. Suddenly, his confusion no longer seemed so important. At least, not alongside the anger that bubbled up within.

"And who the hell are you?" he snapped. "Where have—"

"Thank...the gods," the old man rasped over Patrik's spluttered indignation. He staggered forward again, reaching inside his robes...

"Holy shit!" Patrik leapt back as he saw what the old man had hidden inside the sparkly robes. "Dude, is that a sword? You can't just walk around with one of those in Portland!"

He retreated another step, his heart racing, and bumped into solid stone. Only then did Patrik notice the ring of boulders that ran in a circle around the clearing. No, not boulders, he realised with a chill. The way the stones stood reminded him of a field trip his school had taken to England.

Stonehenge...

"What the..." he muttered, then gave an angry shake of his head. No way he was in bloody Europe. This had to be a prank. "Fuck this," he growled, jabbing a finger at the old man, "I'm calling the police."

His iPhone's glow lit his face as he pulled it from his pocket. He tapped the screen—then tapped it again as the faceID failed to initiate. Typical. It took two more tries before it unlocked. At which point, sparks burst from the screen, crackling in the darkness. Yelping, Patrik dropped the phone. It struck a rock and shattered into a thousand pieces.

"What the hell..."

"Patrik of Portland..." the Dumbledore cosplayer rasped, ignoring the destruction of his precious iPhone. "Know this... I, Tenser the Great...Wizard of the...Four Circles...have summoned you here...in defiance of Fate...to fulfil an ancient prophecy..."

The old man was really struggling now. He wheezed out the words between each strained breath, as though he'd just run a marathon—or dragged an unconscious body for several hours through the forest. Patrik's eyes were drawn again to the sword hilt. What the hell was going on here?

"Look, buddy," Patrik said, trying to keep his voice calm. He held up his hands in a show of peace. "Or...Tencel...whatever the hell your name is, let's just talk about this. I'm sure all this…ah…was meant to be an awesome practical joke, right? But I think you and I can both agree it's gone a bit too far now. My phone just exploded. You know someone's going to have to pay for that."

"Too…far?" the "wizard" wheezed. His eye twitched, a spasm passing across his face. Both hands were clinging to the twisted staff now. "You are…the hero foretold…Champion of Portland…the Chosen One." His eyes fluttered closed as he sucked in a laboured breath. "You are to…destroy…Dark Lord…arggggg—"

The old man's words turned to a moan as he slumped to his knees. Patrik watched, mouth hanging open, as the so-called wizard toppled sideways and crumpled to the ground. His body twitched and jerked. A harsh rattling came from the depths of his throat, slowly fading to nothing…

Silence.

Patrik stared at the man sprawled at his feet, unsure whether to be amused or horrified. Collapsed amongst the leaves and dirt, the man lay completely still. Had he actually passed out from exhaustion?

"Hey man," Patrik muttered, stretching out a foot to give the wizard a nudge. "Come on, that's not funny…"

No response. He nudged the man again. This time it was hard enough to roll the fallen figure onto his back. The old man's head wobbled slightly as he rolled, but otherwise there was no response. He didn't appear to be breathing.

Patrik swore. He wasn't about to leave an old man lying on the cold forest floor, wearing nothing more than a bathrobe. Kneeling, he touched a hand to the wizard's forehead. His skin was damp and clammy. Not a good sign.

"Hey, if you're awake, you need to tell me," he said, giving the old man a shake. "Fine. I'm going to check your pulse. Say nothing if that's okay."

You never knew how people would react to a good Samaritan these days. But his wizard friend remained unresponsive. Pushing aside the collar of the silk robes, Patrik placed a finger to the man's throat.

Nothing.

A frown spread across Patrik's face as he moved his fingers with greater urgency. He tried his other hand. Still nothing.

"Well shit."

Whoever this old man was, he wasn't faking.

"Shit, shit, shit."

Instinct kicked in. He'd been an RA for his college dorm in sophomore year and they'd all had to do a first aid course. Now if he could just remember the basics of CPR…

The wizard was already on his back. That was a start. Patrik checked his pulse one last time. Then drew in a deep breath.

"Here goes nothing."

He entwined his fingers and placed them on the man's chest, then pushed down hard. He immediately flinched as something went *crack*, but the nurse who'd run the course had warned that might happen.

If you break a rib, you're doing it right.

Baring his teeth, Patrik continued the compressions, hoping against hope he was indeed remembering the instructions correctly. How fast were they meant to be again? There'd been a song they were meant to use for the rhythm, but…it had been almost two years and he'd been distracted by other things. Like the curve of her bra as she bent over the CPR dummy…

He shook himself. It had been a song by the Bee Gees, hadn't it? He couldn't remember. Actually, there'd been two! His spirits rose as he recalled the second song. It was far from ideal…

I'm going straight to hell for this.

Patrik started to sing the chorus of Queen's *Another One Bites the Dust*, using the tune to set the rhythm for his compressions.

"Aaaah!"

With a rattling cry, the 'wizard' lurched upright. Patrik toppled backwards in fright as the ancient eyelids snapped open. The frail chest swelled as the old man inhaled a life-giving breath. Relief swept Patrik as he sat back on his heels.

He reached a hand to his own chest in an effort to calm his racing heart.

"Chosen…One, hear me!" The words rasped from the wizard's pale lips as he exhaled.

Patrik frowned. Surely, *surely*, this dude wasn't still playing the whole role playing, fantasy, whatever the hell game was going on here.

"Sir…" he began, but the old man reached out a withered hand and caught Patrik by the front of his shirt before he could continue.

Despite his close call with death, the wizard turned out to be wickedly strong. Patrik cried out at the assault, but could not tear himself loose. Instead, he was dragged down until he was face-to-face with the old man.

"Ring…" the wizard croaked. The icy fingers left Patrik's collar and wrapped around his wrist instead. Patrik flinched as something cold and metallic was pressed into his hand. "Go… Bledross…Please…Protect…Destiny…Save…Circles."

Each word was forced out between strained gasps, before a terrible cough tore from the old man's throat. Bloody droplets of saliva splattered Patrik's face as the wizard crumpled, slipping back to the ground. His eyes fluttered closed. His breath stilled.

"What! *No!*" Patrik cried.

He resumed the compressions. Seconds turned to long minutes. At some point, a second *crack* came from the man's chest, and a third. But this time there was no miraculous gasping for air, no sudden recovery. Finally, his arms aching and own lungs gasping, Patrik was forced to accept defeat.

The old wizard was dead.

Patrik started to stand, only to notice the item he'd dropped when the man had collapsed the second time. A golden ring lay in the dirt at his feet. He bent down and picked it up. It shimmered in the firelight. There seemed to be some text inscribed around the outside, but when he held it up to the light, the gold appeared smooth.

Then to Patrik's complete shock, the ring disappeared. Just

blinked out of existence. He stared at his empty hand, trying to understand what had happened.

Achievement Unlocked! Necromancy. Congratulations, you have successfully brought someone back from the dead. Reward: You have learned the spell 'Raise Dead'. Use this spell to temporarily bring a person or creature of a level equal to or lower than your own back from the dead. Duration: ten minutes. Cost: 10 mana. Note: This is considered a negatively aligned spell. Use will accumulate negative alignment. [-50 Alignment]

Patrik staggered and fell as a voice boomed through the clearing. At the same time, words burst into his vision, flashing a brilliant red. In a panic he lashed out, sure he was under attack. His fingers slashed through the swirling text and while they encountered nothing tangible, the words went flying away.

More immediately appeared to replace them.

Achievement Unlocked! Hell Raiser. Woah, congrats! You have defied the laws of Death and revived a creature more than 50 levels higher than your own. Reward: Your spell, Raise Dead, has advanced to level 2, 3...6! You can now temporarily revive a person or creature up to [your level + 5]. Raising a creature of a higher level than yourself will endure an additional cost of 1 mana per level higher. Duration: ten minutes. Cost: 10 mana [+1 mana per level higher]

Reeling from the volume of the voice, Patrik came to his feet. He swung one way, then another as the text flashed before his eyes. Screaming, he tried to catch hold of his unseen assailant. Instead, the text flashed again and flew off into nothing. Yet more burst into existence.

Achievement Unlocked! First victim. Congratulations, you've made your first kill. I mean, it was an old man, but I guess it still counts. Reward: 10 gold coins.

"What the *fuck* is going on?"

Every time he got rid of one set of flashing text, another appeared—accompanied with that shrieking voice. This was far beyond the realm of a prank now. Had someone drugged him? Yeah, that had to be it. All these wild imaginings were the result of—

Achievement Unlocked! Giant Slayer. Well, look at the balls on you. You have killed a creature more than 50 levels higher than your own. Reward: 1000 gold coins.

Achievement Unlocked! Friendly Fire. You've killed an ally. Shit mate, that's not cool. Why'd you go and do that? [-500 Alignment]

Patrik shook his head, as though that might dislodge the hallucinations flashing in front of his eyes. His stomach lurched and he struggled to keep from hurling. It was a moment before the meaning behind the words finally caught up with him. Had someone just accused him of murder?

"What?" he burst out. "I didn't kill anyone!"

Silence descended on the clearing. By now the fire had burnt down to coals. He stared at the gaps between the standing stones, trying to figure out if this was all some hallucination. Or hell, could someone have set up a speaker and projector in the woods? He couldn't see anything beyond the ring of stones.

"Come out, whoever you—" he started.

Ring! Ring! Ring! Congratulations. You have reached level 2, 3…9! You have been awarded [24 stat points] to assign amongst your attributes. Stat points may be assigned at level 10.

More enraged than confused now, Patrik waved a hand as the text flashed again before his eyes. Like before, the gesture sent it spinning away. By now he was so disorientated he just wanted to sit down and put his head between his legs. But if someone really was out there…

"Look, whatever sick joke you're trying to play, enough!" he called, then made a gesture in the direction of the old man. "Someone is *dead!*"

Patrik stood amongst the stones, keenly aware just how exposed he was in the darkness. The soft pop and crackling of the embers was the only break in the silence. A sudden emptiness hung about the clearing, an eerie stillness.

Geeze, I didn't even know you could do that. This time there was no accompanying text to the voice. It was also softer, where before it had spoken with a cold, detached formality. ***Did you really revive that old dude just so you could kill him again? That's cold, mate.***

CHAPTER 2
HELL IS AN AUSSIE IN YOUR HEAD

"Huh?"

Patrik blinked. He still couldn't locate the speaker. But now that he'd taken a moment to centre himself, he realised the reason for part of his confusion. The man was speaking in a distinctly Australian accent. But that didn't clear up the other part of Patrik's confusion.

The part where someone was accusing him of murder.

"Look, buddy," he said, holding up his hands to show they were empty. "Whatever's going on here, I had nothing to do with your friend's death. I tried to help him."

His words were swallowed by the darkness. The fire was little more than embers now. Hands raised, Patrik edged towards the glow of the coals, intending to feed them more kindling and restore the flames. Then he might catch a glimpse of his accuser.

Hey, no worries, mate. Don't need to get defensive with me. I'm just your friendly, everyday PQA. Who am I going to tell?

Patrik paused. "You're what?"

Personal Quest Assistant. Sorry, forgot you're from off-world. Seriously though, that was some genius experience harvesting. You must have been one cold-ass motherfucker on Earth. What were you, a cartel boss? One of those "enhanced interrogators"? Ooooh, were you a CEO—or what do you call 'em nowadays—an entrepreneur?

By this point Patrik was totally lost. "What the hell are you talking about?" he asked. When his accuser did not respond, he reluctantly added: "And I'm an Arts major…"

An…Arts major? What's…oh, I see. Wow…and you're meant to be the Chosen One? There was a long pause. *Man, we're fucked.*

Patrik opened his mouth to ask what the hell the Australian was talking about, then thought better of it. He was clearly dealing with a madman. Time to try another tactic.

"Look, ah, Mr. PQA, was it?" he said, trying to keep his voice friendly. "It's a little dark tonight. I'm having trouble seeing you. Do you think you could come over here and we can figure out what to do with your friend?"

Silence. Somewhere, a cricket chirped.

It seems we're having a bit of a misunderstanding, mate, the voice replied at last. *Maybe it's this bloody translation magic. I. Am. A. Personal. Quest. Assistant,* the man continued in a deliberately slow tone, as though speaking to an idiot. *I cannot "come over here," as I am currently nestled in the prefrontal cortex of your brain.*

Patrik stood for a long moment, letting those words seep in. His first instinct was to laugh. Bad idea. The Australian was clearly disturbed. Who knew how he might respond?

"Sorry, I *do* seem to be having trouble with your translation. What on earth is a Personal Quest Assistant?"

There came an audible sigh. *Hold on, let me check these records, maybe there's something—oh! That's our problem. Seems you don't actually* have PQAs on *Earth. Guess we're a Four Circles kind of thing.*

This time Patrik couldn't cover his frustration. He raised a hand and rubbed his temples. First the wizard, now someone pretending to be a disembodied voice that lived in his brain. What was next, an Elvis impersonator?

Wow, look at this book! It's like a bloody tomb. Geez, yeah, I really should have done the reading beforehand. That's my bad, mate. Was it Patrik's imagination, or could he hear pages shuffling? *Usually we can just get away with the back page—holy shit, you really don't have magic? How do you kill each other—oh wow, that's* **wild!**

Patrik supressed a sigh at the Australian's antics. He had no desire to engage with the lunatic, but at this stage, the insane, disembodied voice might also be his only way out of this forest.

"Okay, Mr. PQA," he said, deciding to humour the man for now. "So let me make sure I've got this straight. You're saying I am no longer on earth, but somewhere called the 'Four Circles'? And you're meant to be some kind of assistant to help me navigate this new world?"

That's right! See, who says humans are slow? Stick with me, mate, and we'll go far. Well, so long as you don't go stumbling upon a troll or something.

"A *what?*"

Patrik couldn't help but feel a tingle of alarm. He *was* alone in the middle of a pitch-black forest after all.

Oh, I wouldn't go worrying about them. They usually only appear in the higher circles. You'd have to be cursed by Fate or something to encounter one here.

Patrik frowned. Hadn't the old man said something about Fate? He was beginning to think he'd been kidnapped by some sort of cult.

Anyway, I guess we'd better get started on your induction!

Definitely a cult. But before Patrik had a chance to ask what the hell the Australian meant by induction, the flashing words were back. They burst across his vision as though they'd been projected by a thousand laser lights. He waved his hands the way he had before to dismiss them, but this time they remained fixed in place. Mercifully, this time there was no booming Australian voice to accompany the text.

That's an interesting pose...

It took a moment for the words to seep in. Patrik stood with his hands thrust out and head turned away, as though he was about to receive a beating from the schoolyard bully. Despite the ludicrousness of his situation, he felt his cheeks grow warm. He quickly straightened. The words still danced before his eyes. This time, instead of cringing away, he read them.

"What the actual fuck?" Patrik muttered, more to himself than the Australian or PQA or whatever his abductor wanted to call himself.

Then he sat down on a rock. Hard. The words followed him, hanging in the air like…like…

He swallowed. They hung in the air like a menu in a video game.

"What is this?"

Your stat box. It tells you how weak, or powerful, you are. Everyone in the Four Circles has one. As you can see, you're a bit of a noob. But thanks to that stunt you pulled with old Tenser the Great, you're at

least in a mildly better position than your average pimple-faced teenager.

"I…what…means…"

Patrik's vision began to spin. His stomach heaved. Before he knew what was happening, he was bent in two and hurling his breakfast into the dirt. Red pulsed at the corners of his eyes as he choked on half-digested oatmeal. An acrid taste burned his tongue.

You have been struck by nausea [-5 health].

Groaning, Patrik sat back on his heels as the nausea finally passed, the Australian's voice still ringing in his ears. Absent-mindedly, he waved a hand at the new box that had popped up. It flashed out of existence. Drawing in a breath, he closed his eyes and tried to make sense of everything he'd seen.

Except, there was no sense to be made. This was all categorically insane. It simply could not be happening. Maybe there'd been a gas leak in the bathroom. Yes, that must be it! He should have known—

Ha! We both know there was only one source of gas in that toilet, mate.

Patrik opened his mouth to groan, then froze. "How did you…"

Like I said, I'm inside your **brain.**

No, no, no, the words rang through Patrik's thoughts. He squeezed his eyes closed and willed himself to wake up from whatever nightmare he'd slipped into. *This isn't happening, this isn't happening, this isn't happening.*

If you really think this is all some delusion, there's a simple way to find out.

Patrik's eyes snapped open. "How?"

That fire is still burning—just. If all this is just a dream, you shouldn't feel any pain, right? So stick your hand in the coals.

"Stick my hand…are you actually insane?"

I'm not the one talking to the imaginary voice in their head.

A curse formed on Patrik's lips, but he bit it back. He eyed the embers instead. Tongues of fire still licked around the edges of the coals, crackling softly in the night's silence. As he took a step closer and knelt beside it, he could feel the heat radiating against his face. If this really *was* a dream, it was the most realistic he had ever experienced…

…then again, if he was in a coma, it would be like that, wouldn't it? One of his psych classes had talked about people in comas having the most vivid dreams. Some could even hear their loved ones talking to them. Could that be what he was experiencing? He didn't know any Australians, but maybe his subconscious was projecting the accent onto his father or something.

That was certainly a more realistic conclusion than believing the voice in his mind when it said he'd been dragged through a magical portal into another universe.

There was only one way to know for sure.

Gritting his teeth, Patrik thrust his hand into the glowing embers…

Burn damage inflicted [-20 health].

"*Yoooow!*"

Patrik lurched upright as the red-hot coals seared his flesh. His scream echoed from the standing stones as he scrambled back from the flames and tripped over a stack of firewood. He crashed to the ground, but the pain from his fall was like a pinprick beside the agony of his hand. Whimpering, he cradled it to his chest as though that might sooth the pain.

Somewhere nearby—or maybe it really was in his head— the Australian howled with laughter.

Holy shit! Maaaate, I can't believe you actually did it!

"You told me to!" Patrik choked.

Another wave of agony swept him. He clenched his teeth, biting back a sob. He would *not* cry in front of the psychopath hiding in the bushes. His hand was scorched black, his flesh quite literally bubbling in places.

Mate, I'm a random voice in your head. If I told you to jump off a cliff, would you do it?

"Of course not!" The words exploded from Patrik in a rage.

They were followed by a stream of such profanity that he surprised even himself. It had been a long day, even before the kidnapping, with exams and essays and the constant stress of college. Now someone was dead, there was an Australian talking to him in his head, and he'd just stuck his hand in a fire. He'd had enough.

Geez, okay, take a joke much?

This time Patrik didn't deign to reply. Drawing in a long, shuddering breath, he held his seared hand out before him. It still felt like it was burning. He needed to find some running water or he was going to pass out from the pain.

Look, relax, okay? I'm sure your victim has some healing potions.

Patrik was in too much pain to deny the murder accusation yet again. But the mention of "healing" got his attention.

"What…the fuck is…a healing potion?" The words came out between wheezing breaths and clenched teeth.

It's a potion that—get this—heals you.

Patrik squeezed his eyes closed. Swaying on his feet, he felt a bit like he was floating. Not good. His mind drifted, finding its way back to one fateful Fourth of July. He and his older brother, Chris, had been left unsupervised for the morning. They'd used that time to build their own "fireworks" from old cap gun rings and methylated spirits.

When their parents had returned, the family had gone to the river to watch the fireworks over the city. Patrik had waited until his parents had been distracted, then tossed his makeshift "firework" into the fire. Just to see what would happen.

A few hours in the Emergency Department and some light scarring on his shins later, Patrik had come away with a keen understanding that the manufacture of fireworks should be left to the professionals.

Which was all to say that the pain from that day had been like a light carpet burn compared to what he was currently experiencing.

Come on, don't you trust me?

The question snapped Patrik from his drifting thoughts and back to the present.

"Why the fuck would I trust you?" he cried. "You *just* told me to put my hand in the fire!"

It was a trust building exercise!

"I…that…you and I have very different definitions of a trust building exercise," Patrik muttered.

Oh, well, maybe I got that wrong. Sorry, still flipping through the pages on Earth here.

Patrik bit back another torrent of abuse. He was in too much pain to be arguing with the PQA—or himself, if that was where the disembodied voice was actually coming from. His eyes settled on the old man. Exhaling through his teeth, he staggered across the clearing and knelt beside the body. Maybe the dude had Tylenol or ibuprofen or something. He began to riffle through the pockets of the sparkly robes.

Eww! What the hell are you doing?

Patrik paused. "You said he might have…something that could help."

In his inventory! Gods, does everyone on Earth desecrate the corpses of their victims like that?

"It's my first—" He bit back what he'd been about to say and changed tack. "What is an inventory?"

Okay, pervert, step away from the body!

In too much pain to disobey, Patrik did as he was told. He swayed on his feet, vision blurring as much from nausea as the tears that threatened to fall.

Good, good, the voice continued. *Now, focus on your victim, and…there you go!*

Patrik flinched as a new line of text appeared, accompanied by the booming voice.

Would you like to loot the body of Tenser the Great?

"Arg, do you have to shout every time?"

Sorry, part of the job. Anyway, let's see, if you hit

"yes" there'll be an option to—oh wow, okay, you just went ahead and selected "loot all." Right.

Patrik smiled as the text box faded from view. The smile faded when he saw what had changed while he'd been fiddling with imaginary text.

The old man was now completely naked.

"What the fuck?" he exclaimed, retreating a step and looking around. "What did you *do?*"

*What did **I** do? You're the one who decided to loot everything the poor bloke had. Didn't even leave him his undergarments...*

Achievement Unlocked! Grave Robber. Congratulations, you've looted your first corpse. You're going straight to hell! Reward: You just looted a corpse, you must have gotten something good, right? Or are you just into that sort of thing?

The voice was so loud this time that Patrik slapped his hands to his ears. Or at least, he tried. His efforts were foiled by the agony from his burns. Besides, he was beginning to believe the Australian might *actually* be in his head. That did not bode well for the other terrifying things the PQA had mentioned.

"Can you please stop doing that?" he said, removing his hands from his ears.

Oh, fine.

Updates have been muted.

"Thank you," Patrik murmured.

Then he looked at the naked corpse at his feet.

And lost what remained of his breakfast.

By the time he'd finished his second round of vomiting in as many minutes, Patrik was very much hoping that healing potions might really be a thing. Straightening, he drew in a settling breath. Keeping his eyes averted from the wrinkled, desiccated corpse of the old man or wizard or whoever this Tenser person had been, he addressed the voice again.

"So...what happened to his stuff?"

*Oh, so you **do** want to hear from me?* Unless he was

mistaken, Patrik detected a petulant tone to the PQA's voice now.

He was in no mood for it. "For fuck's sake, just tell me what to do."

Fine. You'll have to check your inventory.

"How do I—"

Patrik swallowed the question as another text box sprang to life. This time he managed to keep himself from panicking at its appearance. Just. His heart raced, though, and it took a moment before he could compose himself enough to focus on the contents of the box.

To his surprise, this one included images coupled with little snippets of text beneath each. He couldn't read them immediately, but as he focused on the first item, the words grew larger and the image clearer. It looked suspiciously like a set of blue robes covered in yellow stars. He glanced at the text.

Legendary Wizards Robes. Properties: Unknown. Increase your intelligence to learn more about the properties of this item.

Patrik shook his head and blinked, feeling slightly disorientated. The image shrank back into the rest of his "inventory." He cast a quick look over the other items. They included a sword, dragger, staff, hat, several rings and pieces of jewellery —including a picture that looked remarkably similar to the ring that had disappeared earlier. Curious, he focused on the golden band.

Unidentified Ring. Properties: Unknown. Increase your intelligence to learn more about the properties of this item.

He sighed and turned to the other items. There were several slots filled with what looked to be food—bread, a sack of salt, some chicken legs. There was also kindling and a tinder box. The descriptions aptly described what he saw in each of the images. There were also two rolled up pieces of paper.

Scroll of Lightning Bolt [permanent]: Use this scroll to learn the spell "Lightning Bolt." Requirements: 10 intelligence.

Scroll of Inferno [single use]: For emergency situations only. Hurls an enormous fireball at your enemies. Requirements: none. Effect: massive damage.

"This is…insane."

Weren't you looking for a healing potion? Looks like the old dude had three. Nice, they're rare in this Circle. Too bad you killed him before he could use one.

"I did not…"

Patrik shook his head. There was clearly no use arguing the point. He returned to his inventory and noticed a few jars and beakers. He scanned the labels as they appeared. One was labelled as a mana potion, whatever that was. But the last four were healing.

"So how do I use them?" he asked, feeling in no small part like an idiot, standing in the middle of nowhere talking to an imaginary voice.

Just imagine the potion appearing in your hand—
Pop!

Patrik jumped as he found himself holding a jar of red liquid which looked suspiciously like the image that had just been hovering before his eyes.

"How…." he began, then trailed off.

If not for the very pressing reminder of his scorched hand, he would have been seriously reconsidering the dream theory. Swallowing, he glanced at the fading coals, but decided there was no need to revisit that particular piece of stupidity.

"So I drink it?"

No, you take it as enema…no, no, stop. Yes, you drink it. Geez, do they not have sarcasm where you're from?

"Sarcasm, yes. Magical potions, definitely not. Unless the billionaires are hiding them, which actually might make some sense. Never mind."

He popped the seal on the vial before the conversation devolved into another argument. A strong smell of ash and hospital-grade disinfectant wafted up from the mouth of the jar. He wrinkled his nose.

"Err, you sure this isn't poison?"

It's labelled as a healing potion, isn't it?

Patrik hesitated, but another pulse of agony from his hand convinced him to throw caution to the wind. He raised the jar to his lips. The scarlet liquid disappeared down his gullet in a single gulp—

*Then again, you **did** kill the dude. And he **was** a wizard. Could have safeguard spells on his items. Something that switches labels between the potions and the poisons—oh you already drank it? I'm sure it's fine.*

"I swear to—"

Patrik broke off as a tingling began in his hand. He watched in stunned amazement as the scorched flesh turned pink, and then in further wonder as his skin began to knit itself back together. Just a few seconds later, he held up his hand before his face and clenched it into a fist. He grinned like a kid who'd just raided his dad's beer stash.

Hey, look at that, it worked! Your health is back to full.

"That's amazing!" Patrik whispered, before frowning at something the PQA had said. "What was that about my health?

You know, how close you are to death. You can see your health bar by—

"Imagining it. Got it." He was beginning to get the hang of this.

A simple box appeared in the corner of his vision. It glowed green, with little numbers beneath that read 90/90.

"Wait, you said something about 20 burn damage. So… that fire took down a fifth of my health?"

Yep! You'll gain ten health points per level increase.

"And if it hits zero…"

Caput, game over, no more Mr. Chosen One.

Patrik's mouth suddenly felt dry as sandpaper. Choosing to ignore the fact he now had a direct measure of how close to death he was at any given moment, he moved on.

"And mana? There was a box for that too, right?"

Exactly!

At his words, another bar appeared, this one blue. The numbers beneath read 10/10.

"Ah, and what is mana, exactly?"

Mana…he'd heard of it somewhere…*Fable*! He remembered belatedly. It was a video game of his brother's that he'd played a few times—well, actually, being a single player game, he'd mostly just watched his brother play.

Mana is the energy you use to cast magic. It's connected to your Intelligence—for every increase in your Intelligence attribute, you'll add five points to your mana pool.

Patrik nodded slowly to himself. That linked up with what he remembered. In fact, now that he'd made the connection, everything about this place was reminding him more and more of the video games from his youth. Fable. Oblivion. RuneScape. Halo—okay, not so much Halo. Maybe the holographic displays that kept popping up before his eyes?

He drew in a breath. "Okay, so what about those other numbers, the ones that popped up in my stat box?"

Well—

The voice broke off abruptly. Patrik waited for the PQA to continue, but the silence only stretched out.

"Ah, were you going to finish?"

Oh, now you care about people finishing? the PQA muttered. ***Look, I'd love to continue this little tutorial, but there's a small problem.***

Patrik sighed. "And that is?"

For some unknown reason, it seems your dead wizard friend summoned you into the middle of the Enchanted Forest.

"Great. And what exactly does that mean?"

Well, given you've been standing here for a good

twenty minutes talking quite loudly and occasionally screaming, it seems your presence has been noted. There was another pause. ***Sorry, this one overrides the mute setting.***

Warning: Monsters sighted in your area!

CHAPTER 3
MONSTERS SIGHTED IN YOUR AREA

Warning: Monsters sighted in your area!

"Monsters?" Patrik spun one way, then the other, but the pale trees around the standing stones revealed nothing. "What the hell are you talking about?"

Let's see here… That was definitely the sound of flipping pages now. ***Ah, yes! You know all those myths and fairy tales you have in your world?***

"Yes…"

Well, they're like, totally real, dude! For some reason, this time the PQA spoke in a bad impression of an American accent.

"Are you…trying to be funny right now?"

Just bringing some levity to the situation, mate.

Patrik rubbed his forehead. He was still reeling from every-thing the PQA—*the voice in his head*—had told him. Now there were apparently *monsters*? He strained to pierce the shadows beneath the trees. There seemed to be a faint glimmer of light through the branches overhead, but daybreak must still be hours away.

There's no such thing as monsters…

The thought ran on repeat at the back of his mind, but after everything Patrik had witnessed in the last half hour…

well, he figured it was probably best to trust the asshole in his head.

"Where are they coming from?" he croaked.

I'd say you have about a minute, came the reply. ***It's approaching from the west.***

"Which is in…what direction?"

Your left, no, your right…there! May I suggest you equip a weapon?

"I don't have a weapon—"

Patrik broke off as he recalled the contents of his "inventory." Determined to avoid further rebuke from the disembodied Australian, he willed his inventory box into life. As the items appeared before his eyes, he scrolled through the contents until he came to the sword.

Iron Short Sword. A plain sword forged from iron ore. Not bad for a noob. Effect: +3 to strength. Requirements: must be level 15 to wield.

Doing the same as he had with the health potion, Patrik focused on the item, and grinned when its weight settled in his hands.

Dismissing the text box, he took a moment to contemplate the weapon. It was heavier than he'd expected. There was no way the frail old man could have wielded it—in fact, Patrik himself was struggling with its weight. He wasn't exactly a gym fanatic. He preferred working out his brain over his muscles.

In hindsight that might have been a mistake.

Still, there was a firmness to the sword that was reassuring. Its blade had been honed to a fine, razor-sharp edge. And the weight seemed to scream: "hit something with me and it's not getting back up." Which, if Patrik was about to fight *literal* monsters, was exactly what he wanted.

Ahem, I hate to interrupt…

Patrik scowled. "What now?" he grated, eyes fixed on the trees the PQA had said the monster was approaching from.

Well, it's great you're all gung-ho to kill some monsters and that you're ignoring my ever-so-helpful

prompts, but I feel it's my duty to inform you that that sword can only be used once you reach level fifteen.

"Wait…what?" Patrik paused. "What the hell do you mean? I'm holding it just fine." He laughed. "What, is your king going to come and punish me for using the wrong sword? Or does he have soldiers patrolling the so-called Four Circles looking for rule breakers?"

We don't have a king. We have a Dark Lord.

"Cause that's so much better."

Yes, well, it's not the Dark Lord who makes the rules—

The PQA's explanation was interrupted by a dark shape exploding from the undergrowth to Patrik's left. A high-pitched scream that was definitely *not* in Patrik's head echoed through the clearing. His blood turned to ice and he couldn't help but stumble back a step. The creature standing beyond the ring of stones loomed over the clearing. His mind reeled at its enormity.

Black fur bristled over countless long, reaching legs and a dozen enormous eyes swivelled in the centre of a monstrous face. Great fangs stretched wide, a bright green liquid dripping from their razor points. The drops *hissed* where they struck the ground, letting off an acrid stench of burning. A low growl vibrated from the creature as it skittered forward on those terrible legs.

Patrik shuddered as the monster's attention settled on him. It was a spider. A *giant* spider. A giant spider somewhere around the size of a bear, to be more precise. Worse than anything that had ever crawled out of the hellscape otherwise known as Australia. Was that why his PQA was Australian? Was this entire kingdom a parallel fantasy version of Australia?

Such idle thoughts were chased from Patrik's mind as the giant spider made a low hissing noise and skittered towards him.

"*HOLY SHIT!*" Patrik screamed.

Instinctively, he lifted the iron sword and slammed it into the hideous face. *Thwack.* Patrik's arms jarred as the blade struck solid flesh. A green bar sprang up over the spider—based on his own similar bar, he guessed that was its health. Text also appeared alongside the beast.

Giant Silk Spider Queen [Level 5]

Unfortunately, the sword seemed no more effective than a toothpick against a lion. Patrik gaped as the spider reared up, its front legs clawing the air, and gave another high-pitched scream. He tried to retreat, but his foot caught on a loose rock and he crashed to the ground instead, landing hard on his ass. Somehow he managed to scramble through the dirt away from the beast.

Coming to his feet, Patrik faced the spider again. It hissed, spitting drops of acid across the dirt. Patrik skipped sideways out of the way, then swung again, aiming for its legs. Surely the weighty sword could break the slender limbs…

Bong!

To Patrik's dismay, the sword bounced clear again without doing any noticeable damage. The green bar above the spider's head certainly didn't change.

So, as I was saying…

"Kind of busy here," Patrik grunted.

Sweat dripped from his forehead. He tried to blink it away, not daring to take a hand off the heavy sword to wipe it. The spider crawled behind one of the standing stones and attempted to enter through another gap, but Patrik leapt to intercept. Despite having done absolutely no damage to the monster so far, the sword at least seemed to be deterring it.

I know mate, I know. But it's just, if you really want to kill that thing, you're going to have to use something within your capabilities.

"What the fuck are you talking about?"

That sword won't deal any damage until you reach level fifteen.

"That's the most ridiculous thing I have ever heard," Patrik panted. "What difference—you know what, never mind." He batted back the spider a third time. "What *am* I allowed to use?"

You're in luck. There's a bronze dagger in your inventory that should work. That old wizard must have stocked up on equipment for you before the summoning. I'm sure he would have been a wonderful mentor if you hadn't, you know, murdered him.

"Great," Patrik muttered.

Ignoring the PQA's repeated accusations, he dived back into his inventory and found the dagger—which was an appropriately copper colour. He concentrated a moment, and the sword disappeared, only to be replaced with the dagger. It was tiny.

Bronze Dagger: A dagger made from bronze. What else do you need to know? Effect: +1 to strength. Requirements: none.

"You've got to be kidding me."

He glanced from the puny weapon to the enormous spider. Its beady eyes watched him through the ring of stones, obviously looking for a way in. If the enormous iron sword had left that thing untouched, what could this toothpick possibly achieve?

But there was no help for it.

Letting out a high-pitched battle cry that was most definitely not a girly scream, Patrik leapt at the beast, dagger raised high. The copper blade flashed brightly as the first rays of morning sun pierced the canopy, then plunged towards the maw of the monster…

…and unlike the sword, sank to the hilt in spider flesh.

Shocked that he had succeeded, Patrik froze. The spider was not so calm. A bloodcurdling shriek tore through the forest as it reared back, feet flying, blue haemolymph—assuming that was what spiders had for blood here—spraying everywhere, including all over Patrik.

Fortunately, the blue liquid didn't prove acidic like its venom.

Unfortunately, Patrik was caught with his mouth open at the wrong moment and caught a mouthful of the stuff.

When he recovered from chocking on spider blood, he

found the enormous spider crumpled before him, its legs all folded up and broken. It seemed dead, until it gave a quiver. The legs thrashed weakly as it tried to stand. Thankfully it failed. He noticed its previously green health bar had dropped deep into the red.

Grimly, Patrik fingered the hilt of his dagger and stepped up to the creature. Collapsed in the dirt with the blue liquid still pulsing from its wound, the monster no longer looked so terrifying. The uncountable eyes seemed to contain an ocean of sadness. They stared up at Patrik, and it seemed to him that something passed between them in that glance. A pang of guilt touched his heart. Like the great lions and elephants of the Sahara, it would be a shame to slay—

Patrik screamed as the monster lurched suddenly towards him. His dagger flashed out and pierced it through one giant eye. With a final shudder, its health bar vanished. The beast lay still.

His shoulders sagging, Patrik let out a heavy sigh and stepped back. It was done. Somehow he had defeated the terrible beast and saved himself. Maybe even saved others! This monster would not have stopped with a single victim— such a behemoth needed sustenance. It would have struck again.

Well that was…messy.

Patrik sighed, taking in the state of his clothing. "I killed it, didn't I?"

I mean, I guess so?

"Are there points for style or something?"

Don't be ridiculous. Anyway, would you like to loot the corpse?

"It's a spider, what could it possibly—you know what, yes, yes I would like to loot the corpse."

The familiar text boxes popped up and he selected the "loot all" option. Why not? All the hair on the spider disappeared and its swollen abdomen caved in as though suddenly hollow. He was about to open his inventory to see what he'd received when the Australian began to shout again.

Warning: Monsters sighted in your area!

"I know, I already fought it, remember?" Patrik paused. "Shit, there are more, aren't there?"

They're coming from the east.

Patrik drew in a measured breath and tightened his grip on the bronze dagger. Fear fluttered in his stomach. He struggled to push it down. He'd already killed one monster. And it had died surprisingly easily—once he'd been equipped with the right weapon. He could do this.

Oh, look at that—they're also coming from the west. And the south—actually, you know what mate, they're just all around you at this point. There was a long pause. *I think it might have something to do with the dead spider. Wasn't it a queen?*

Butterflies whirled in Patrik's chest. "How many?" he asked, trying to still the racing of his heart. After living off campus food for five years, he was not in the greatest of shape.

I'd say a dozen or so.

Patrik glanced at the dagger in his hand. "Can I fight that many?"

I wouldn't count on it. Why don't you try your spell?

"What spell?"

Raise Dead. It'll summon something dead to fight for you. With your current mana you'll only be able to cast it once, but...

A leaden weight fell into the pit of Patrik's stomach. He found himself staring at the body of the wizard. The thought of the old man rising again as some kind of demented zombie...

What—no! The PQA interrupted his thoughts. *You're way too weak to bring him back. Still don't know how you managed it the first time. Luckily for you, there's another fresh corpse available.*

It took longer than Patrik cared to admit to figure out what the PQA meant. His eyes fell to the grotesque remains of the spider at his feet. "Oh, you've got to be kidding me..."

CHAPTER 4
MURDER MOST FOUL

SEVERAL HOURS LATER, COVERED HEAD TO TOE IN BLUE BLOOD and utterly exhausted, Patrik stumbled from the Enchanted Forest. Aching from exertion, he still managed a little *whoop* of joy as he stepped into the light. Closing his eyes, he slumped to his knees and basked in the warming rays of the sun.

Freedom.

His arm burned from the hours of slaughter. There had been a lot more than just a dozen of the vile spiders. Only use of the "Raise Dead" spell had saved him.

The sight of the *very* dead spider lurching to its feet and looking at him with dozens of bright red eyes had been beyond creepy. It moved more like a puppet on strings than a real living creature. But monstrous as it was, the thing had guarded his back while he fought off its fellows. Well, at least until they'd torn it to pieces. But by then his "mana" had regenerated—mana apparently regenerated at a rate of one mana per minute—and he'd been able to cast the spell again on another of the fallen monsters.

Truthfully, it hadn't been so bad. Most of the giant spiders were only level 3—which apparently meant they were as weak as newborn kittens. Many were also too busy screaming to actually attack him. They'd fallen to his dagger by the dozens. He would have almost felt bad, if they hadn't just kept coming and coming, swarming into the little clearing to fall upon him. Or rather, fall to his dagger.

When the waves had finally begun to slow, the PQA had prompted him to loot the corpses. Then he'd made his way through the trees towards the growing light, pausing only occasionally to knock off stragglers. By the time he stumbled from the trees, Patrik was pretty sure he'd cleared most of the forest of the monsters. At least future travellers would not have to fear the beasts.

Though anyone who travelled through those trees was surely one neuron short of a synapse. There was very little "enchanted" about the dark forest. And he did mean *dark*—the canopy was so dense almost no sunlight reached the ground. Fine silken webs hung everywhere, just waiting to snare unsuspecting humans in their sticky nets. Which had happened to Patrik on no less than a dozen occasions. Without his trusty dagger, he would have been spider food in no time.

But here he was, sitting on the grass, enjoying the warm sunlight of another world, the forest at his back…

He frowned. "They can't follow me out here, can they?" he asked, casting a glance over his shoulder.

There are currently no monsters in your vicinity, his PQA announced cheerfully. ***Well done in there, by the way. As this Thor bloke would say: hell is filled with the screams of your victims.***

Relaxing at the news, Patrik settled back on the soft ground. He had emerged from the forest at the top of a broad hillside. Grassy slopes stretched out below him, forming a broad valley in which the thatched rooftops of a village could be seen in the distance. Smoke drifted from the chimneys of several buildings and the *clang* of a hammer carried on the breeze to where Patrik sat.

Despite the generous coating of web and ichor that clung to his clothing, Patrik found himself smiling. Civilization. After spending the last few hours carving through monsters, it was more than he'd hoped for. Though…the prospect of trudging into town looking as he did was not so exciting. First impressions and all.

Away to the right, a stream emerged from the forest, before curving down around the valley and past the village. He should be able to wash off the worst of the gunk, though his clothes were most likely stained beyond rescue. He started to rise, when a scream from the forest behind him broke the silence.

"What the hell was that?" He spun towards the trees, raising his dagger.

For once the mouthy PQA did not reply. Patrik stood, blade poised, eyes fixed on the shadows. The scream came again. A man's voice this time—he could have sworn the first had been a woman. Patrik cursed. Somewhere in the forest, people were in trouble.

Another scream. A woman's again. This time it went on for longer. Much longer. Patrik hesitated. That hadn't sounded like someone in pain, or even terror. The way it trailed off…and at the end, it had seemed more like a wail of grief, than of someone facing a monstrous spider.

"Hello, Mr. PQA? What the hell is going on in there?"

Ah…well, I was going to mention it earlier, but… you should really check your muted notifications.

"My what?"

You asked me not to update you with every little notification, remember?

"Right…and?"

Just…can I catch you up? I should really catch you up, mate.

Patrik sighed. The Australian accent was really beginning to grate on him. How did anyone stand it? "Fine. Just don't scream."

Great! Now where were we—there!

Achievement Unlocked: Potions Apprentice. Congratulations, you've used your first potion. Reward: Your hand is better, isn't it? What more do you want?

New Quest: Escape the Enchanted Forest.

Congratulations, you have received your first quest. This one is pretty simple. You've stirred up a nest of Giant Silk Spiders by killing their queen. You must escape the Enchanted Forest. No worries if you lose some limbs, but you must escape alive. Reward: 10 gold coins.

Achievement Unlocked: Bladesman. Congratulations. You have successfully wielded a weapon suitable to your rank. This isn't really meant to be a challenge, but you seem to be the extra special kind of hero. Reward: A valuable lesson about your own limitations.

Achievement Unlocked: Beast Slayer. You have killed 20 creatures of the same race. Reward: 100 gold coins.

Achievement Unlocked: Killer. Wow that's cold, mate. You've accumulated twenty kills of positively aligned individuals. Reward: 100 gold coins. [-100 Alignment Points]

Congratulations! You have learned the skill Hack and Slash! You are now [passable] with edged weapons.

Congratulations! Your skill Hack and Slash has increased to level 2!

Congratulations! Your spell Raise Dead has increased to level 7!

Ring! Ring! Ring! Congratulations. You have reached level 10! You have been awarded 3 stat points. You have 27 stat points to assign. You may now distribute stat points between your attributes.

Quest Complete: Escape the Enchanted Forest. Congratulations, you have escaped the Enchanted Forest alive. Reward: 10 gold coins.

"Wait, wait, wait, what was that killer crap?" Patrik interrupted the stream of text that was scrolling past his eyes. The PQA's volume had dropped maybe one percent. He would take it.

You know, it's rude to interrupt. But I guess you're not too worried about that, being a mass murderer and all.

"Are you talking about the spiders?" Patrik asked. "In what world were they friendly?"

Hey, I don't make the rules. The Giant Silk Spiders in this region are classified as friendly monsters. It's not my fault you went all... There was a pause as some pages were flipped. *"Leeroy Jenkins" on their queen.* Another pause. *Did I get that reference right?*

Patrik groaned and ran a hand over his face. "You said they were enemies!"

I said they were monsters. *That doesn't mean they're enemies. What would make you think that?*

"Because they're *monsters!*"

That's speciesism.

"Spec…"

Patrik trailed off as a commotion came from farther along the treeline. Half a dozen people burst from the forest and staggered into the sunlight. Their wails carried across the slope, tugging at the heartstrings of any who heard them. The men and women wore surprisingly modern looking clothing—including one woman in a pair of yoga pants. Patrik had little time to appreciate their fashion sense, however, as the group stopped only long enough to exchange hugs and sobbing tales of woe, before taking off down the slope towards the distant village.

A lump lodged in Patrik's throat. He slipped silently back into the shadow of the trees. He might not understand everything that was happening here, but he had a suspicion things would not go well for him if those people found him covered in the ichor of the dead spiders.

"*Goddamnit, man,*" he hissed beneath his breath. "Why didn't you tell me they were friendly?"

Well, the description was quite detailed. I figured you knew! You were quick enough to kill the poor wizard. It only seemed natural that you'd leap at the chance to butcher some helpless little spiders.

"Little? Those things were little?" Patrik let out a long exhalation, seeking to calm himself. "The thing was attacking me, I didn't exactly have time to read the description."

Well, there we go. Reading is important, you know.

Patrik would have spent the rest of the day cursing the PQA, but the people from the forest were already drawing close to the village. And their cries had apparently alerted those within, for several figures emerged from the buildings and raced to meet them.

"So those villagers…what exactly do you think is going on down there?

You ah…might want to check the description for the Enchanted Forest.

A feeling of dread settled like day-old Taco Bell in Patrik's stomach as he glanced at the trees and a new text box popped into existence.

The Enchanted Forest of Monmouth. The Enchanted Forest of Monmouth is home to many friendly critters—most famous of which is the indigenous Giant Silk Spider. These spiders are famed for their eight-legged hugs, the experience of which is said to be lifechanging. The Giant Silk Spiders are also essential to the local economy, specifically through Arachniculture—the growing and raising of giant spiders for the harvest of their silk. This practice has long formed the backbone of the economy in the nearby town of Monmouth.

"You've got to be shitting me," Patrik murmured.

You really went all in on the bad guy narrative, didn't you?

A groan built in the back of Patrik's throat. If the PQA had been a physical entity, he might have strangled it. As it was, he barely had time to curse the disembodied voice for a few seconds before he noticed a fresh commotion in the town.

Several dozen men and women had disengaged from the

rest of the crowd and were starting towards the forest. Their voices carried up the hill, pitched now towards anger. Even from a distance, Patrik caught a few of their muttered words. "Queen," "dead," and "justice" were just a handful of those he understood. Several amongst the crowd carried literal pitchforks and flaming torches. Apparently, the villagers of Monmouth had decided to hunt down the one responsible for the murder of their precious spiders.

"Shit, shit, shit," he muttered under his breath.

Patrik's clothes were completely soaked in spider ichor. If they found him like this, there would be no doubt as to his guilt. He had a feeling they wouldn't be interested in excuses.

Yeah, this is quite the situation you've gotten yourself into, mate.

Patrik exhaled a long breath. He glanced at the stream, but at the pace the villagers were coming up the hill, they couldn't be more than ten minutes away. There just wasn't enough time to wash away all the haemolymph and spider carapace.

"Well, you're the Personal Quest Assistant," he said. He held out his arms in a gesture that indicated the gunk covering him from head to foot. "You got any suggestions?"

I would suggest you avoid murderhoboing your way through a nest of friendly monsters in the future.

"I meant for right now," Patrik grated through clenched teeth. "You know, some advice about avoiding the literal mob of villagers screaming for my blood."

Yes, they do look rather angry. If they see you covered in the blood of their beloved spiders, they will become your most bitter enemies.

"Yes, I already pieced that one together myself."

Well, I guess it's a good thing you have a spare set of clothes!

Patrik opened his mouth to deny the claim, then paused. A frown touched his forehead. His skin crawled.

"You don't mean…"

Well, you did loot everything *from the poor bastard.*

CHAPTER 5
THE CHOSEN ONE

Warning: The requirements of a piece of equipment you are wearing exceeds your current attributes.

Patrik shivered as his clothing flickered, then disappeared, only to be replaced instantaneously by the bright blue robes of the wizard. He'd just moved the items around in his inventory, swapping his 'everyday earth clothes' that were apparently 'equipped' around with another set of clothing labelled as 'wizard's robes'. After a moment's hesitation, he added the hat and ivory staff for good measure.

"This better work," he muttered. "I look like I'm wearing pyjamas."

His skin crawled as the silk robes settled around him. He was wearing the clothes of a dead man. An old, dead man. Gross. At least it was better than the alternative. Not that this plan was by any means foolproof. The PQA had given it a 65% likelihood of success—whatever that meant.

He felt his terror rising as he continued down the hill and closer to the mob. It wasn't long before those in the lead noticed him. If anything, they seemed to pick up the pace. Patrik swallowed and resisted the temptation to draw the dagger from his inventory. There were far too many for him to fight.

As the group approached, text boxes began to pop up

above the heads of the lead villagers. Ice spread through his veins when he saw their levels. Most were in the low teens, but several were at twenty or even closing on thirty. He was still learning the basics of this world, but it didn't take a genius to realise he would have a lot more trouble with a bunch of high-level humans than he'd had with the level 3 spiders.

"You there, wizard!" the lead villager called as Patrik drew to the side of the road in an effort to let the mob passed. "What are you doing in these parts?"

Patrik had memorized an explanation for his presence, but being called a wizard momentarily threw him off-balance. His face flushed. The bright blue, starry robes were nothing short of a travesty. The PQA claimed that each piece of clothing was a powerful magical item, but their requirements were so far above Patrik's attributes that he couldn't get any information about what exactly they did.

Stilling his thoughts, Patrik took a firmer grasp of Tenser's ivory staff and drew on everything he recalled from second grade drama classes to put on his best angry Dumbledore face.

"Who are you to question me?" he bellowed, eyes bulging, magical staff thrust out before him. "I came to this place seeking demons, not to answer the questions of a bunch of daft country bumpkins. Now get out of my way."

Silence fell across the roadside. Patrik stood there a moment, breath coming in soft gasps. He'd had to yell to ensure his words would be heard by everyone and now his throat was hoarse. But from the stunned faces of his audience, he thought he might just have gotten away with the act.

You know they can see you're only level 10, right? Hardly demon hunter material.

Ahhhh... He had not, but Patrik wasn't about to admit as much.

A long, long moment passed, then two of the men at the front of the crowd turned to one another and began whispering. This continued for a few seconds, before one nodded and stepped towards Patrik. A grin that was quite obviously forced appeared on the man's face as he spread his arms in a welcoming gesture.

"Our ah…apologies, Mr. Chosen One. We did not realise with whom we spoke. Please, make yourself welcome in our village. We must be going—there are urgent matters we must attend to in the Enchanted Forest. But ah…I am sure our apothecary may have a potion that could help with your demon problem."

Patrik blinked, not sure he fully understood the villager's words. His harsh accent sounded like it came from somewhere in Eastern Europe. But sure enough, one by one the villagers stepped aside to grant him passage. Still wearing the haughty face of the second Dumbledore actor, Patrik offered the lead villager a curt nod and strode forward through the mob.

He kept the expression fixed in place until he passed through the last of the pitchfork-wielding men and women. Only when he was another hundred yards down the road did he dare to breathe.

"Holy shit," he burst out, laughing despite himself. "I can't believe that worked!"

I know! the PQA chirped in. *Honestly, if you'd told me you were going to pretend to be a mental patient, I would have said you were mad. Hey, maybe that's why it worked so well! You sure you didn't escape from a State Mental Institution?*

"We don't have those anymore, Reagan closed them all," Patrik said, then frowned. "Wait, what was that first part?"

Reagan, Reagan, Reagan…oh wow, that's like…a whole chapter. I'll read it later, or maybe you can just give me the summary? And where do you send the crazy people then?

"You're not meant to call them crazy anymore," Patrik chided. "And all over. There are some private places, you know, if they've got rich family. Or the libraries if they don't. Or the streets. Or—hey, stop changing the subject. What did you mean back there?"

That little act with the villagers. Seriously, hilar-

Patrik stopped dead in the trail. "They didn't believe I was a real wizard?"

Rather than a response, actual laughter echoed in Patrik's mind, followed by a distinct *thump*, as if someone had just fallen off their chair.

Patrik's heart sank. He'd been quite proud of his Dumbledore impersonation, and the PQA's mocking left him oddly despondent.

Letting out a pained sigh, he continued towards the picturesque village. "Well, at least they let me past," he said after a while, then as an afterthought. "What was it he called me, 'Mr. Chosen One'? What's that all about?"

Mate, come on, did you not read your title?

Patrik scowled at the PQA's tone. "Of course I read it…" He trailed off as he pulled up his stat box.

"Patrik the Chosen One...wait, so that's what everyone sees when they examine me?" he exclaimed.

Ding, ding, ding, correct! You might just get the hang of this yet, mate!

"What the hell!"

He remembered the wizard rasping something about a saviour or chosen one when Patrik had first landed in the stone circle. At the time, he'd assumed it was the ravings of a... mentally ill person. Now it turned out he'd literally been labelled as the "Chosen One" for everyone else to see. That sort of attention was the last thing he needed.

But there didn't appear to be anything he could do about it just now, so pushing the concerns aside, he set his thoughts on the village instead.

Truthfully, "village" seemed an overly generous description for the collection of buildings known as Monmouth. The trail leading to the village was worn and pitted with use and there wasn't so much as a garden wall or ditch to mark its boundary. The road just led right up to the first of the buildings and continued on through the town. Considering they lived right next to an Enchanted Forest filled with monsters, that seemed somewhat naïve. Sure, the monsters were supposedly friendly, but could you ever *really* trust a wild animal? What was to stop a few hungry spiders from wandering down one night and eating some poor family?

You know, this line of thinking feels a lot like trying to justify the wonton slaughter of a nest of friendly spiders.

Patrik startled at the PQA's interruption. *Wait…so you can hear* all *my thoughts?*

I am quite literally inside your head, mate. And yes, that means I can read all your thoughts. Including what you did with your cousin in tenth grade.

"She was my cousin by marriage—" Patrik bit off what he'd been about to say.

He'd just passed through outermost buildings of Monmouth and his outburst had drawn the attention of a nearby group of villagers. They stared at him, eyes wide in surprise. He gave a little wave.

"Hey there," he said, "I'm ah…looking for the apothecary? Bit messed up in the head, apparently." He wrapped his knuckles against his skull for good measure.

The villagers stared at him for another full minute before one finally lifted a hand and pointed down the street.

"It's next to the inn," the man offered hesitantly.

His cheeks hot with embarrassment, Patrik nodded his thanks and continued on his way. The streets of the village were similar to the road outside—unpaved, dusty and pitted so badly he had to watch his step lest he break an ankle.

In contrast, the buildings themselves seemed to be built solid enough. Most were single story, though he noticed a few clustered further towards the centre that stood taller than the rest. The wooden walls reminded him of the log cabins up Mt. Hood, though here the roofs were of thatched straw rather than steel. He wondered how they stood up to snow in the winter. Did they even have snow here? Or winter, for that matter?

Information requested: Monmouth winter. In the depths of winter, the people of Monmouth often find themselves cut off from the world by heavy snows. During these months, many spider caretakers move to the Enchanted Forests and light fires to keep their precious spider friends warm. Others hunker down and ration their supplies until the spring melt arrives.

Patrik blinked. "Hey, that was surprisingly helpful."

That's what I'm here for, isn't it?

Patrik kept his mouth shut. No point answering to that question. Instead, he asked another that had sprung to mind when the villagers were staring at him.

"So does everyone here have a PQA?"

Nope! Just those of you who cross the void between worlds and find yourselves stranded here in the Four Circles. And a few of the richer adventurers in the higher Circles, of course.

"Wait, so there are others like me? From Earth?"

From Earth, no. No one's poked that nest of hornets since the Thousand Years War. Old Tenser must have been desperate to dig up a spell that could crack open your universe.

Patrik sighed. "That's just great." He hesitated. "So, ah, I probably should have asked this earlier, but do you have a name?"

A long silence followed. *I'm a Personal Quest Assistant. We don't have names.*

"Well, I can't just keep calling you 'voice,' now can I?" He frowned as he walked, trying to think of something creative and interesting to call the magical all-knowing voice inside his head. He came up blank. "How about Steve?"

...Seriously?

"Great, then it's settled!" Patrik exclaimed, then quickly lowered his voice when he noticed a pair of villagers watching him. "Steve it is." He took no small amount of pleasure in the silence that followed.

Hey, remember how you're wearing the clothes of a dead man?

Patrik wrinkled his nose. For just a moment, he'd managed to forget that. "I don't suppose this place has a laundromat..." he trailed off as he finally took note of his surroundings.

All was not well in the village of Monmouth.

Patrik came to a stop in the middle of the road. Across the street, a man was busy fixing wooden boards over his windows. He was already halfway finished. A crudely painted sign hanging from the front door read "Out of Business." As he stood there, a text box popped up in Patrik's vision asking whether he'd like to examine the store. He selected "yes."

The Blacksmith of Monmouth [closed]. Fredrick the Blacksmith first came to Monmouth in search of a suit jacket made from the town's famed spider silk. While visiting the town, he ventured into the Enchanted Forest and was blessed with a hug by one of the Giant Silk Spiders—from the queen, no less. He instantly fell in love with the region and decided to set up shop as the local blacksmith. For thirty years, his business has forged iron armour renowned for its high quality. However, due to the wanton slaughter of the Giant Silk Spider population and the collapse of the local economy, he has lost everything. With the Dark Lord's tax collectors due any day, he must flee the town or risk being detained for tax evasion.

"What the hell?" Patrik muttered. The blacksmith finished boarding up the last window and cast a glance in Patrik's direction. He gave a little wave but the man disappeared into the shop without a word. "His business doesn't have anything to do with the spiders. Why would he be closing? Why would anyone be closing, for that matter—it's barely been a few hours since I umm…well, you know."

That guilty conscience finally catching up to you, Mr. Chosen One? Steve piped up. *But by way of answer, think about this. Spider silk is estimated to make up 80% of Monmouth's income. Without it, there will be no inflow of gold. That means no clientele for other store owners such as the blacksmith, or jeweller, or baker—or just about anyone in town. As for why it's happening now…well, the Dark Lord likes efficiency. No point drawing things out, right?*

"This is ridiculous," Patrik muttered. "I did *not* bankrupt an entire town."

Keep telling yourself that, mate. Whatever helps you sleep at night.

He was about to give a snide reply when the sound of others approaching distracted him. At first glance he thought it was another mob preparing to follow the others into the Enchanted Forest. Then he noticed that instead of pitchforks, these villagers were carrying bundles of random belongings hoisted on their shoulders. Some of the men were even dragging wheeled carts behind them. Each was stacked high with furniture—chairs and tables and cabinets, even a few trunks that presumably contained yet more of their personal belongings.

Patrik swallowed a sudden lump in his throat. "So much for the laundromat."

The forlorn villagers continued their march. Patrik let them pass. A few cast glances in his direction, but most kept their heads down. Misery hung over the group like a cloak. Several were even sobbing, as though it had been their friends and family they'd lost in the forest. A leaden weight settled in Patrik's stomach.

"How can it be this bad?" he muttered beneath his breath.

Sure, the forest's description had mentioned the town's

reliance on the spider silk. But it wasn't like he'd killed *all* of the creatures. Had he? No, this was an overreaction. Surely they could rebuild…

The next cluster of villagers brought Patrik's thoughts careering to a halt. There were seven of them in all, each carrying a massive backpack loaded up with hatchets and pick-axes and all manner of tools. Those packs had to weigh at least eighty pounds—a feat made all the more incredible as not one of this group stood taller than five feet.

"Wait," Patrik said, "are they…"

They're dwarfs, Steve offered helpfully.

"I…ah, think we're meant to call them 'little people,'" Patrik coughed.

These are the more fantastical variety, the PQA replied. ***Also, don't go calling them "little people," mate. They'll rip your head off. And if you recall, there are two of us in here now.***

Patrik nodded absently, still staring at the dwarfs. The other villagers seemed to be giving them a wide berth, though he couldn't say whether that was down to some bias or because each dwarf wore a scowl that could strip paint. Thick, wiry hair covered their arms and tumbled down their faces in matted beards. Golden rings and bracelets adorned their stubby hands and several clutched weapons of forged iron—short swords and daggers for the most part, but one held a hatchet as though he was prepared to change its diet from wood to blood. Most of the group seemed young—or rather, their features were young by human standards. He couldn't be sure whether aging held true across species…or which were men or women, for that matter. If they followed some of the mythology on Earth, beards weren't necessarily exclusive to men in their species. If they were in fact considered a separate species…

"This is definitely going to get me in trouble with Peter Dinklage—"

"What was that, rubberneck?"

Patrik jumped as one of the dwarfs stopped dead and

turned to stare at him. The one with the hatchet. He was not happy.

"Ahhh, nothing, nothing!" Patrik said hastily, raising his hands in what he hoped was a universal sign of peace.

The dwarf watched him with its beady eyes as the rest of his column marched past. Finally he snorted and rested the hatchet on his shoulder.

"Mongrel," he spat.

He turned and marched after the others without so much as a backwards glance. Patrik stared after the departing dwarfs as the next group of villagers approached. Like those in front, they gave the dwarfs a wide berth. He caught snatches of their comments as they trudged past.

"Bet it was one of the little bastards…"

"Never can trust their kind…"

"…would do such a thing. Never seen the like. All torn to pieces."

They don't seem to like each other much, Patrik said in silent communication with his PQA.

There are four humanoid races in this world— humans, dwarfs, elves, and dragons. For the most part, they tolerate one another. But in times of stress…well, you saw. Old prejudices run deep, they say.

"So elves are real here too—wait, did you say *dragons?*"

Yes, although you'll generally only find the last two in the inner circles. They live exceptionally long lives, so tend to max out at higher levels.

"Sounds like a pretty raw deal for us humans. Also, what was that about inner circles?"

Sorry, yeah, the whole circle thing is a little misleading. It's really more of a spiral.

"Helpful as usual, Steve. I still don't know what the hell you're talking about."

An audible sigh came from Patrik's mind. He shivered. Steve's voice was one thing, but the actual noises the PQA occasionally made were an unnerving reminder it was actually lodged in his brain. The implications of that were truly terrifying.

Before the PQA could make whatever snide comment it had been about to offer, shouting broke out down the street in the direction the crowd was moving—which was thankfully back the way Patrik had come. The ring of clashing weapons followed. A fight had broken out.

Ah, might I suggest you find someplace safe to hold up while the consequences of your actions play out? Steve offered. *Then I'll be more than happy to go over everything you need to know about the Four Circles and those attribute points you've been ignoring.*

"Yeah, that's a good idea. Do you have any suggestions?"

The local inn would be a good place to start.

Patrik nodded. "Lead the way."

CHAPTER 6
LOCAL DELICACIES

OF THE HANDFUL OF SHOPS IN MONMOUTH, THE LOCAL INN was one of the few that remained open. Steve helpfully explained this was because the Dark Lord's government funded a network of lodging houses throughout the Four Circles. Publicly, this was to encourage merchants to trade with every corner of the strange nation. According to Steve, everyone knew this was actually just a front to create safe houses for tax collectors in every town they visited.

All of which meant little to Patrik, other than he would have a bed to sleep in tonight. That was the only thing on his mind as he stumbled headfirst through the old western style double doors of the Dancing Spider—which *of course* was the name of the inn.

He found himself blinking in the gloom on the other side, struggling to adjust from the bright afternoon sun. Several candles dotted the tables but otherwise the place was unlit. A dozen tables filled the common room, which according to the place's description, doubled as the town's tavern.

Today, unsurprisingly, the place was deserted. A fine layer of dust already covered every surface, as though time had somehow accelerated inside the tavern in order to demonstrate its newfound deprivation. Even with the Dark Lord's subsidy, it seemed like for the foreseeable future the owner would be living like a college student cut off from their trust fund.

Patrik knew more about that than he cared to admit.

A creak from the wooden floor drew his attention. A silhouette moved in the shadows behind the bar, before a candle flickered to life, illuminating the man who stood there. He was human and huge—though more due to his girth than his height. Smile lines spread from the corners of his broad lips, but there were no smiles now as he stepped from behind the bar. In his left hand he held a club wrapped in barbed wire. His right hand was missing.

Johnny the Bartender [level 20]. Once a budding adventurer in search of monsters to slay, Johnny's career was quite literally cut short in a brief and brutal encounter with a Dark Elf. Johnny left without his good arm and the Dark Elf left with a broken heart. Some would call that a mutual separation. Johnny is probably not one of those people. At least it allowed him to finally pursue his passion in the kitchen. See, everything happens for a reason.

"I'm not taking refugees," the bartender grunted, his voice hoarse and unwelcome. "Times might be tough, but it's paying customers only. Can't have the Dark Lord on my case. Still got my own taxes to think about." The barbed wire bat came up to point at Patrik's chest. "Now out with ya, and there won't be no need for violence."

Stunned by the unexpectedly frosty welcoming, Patrik stood with his mouth hanging open. It took a growl and the bartender advancing a step to snap his mind back into gear.

"Wait, I ah…" *Shit, shit, shit, Steve, what do you even use for currency here?*

Gold, duh. Board and meal is usually fifty coins in these smaller places.

I don't have any gold!

What are you talking about? Of course you do! Did you miss the little "inheritance" you got from the wizard?

"I can pay!" Patrik spluttered as the bartender advanced another step, though he still didn't know what Steve was talking about.

Raising his hands to show they were empty, he pulled up his inventory and finally noticed what he'd missed earlier. Above the boxes and images of all his supposed items was a counter in the top right corner, along with a stack of yellow circles he now realised were meant to represent gold coins. His eyes widened as he saw the number on the counter.

17,567 gold coins.

"Holy shit," he exclaimed. "I'm rich."

"Huh?" Johnny the Bartender asked.

Hardly. A snort sounded inside his head. ***It should be enough to survive for a few months, so long as you don't go blowing it all on hookers and fairy dust. I wonder where the wizard kept the rest of his treasure.***

He mentioned something about Bledross—

"Listen, friend," the bartender interrupted. Despite Patrik's announcement, he was still brandishing the club. "Either I'm going to need to see some gold, or some brains are going to be getting smushed in about ten seconds."

"Okay, okay, here, what is it, fifty gold?"

Patrik held out his hand and hoped the gold system worked like the inventory one. Five heavy coins appeared in his palm, each marked with an X he assumed was the Roman numeral for ten. Grinning, he held them out for the bartender to see.

"There, is that enough gold for you?"

The man stared at the gold for a full ten seconds, eyes narrowed as though he didn't quite trust what they were telling him.

"It's sixty gold now," he grunted finally, brow still creased in a heavy frown.

At Patrik's command, another X-marked coin appeared. That at least finally seemed to satisfy the bartender, who promptly reached out and swept the coins into his hand. Still grumbling to himself, he stomped his way back behind the counter. Patrik followed, taking one of the stools at the bar for himself,

"So what's on the menu?" he asked hopefully.

It was still hours from sunset, but after his exploits in the forest Patrik's stomach was about ready to start eating itself. He had a few potentially edible items in his inventory, but consuming condiments pulled from some mystical void wasn't at the top of his to-do list.

Johnny's face lit up at the question. "Oh, you're hungry? Yes, yes, of course, I'm sure you've had a long day, Mr. Chosen One. You're in luck. Got some stew simmering that'll melt your tastebuds good. There isn't much—was only expecting to be cooking for myself."

"Oh…" Patrik's heart sank, but he didn't want anyone going hungry on his behalf. "No, I couldn't—"

"Nonsense!" Waving a hand, the innkeeper disappeared through a door behind the bar. He reappeared a few minutes later with a steaming bowl of broth and a plate of dark bread. "I'll set another pot to boiling," he announced as he placed bowl and plate on the wooden bar. "Ain't no rush. Can have supper a little later tonight."

Patrik stared, shocked at the transformation from unwelcoming bouncer to jovial innkeeper. There was no sign of the scowling man who had greeted him a few minutes ago. Excitement now twinkled in Johnny's eyes and he seemed to have lost 10 years in the space of a heartbeat. He nodded enthusiastically at the food he'd set in front of Patrik.

"Go on, let it not be said old Johnny ever let a guest go hungry! No siree, Mr. Chosen One. Say, that is an unusual name. From your father's side? Have a cousin one town over, last name Assman. I tell ya, he never hears the end of it…"

Listening to the innkeeper drone on, Patrik found himself smiling for the first time since he'd been dragged off that fateful toilet. Taking up his spoon, he reached for the bowl. The rich aroma of cooked meat wafted from the stew as he dipped his spoon. He was just about to lift a spoonful to his mouth when he noticed something bobbing in the thick, gravy-like liquid. It looked like a ball of tofu.

"Ah, what sort of meat did you say this was again?" he asked, prodding at the floating ball.

It spun at his touch, still floating—

"What the *fuck!*"

Patrik lurched back from the bowl as though it had bitten him. The ball bobbed in the liquid, the dark iris in its centre now face-up. An eyeball. There was a goddamn eyeball in his soup. And it looked frighteningly human, almost as if…

"Oh, that's some high-quality centaur meat, Mr. Chosen One," Johnny replied as though cooking up a half-human crea-ture was the most normal thing in the world. Which it appar-ently was, in this universe. "Nothing but the best for my customers. Even picked out the eyeball for ya, see?"

For some reason, Patrik found his appetite had suddenly vanished. He looked from the bowl to Johnny, at a loss for words. The innkeeper smiled back at him. His eyes shone with expectation.

Ahhh, I get it, you don't like to eat things that look like humans. But…people on Earth eat dolphin still? Hell! Talk about double standards. Okay, just stay calm. Think this through, mate. What's more impor-tant: a few outdated scruples, or not crushing the last good thing left in this poor bastard's life?

Is that a serious question? Patrik cried. *Centaur, right? As in half horse, half human? As in THIS IS A HUMAN EYE!*

Oh, it is not. You're being dramatic. It's a centaur's eye. Completely different. The things are dumb as… cows. Which, by the way, ugly much? What on your Earth made people think they were in the least bit edible?

I'm not eating something that looks like a bloody human!

There was an audible sigh. **Sorry, my bad. I thought you liberal sorts were meant to care about people's feelings. How about this then—Johnny here is clearly at the end of his rope. One arm or not, he's level 20.**

As in, he will really fuck you up when he snaps. And you haven't even assigned your attributes yet.

You haven't even told me what…

The thought trailed away as Patrik looked at the bartender. Really looked. The smile he wore was genuine enough. But the way his lips drew back, revealing yellowed teeth beneath, seemed just a little forced. And that excitement shining in his eyes…didn't it seem…feverish at all?

"Is something the matter with the food, Mr. Chosen One?"

The smile flickered. The mask cracked, just a little.

Patrik swallowed. "No, no, not at all!"

He took up the spoon and very deliberately scooped the eye from the stew. His stomach heaved, but keeping his eyes locked to Johnny, Patrik took a bite.

Squelch.

It was squishy. And crunchy. Worst of all, it was actually quite tasty. Like beef, but…more gamey…

…it took all Patrik's willpower to keep himself from throwing up in his mouth.

"Yummy," he croaked instead, and offered a weak smile. "Got anything to drink?"

The innkeepers face brightened further. "Of course, Mr. Chosen One!" He rummaged around beneath the bar and came up with a large glass mug. "Ale or mead?"

There were two brass taps behind the bar, presumably connected to a couple of kegs out back. Having never tried mead, Patrik considered his options. Mead came from honey, but who knew what messed up version of bees made honey in this world. Ale was made from barley. That seemed like the safer option. Or so he hoped.

"Ale, thanks," Patrik said at last, and Johnny filled the glass with a golden liquid from one of the taps.

He set it on the bar in front of Patrik, who promptly took an oversized gulp. It was blessedly cold and—most importantly—tasted like actual ale. That would have to be good enough, since Patrik was most definitely not game to ask for any further details. For all he knew, Johnny had brewed it from his own urine and would throw a tantrum if Patrik didn't like it.

Yep, ignorance is bliss, Steve remarked as Patrik chugged another mouthful, making him think there was most definitely something wrong with the bloody ale.

But Johnny the Bartender was still watching him. He sighed and ate another spoonful. It really was rather tasty, if he could just forget what creature it had come from. At least there were no more eyeballs. But every time he encountered a chunk of meat, his stomach heaved and he chugged another mouthful of ale. He went through three mugs like that before he emptied the bowl.

And they said college drinking wouldn't pay off…

Only when he finished the bowl did the bartender return to the back room. Patrik prayed it wasn't for a refill. His stomach gave a little rumble as he lounged on the stool. He placed a hand to his belly, a sense of dread settling in. Finding out how the plumbing worked in this world wasn't at the top of his priorities—quite the opposite in fact.

The squeal of iron hinges, long unoiled, announced the arrival of a new patron. A man stood in the entrance, blinking in the gloom. He seemed normal enough, as far as people went in this world. He squinted in Patrik's direction.

"Any food left?" he asked.

"Ah," Patrik hesitated, glancing at his empty bowl. "I think Johnny said there was only enough for one." He scrunched up his face. "Wouldn't recommend it—he's serving centaur."

"Aww, centaur? That's my favourite!" the man exclaimed.

Patrik shook his head. "You don't think there's something innately wrong about eating half-human creatures?" he asked.

A frown touched the stranger's lips. "I guess I never thought of it that way."

"Seems a little messed up to me," Patrik said, idly scratching at his chin. He was already growing stubble. Were there barbers in this world? "I mean, they've got *faces*."

The man's eyes widened. "They *do* have faces."

Before Patrik could say anything else, the stranger vanished through the swinging doors out into the street.

Patrik stared at the patch of light shining above the door, then offered a shrug. "That was weird," he muttered, before returning to his mug. There was still a swig of ale left at the bottom.

You should probably refrain from rocking people's world if you want to remain inconspicuous, Steve remarked.

"Sure, cause inconspicuous is possible with a name like 'the Chosen One'," he chuckled to himself. The ale must have been stronger than he thought.

His vision blurred a little, but by now he was quite enjoying the buzz. That, and the news he was rich. Well, not rich, if the PQA was to be believed. But financially independent at the very least. Grinning, he summoned a gold piece from his inventory. Just one this time. Sure enough, the coin was marked with a Roman I. Patrik turned it idly in his hand, then froze as he saw the image stamped on the other side. He hadn't noticed it earlier.

It was a face of absolute perfection and…absolute evil, somehow? Like, the man staring at him from the gold coin was at once stunningly, irresistibly attractive—and also the physical embodiment of the devil. Magic must have been involved in its creation, as despite being etched in gold, the eyes were a bright blue. His cheekbones were prominent and perfectly symmetrical, while his short cropped blond hair practically shone in the faint light of the inn. Narrow lips were twisted into what was probably meant to be a benevolent smile.

But anyone who took the time to look closer could see the devil in the details. Under closer inspection, the benevolent smile seemed more like a leer from one of those guys in the club who spent all night staring at the women. And there was an emptiness to the eyes, a soulless quality that suggested this was someone who could happily murder a roomful of people and then go enjoy dinner with his children without so much as batting an eyelid.

And then, of course, there were the horns.

Probably should have started with those.

The dude had horns that looked very much like those of the devil himself.

"This ah…this is your Dark Lord, I take it?" Patrik whispered to Steve, too stunned to remember to speak in his head.

Thankfully Johnny was still out back and didn't hear the comment.

Yep, that's him! The Dark Lord Malus in all his unholy glory. I'd suggest turning it facedown. Those eyes are always watching, even if he isn't.

His mouth suddenly dry, Patrik tucked the coin back into his inventory. He reached for another swig of his ale, only to find it empty. His heart was inexplicably racing and he couldn't find the voice to call out for another. There was something about that face. Something dark, something evil. Something that filled him with dread.

Words he'd barely paid attention to at the time trickled back from some hidden alcove in his memory. The words of Tenser the Great, who had summoned him to this world for some secret, unknown reason.

You are…the hero foretold…champion of Portland…the Chosen One. You are to…destroy…Dark Lord…

"Steve," he rasped, "what exactly does my full description say? The one people see when they examine me?"

The words popped up without the PQA's usual cheerful screeching to accompany it.

Patrik the Chosen One [level 10]. Summoned from another universe, Patrik may look like a nothing nobody from nowhere. And he probably is. But Tenser the Great didn't seem to think so. And you don't earn a title like "the Great" by being a chump. Due to the legendary wizard's interference, Patrik the Chosen One has now become a pebble in the pond of Fate. She's going to be pissed. And until she finds a way to burn him to cinders, his actions cannot be predicted. Which, of course, means your usual collec-

**tion of fortune tellers, prophets, and doomsayers
have all made about a thousand prophecies about
this dude's arrival. Most of them are worthless. The
one old Tenser cared about, however, claims he is
destined to bring about the fall of the Dark Lord
Malus. Good luck with that one, mate.**

Patrik sat in his chair for a full minute after the PQA had
finished speaking, staring into his empty glass. Suddenly, eating
centaur and angry villagers discovering him no longer seemed
like his biggest concerns.

"Fuck me," he whispered.

CHAPTER 7
TUTORIAL

"So. Stat points. Attributes. Levels. Give it to me straight, Steve. Just how fucked am I here?"

Patrik lay on his bed staring up at the thatched roof of the inn—although calling it a bed may have been overly generous. What passed for a mattress in this world was actually just a sack of straw stitched closed so the contents wouldn't escape, and then pressed down until it vaguely resembled a bed. It was about as comfortable as it sounded. Straw spiked him through the weaved cover and he was still trying to flatten out all the lumps.

But at least he had some privacy, a room to himself. Which was more than he'd managed in the whirlwind of hours he'd experienced since first faceplanting into this world. Given the time to breathe, he could finally attempt to gain some understanding of where he was—and how he could get home.

Yes, now you are at level ten, we can actually do something about all that. Let's start from the beginning, shall we?

"Nah, I thought starting at the end might be better…"

Really? Well then—oh, that was sarcasm. You know, that's not very nice. Maybe I shouldn't be trying so hard to help you.

Patrik suppressed a sigh. He was exhausted. The last thing

he wanted was a lecture. But Steve was right. He needed to learn the rules of this place. Since apparently it was shockingly easy to go on an accidental killing spree.

"Sorry, I'll try to keep my mouth shut."

Humph. Good. Right, from the beginning. Your overall level. As we already discussed, each time you advance a level, you will also increase your base health by ten points. By slaughtering the spiders, you gathered enough experience to reach level ten, so you now have 100 health points. You can also now assign those extra stat points you've gathered. Who says mass murder doesn't pay?

"Great. So these other stats…Intelligence, Strength, Constitution, Dexterity, Charisma and mana—"

You can't assign stat points to mana. Remember, we went over this. Your mana stock will increase by 5 points for every increase in your Intelligence.

"Okay…so Intelligence is linked to mana and magic?"

It's linked to faculties of the higher mind, Patrik. Mystical powers, divine connections, what to do when a room full of people start to sing you Happy Birthday. That kind of stuff. Also being able to follow along with a simple explanation about astrophysical principles.

"Hey, stop digging around in my memories."

Sorry, I thought they would be more interesting than this dusty old book, but…

"…"

…

"You're an ass," Patrik muttered, then because he didn't have the energy for bickering, pushed on. "So mana, I used that when I cast this Raise Dead spell. But its back to ten now. You mentioned something about it recovering…"

At a rate of one mana point per minute, yes. Your health points also recover over time, but at a rate of one point per ten minutes. You can also use potions to replenish both. You got a mana potion from the

wizard, but I would recommend saving it for an emergency situation, since they're quite rare in these parts.

"Okay…" Patrik mused as he opened his inventory and confirmed Steve's words. "And what about health potions? Are they rare?"

If you need to use one of those, I wouldn't go worrying about a potion's rareness. If your mana bottoms out, you can't cast your spells. If your health hits zero, you're dead. In fact, I recommend adding the health potions to your hotlist so they can be taken without the hassle of actually drinking them. You have three left.

"The…wait, you lost me there."

An audible sigh came from inside his mind. *Open up your inventory…good, scroll to the health potions… now, concentrate, there! See?*

To his surprise, Patrik did. The health potion had been added to a little list of five boxes at the top of his inventory.

Now, when you're in a tight spot, you can just concentrate on your hotlist to use the items there, rather than scrolling through your inventory. If it's a potion, its effects will begin immediately. You can also add scrolls and weapons if you'd like to be able to cycle between them.

"Great," Patrik muttered. Hopefully he wasn't going to see enough combat for any of this to matter, but he'd promised the PQA he would listen. "I suppose that makes sense. And what's this about a four spell limit in my stat box?"

Correct. Since you're human, once you learn four magical spells, you'll need to replace one if you want to learn something new. Thankfully there are no limits to the number of skills a human can learn.

"Oh, so like Pokémon?"

There was another audible sigh. *Yes, like Pokémon.*

"Okay, think I'm beginning to get the hang of this. What

about my other stats? Like Strength? If I dump all my stat points into it, will I become Captain America?"

Captain...America? Is that some kind of...breakfast cereal—oh wait, holy crap, how many of these movies are there? Umm, let me see, no, looks like Cap is 'peak human,' so going by the standards of your world, he would be a fifteen in every attribute.

"So..." Patrik thought for a second. "So overloading on strength, we'd be talking more along the lines of the Mountain then?"

The Mountain, I don't see him in these movies...

"Oh, right, no, it's a Game of Thrones reference," Patrik chipped in.

By Fate, how much of this television crap do you people watch on Earth. Actually, don't answer that. Yes, you would be just like the Mountain. All brawn, no brains. Clearly why he's getting his ass handed to him by this Viper dud—OH BLOODY FATE, WHAT THE HELL—you know what, scratch that, this dude can take a beating. You'd have to dump a few points into Constitution as well.

Despite the gravity of his predicament, Patrik found himself chuckling. "You, ah, watched the fight between those two, didn't you?"

I don't want to talk about it.

"Yeah it was pretty traumatising. Right, so Constitution what, helps me resist damage?"

Yep! Whereas Dexterity will improve your mobility and is useful for skills involving swords or bows—like that skill you levelled up slaughtering the spiders... what was it...Hack and Slash. It also helps you avoid more powerful attacks if you're facing a stronger enemy.

Patrik sighed. The more he learned about this world, the more it seemed like one of his brother's video games. Maybe that was where the spell had gone wrong. Had it been looking for Chris instead of him? He swallowed as a lump lodged in his throat. If so, it had been five years too late.

"Okay, what about this last one, Charisma?" he asked, forcing the memories to the back of his mind.

You ever wonder what those high school jocks had that you didn't?

"Ha, ha, very funny," Patrik muttered. "So what, increasing my Charisma will make me better at talking to people?"

Something like that.

"Great, then let's worry about Charisma when the Dark Lord that rules this entire world *isn't* hunting me, shall we?"

Patrik fell silent as he considered his options. There were no doubt dozens of different combinations and specialisations in this world that would make the distribution of points important. He'd barely scratched the surface of this universe. He definitely didn't know enough to be making this decision.

But he also couldn't afford to wait. Despite the mix-up in the forest, this world was clearly not a safe place. These attributes were his only chance of holding his own with the monsters he would encounter. So not knowing enough to make a decision, Patrik decided to hedge his bets.

"Can I just spread the points across my attributes for now? Except Charisma, of course. The jocks always were overrated."

Sure, that'll give you 6 points per stat, with 3 left over. Did you want to put those into your Charisma?

Patrik gave it a moment's thought. "Nah, put them into Strength."

Done!

A bright light flashed across Patrik's eyes. He felt a surge of…everything. Energy washed through his body, leaving him feeling strong, invigorated. The various aches and pains he'd picked up from his battle in the Enchanted Forest vanished. His body seemed lighter, as though gravity no longer pressed so heavily on his shoulders. Even his mind was more alert, more awakened, like the feeling of waking up from a full night's sleep to a strong cup of coffee.

A few moments later, that alertness sadly faded back into the slush of his current exhaustion. His mind remained… different, which was only slightly worrying. At least whatever magical or mystical forces were augmenting his body didn't seem to negate the need to sleep. It was his favourite activity. Still, pushing through the weariness, he pulled up his stat box to check that Steve had made the changes he'd asked for.

Of course I did, the PQA grumbled as the menu appeared. *You have just become faster, stronger, smarter and more durable. Sadly your social skills have not been improved.*

PATRIK THE CHOSEN ONE   LEVEL 10

PROGRESS TO NEXT LEVEL 30%

RACE	ALIGNMENT
Human	-875

HEALTH	MANA
100/100	40/40

STR	CON	INT	CHA	DEX
10(+1)	7	7	1	7

Equipped: Bronze Dagger (+1 STR)

You have no stat points to assign.

SPELLS [LIMIT: FOUR]

RAISE DEAD
level 6

SKILLS [UNLIMITED]

HACK AND SLASH
level 2

Satisfied, Patrik willed the menu away. "Just checking. I don't know if you've seen *Terminator*, or *I, Robot*, or any other movie involving artificial intelligence yet, but they tend to have a common theme."

I am a most certainly not an "artificial intelligence." I'm a PQA. Completely different.

"How?" Patrik asked, suddenly curious. "What exactly are you, anyway?"

We are not allowed to discuss that.

"Aha," Patrik replied somewhat sceptically. That sounded exactly like something an evil AI intent on conquering the world would say.

He wriggled in place again, trying to get comfortable on the lumpy bed. There was a strong smell of must and dampness to the room, which was really just a space about the size of a walk-in wardrobe with the mattress shoved into the corner. It didn't even have a window. If not for the oil lantern Johnny had provided, it would have been pitch-black. Not that Patrik was entirely comfortable with the flame—between the wooden walls and thatched roofing, the entire village was one toddler-playing-with-matches away from becoming a pile of ash.

"So, this place is the 'Four Circles.' You mentioned something about higher and lower circles earlier. I take it those are connected."

Hey, would you look at that, your upgrade must be working, you finally put two and two together!

"Asshole," Patrik muttered.

Yes, the "Four Circles" is more than just a name, Steve continued as though he'd said nothing. ***Although no one is entirely sure why we call them circles. The kingdom is really shaped more like a spiral. We're currently located in the outermost loop, also known as the "First Circle." Again, don't take these terms too literally.***

"Okay, so we're in the First Circle, which is really just the outer loop of a giant spiral. What does that actually *mean*, Steve?"

A sigh whispered through Patrik's thoughts. Steve seemed to do that a lot. ***Well, it means there are combat restric-***

*tions in place. **The Four Circles were forged to create a just and equitable society.***

"Wait, aren't you ruled over by a Dark Lord?"

Don't interrupt, Steve rebuked. ***And I hardly see how that's relevant. Anyway, these egalitarian objectives are the reason for our levels, attributes, and skills. To give all who exist within this realm a fair shot at success. Upon coming of age, citizens of the Four Circles—that is, the four humanoids we talked about—each start out at level one. Most will travel to the First Circle to begin their journey, as combat within this zone is restricted to individuals lower than level 30.***

"I see…" Patrik frowned as he processed the PQA's words. "So what happens once someone hits level 30? Are they just… teleported to the next Circle?"

Of course not. They're simply prohibited from participating in combat.

"That's…weirdly humane. So basically, a master wizard like that old dude couldn't go on a killing spree in this First Circle of yours?"

Exactly. Apparently it takes the Chosen One for that. There was a long pause. ***But in all seriousness, yes. That is not to say they do not have a presence in this Circle. The powerful in the higher circles tend to recruit apprentices or send their own children to exert their influence here. Proxy wars are even fought in some areas, though you should avoid them. Those sent by the powerful are inevitably far better equipped and trained than others you might encounter in the First Circle.***

"Not so egalitarian after all," Patrik said. "Hardly seems fair."

You clearly weren't paying attention to the moral of this* Game of Thrones *show. Life ain't fair, mate.

"Hey, things turned out pretty well for the Starks in the final season."

Probably why everybody hated it.

"Yeah, well, good thing my life isn't a George RR Martin novel, isn't it?"

Ahhh, well, Fate does consider herself something of a novelist.

"What's that supposed to mean?"

What? Oh nothing, I'm sure. Anyway, you still haven't asked about that last little box. Your Alignment.

Patrik's stomach twisted in a knot. He knew what that was. That was something, at least, that he remembered from Fable.

He still had to ask the question. "It's how good or evil I'm considered, isn't it?"

Exactly! Steve exclaimed, unusually excited by his question. *You probably don't need me to say this, but I will anyway. You've been a baaad boy.*

"So what does my Alignment actually do?" Patrik pressed.

At first it will only affect how others react to you. Yours is pretty bad—it's probably why Johnny the Bartender's first instinct was to throw you out rather than serve you. You should balance that out with better Charisma if you intend to continue down the dark side.

"Wasn't really in the plans," Patrik replied. "So what do I need to do to improve my Alignment?"

Well, as Chidi on *The Good Place* was fond of saying, to be a good person, you have to do good things.

"That shouldn't be a problem. I've been doing good things all my life. How hard can it be?"

That's what Chidi thought, and he still ended up—

"Spoilers!"

We're in the Four Circles, Patrik. They don't exactly get reception for Netflix here. Shame, some of the stuff in here is actually pretty good.

Silence fell. Patrik lay back on the straw-stuffed mattress, staring at the flickering candle. Exhaustion weighed on him like a lead blanket, yet for now his mind did not seem ready for sleep. Truth be told, he wanted nothing more than to slip into that sweet escape. Maybe when he woke, this would turn out to be a dream after all, and he'd be back home in his student apartment in Portland…

…but no, sleep wouldn't come. There was just too much. Too much insanity. Too much fear.

"So, this Dark Lord…he's the real deal?" he asked at last.

A long silence stretched out before Steve replied, as though the PQA was weighing his words carefully. ***He's real. He's powerful. And like all power-obsessed tyrants, he doesn't like being challenged.***

"No, I suppose not," Patrik replied, then frowned as a thought came to him. His heart quickened. "Wait, if he's that powerful…"

He's the Dark Lord. I'm afraid the rules of the Circles do not apply to him. Though unless you threaten to become a true challenger to his rule, I doubt you'll have to worry about a direct confrontation.

"That's something."

Yeah, he'd probably just send his hellhounds or Demon Prince to deal with you.

"Well, that's just great," Patrik muttered. Pulling up his inventory, he cycled to the ring the wizard had given him in those last, dying moments.

Unidentified Ring. Properties: Unknown. Increase your intelligence to learn more about the properties of this item.

"Any idea what this is?" he asked, not very hopeful about the answer.

No more than you, mate.

"Tenser seemed to think it was important."

Shame someone went and murdered the poor guy. Why don't you put it on and find out what it does?

"You're kidding, right? Have you not read up on *The Lord of the Rings* yet? Putting on the One Ring is *never* a good idea."

Oh stop being such a baby. There's only like a... 25% chance it'll turn you into a demon enslaved to the Dark Lord.

"Great."

He stifled a sigh. The PQA was right. Not about the ring, but the part about Tenser being dead. Without the wizard, he was up shit creek without a paddle. Everywhere he went, people in this land would see his title as "the Chosen One" and read a description that claimed he planned to assassinate their Dark Lord. And while he had little doubt the dude was generally loathed, there would also be plenty who supported their dictator. That was usually the way. People liked strong leaders. Eventually someone would tattle.

"Don't suppose you know how I could get back to Earth?" he asked without much hope.

Information Requested: Portal to Earth. Error. Forbidden information. Locate Tenser the Great if you would like further information on this subject.

"The wizard again? *Shit!* Seriously, he's the only guy in this entire kingdom who knows how to open a door to my world? And of course he's dead." He sighed, slipping his hands into the pockets of the sparkly robes. "I just can't get a break—hey, what's this?"

His fingers had just encountered something in the pocket of the robes. There was a tag on the inner lining. When he turned the pocket inside out, he saw the writing scribbled on the back.

Property of Tenser the Great. If found, please return to the House of Great in Bledross.

"Who still puts a lost property label on clothes?" Patrik muttered to himself.

Have you never used a laundromat?

"Huh." He had to admit, that might have put an end to his collection of disappearing socks and underwear. "Well, anyway, what's this Bledross place? I think Tenser mentioned it too, at the end—"

Right after you bludgeoned him to death, yep.

Bledross is the capital of the human alliance, the seat of the royal family.

Patrik's heart sank. "So…the Dark Lord's house?

No, no, don't be silly. He has a fortress all of his own in the centre of the Fourth Circle.

"So what's this royal family?"

Hmm, how to explain it…oh, here! It's like the British monarchy, really. A remnant from when humanity ruled themselves. They don't have much of any sort of power outside Bledross nowadays. People just like keeping them around because the queen is hot and the king occasionally gives these inspiring speeches. Much like the Queen of Britain really—by the way, from what I'm reading, I'm pretty sure she's actually a vampire. Might want to get some people to look into that.

"Do you think Tenser could have been in contact with them?" Patrik asked. "That could be why he told me to go there."

I wouldn't be surprised. Was probably their court jester or something.

"But this is great!" Patrik exclaimed, sitting up in bed. "I can take the ring to them. They'll know what to do with it. I bet there'll be a reward for returning it, too. Maybe they even have some of Tenser's notes, something that tells me how to get home."

Well aren't you chipper all of a sudden.

"Obviously. Now, how do I get there?"

Oh, you just pull up your map. It'll show the general layout and locations of villages and cities. Finer details like buildings and trails won't be revealed until you've explored a region yourself. And the higher circles won't be shown at all until you enter those realms.

"Wait, wait, wait. I have a map?"

Yet another sigh came from inside his head.

"Okay, okay, I get it," Patrik snapped. "Let's see. Just imagine it, right?"

Lo and behold, a holographic map popped up in Patrik's vision. It took him a few moments to come to grips with what he was seeing. Eventually he realised the blue dot was his current location, as it was set amongst a cluster of buildings labelled as "Monmouth."

He imagined the map zooming out as he would with Google Maps and watched in fascination as his viewpoint expanded. The boundaries of Monmouth appeared, then the Enchanted Forest. Beyond that it was like viewing the map through a fine mist. Dots appeared with labels for other towns and cities, along with a coastline and mountains, but the rest was concealed. Eventually he found the dot labelled as Bledross away to the east.

"How far would you say that is, Steve?" There didn't appear to be a scale.

A little under three hundred miles by the Lord's Highway, Steve replied, then being actually helpful for once, added: *A week's travel if you're fit and don't stop much for rest. Two if you're not in a hurry.*

"Great," Patrik muttered. "I hate walking."

At least you aren't in a desert.

"What's that got to do with anything?"

Oh nothing, I just hate sand.

Patrik rolled his eyes and returned his attention to the map. He wasn't exactly what you'd call a hiker. In fact, as much as his Hinge profile might profess his love of nature, he was a city boy at heart. This was going to be a long journey. Turning the golden ring between his fingers, Patrik consoled himself with the hope it would be the *only* journey he needed to make in this messed-up world.

New Quest: Journey to Bledross. Deliver the [Unidentified Ring] to the House of Great in Bledross. Reward: 5000 gold coins.

"Well at least that'll cover the costs." He sighed, before the gesture turned into an enormous yawn.

Worries about the journey could wait until morning. New magical powers and enhanced body or no, he desperately needed sleep. Another yawn overtook him as he lay back on the lumpy mattress and returned the ring to his inventory.

"Let's deal with Bledross in the morning," he murmured. "Sleep comes first." He closed his eyes.

How long would you like to sleep for?

Patrik grunted. "Oh, I dunno, after all the shit that wizard dropped me in, a week would be good—"

The world abruptly went dark.

FAR TO THE SOUTH, a battle raged on the outskirts of Solime. For five long days and nights, the forces of good and evil had clashed, both sides fighting with a terrible ferocity. Magical spells and secret abilities lit the battlefield with an eerie, unending glow. And yet the days passed, and neither side seemed able to gain an advantage.

Until the Demon Prince Rhian arrived upon the battlefield.

A roar of thunder announced the arrival of the demonic prince. Encased in black-forged iron armour and wielding the mighty blade *Annihilation*, he strode across the green fields of Solime, bringing death and destruction wherever he passed. None could stand against him. The forces of good tried, of course, but with one swing of his enormous sword, Rhian smashed their lines asunder. Screaming their triumph, his followers poured into the gap and fell upon the flanks of the enemy.

Chaos engulfed the armies of the light. Within seconds they were broken, their members fleeing in disorganised panic. Hordes of orcs and goblins chased after them, slaughtering hundreds before they could escape the field.

Amidst it all, Rhian stood and watched the confusion and disarray of the enemy. This…this was not how he had expected the battle to unfold. The enemy's Dues Ex Machina always intervened before he broke their line. But not today. So where was she?

An orcish aid approached, bowing low. "My prince, the day is won!"

"I can see that, Garfunkel." Rhian did not deign to look at the creature. His lips turned down to show his displeasure. "The Elven Princess did not come."

"No, my prince," The creature exclaimed. "Your father be blessed, Dues Ex Machina could not thwart our victory this day!"

He grated his teeth. Fate, but it was hard to find good help in this Circle. "Yes," he said, as though talking to a simpleton, "so what happened? Did she advance early?"

"Not to our knowledge, my prince!"

"Then where is she?" he asked, truly exasperated now. "Are you telling me a Warrior of the Light just up and abandoned her people without a moment's notice?"

"It…ah…would appear that way, my prince," the orc stammered.

Rhian groaned. Father was not going to be happy about this. He fixed the orc with a glare that could melt rock. "Garfunkel, do you know what my father does to those who upset his precious balance?"

The orc swallowed at the Dark Lord's mention. "No…no, my prince."

"Would you like to find out?"

"No…no!"

"Then I suggest, Garfunkel," Rhian said politely, before his voice rose to a bellow that echoed across the hillside, "that you *go and find out what happened to the damned elven princess!*"

CHAPTER 8
ONE WEEK LATER

Patrik woke with a start—and a terrible rumbling in his stomach. A spasm ripped through his gut as he struggled to sit up. It felt like he'd swallowed a tiny mouse that was now trying to tear its way out of his insides. Darkness clung to the room, absent of the ever-present streetlights outside his window. Had there been a power outage—

Sleep complete: You are fully rested.

"Jesus!" Patrik flinched as the voice sounded through the silence. "Who the fuck—"

He broke off as another spasm racked his stomach. Bending in two, he gasped for air and prayed for the pain to pass.

Achievement Unlocked! Rape and Pillage. Congratulations, you made an entire village destitute. Reward: 1000 gold [-500 Alignment]

Ring! Ring! Ring!! Congratulations. You have reached level 11,12...13! You have been awarded 9 stat points. You have 9 stat points to assign.

Warning: A week has passed since you last consumed food. You are [famished]. Please consume food immediately. You will lose 5 health per hour until you consume a meal.

Warning: A week has passed since you last

consumed water. You are [dehydrated]. Please consume water immediately. You will lose 10 health per hour until you consume a meal.

Warning: A week has passed since you last defecated. You are [constipated]. Please defecate immediately. You will lose 5 health per hour until you defecate.

"What the actual fuck is going on?" Patrik gasped.

Oh, come on, don't tell me we have to go through the whole hand-in-the-fire thing again.

Patrik groaned. Fuck. It hadn't been a dream. He'd been so, so hoping. But it was all real. Another wave of agony rolled through him. He bit back a scream and clutched his stomach. What had the PQA said?

"How have I not eaten or drank anything for a week?" he said as the wave passed. "I can't have been out more than a few hours, surely..." As a student, he rarely managed more than six hours a night, much as he might have liked more.

You said you wanted to sleep for a week.

"I...what...that's...*what?*" Patrik spluttered.

As your PQA, one of my functions is to regulate your sleep. You set the hours and I ensure your body fully rests for that amount of time. Although, you should be more careful in the future. Such a long period of rest isn't really good for you. Plus your environment can change while you sleep.

"That's..." Patrik wheezed. "That's..."

Warning: you have lost 5 health due to starvation.

Warning: you have lost 10 health due to dehydration.

Warning: you have lost 5 health due to constipation.

The loss of health came with a fresh belt of agony, as though the mouse had just found a red-hot poker and begun to stab him with it. Deciding it was better to argue with the PQA later, Patrik stumbled to his feet and lurched in the direction he hoped was the door. He found it with his face and shoved it open.

He stumbled into the corridor and across to the stairs, then practically crashed his way down into the dining room. Two men and a women looked up from where they were sharing a meal in the corner. So he was no longer alone at the Dancing Spider. Had things improved in the *FUCKING WEEK* he had slept?

Another spasm reminded Patrik that he was on a timer and he staggered across to the bar where a familiar face waited.

"Mr. Chosen One!" Johnny the Bartender exclaimed. "Great to see you again! I do hope you enjoyed your sleep. I hadn't realised you'd be staying so long—rent is generally paid in advance. But I'm sure you're good for it." Despite the subject, he didn't seem overly upset. "If you could please pay your tab, I have another stew on the hob that is guaranteed to refresh a hungry young lad such as yourself!"

Patrik opened his mouth to apologise, but a groan came out instead. Willing several hundred worth of coins into existence, he banged them down on the counter. The stew could be unicorn meat for all he cared.

"Stew. Please," he croaked. "And. Water." He licked lips parched with thirst. "Quick."

The bartender chuckled as he scooped the coins into his own inventory, then turned and swept into the back room.

Closing his eyes, Patrik gulped down great lungfuls of air. He'd never experienced pain like this. And they made the elderly and terminally ill finish themselves this way? Starving and dehydrated to the point of death? Holy shit.

He'd never been so glad to see someone than when Johnny returned with a mug brimming with water.

"Thought you'd want this first," he said, placing it in front of Patrik.

He scooped it up and downed it in one long gulp. Yet another skill hard learned from college. A flashing red light he hadn't even noticed in the corners of his vision flickered out. Two fainter ones remained.

The starvation and constipation debuffs, Steve explained helpfully.

"What the hell is a debuff?" Patrik gasped.

Conditions that damage or negatively impact your stats or health over an extended period of time.

"Great."

Placing the glass back on the bench, Patrik rose and staggered across to the restroom in the corner. He'd glimpsed the door the night before, but had fallen asleep before coming back downstairs to actually use it. The stew might take a minute, and he had business that couldn't wait. Ignoring the other patrons in the corner, he forced the squealing hinges of the door open and stumbled inside.

He almost wretched as a terrible stench struck him. Wow. The air was so rancid it was practically soup. The room was also tiny, barely bigger than a single bathroom stall back home. A scattering of straw covered the floor, while on the opposite wall was what at first glance looked like a wooden bench.

On second glance, he noticed the gaping hole in the middle. Patrik did *not* want to know what was down there. But he could guess its purpose.

Any other day, he might have decided to hold it, but another bout of crippling agony from his stomach convinced him otherwise. Eyes watering, he stumbled across to the bench, pulled up his sparkly robes, and angled his ass over the hole.

Ten minutes later and a full pound lighter, Patrik staggered from the bathroom. "Never again," he croaked as he stumbled back to his seat at the bar. There hadn't been any toilet paper. Or soap. At least he'd had the spider silk in his inventory. It had proved an adequate…sanitary product. "That…that had to be one of the most awful things I've experienced in my life."

Steve snorted in his mind. ***Worse than seeing that old dude you killed naked?*** The PQA laughed. ***Maybe if you hadn't gone and slept for an entire week, it wouldn't have been so bad.***

"I was joking about sleeping for a week!" Patrik snapped. "Never do that again."

Yes, boss! came the reply, then: ***So long as you, ah, don't ask to sleep for a week again. I'm kinda contractually obliged with that stuff.***

Patrik groaned. "You know, you're not very good at this whole PQA thing."

Hey, that hurts my feelings! Steve replied. ***I'm doing my best. It's not my fault you keep going off the rails. Besides, if you must know—***

"Here you are, Mr. Chosen One!"

Patrik jumped as Johnny reappeared, a fresh bowl of stew held lovingly in his mittened hands. He set it in front of Patrik with a broad grin.

"Manticore soup. Good enough to wake the soul. Just what you need after a long sleep."

Patrik couldn't remember exactly what a manticore was. There was a lion in there somewhere. And he was pretty sure it had wings. At least it wasn't something with a human face this time. He swept up the spoon and started ladling mouthfuls of the heavy broth into his mouth, unconcerned if the other occupants of the tavern stared. So long as he did away with that last damned mouse in his stomach.

For this reason, it wasn't until Patrik's fifth or sixth mouthful of broth that he began to notice the burning.

Now, Portland might not quite be California—or Mexico for that matter. But Patrik had enjoyed his fair share of tacos laveered in Habanero sauce in his time. He'd even dabbled in ghost peppers on the occasion.

But none of that held a candle to the heat of the manticore meat.

"*Fuuuuu—*"

He couldn't even get out the whole word. Fire engulfed his entire mouth. His tongue hit some threshold and went so numb that he feared it had melted away entirely. Coughing and choking, he reached for the glass of water before realising he'd already downed it. Wouldn't have helped anyway.

"Miiiilk," he tried to rasp, but it came out more as a high-pitched whining than anything intelligible.

Thump.

A half-drunk mug of ale banged onto the counter in front of Patrik. One of the men from the occupied table had apparently noticed his distress and come to his aid. Unable to even gasp out his thanks, Patrik snatched up the mug and practically poured the amber liquid down his throat.

It helped, a little. Although only with the fire in his mouth. Which meant he finally noticed the burning from his throat all the way down to his stomach. He shuddered to think about what would come tomorrow.

"Thank you," he gasped as he set the now-empty mug back on the bar. "Gods, what the hell was…" Patrik trailed off as he saw who had come to his rescue.

His first thought was that Steve had neglected to mention a fifth human species called *giants*. The man loomed over the bar to the point he had to bend his neck slightly to avoid the crossbeams that supported the second floor. A wiry beard that would have given the dwarfs a run for their money matted his face, though thankfully his expression was friendly.

"You must be from elven territory," the giant chuckled, then slapped Patrik on the back. "Those old bags wouldn't know flavour if it smashed them in the face. Not to worry, ya back amongst your own kind now. We'll sort ya out. Few more meals like that and you'll remember what real food tastes like!"

Patrik sat frozen in place, still staring. Scars covered the face of the giant—or he supposed 'overly large human' would be more correct—and a mop of tangled brown hair tumbled down almost to his waist. His eyes were so dark as to almost be black and despite the smile, there was a fierceness to his face. He also wasn't wearing a shirt. His half-naked state revealed a stunning array of muscles rippling across his chest and shoulders. He reminded Patrik of the paintings of Norse Vikings. The man wore no sword or other weapon that could be seen, though of course that meant little with the inventory system. Or perhaps this man simply didn't need a weapon to dispatch his enemies. Patrik could well imagine those fists cracking skulls.

"O…kay?" he offered at last.

"A man of few words I see," the man laughed again. "Not to worry, my friend. The name's O'Malley the Bard." Patrik blinked, only now realising the man did indeed wear a lute strapped over his shoulder. He made a quick examination of the man's description.

O'Malley the Bard [level 24]. Ever since he was a child, O'Malley has been the biggest kid on the playground. Packed with muscle and brawn and little else, he could have been one of the greatest fighters of the age. That's what his Barbarian parents raised him to be, after all. But don't let his appearance fool you. Inside that barbaric body is the heart of a musician—and a pacifist. O'Malley wouldn't hurt a fly. That's what his companions are for.

O'Malley pointed a thumb over his shoulder. "My friends over there say hi. Might I introduce Thalia the Sorceress, and Giovanni the Great…"

Hey what do you know, they do give that title to any old chump, Steve interjected. *Probably doesn't bode well…*

"…we're here on a quest," the bard continued in his easy manner. "How about yourself…?"

He left the last part hanging, which seemed to Patrik must be more a matter of manners than an actual question, given anyone could read his ridiculous description.

"You can call me Patrik," he said anyway and held out his hand.

The giant stared at the outstretched hand. "Ahhh…" He slapped it with his own giant mitt, giving Patrik a low five. "Is that some kind of weird elf tradition? You really were with them a while, weren't ya?"

"Hey, O'Malley!" A shout from the woman at the table saved Patrik from his embarrassment. She rose and stomped over to join them. She did not have a friendly expression. Patrick quickly examined her.

Thalia the Sorcerous [level 25]. Growing up the

daughter of a noble family, one might think that the young Thalia had everything handed to her on a plate. And she did. The best spells, armour, weapons, she got all of that shit. But one thing you can't fake in the Four Circles is Alignment, and the spoilt sorceress has wanted to be a Warrior of the Light since she was five. She'll do whatever it takes to earn the title—even if she has to murder her way through an army of negative Aligned creatures to do it.

"What are you doing, idiot?" she snapped at the giant bard when no one said anything. "Where's the innkeeper? We need to settle our bill and get out of here before this pipsqueak poaches our quest."

"Or we could do the neighbourly thing and ask him to join us!" O'Malley exclaimed, apparently unperturbed by the woman's snarling.

The sorceress stared at the bard until his shoulders slumped and the bright look on his face crumpled. Then she turned her bright blue eyes on Patrik. He swallowed at the rage he glimpsed there. It was completely at odds with the rest of her complexion. Brunette bangs framed her face and tumbled down around her shoulders, while her overly large, thick-framed glasses gave her more of a librarian look than that of a sorceress capable of wielding arcane magics. Hell, she barely came up to his shoulders, and was even wearing a red sweater and backpack.

Man, her alignment is something else. Steve cut in. *It's over 9,000! You should get some pointers from this chick.*

"This level ten idiot looks like he's about an hour away from being murdered by a horde of ghost orphans," she snarled. "He can join us over my dead body. Now get the bill, O'Malley. We're leaving."

Or not...

Patrik swallowed as the woman turned and swept across the room. The man who'd remained at the table, Giovanni the Great, didn't look up as she sat across from him. Tucked away in the corner, Patrik could see little of the man, other than that he wore a brown leather jacket and had a sword strapped over his shoulder. Patrik wondered why these three kept their weapons—or in O'Malley's case his lute—outside their inventory.

"I am sorry, my friend. Seems we won't be getting to know each other after all."

Patrik looked around as O'Malley lay a giant hand on his shoulder. Johnny had reappeared and was just now sweeping a pile of coins from the countertop. The innkeeper was whistling to himself and seemed to be in a much better mood than when Patrik had first seen him.

"What is your quest?" he asked, raising his eyes to meet O'Malley's gaze. "I promise I won't poach it. I've already got a long journey ahead of me."

The giant hesitated. It was impossible to miss the quick glance he cast over his shoulder. But finally he shrugged.

"We came to cleanse the town's infestation," he said.

That brought a frown to Patrik's face. "Infestation?" he asked. "What infestation?"

"Ha!" To Patrik's surprise, the giant burst into laughter. "What infestation, right! That's a good one, my friend." Still chuckling, O'Malley clapped Patrik on the back again. "Damn shame you won't be joining us. But perhaps we will meet again. Till then, I wish you luck!"

With that he turned and wandered back to the table of adventurers.

Patrik watched him go, still wondering for the life of him what exactly he'd said that had been so funny. As O'Malley returned, the other two rose and marched out the front doors. Patrik caught a glimpse of mist swirling outside and shivered.

He shook his head as the double doors swung closed again behind them. "Seriously," he muttered. "What infestation?"

CHAPTER 9

THE INFESTATION OF MONMOUTH

PATRIK STILL ONLY HAD THE RIDICULOUS WIZARD'S ROBES FOR clothing. He wasn't looking forward to venturing out into the elements in the thin silk, especially not with the dense mist he'd glimpsed outside. Hopefully a local clothing store or tailor had survived. It wasn't like he was short on gold. And—he suddenly started getting excited—maybe there was a horse trader or whatever they called it. A mount would cut his journey time in half.

"Johnny," he called. The innkeeper reappeared from out back a few seconds later. "What stores are still open in Monmouth?"

"Stores, Mr. Chosen One?"

"Please, you can call me Patrik," he replied wearily, "and I mean, is there still a tailor? A laundromat? Food stores?"

The innkeeper did not immediately reply. He just stood there, staring at Patrik. Finally he gave a slow shake of his head.

"No stores, Mr. Patrik," he said. "No nothing."

An icy chill blew across the back of Patrik's neck. "What?"

"Alas, I am all that is left now of Monmouth," he replied. "All the others…" He trailed off. A heavy silence hung over the room. Then the man's eyes settled on Patrik's half-finished bowl of stew. When the innkeeper spoke again, there was an edge to his voice. "Did you not like your meal, Mr. Patrik?"

"Ahh…" *Shit.* "No, no, I was just going to ask for a glass of ale to help wash it down."

The innkeeper's face brightened. "Of course!" He moved to fill a glass, then plonked it down in front of him. "Eat, eat!"

Grimacing, Patrik took up his spoon again. The fire in his mouth had barely begun to lessen. Deciding the best course of action was to get it over with, he began to shovel spoonful after spoonful down his gullet.

"If you're looking for supplies for a journey," the innkeeper mused as he ate, "I'm sure I could help. Where are you heading?"

"Bledross," Patrik gasped, struggling to breathe between each spoon of fire.

"Ah, then you'll be passing through Anchorpoint along the way." Patrik hadn't checked the exact route on his map, but he nodded, trusting the man's geographical knowledge. His eyes were watering so badly he could barely see the bowl in front of him. He prayed to whatever gods existed in this world that it was almost empty.

"A week's supply should do it then. Wait here, I'll go put together a bag. Geez, you really like the manticore, don't you? Think I've got some jerky, I'll make sure I include some."

Patrik stifled a groan as the blurry shape of the innkeeper disappeared. By the time he returned, Patrik had finished off the bowl of *literal fire*, and was halfway through chugging the ale in a desperate attempt to quinch the flames. Johnny chuckled as he placed a mesh bag on the benchtop.

"There ya are, Mr. Patrik. Enough food for a week's journey. You're young though, should really only take three or four days to reach Anchorpoint. Be sure to stay at the Sailor's Wife when you're there. Old friend of mine runs the place. She'll take care of ya. That'll be sixty gold for the supplies, by the way."

Eyes still tearing up, Patrik handed over the coins. Then he took a moment to check his map and found there was indeed a village about halfway to Bledross. Anchorpoint appeared to be nestled in a little cove alongside the Mermaid Isles. Hopefully he could get a horse and some food that didn't burn his mouth with hellfire there. Maybe even some fresh clothes.

Rising from his chair, he offered his hand. "Thanks for everything, Johnny. I hope things improve soon for Monmouth."

The innkeeper stared at Patrik, frowning, before he finally picked up the sack of food and placed it in his outstretched hand.

"You're a strange one, Mr. Patrik," he murmured. "Still, one can hope, I suppose."

With a sigh, the innkeeper turned and wandered out back, leaving Patrik standing there with his hand still outstretched.

"Handshakes aren't a thing here, are they?"

Is* that *what you keep trying to do!

Shaking his head, Patrik pulled the bag of supplies into his inventory and headed for the door. The food might not be to his liking, but at least he had enough to get him to the next town. If he could get a full day's walking in, he could be in Anchorpoint—

Patrik stumbled to a stop in the doorway of the Dancing Spider. Outside, the mist was so thick he could hardly see a few feet beyond the entrance of the inn. He stepped onto the porch with a frown, allowing the door to swing shut behind him. When the wooden planks groaned ominously beneath him, he quickly moved down the steps into the street.

Silence.

There was no gentle buzz of voices in Monmouth now, no banging of hammers as houses were boarded up or squeaking of wheels as refugees loaded their wagons. O'Malley and his friends had left no sign of their presence. They must be long gone by now.

Waving his hands in front of his face, Patrik confirmed he couldn't see jack shit, let alone figure out which direction to take to leave the village. He was as likely to walk face-first into a wall as he was to navigate his way down the road.

Thankfully, he was beginning to get the hang of his newfound abilities. Pulling up his map, he found his dot and moved a few steps in one direction, then the other. The positioning seemed to be far more accurate than Google Maps, and he was able to orientate himself from the movements of the dot. Satisfied, he turned until the dot showed him facing towards the edge of the village and then set off at a cautious pace. Knowing he would see nothing in the heavy fog anyway, he left the map in place. It felt weird at first, navigating by the projection alone, but he was just beginning to get the hang of it when Steve's voice rang in his mind.

Warning: Monsters approaching.

"What the hell?" Patrik stumbled to a stop and dismissed the map.

The mist closed in on him. It might have cleared a little, as he could see the silhouettes of a few buildings now. The wooden walls loomed around the street, windows boarded up, silent—

Patrik spun as the soft whisper of laughter came from behind him. Instinctively he summoned the bronze dagger from his inventory, but the street was empty. Or…was that a flicker of movement in the mists? He took a step towards it, dagger raised, when a thought occurred to him.

"Wait, you said monsters. And we're still in the village. This isn't the *good* kind of monster again, is it?"

Ah, well, that depends…

"On what?"

The laughter came again. A different direction this time. He spun towards the noise, heart racing. More silhouettes moved amongst the mist. The laughter sounded like that of a child. Patrik forced himself to relax. Obviously Monmouth wasn't as deserted as he'd been led to believe.

You should probably read the town's new description.

Clenching his teeth, Patrik pulled up the text box.

The village of Monmouth. Once a wealthy village, Monmouth was known as a rare gem of civilisation in

a brutal and unforgiving world. The villagers lived peaceful lives, prospering from the trade of silk from the local population of Giant Silk Spiders. That is, until a wicked fiend slaughtered the spiders and their queen, driving the creatures to extinction and destroying the town's economy. With their livelihoods ruined, the villagers fled the town for brighter horizons. However, not everyone was remembered in the exodus. The children of the local orphanage were abandoned in the chaos, left to perish. Cursed to haunt the town forever, they are Monmouth's only remaining residents.

"What, it's only been a week—" Patrik exclaimed.

New Quest: Cleanse the village of Monmouth. Monmouth has been overrun by the ghosts of abandoned children, turning the once prosperous village into a literal ghost town. Do not let this darkness thrive. Exorcise the ghosts by whatever means necessary. Reward: 1000 gold coins.

"You've got to be shitting me," Patrik muttered.

I told you the environment could change while you sleep.

A shadow flittered through the mists. Patrik swore, bringing up his dagger. He could barely see anything in the swirling white. An icy breeze blew across his back, raising hackles on his neck. His intuition screamed a warning and he spun, bringing up the copper-coloured blade.

Tendrils of cloud shifted in the gloom, coalescing into a pale silhouette. Patrik's heart practically stopped in his chest as he found himself looking upon the translucent face of a little girl. Sunken pits of shadow swirled where cheeks should have been, and bright blue eyes stared at him from a terrible, hollowed-out face. A faint laughter carried through the air as the child opened her mouth, though she did not speak.

"Is it…is it, ah, friendly?" Patrik rasped.

His heart was racing so fast he thought it might explode. This was some shit torn straight out of *The Shining*. But he had already learned a hard lesson about first appearances in this world, and the ghost child hadn't yet made any move to attack him.

That depends.

"Depends on what, exactly?"

On whether it recognises you as the cause of its torment…

Patrik swallowed, then forced himself to let out a long breath. His heart slowed somewhat. No one in the village had seen him leave the forest. There was no way it could know—

Or your soul, actually. Yeah, your soul could totally give you away.

At that moment, a bloodcurdling cry echoed through the street. Before Patrik's eyes, the mouth of the little girl distorted, stretching wider and wider. The shrieking grew in pitch until all Patrik could do to endure it was to slap his hands over his ears and squeeze his eyes closed.

Abruptly, the shrieking cut off. Silence fell over the town. Hesitantly, Patrik opened his eyes and faced the little girl again.

She was no longer alone.

Patrik stared in horror as the ghosts of a dozen children coalesced from the mists. Faces hollowed out and lit by a sapphire glow, they drifted towards him with arms outstretched. There was no mistaking the murderous glint in their eyes now.

"Well, fuck."

I would suggest you run?

Patrik ran. For once, there didn't seem to be any point arguing with the PQA. Sadly, running from a handful of ghosts proved far more difficult than expected, as an invisible force picked him up and hurled him sideways. Before Patrik could so much as scream, he crashed through the boarded-up front door of an enormous building on the street corner.

Crack!

Blunt force damage inflicted [-15 health]

A groan rasped from Patrik's throat as he picked himself up from a pile of rubble. His health meter was now flashing in the corner of his vision. It was still green, thankfully, but he hadn't fully recovered from his earlier deprivation. A third of his health was now gone.

Staggering to his feet, he gathered up the fallen dagger. Dust billowed and the floorboards groaned ominously as he shifted his weight. It was dark inside the boarded-up building. The only illumination came from thin slivers of light filtering down from somewhere above. Patrik wasn't sure where it came from, considering the gloom outside, but he wasn't about to question the blessing.

With the windows all boarded up, the door through which he'd 'entered' was the only exit. His body aching, Patrik started towards it, but the little girl was faster. Her ethereal form appeared in the doorway, pale eyes burning with a fiery intensity. Her translucent form flickered like an old CRT television with bunny ears.

"Oh, fuck this right to hell," Patrik muttered as he finally examined the ghost.

Orphaned Ghost [Level 12]: Once upon a time, Samantha dreamed of a nice couple coming to the orphanage and adopting her. She would have lived a life of joy and laughter. Instead, she and the other orphans were abandoned. Now she has only her laughter. That, and an unquenchable thirst for blood. Warning: this is an incorporeal monster.

"Sorry, kid," Patrik growled, raising his dagger. "Nothing personal."

The thought of stabbing a child—even one that was clearly a ghost—was unnerving, but he had to remind himself she was already dead. Having apparently starved to death in less than a week…

Anyway, these things had shown they meant business. He had to act before they used their psychic telekinesis or whatever it was again. Lunging forward, he drove the bronze dagger at the creature's throat. As the blade connected, the creature blinked out of existence. Howling a cry of triumph, Patrik swung on the next—

Raarrgg!

This time, the screaming was right in his ear. He staggered as the little girl reappeared right beside him. Her face distorted, mouth stretched unnaturally wide, she drifted forward, a pale hand catching him by the throat. Icy fingers began to squeeze.

He lashed out again with his dagger. The ghost flickered as the blade passed through her arm, but she did not release him. Screaming so loud Patrik felt that blood must erupt from his ears, she tossed him bodily across the room, where he slammed into the wall with a crash that must have echoed through half the town.

Blunt force damage inflicted [-15 health]

The iron tang of blood filled Patrik's mouth. He coughed, each pained inhalation rasping in his throat. His health was in the orange now.

"What the hell?" he gasped.

You did read the incorporeal warning, right? As in, immune to physical attacks…

"So how—"

Patrik broke off as he felt a terrible cold spread through the room. The fog from outside billowed through the doorway, bringing with it the other children. Their burning eyes lit the room a pale blue. Patrik found himself shivering on the floor as the temperature plummeted, his breath misting on the air. It reminded him of a scene from a horror movie…or that episode of *Supernatural* when Sam and Dean went up against a ghost…

…which gave him an idea.

"Come on, come on," he muttered to himself as he pulled up his inventory.

The system window was only partly transparent. He could see the shapes of the little children drifting towards him, but in his desperation, he forced himself to ignore them. Scrolling through the dozens of items he'd looted from the old wizard and dead spiders, he finally came to what he'd been seeking.

A heavy fabric bag appeared in his hands. The little girl

screamed. The sound cut through Patrik like a two-day old burrito. He slapped his hands to his ears, sending the bag tumbling to the ground, where it burst open. Salt rained across the floorboards.

Well, that's gotta be at least ten years of bad luck... Steve began.

Patrik didn't listen. As the ghostly scream cut off, he scrambled for the spilt salt, pushing it into a messy line between himself and the pale-faced children. They screamed again, all of them together. Pain split Patrik's head in two, but he couldn't spare his hands now to block out the sound. One of the children blinked out, then reappeared just beyond the line of salt. He had only seconds.

His hands dragged salt from the pile and drew it around himself in a circle, praying there was enough, that he could get it to join, until...

Done!

Panting, Patrik sat back on his haunches. Only then did he dare to look up.

The ghostly children stood in a ring around his circle of salt, pale faces staring, eyes burning. His heart racing so hard he could barely hear himself think, Patrik waited for them to spring. Fear filled his throat. Surely it couldn't be so simple. And yet...seconds ticked by and still the children did not move. They didn't even blink.

Ha, I can't believe that actually worked.

CHAPTER 10
SAM AND DEAN WOULD BE PROUD

Cursing, Patrik closed his stat box. Nothing there would help him with his incorporeal ghost problem.

Seriously, I still can't believe that worked. Sam and Dean would be proud.

Patrik exhaled. "Me neither," he muttered. "Who says watching 14,600 minutes of Supernatural doesn't have its benefits." Chris might have been the gamer, but Patrik was the television fanatic.

He returned his gaze to the ring of pale faces. His heart sank. Ten minutes had passed since he'd created the salt circle and not one had so much as blinked.

"Now if only some wise, all-knowing PQA could find us a way out of this mess…"

Well, if you had an enchanted weapon, it would be easy, Steve replied. *Maybe some decent magic… although they're resistant to the spells common at your level. And you ah, only have Raise Dead. Which doesn't work so well without a body.*

"Great." Patrik glanced at his pile of salt. "Don't suppose they have shotguns in this world?" The Winchesters loaded them with rock salt shells.

They don't really go with the medieval theme, do they?

Patrik sighed. "You know, Clippy was more helpful than you, Steve."

Hey, don't go lashing out at me. I wasn't the one who in the space of a week turned a thriving metropolis into a ghost town.

"Touché."

A shout came from outside before either could continue. Trapped in his circle of salt, Patrik could only watch as first Thalia, then O'Malley, and finally the swordsman Giovanni entered through the busted-in door. The sorceress's face hardened when she saw him standing amidst the ring of pale children.

"Damnit, O'Malley. I told you he was trying to poach our quest. What did you tell the little asshole?"

"Hardly nothing—" the giant bard began, but by then the ghosts had taken note of their presence.

As one the children turned—or rather, their heads turned, each twisting unnervingly on their necks to stare at the intruders with those unblinking eyes.

"Ah…that's a lot more than we thought…" O'Malley whispered in a conspiratorial manner to the sorceress at his side.

"That's a lot more than *you* thought," Thalia growled. "*I told you a quest worth 1000 gold was going to be a bitch.*"

Giovanni said nothing, but he drew his sword. It glinted strangely in the gloom of the house. Almost as though…

Giovanni the Great [level 24]. Abandoned as a baby in the wilds of Tergaron, Giovanni was adopted by a pack of wolves [*holy…literal wolves?*], and raised as one of their own. However, upon reaching maturity and learning he was adopted, Giovanni returned to civilisation seeking answers. Blessed by the creatures of the wilderness and a master of shadows, the mysterious swordsman has sworn a vow of silence until he can resolve the secrets of his birth.

Ooh, that's good fortune. He's got an enchanted blade.

So he can kill them?

Geez, were you always so eager to slaughter children? But no. The blade will only banish the ghosts for a few hours. At least you'll be able to escape. Good thing I didn't make that bet.

What bet—

"Wait!" O'Malley stepped between the ghosts and Giovanni. He flashed the silent warrior a look, then turned to the ghosts. "Look at them! They're just children." His voice cracked as he spoke.

"They're not children anymore, O'Malley," Thalia growled.

"But they were!" the bard insisted. "In all this world, nothing is beyond redemption. Look, they haven't attacked us. They know. They know we can help them!"

"We help the poor bastards by banishing them all to the cleansing fires of hell," Thalia growled. A flickering light appeared in her hands. "Now play your damn lute before they attack."

The pair locked eyes, and for a moment it seemed the gigantic O'Malley would refuse the sorceress. The atmosphere in the room grew increasingly tense as the ghosts began to flicker and make soft moaning noises. Patrik shivered as he watched the silent conflict. The ghosts were getting ready to attack. Even at their higher levels, the adventurers were clearly outnumbered…

"Oh, fine," O'Malley muttered, reaching for his lute.

As one, the ghosts all disappeared.

"Look out—" Patrik started.

Chaos erupted as the sounds of children's laughter echoed through the room, growing louder and more shrill, until Thalia and Giovanni were driven to their knees. They clutched at their ears, eyes clenched closed in apparent agony. The enchanted blade clattered to the ground and Thalia's magical light flickered and died. His lute clutched in hand, O'Malley seemed unaffected by the sound-based attack. Was that because of some kind of bard magic, or because there was no hatred in his soul? Patrik didn't know, but either way, the giant stood frozen as the ghosts appeared around his companions.

Isolated in his ring of salt—and apparently protected from even nonphysical ghost attacks—Patrik watched in horror as the children approached the fallen pair, arms outstretched. Green health bars appeared over their heads, just like they had with the spiders. As the first ghostly fingers laid hand to flesh, the green bars rapidly began to plummet.

He had to do something.

Patrik's mind raced. Crouching, he reached for the leftover pile of salt. Separating it into smaller piles, he drew in a breath, then touched a finger to the first and drew it into his inventory. It appeared as a small pile of salt in his list. He touched the next and did the same. To his relief, a x2 marker appeared next to the small pile of salt. He repeated the process until the counter struck x20, then scooped the remainder back into the bag and took that as well.

Only then did he look up again. Barely a minute had passed, but the health bars for both Thalia and Giovanni were already in the orange. The bard still stood nearby, ringing his meaty hands as he looked from one to the other in a state of indecision.

"O'Malley!" Patrik shouted. The sound echoed loudly in the silence. At least the screaming had stopped. On the floor, the pair stirred, but they were surrounded, their health already below half. "Get your friends into the circle!"

Then Patrik leapt from his protective ring of salt.

The reaction was immediate. Patrik had been hoping for it, but even so he was taken by surprise. Across the room, the ghostly faces snapped around as the object of their hatred became vulnerable.

Then they all blinked out, disappearing without a trace.

Only to reappear directly in front of Patrik.

Crying out in terror, he threw up a hand and at the same moment, tore open his inventory. Salt slashed the air as he summoned the first small pile to hand. It struck the little girl and several of her ethereal companions, who promptly flickered and disappeared. Patrik didn't pause. Hoping O'Malley was doing his part, he sprinted for the door.

He almost made it.

He had just reached the doorway when an invisible hand grabbed him by the back of his shirt and hurled him aside. Crashing bodily into a wall, he slumped to the ground and groaned, the wind driven from his lungs. The pain redoubled when he tried to sit up and found his breath would not come. Stars danced before his eyes, slowly clearing until he could see his health had dropped another twenty points. It was into the bottom of the orange now.

And the children were coming.

Might want to think about a health potion, Steve piped up.

Patrik didn't have the energy to curse the disembodied

voice. Oxygen filled his lungs as he finally managed to inhale. It was icy cold, burning. Fiery blue eyes surrounded him on all sides. Pale hands reached for him. His skin tingled where they touched.

"O'Malley!" he cried, watching his health plummet. "Did you do it—arghhh!"

He screamed as the tingling turned to icy fire. Thrashing, he tried to escape the outstretched fingers of the ghosts and almost missed the bard's reply.

"We're in the circle…hey what is this…is this salt?"

There was no time for Patrik to reply. His health flashed red as he pulled up his inventory. Ignoring his little piles of salt this time, he went for the bag—or what remained of it anyway. As its weight settled in his hands, Patrik slammed it into the floor. Salt exploded outwards in a cloud of dust. A collective moan rasped from the ethereal children as they flickered out.

Nicely done! Steve encouraged. ***Just cost me ten gold, but still…***

Ignoring the voice, Patrik scrambled to his feet. If these things really went by *Supernatural* rules, he had anywhere from a couple of seconds, to a few hours. Agony racked his body and his vision spun. Recalling Steve's earlier suggestion, he flicked open his hotlist and clicked on the health potion he'd put there. Strength flooded back into his body, the aches and pains he'd picked up vanishing in seconds as his health returned to full.

Heart pounding, he staggered back to the salt circle, where he found O'Malley standing over the unconscious bodies of Thalia and Giovanni. Thankfully the bard had been aware enough to lift their bodies over the salt, leaving the ring intact.

The pair were just beginning to stir as Patrik joined them in the circle. It was far too small for four people, but given he'd just used up the rest of his salt, there was no help for it but to cram themselves inside.

"You saved us!" O'Malley exclaimed, engulfing Patrik in a bearhug. The giant released him just as quickly. "I have no idea how, but thank you, my friend!"

A groan came from Thalia as she sat up. She appeared to

have knocked her head—either when she'd fallen or when O'Malley had carried her—and a trail of blood ran from a cut on her forehead. A scowl crossed her face when she noticed Patrik standing over her, only to change to confusion when she saw the ring of salt around them. She reached out a finger and dipped it in the white substance, then gave it a lick.

"Salt?" she asked. "None of the handbooks mention salt." She seemed more angered by the discovery than confused.

Patrik allowed himself a smile. "I learned from the best."

"I'm sure," she muttered. Something flickered behind her eyes, then the health bar over her head started to refill.

"So where—" Thalia began, then trailed off as a cold breeze blew through the room.

Patrik didn't need to turn around to know the children were back. Drawing in a breath, he faced them. They stood as before in their silent circle, waiting.

"So salt protects against them," O'Malley was saying, "but…I don't understand. Why did they chase you, Patrik? Instead of finishing us off while we were incapacitated."

The words barely registered on Patrik. The icy blue eyes watched him. They knew, these children. They could read his soul, Steve had said. They knew he was responsible. His stomach tied itself in a knot.

"O'Malley," he said at last. "Did you mean what you said earlier? About redemption?"

A frown creased the big man's face. "Of course. How can the world become a better place if we cannot forgive those who have done wrong?"

Thalia snorted. Giovanni kept his silence.

Patrik clenched his fists. It would have to be enough. "I think I know how to stop them, for good," he said at last. "But…" He sighed. How could he explain it? "They're here because of me, O'Malley. That's why they attacked when I left the circle. It is my fault they're ghosts."

"But…that's…" The bard's frown deepened.

Drawing in a breath, Patrik squared his shoulders. "And if

my hunch is right, I'm the reason they remain on this plane. They want vengeance. But maybe…"

Exhaling, Patrik stepped from the circle.

This time the ghosts didn't react. Or at least, not immediately. O'Malley cried out in warning, but Patrik didn't look back. The little girl, the first to have recognised him, stood before him, eyes burning in the darkness. Waiting.

"I'm sorry," Patrik whispered, bowing his head. "This is all my fault. I'm sorry I killed the spiders. I'm sorry I ruined your town. It was an accident and I wish I could take it all back. But I can't. All I can do is offer my sincerest apology."

Silence. Behind him, the three adventurers said not a word. Patrik could sense their eyes on his back. But it was not their judgement he feared. At least, not just yet. He could feel the collective weight of the spectral children as they watched him, could sense their rage, their yearning for revenge. It bound them to this world as surely as Patrik's gym contract tied him to the gym he hadn't visited in three years.

But unlike a gym contract, theirs could be broken.

"Please," he continued. "Know that for as long as I live, I will dedicate myself to healing the evil I wrought here. Please, know that, and know peace."

Shivering in the icy air, Patrik closed his eyes and waited. It was a risk, he knew, exposing himself like this. After all, there were three adventurers watching him who might decide that Monmouth needed justice. And any one of the ghosts might decide they preferred his blood to an apology. Still, he was pretty sure—

Thump!

Eyes closed, Patrik didn't see the blow that struck him. But he sure as hell felt it. The impact drove the air from his lungs and hurled him backwards. Giant arms caught him before he could slam into the ground again, but he was still left reeling and struggling to breathe.

By the time he recovered enough to open his eyes, the ghosts had drawn up right around the edges of the circle. Their mouths stretched wide when they saw him alert, and the screaming began again. Even within the protection of the salt, Patrik felt fresh pain in the base of his skull.

"What the hell was that all about?" Thalia snarled. "You have a death wish or something, idiot?"

"Thalia is right. That was most unwise, my friend," O'Malley added as he set Patrik back on his feet. The bard had been the one to catch him.

Giovanni said nothing, but Patrik noticed the man was holding his sword again.

"I didn't…" He trailed off, glancing at the ghost. Swallowing, he forced himself to continue. "I thought by making amends, it might free them from their curse.

Thalia snorted. "Not many ways to kills a ghost. Love ain't one of them."

"Great," Patrik muttered, teeth clenched against the pain radiating through his chest. His health had dropped at least twenty points from the blow, but he only had two health potions left and he didn't want to waste one just yet. "Now I know."

"At least you tried," O'Malley offered, placing a giant mitt on Patrik's shoulder. "It is not an easy thing, to admit what you did. For what it is worth, you have my forgiveness. And should we escape this trap, I will help you seek the redemption you crave."

"Ah…thanks?"

Thalia made a sound that might have been a growl, or could have been laughter. It was difficult to tell with her. "Let's survive this mess before you go inviting any more liabilities onto our team, shall we, O'Malley? Or did you forget what happened to Gary?"

"He wouldn't be another Gary!" O'Malley exclaimed.

"Wait, what happened to Gary?" Patrik asked.

"Don't worry about it," Thalia muttered. Folding her arms, she studied the ghost children. "Some mess you've gotten us into, amateur. Did you have a plan before you got us surrounded by ghosts, or was begging for mercy your entire strategy?"

Patrik was about to snap back something about saving their hides with his salt circle, before thinking better of it. Now was not the time for a debate about whose actions had put whom in terrible danger. Letting out an angry breath, he looked from the sorceress, to the warrior, to the bard, then back to the enraged children. Finally he looked around the boarded-up building. The orphanage…

"Well, Mr. Child Murderer?" Thalia asked, tapping her foot impatiently. "Any other bright ideas?"

Patrik grimaced. "Well, I don't think you're going to like it, but yeah, I might have one…"

***

SEVERAL HOURS LATER, they stood on a hillside outside of Monmouth, looking down at what had once been a thriving village.

"Huh," O'Malley murmured. "That ah…that went up real fast."

"So much for redemption," Thalia muttered.

Giovanni grunted.

Are you **sure** *you're not trying to be evil?* Steve asked silently. *Oh, hey, you can use your sword now!*

Patrik sighed.

Quest Complete: Cleanse the village of Monmouth. Reward: 1000 gold coins. [+200 Alignment]

Achievement Unlocked: Rape and Pillage II. Wow, that was quick. Seems like you're already moving up in the world. Congratulations, you have razed an entire village from the map. Nothing remains but ash. Reward: 1000 gold. [-1000 Alignment]

Congratulations! You have learned the skill [Arson]! You know how to light shit on fire. Well done…

Congratulations! Your skill [Arson] has increased

to level 2, 3…6! Fires will now be easier to light and will burn 25% hotter and faster.

Ring! Ring! Ring!! Congratulations. You have reached level 14…15! You have been awarded 6 stat points. You have 15 stat points to assign.

Below, the last of the embers that had been Monmouth glowed in the darkness. The inferno had swept through the town in a matter of minutes. It had started in the orphanage—the only building he'd actually meant to burn. It was another trick from *Supernatural*. When in doubt, burn the body…and everything attached to it.

Patrik had used the last of his salt to temporarily expel the ghosts, and while the others had escaped through the front door, he'd readied his plan B. He'd already checked with Steve and knew the most flammable material in his inventory was the spider silk he'd collected in the forest. Pulling masses of it from his inventory, he'd tossed it all around the orphanage. Then he'd pulled out his tinder box.

By the time Patrik joined the others in the street, the orphanage had become a merry little blaze. Not long after, the ghosts had reappeared. Thalia and Giovanni readied themselves for the battle, but this time Patrik's hunch was proven correct, as one by one the ethereal figures burst into child-sized flames.

And things would have been all well and good, job done… if not for the wind. And the tinder-dry construction materials of Monmouth.

One good gust had sent embers spiralling into the sky, where they had soon settled in the thatched roofs of the nearby buildings. Within minutes those too had been aflame.

Patrik and the others tried to save the village, of course. They had spent long hours battling the growing blaze. But apparently none of Patrik's new companions had a spell suitable for fighting fires. It had been a losing battle from the start, and one by one, they had surrendered to the inevitable.

"Hey, Thalia, look at that!" O'Malley cried. "We

completed the quest. Does that mean we can keep him? You said if he was useful we could keep him!"

"Ahh…" Patrik looked from the bard to the smouldering sorceress and silent murder assassin. He wasn't entirely sure these were the people he wanted to be spending his time with.

Thalia clearly harboured her own doubts. Crossing her arms, she glared at the giant bard. "He'll be your responsibility," she growled. "And if he burns down one more town…"

"I'll take care of him, I promise!" the bard exclaimed.

"Ah…do I get a say?"

"Fine," Thalia muttered, completely ignoring Patrik. "Then he can stay."

Congratulations! You have joined the fellowship of Thalia the Sorceress. Members of fellowships share experience and feats earned while in close proximity to one another.

"Hurray!" O'Malley exclaimed. The bard bounded over and swept Patrik into a hug. "You hear that, Pat! You're coming with us!"

Oh, this is going to be fun. There was laughter in the PQA's voice.

You know what, Steve? Fuck you.

CHAPTER 11

WAIT, YOU'RE FROM EARTH?

PATRIK THE CHOSEN ONE — LEVEL **15**

PROGRESS TO NEXT LEVEL: 70%

RACE	ALIGNMENT
Human	-2077

HEALTH	MANA
150/150	55/55

STR	CON	INT	CHA	DEX
16(+1)	10	10	1	10

*Equipped: Bronze Dagger (+1 STR)

You have no stat points to assign.

SPELLS [LIMIT: FOUR]

RAISE DEAD
level 7

SKILLS [UNLIMITED]

HACK AND SLASH
level 2

ARSON
level 6

PATRIK FELT HIMSELF GROW STRONGER AS HE ASSIGNED HIS points. It was actually kind of exhilarating. He hadn't seen a mirror yet in the Four Circles, but he imagined this must be how Tobey Maguire felt the morning after being bitten by the radioactive spider.

What a rush. He might be new to this world, but for the first time since crashing through the gateway with his trousers around his ankles, Patrik thought he might be getting his feet underneath him. He'd split the extra stat points from the ghost infestation quest—and the complete destruction of Monmouth—between his three physical attributes and intelligence, bringing them each up to ten. According to Steve, he was closing in on peak physical and mental conditioning for a human in his own universe.

He then dumped his remaining points into strength. Given his lack of knowledge on the system—to the point that he didn't even know enough to ask Steve what he might be missing—allocating stats to an attribute that would give his attacks a little extra oomph didn't seem like the worst idea. He was now stronger than any man to have ever lived on Earth—

Riiiiip!

He winced as something tore. Thankfully, not a muscle. But definitely his underwear. They were the only piece of clothing he was still wearing from his own world. Apparently they hadn't been fabricated to survive all of his muscles suddenly growing several sizes. The robes, however, were fine.

Good thing you've got that extra pair! Steve offered helpfully.

Nope. Patrik shot back. *Guess I'm free-balling it.* He used his inventory to remove the offending undergarments. There was no way in hell he was wearing the old dude's underpants. The sparkly robes were bad enough.

He didn't linger long on the issue. Striding up the hillside away from Monmouth, Patrik savoured his newfound energy. Suddenly his stride was longer, each step sending him bounding forward. He held himself a little taller, and while Steve had claimed that improving his Intelligence didn't actually make him smarter, affecting instead his ability to cast magic, his thoughts did seem clearer. Crisper. Even that ache in his neck he'd been suffering since secondary school had faded.

It was a somewhat novel, the prospect of life without constant pain.

Sadly, it was not to last.

He had Thalia to thank for that. The sorceress soon proved herself sterner than the drill sergeant in Full Metal Jacket. Insisting they put as much distance between themselves and Patrik's 'crime scene' as possible, she had them set off immediately. Barbed words and the occasional well-placed kick up the backside drove them down the road from Monmouth, even as night set in.

Soon Patrik was stumbling and tripping over himself in the darkness—but even that proved not enough for the angry sorceress. Before they'd travelled a mile she had them leaving the road and setting off into the forest. This one was unenchanted, whatever that actually meant, but a forest all the same, with all the creepy crawly bugs and monsters that apparently came with them in this world.

If keeping up with the level 26 sorceress and her companions had been difficult on the road, doing so while unseen branches whipped at his face and his feet tripped in twisted roots was all but impossible. It took all of Patrik's newfound Strength and Dexterity just to keep them in sight.

Though they had only a single burning torch held by O'Malley for light, his companions seemed unaffected by the dark. They leapt and dodged and bounded past unseen obstacles, leaving Patrik to stumble along in their wake, crashing into every rock and tree trunk.

The gloom only deepened as the night stretched out. It wasn't long before Patrik's old friend, pain, returned. It began in his legs and his poor, poor feet. His lower back soon joined in, followed by the hateful crick in his neck.

More than once in that long night, Patrik considered surrender. Exhaustion became a rock on his shoulders, his head bowed ever lower by its weight. His lungs gasped and his heart pounded so hard in his chest that at times he feared his earthly body was rejecting the enhancements he'd placed on it. He might have even given up, had Thalia not made it clear from the start that this was all a test, one she assumed he would fail.

That alone was enough to keep Patrik going. All his life, he'd been surrounded by men and women like her. People who assumed he wasn't capable, who dismissed him as a bum and a loser. And maybe he had been, once. Sure, he'd coasted off his trust fund for a few years after school. But they were hardly wasted years. He'd travelled the world, backpacked through Asia and learnt Spanish while sipping mojitos off the coast of Mexico. Well, a few phrases at least…

…anyway, none of that mattered. That was the old Patrik, before…before things had changed. He was a college student now. He might still be a few credits short of a degree, but damnit, he had applied himself. He would not let this world treat him like its personal trashcan.

And so he prevailed. To his pride, he stopped only once, and that was only to confirm that the Manticore meat did indeed burn as hot coming out as it did going in. Other than that one, painful, break, he allowed spite to fuel the unending chase. Well, spite, and no small degree of desperation for some *actual* guides to help him navigate this world.

Hey, you know I can hear you right? It's not my fault you never listen to my advice.

Name one time I didn't listen to your advice!

Just yesterday I told you to put some of your stat points into Charisma!

Just yesterday I was almost murdered by a pack of bloodthirsty ghosts, Patrik snapped. *I need to learn how to fight and throw fireballs, not flirt with girls.*

It's more than—you know what, fine. It's your funeral.

Patrik could only shake his head. It turned into a yawn that he quickly covered with his hand. Hours had passed and while he did not regret neglecting his Charisma, he was seriously rethinking his dumping of stats into Strength. With a bit of extra Constitution or Dexterity…

His heart lifted as he noticed a glint of light ahead. It grew steadily as they ran. Dawn had come. Patrik wasn't entirely certain he was reading his map right, but he thought it was coming up in the east. At least some things in this universe were the same as back home.

With the sun's awakening, he could finally see the details he'd missed during their nocturnal march. They had left the road some time ago, but they were still following a narrow track that wove through the trees. Beyond the path, vegetation pressed close, so dense as to be all but impassable. Shadows clung to the undergrowth, and while there were no spiderwebs here, to Patrik this seemed like an altogether darker place. There was an unnatural stillness to the trees, as though not even the breeze could penetrate the dense canopy. The air was hot and humid, the chill of the haunted town long forgotten.

Pins prickled Patrik's neck as he watched the trees. He thought he caught a flicker of movement, but when he looked again there was nothing. He waited for Steve to announce the presence of enemies or monsters, but no warning came. Even so, some second sense was screaming at him to beware. He had never been so glad than when the trees opened out and they found themselves back on a road. Sure, it was only packed dirt, but it was at least as wide as a car and a massive improvement on the tiny track that had seen him beaten black and blue by the overgrown forest.

Fine, I'll drop the Charisma thing, Steve announced as Patrik drew alongside O'Malley. ***But hey, can we at least agree that whole thing with the ghosts was…scarring?***

A shudder ran down Patrik's spine as an image of the little girl—her mouth stretched unnaturally wide and screaming—popped into his head.

"Oh, yes," he muttered. "One hundred percent agree. I'm going to need some serious therapy when I get back home."

"Back home to the elves?" O'Malley interrupted. Patrik's head jerked up. He'd been in such a daze he'd hardly noticed the bard. The man wore a look of surprise. "Why would you want to go back to those old windbags?"

Patrik hesitated, but it was probably best to correct the record now, rather than wait for his obvious ignorance of the elves to give him away.

"I'm not actually from the ah…what did you call them, the elven lands?"

"Huh?" O'Malley seemed genuinely confused. "But…the dwarfs would never take a human…and the dragons would have eaten ya long before you came of age. Don't tell me you just don't like Manticore! What kind of a human doesn't like Manticore?"

"One from another universe entirely?" Patrik offered. "I'm, uh…how would you put it…new to the Four Circles?"

"Is that so?" Thalia interrupted, appearing at his shoulder. She cast a measured eye over Patrik. "It's been a while since anyone's seen an outworlder. Which universe did you get dragged from, then? Turtleback? Circle World? Burning Eye?"

"I, ah…no, I'm from Earth."

The others came to an abrupt halt. Patrik came to a stop with them, frowning as he looked from one to the other in question, but neither said anything. Even Giovanni, who had been leading, stopped to stare at him.

"You're joking, right?" O'Malley said at last. He looked from Patrik to the sorceress. "He's joking, obviously!"

"Shut it, idiot," Thalia snapped. She advanced until she stood directly before Patrik. Only then did he realise just how much taller than her he was. Despite all her power, all her anger and, well, meanness, he practically *loomed* over the woman. Of course, that didn't stop him shrinking back at the venom in her voice when next she spoke: "Are you joking, Patrik the Chosen One?"

"I…ah…" He flicked a glance in O'Malley's direction, but the giant bard only stood by, helpless. "I…yes?"

Thalia's eyes never left his own. She snorted. "By the Dark Lord, O'Malley, who have you invited into our fellowship?"

To Patrik's relief, she said nothing else, only turned and

marched up the road past Giovanni. The silent swordsman continued to stare intently in Patrik's direction, before he turned and followed Thalia. O'Malley remained at Patrik's side. He watched the others draw ahead for a few silent seconds, then offered a nervous laugh.

"So, Earth, ay?" he muttered, placing a tentative hand on Patrik's shoulders. "No wonder you have such ah…violent tendencies."

"I do not…" Patrik trailed off. "Look, I didn't mean to destroy the village, okay? It was an accident."

"Just like it was an 'accident' when you slaughtered an entire forest of cute little spiders?" O'Malley pressed, his voice touched by sadness. Patrik had told them the full story on their way out of Monmouth.

"It wasn't like that—" Patrik bit off the excuse he'd been about to give when he saw the tears beading O'Malley's eyes. He swallowed. "It's just, I don't know what the hell I'm doing here. A week ago I was living an ordinary life on Earth. Then suddenly this old dude in wizard's robes is having a heart attack and a voice is talking in my head and monsters are real. It's all just a bit…overwhelming."

"Not to worry, my friend, you have us now," O'Malley said with a smile. The giant bard started off down the road after the others, drawing Patrik with him. "We will help you curb those violent Earthen instincts. You are truly from that awful place? One can hardly imagine. Our legends speak of the slaughters perpetrated by Earthlings in olden times."

"Oh…" Patrik replied. "Then, ah, why are you helping me? Aren't you afraid I'll go bad?"

"What? Us? Afraid of little old you?" O'Malley howled with laughter. "Don't you worry, Patrik. If you go too far down the dark path, we'll put things right."

"I…ah…that's…reassuring…"

"And besides, we're not illiterate. That's some description you've got. Destined to confront the Dark Lord! How about that?"

"You read that?" Patrik swallowed.

"Of course! Now that's a cause even this old pacificist could get behind. Us humans have suffered too long under the bastard's yoke. So many of us crammed into this outer circle with the damned dwarfs. It's not right, I tell you."

"Okay…" Patrik decided it was best to stay out of whatever passed for local politics between the humanoid species. He still struggled to understand the Electoral College. "Anyway, I'm not sure where my description really came from. I'm not a big believer in prophecy. All I know is I have a quest—"

"A quest?"

Patrik jumped, surprised to find that Thalia had returned to his side. The sorceress sure could move quietly when she wanted. She stood with her arms folded across her chest, one eyebrow arched high above her thick-framed glasses.

"And what kind of quest does our brave level 15 have to complete? Is there a farmer who needs the rats cleared out of his barn? Or maybe someone's cows have gone missing—"

"Wait, wait, wait," Patrik interrupted, holding up a hand. "You have *cows* here? Then why the hell are you eating *centaurs?*"

"You only get centaurs at the high-quality places," O'Malley said sadly. "Like old Johnny's. Shame really, spots like his are so hard to come by." He wagged a finger at Patrik. "You see, the ends do not always justify the means, my friend."

"Wait, what happened to Johnny?" Patrik asked, suddenly concerned. "There was plenty of time to get out, right?"

O'Malley and Thalia exchanged a look. "Ah…sure, buddy," O'Malley offered.

"The innkeeper always goes down with the inn," Thalia said matter-of-factly, then: "As for your supposed quest, we do not waste our time on country bumpkin missions to help Old McDonald. We are serious adventurers, and you are here because you have proven useful. The moment you prove otherwise…" She made a violent hacking movement across her neck.

"Ahh…" Patrik was still reeling from the news Johnny the Bartender was probably dead.

"And before *either* of you go there," Thalia continued, glaring now at O'Malley, "nor will we be helping anyone with suicidal quests that involve taking on the Dark Lord, got it?"

The woman's words shook Patrik from his stupor. Despite also having no desire to face the Dark Lord, he found himself scowling at the sorceress. Her attitude was really beginning to grate on his nerves.

"I thought you were supposed to be the good guys," he snapped.

Folding her arms, Thalia stared up at him from behind her glasses, in much the same way his secondary school teacher once had.

"We *are* the good guys," she said slowly. "That means we do not go burning down villages or slaughtering endangered species. It means we do good things. Do you know what we call an act of violence committed in order to destabilise the governmental regime of a kingdom?"

"Ahhh, in my world we'd call it the Fourth of July?"

"Good for you, Mr. Chosen One," Thalia replied in that condescending tone of hers. "We have some words for it ourselves. Terrorism. Sedition. Insurrection, to name a few."

"The dude literally calls himself the Dark Lord. You can't tell me the Galactic Empire was better off with Darth Sidious in charge!"

"Yeah—wait, what?" O'Malley said.

Ahh, don't think they're going to get that reference, mate, Steve interrupted. ***Also, wait, this can't be right— it says the Resistance slaughtered tens of thousands of civilian units—***

"I don't know what the hell you're talking about, so I'm going to assume it's nonsense," Thalia spoke over Patrik's silent advisor. "But you of all people should know by now that even the smallest actions can have enormous consequences. Yes, not everyone *likes* the Dark Lord's regime. Certainly, no one enjoys paying taxes."

"Exactly!" O'Malley tried again.

Thalia silenced the bard with a scowl. "But to kill him…"

she continued. "Even *if* such a thing were possible, then what are you left with? Chaos!" She shook her head. "No, we're small time. Tadpoles in a pool of crocodiles. We keep to our Circle, complete our quests for the side of good, and hope to advance enough to hopefully earn a title, maybe settle down with a nice palace in the Second or Third Circle. We leave the big stuff to those in the big leagues. Got it?"

"Aww, come on, Thalia," O'Malley muttered. "You never let us have any fun."

Patrik stayed silent. The woman's words had hit a little too close to home. When he'd first crash landed in this place, he'd lashed out like a wounded animal. And his recklessness had cost lives. Maybe Thalia was right. Maybe this Dark Lord really *wasn't* so bad.

He's still going to try and kill you the second he hears about that description of yours.

A lump lodged in Patrik's throat. In that much, the PQA was right. But if he could get to Bledross before the Dark Lord learned of his existence, maybe it wouldn't matter. Once there, all going well, he would find some note or clue Tenser had left behind that would let him return to Earth.

He drew in a breath and looked at Thalia. "You're right," he said, dipping his head in what he hoped was a show of respect. "I want to do the right thing. Please, will you show me how?"

Thalia's eyes drilled into Patrik, as though she thought he might yet prove his universe's reputation and turn on them in a violent rage. Finally though, she snorted.

"Very well, Earthling," she snapped. Continuing after Giovanni, she waved for him to follow. "The next quest on our adventurers' list is to clear some Harpies from the cliffs around Tunstead. Work hard, and you might be able to improve some of that negative Alignment."

Pulling up his map as they walked, Patrik's heart sank. Damn, Tunstead was in basically the opposite direction of Bledross. That was a detour he couldn't afford, not when he was walking around with a giant sign that read 'enemy of the

Dark Lord'. He hesitated on the path, but only briefly. He could set out on his own, and leave his new companions behind…but…Harpies? What next, a bloody troll? The more he learnt about this dark and violent world, the less he liked the idea of wandering around by himself.

"A quest, you said?" he called, an idea coming to him. "So we'll get some gold for completing it? Can I ask how much?"

Back in Monmouth, Thalia and O'Malley had mentioned something about the ghost quest being worth a lot. That had been a thousand gold coins. If he could share his quest to reach Bledross, they stood to earn five times that amount.

Thalia paused, flashing him a scowl over her shoulders. "We're adventurers. We do not do good things for the gold. We do it for the Alignment." Her scowl deepened. "But if you must know, there's a few hundred gold in it for us. These dwarven villages don't pay like they should."

"A few hundred gold?" Patrik mused. He allowed the slightest of smiles to touch his lips. "I thought you didn't bother with quests from Old McDonald?"

The sorceress slowed, then stopped again in the middle of the road. "What did you say that quest of yours was again?"

Patrik pretended to inspect his fingernails for dirt. "Oh, I think the better question would be: how much is it worth?"

A grin spread across Patrik's lips at the sorceress's expression. He was enjoying—

Suddenly Thalia had her hands around the front of his shirt. Despite being more than a foot shorter than him, she lifted him with ease. Her eyes flashed. "Talk, noob."

"Ah…well…where…" Patrik spluttered, panicked by the woman's reaction. All of a sudden he wasn't sure whether it was a good idea to share the quest with them. Afterall, it wasn't *Patrik* that had to go to Bledross. It was the ring.

Yeah, probably not a good idea, Steve chirped in happily. ***Fun fact, quest rewards are set based on difficulty. A 5000 gold coin reward is pretty much unheard of in this Circle. It means it's basically a suicide mission.***

Wait, WHAT?

Yeah, mate! What, you didn't realise?

What part of—you know what, never mind. Shit. Shit, shit.

He still swung slowly in the sorceress's grip. Thalia's teeth were bared.

"It's not a farmer's quest, alright!" he said quickly, trying to stall Thalia while his mind sought a solution.

Steve, what happens if they accept the quest? He asked the PQA desperately.

Then they'll each receive the quest notification telling them what is involved, and the reward for their service.

That did not help. There were three options here: either they rejected his quest outright, accepted it and then killed him so they only had to split the bounty three ways, or they completed the quest together. Based on what Steve had told him, they were likely to reject the quest the second they heard the reward. If that happened, he would have to travel to Bledross alone, and most likely be slaughtered by monsters along the way.

"I'm still waiting for an answer, Earthling," Thalia growled. She looked about half a second away from tearing out his throat.

Who makes up these stupid quests!

Information Requested: Quests. Quests are initiated by substantial need in an individual, populace, or otherwise collective group. In the most simple cases, an individual (such as Old McDonald the Farmer) may offer a bounty to complete a task. In other quests, such as your escape from the Enchanted Forest or your quest with the ring, both quest and bounty are generated by a collective of PQA's who monitor the fluctuating ether of the Four Circles...

That sounds like something you pulled entirely out of your ass, Steve, Patrik muttered silently. But...actually, the PQA's words had given him an idea. *An individual need...so basically anyone can create a quest?*

Well, it's not quite that simple—

"*I* have to go to Bledross!" Patrik cried out as Thalia gave him a violent shake. "And *I* could really use your help to get there! *I'll* even offer you 1000 gold coins."

He forced a cheerful grin to his lips. But of course, Thalia would not be so easily convinced.

"An escort quest?" she asked, pursing her lips. Abruptly she released him, allowing Patrik to drop back to the ground. Crossing her arms, she watched him. "What could possibly be in Bledross that is worth 1000 gold coins to you, Earthling?"

"Is it Minotaur meat?" O'Malley asked excitedly.

The sorceress pursed her lips. She was still studying Patrik with those sapphire eyes of hers, as if by watching him for long enough, she might unlock some hidden secret of his.

"No," she said at last, giving a curt shake of her head.

Patrik's heart lurched, his hopes curdling at the rejection.

Coming alongside the sorceress, Giovanni flashed her a subtle look. O'Malley was not so subtle.

"What, come on Thalia! 1000 gold coins? For an escort quest? When do we ever get that kind of money for an escort quest!"

"Exactly my point, idiot," Thalia snapped. "What's his angle? Who knows what dastardly plans he has simmering in that Earthling brain of his?"

That was it. He'd had enough of this bloody woman. What had Patrik ever done to her to earn such venom?

"Look, join me or don't. It's no skin off my back. I have no idea why I have to go to Bledross, only that that's where Tenser the Great bloody well told me to go—"

Patrik broke off as he was once again hoisted into the air— though this time it was Giovanni who had grabbed him, rather than the sorceress. It didn't make the experience any more dignifying. Well, maybe a tiny bit. Thalia was a five-foot-four-inch-tall woman with glasses, after all.

"Did you say Tenser?" Thalia whispered, coming alongside them.

"As in 'Tenser the Great'?" O'Malley added.

"Ah…" Patrik swallowed, glancing nervously from one face to the other. Of the three, only Giovanni seemed genuinely angry—the other two only surprised—but of course, the silent swordsman said not a word. "Yeah, ah, do you know him?"

Thalia and O'Malley exchanged a glance before looking at Giovanni. "You could say that."

Patrik swallowed. All the colour had drained from Giovanni's face and his fists were clenched so tight they shook. Veins bulged on his forehead, while a strange energy crackled on the air. Suddenly releasing Patrik, he took a step back.

Landing lightly on his feet, Patrik studied the warrior. "You…okay there, buddy?"

Giovanni's iron eyes burned as they returned Patrik's gaze. Helplessly confused, he looked to the others.

"That's why he swore the vow of silence. You know, to find out about his parents," O'Malley explained helpfully. "Tenser is his dad."

"Allegedly," Thalia added, earning a growl from Giovanni. "But the resemblance is there," she said with a roll of her eyes.

"Oh," Patrik said, before recalling the warrior's description. "Ohhh…"

Fuck.

Ooh, ooh, you should tell him the good news!

Good news? He's been trying to find the dude for how many years? How would you react if you found out someone had killed him?

I guess I'd be a little miffed…

Huh, do you actually have a father?

That would be classified.

"Oh, oh, do you know where he is now?" O'Malley was practically bouncing with joy. "I do so love family reunions!"

Giovanni still hadn't taken his eyes off Patrik.

"Ahh…he kinda just took off, sorry," Patrik said quickly. "Didn't say where he was going." Then, thinking quickly, he diverted the conversation back to the original topic. "Only that I needed to meet him in Bledross."

An almost animalistic growl rumbled from deep in Giovanni's chest. Without a word—obviously—he turned and stalked off up the trail.

You know, I'm not sure that's going to be such a happy family reunion. Seeing as you already murdered the dude.

Patrik watched the swordsman go, not entirely sure what to make of the silent warrior. Steve was right about one thing—he was not looking forward to that man finding out Tenser was dead. And that Patrik may have had a hand in it…

"Looks like you win, Earthling," Thalia muttered. "Congratulations, it seems you've railroaded us into accepting your quest after all. You have my magic staff."

"And my lute!" O'Malley exclaimed.

Thalia stalked off without dignifying the bard with a response.

"And…ah, I guess his sword?" O'Malley added as they watched the pair leave the road and head back into the trees. Whistling a tune to himself, the bard set off after them.

Patrik breathed out a long sigh of relief. He couldn't believe he'd actually managed to win them over. O'Malley had entered the trees now and not wanting to be left behind already, he started after his companions. It was only a few minutes later that something struck him from Thalia's earlier words—she'd mentioned being railroaded.

"Wait, do they have trains here?" he exclaimed. "Then why the hell are we doing all this walking?"

Because it builds character, Patrik. Because it builds character.

CHAPTER 12
FINGER LICKING GOOD

JUST BECAUSE DAYLIGHT HAD COME AND THEY HAD A NEW destination, didn't mean that Thalia would allow their pace to slow. Though it did at least mean that Patrik could see the branches before they struck him in the face. Except the ones O'Malley deliberately held back as part of some childish game to "test the Earthling's self-control." If the man hadn't been twice his size and a good number of levels higher than him, Patrik might have been tempted.

Despite the bard's antics, all in all the daylight march proved far more pleasant than the night. As the sun grew higher overhead, the shadows of the forest no longer seemed quite so dark, its hidden dangers not quite so omnipresent. If he squinted, he could even pretend the long-leafed trees were similar to those in Oregon. Although their purple tint somewhat spoiled the illusion. As he walked, Patrik found himself wondering whether this was some seasonal change, or if plant cells in this world had evolved a different photosynthetic mechanism for energy production.

The company paused only occasionally to eat. The others had their own supplies, which Thalia did not offer to share. This left Patrik snacking on the Manticore jerky Johnny had packed for him. He suffered the meat's fiery spice without complaint as penance for the man who had dreamed of being a chef.

Finally, as the forest opened up somewhat and the sunlight faded between the overhead branches, Thalia called that it was time to make camp.

By then, Patrik could have slept anywhere. Just give him a patch of ground and he would have been gone with or without the help of his PQA. But much to his chagrin, Thalia had other plans. It took at least another thirty minutes before they found a site the sorceress judged acceptable. Giovanni had spotted an outcropping of rocks through the canopy. Ten minutes of hacking and slashing their way through dense bush brought the fellowship to the shelter of a cliff face, and there they finally made camp.

Patrik let out a long groan as he leaned against the cliff. Pressing a cheek to the cold stone, he slid down until his knees touched the ground. Everything hurt. How did people do it, those long, five, ten, *fifty* day hikes through the wilderness with only their wits and a massive bag of supplies to keep them alive? Most of them weren't even close to "peak human" like he supposedly was now. Was this why superheroes still used cars and planes to get around in the movies?

Giovanni and Thalia of course ignored him as they went about preparing the camp. Giovanni disappeared into the forest and soon returned, apparently emptyhanded—until stacks of firewood popped into existence and crashed to the ground beside him. Much of it looked pretty green and damp from recent rains, but the silent warrior was not perturbed. He knelt, taking a few handfuls and stacking them into a smaller pile, though just as haphazardly. Patrik had spent a few seasons in the scouts when he was young and was about to tell the swordsman it would never catch light, when Thalia stepped forward and gave a flick of her hand.

A small, tightly controlled lance of fire leapt from her fingers to strike Giovanni's pile. The wood caught light with a *whoosh*. A wave of heat swept over Patrik as he rearranged himself, settling into a more comfortable position. Twigs crunched under foot as O'Malley wandered over to join him.

"Ah, but that was a lovely journey, wasn't it? Always fascinating to see those night critters out wandering."

"What night critters?" Patrik asked. "I couldn't see crap."

O'Malley frowned. "You don't have Dark Sight? I thought you lived with the elves—no, wait, Earth, right. How do I keep forgetting that? Guess I just expected Earthlings to be a little more…intimidating."

"Thanks, I guess," Patrik muttered. Leaning against the cliff, he eyed the flames. "So is that to cook our dinner or what?" he asked. He had an item that looked like chicken drumsticks in his inventory, one of the many random items he'd looted from the wizard. His mouth practically salivated at the thought of eating something that didn't taste like he'd just swallowed a match.

"Oh yes, Giovanni is a wonderful cook. We've still got some centaur meat from Johnny—"

"Nope."

Letting out a groan, Patrik pushed himself to his feet. Hands on his hips, he did his best to stretch out his lower back, which now felt like a rock had been permanently dug into his spine. Then he walked—staggered more like—to the fire where Giovanni was already pulling items from his inventory in preparation for a meal.

You know, it's rude in pretty much every culture—

Don't care, Patrik spoke over the PQA. Just this one time, he was going to have his way.

"Mind if I share your fire?" he asked the mute warrior. "I've got something from back home I'd like to cook."

Giovanni just stared at him with those cold eyes of his. Thalia, who had dragged over a fallen tree trunk that she was now using for a seat, only snorted.

"So long as it's not human babies or something, you can cook whatever you like," she said, stretching her feet out towards the fire.

"Jesus," Patrik swore, "who…you know what, never mind. I don't want to know."

He opened his inventory instead and quickly scrolled down to find the chicken. As he did so, he passed the iron sword and recalled with a jolt that since he'd reached level 15, he could in fact wield it.

Pretty sure I already mentioned that…

On another occasion, Patrik might have pulled it out and given it a try, but just at that moment there were more important things on his mind. Finding the item he'd been looking for, he drew it from his inventory. To his joy, several drumsticks of what indeed appeared to be chicken appeared on the rock beside the fire. Although given the nature of this place…

Yep, that's chicken alright! See, useful.

Patrik could only roll his eyes. Sadly, Tenser had had no spices or even herbs with which to flavour the meat, and he'd used up all his salt in Monmouth. Still, it was better than nothing, so he summoned his bronze dagger and stabbed it through all four drumsticks. Moving a few rocks, he then laid the dagger so the chicken dangled over the flames, and placed a few more to hold it there.

"Ewww, is that what I think it is?" O'Malley asked as he wandered over to take a look.

"I'm hoping you think it's chicken," Patrik said. "In which case, then yes, yes it is!"

He took a step towards the tree trunk that Thalia was sitting on. Her eyes flashed beneath her broad-rimmed glasses. Ignoring the violent look on her face, Patrik took a seat…at the end of the trunk farthest from the grumpy sorceress.

"Yuck, that stuff has no flavour," O'Malley grumbled. He picked up an enormous boulder that had probably fallen from a crag in the cliff and tossed it down beside Patrik, then took a seat. "Perhaps this is the reason for the terrors of your universe. Such bland food can only breed malcontent."

As he spoke, the giant lifted the lute from his shoulders and gave it a practice strum.

Considering the giant's words, Patrik found himself chuckling. "I guess there's a little truth in that," he admitted. "Once upon a time, wars *were* fought over spices—which many cultures use to add flavour to their food." He looked at his chicken. "I'm not much of a chef, but bit of paprika and oregano wouldn't go a miss with this."

Giovanni grunted. He remained his usual silent self, but the way he wrinkled his nose said enough. O'Malley wore a similar expression, but he left no doubt as to his repulsion.

"Dude, that is gross."

He strummed his lute again. The sound rang out across the campsite. Then softly, gently, O'Malley began to play. Patrik listened, momentarily paralysed by the sweet tunes that leapt from the soundboard of the lute. The stone wall at the bards back reflected and amplified the sound, somehow creating the perfect acoustics for the instrument.

Truth be told, Patrik had expected O'Malley's playing to be some horribly twisted version of music in his own world. But this…the bard's fingers leapt between the strings, his strumming carrying Patrik away in a wild jig reminiscent of country music. And when O'Malley began to sing, it was not the harsh, deep voice Patrik had come to expect from the giant, but soft and suave. It was almost…almost like being serenaded by a young Miley Cyrus.

Not that Patrik had ever listened to her in his life.

Sure, sure, and I suppose those aren't Hannah Montana blankets on your childhood bed.

Patrik ignored the PQA. O'Malley's music had touched something deep within him, some hidden, childhood innocence he had thought long forgotten. Listening to the sweet sounds, he wondered how anyone could ever consider violence. Why couldn't they all just get along and love each other—

"By Fate, that's enough, O'Malley," Thalia interrupted. "I think he's tuned. Fuck."

Blinking, Patrik looked around as the music faded, aware something had changed, but struggling to figure out what exactly. For one brief moment in time, he'd felt light as a feather, all of his Earthly concerns forgotten. He turned to the sorceress. She wore the familiar scowl on her librarian-esque face, as though she'd just eaten a lemon. An ember of anger took light in his heart. How dare she disdain something so beautiful—

"Don't you start," she snapped, swinging her sapphire eyes on Patrik. "It was a charm spell, not the fifth coming. We just needed to make sure you were tuned to O'Malley's music, so when the fight starts you won't be affected."

"Oh…" Patrik trailed off. The fleeting joy he'd experienced during the song was well and truly fading now. He was left feeling deflated and empty, as though something wonderful had been stolen from him. "Okay then…" He paused. "Wait, did you say fight?"

"Yes," Thalia replied.

Patrik frowned. She was eating from a bowl of what looked like stew. Turning to the fire, he found his chicken drumsticks beginning to blacken. Shit, how long had he been daydreaming to that damn song? He scrambled to save them, grasping the hilt of his dagger and dragging it from the flames. Unfortunately, the weapon was now scorching hot. He yelped as the pain struck, tossing it down on a rock.

Burn damage inflicted [-5 health]

A curse was on Patrik's lips, though after the moment of shock passed, he realised the burn hadn't hurt anything like the last. He hardly dared to look, but he forced himself to open his hand. The skin was a bright red, even slightly black in places, but nothing like the terrible, melted flesh he'd experienced when he'd put his hand in the fire.

"Still burn from regular fire, ay?" O'Malley asked, walking up and clapping him on the shoulder. "That should stop once you get your constitution to around 15. Fire spells, burning arrows, or anything lit by someone with an Arson skill will still inflict damage, but at least you won't need mittens for cooking that terrible food of yours." He chuckled to himself at the notion.

Patrik nodded slowly, still staring at his mostly unburnt hand. This was the first, visible sign of his newfound powers.

Incredible. Finally he gave his head a shake. The miracles of…
magic? He supposed this wasn't strictly *magic*, since it had
nothing to do with his Intelligence attribute. Maybe this was all
some impossibly advanced technology, a kind of genetic modi-
fication or mech augmentation to improve the human body…

***It's probably best if you don't think about this
stuff too much,*** Steve offered. ***Wouldn't want to strain a
brain muscle.***

The PQA was probably right. For once. And a rumble from
his stomach reminded Patrik he had other concerns.
Crouching beside the stone where he'd dropped the chicken,
he gave the hilt of his dagger a little test pat and found it had
cooled considerably. Probably not for a regular human, but he
was hungry enough to take the risk. He reached for the first
drumstick—

Thwack.

For a full second, Patrik stared at his arm, where, somehow,
an arrow had just sprouted. From his flesh. In his arm. An
arrow.

Another full second passed. Then the screaming started.

CHAPTER 13
AND YOU THINK I'M THE EVIL ONE?

"WHAT THE FUCK?" PATRIK SCREAMED. THE BURNING HOT dagger might not have hurt that badly, but an arrow through his arm sure as hell did.

Warning, enemies detected!

"Looks like they're here, boys," Thalia replied, standing calmly.

Giovanni grunted and unsheathed his sword.

O'Malley gave his loot a practice strum, then sighed. "Can we spare at least a few of them this time?"

"No," Thalia snapped. "We need the experience."

"*What the hell is going on?*" Patrik screamed again.

Thalia rolled her eyes. "I suppose we'd better share the quest with the noob."

New Quest: Exterminate the Riffraff. Due to recent economic deterioration, the forest between Monmouth and Anchorpoint has been overrun by bandits and highwaymen. Clear the ruffians from the forest so the citizens of the Four Circles can once more travel the roads free of fear. Reward: 200 gold coins.

"Thalia picked it up a few hours ago," O'Malley explained mournfully.

Patrik was still staring at his arm. More precisely, the *arrow in his bloody arm.* Blood dripped from the wound onto his chicken.

Piercing damage—

"*I fucking know!*" Patrik yelled, cutting off the PQA.

He staggered upright. There was a narrow space clear of trees close to the cliff face, but beyond the pale light of their fire, shadows danced in the forest. At first glance—without night vision, at least—it was impossible to tell the silhouettes of the branches from whoever might have fired on them.

Another arrow flashed from the dark.

This time the company was ready. Or rather, the others were. Patrik flinched as the bolt slashed towards him, but Giovanni leapt into its path. His enchanted blade hissed as it cut the air, and the arrow fell to the ground in two pieces.

"Come on then!" Thalia screamed at the shadows, arms spread in challenge. "Come, you cowardly bastards, show us your balls. Don't you want some of this gold?"

Golden coins poured from the sorceress. They made a delightful ringing sound as they tumbled to the rocky ground, where they shone in the firelight. Patrik could only stare in absolute bewilderment at the little horde of wealth. What the hell was that crazy bitch up too?

The answer came as dark-cloaked men stepped from the darkness, one after another. Their faces were masks of shadows in the gloom, but each held a sword. The blades glinted bronze in the firelight. Some carried wooden shields on their arms and others wore vests of leather hide. The last to emerge lifted a massive longbow, an arrow already nocked. He moved until he stood in front of the others.

"Look, lady." When the man spoke, Patrik was surprised at the softness in his voice. "We're not really looking to make a fuss. Don't need all that there gold ya showing off. Just a handful would be nice, ya know? Hungry mouths to feed and all."

If the man thought he was going to get any sympathy from the sorceress, he was sadly mistaken. Her answer came in the form of the spell she'd used earlier to light the campfire. A lance of flame lit up the night as it tore across the open ground and caught the bowman in the chest. *Boom.* Leather vest aflame, the bandit flew back into the shadows. An orange bar appeared above his head, showing his health was not entirely depleted, but amongst the trees, the fire continued to burn.

"Holy shit," Patrik looked at the sorceress, then back at their assailants. He quickly examined the nearest.

Highwayman [Level 18]: Depending on who you ask, these guys are either vicious criminals—you know, murders, rapists, serial killers and lawyers—or they're desperate men forced into a life of crime to feed their families. Like most things, the truth probably lies somewhere in the middle. Either way, they'll try to rob and kill anyone they encounter on the roads around the Four Circles.

"Well, that's just wonderful," Patrik muttered as the men began to advance.

Thankfully, the pain had actually receded from his arm. And when he clenched his fist, he found that everything inexplicably still worked. A quick check of his health showed it still more than three quarters full. He had two health potions left, both hotlisted, but given they could heal him fully from the brink of death, he reluctantly decided to save them.

Even though there was a *fucking arrow* in his arm.

Instead, he dove into his inventory and equipped his new weapon.

Iron Short Sword. A plain sword forged from iron ore. Not bad, for a noob. Effect: +3 to strength. Requirements: must be level 15 to wield.

He felt a strange burst of strength as the blade settled into his hand. A smile touched Patrik's cheeks and he gave the blade a few practice swings. It made a satisfying *hiss* as it cut the air. Compared to when he'd held it before, he could *sense* the difference. It was as though the blade had gained some kind of substance since he'd levelled up to 15.

His smile faded as the lute chimed out. O'Malley had begun to play. It still sounded lovely to Patrik's ears, but this time there was no soaring elation or otherworldly experience to go with it. It was just…music.

You should probably do something about that arrow.

Have you not gotten to Bear Grylls yet? You never _pull out the stabby thing._

The PQA would have likely argued further, but with a disjointed bellowing of war cries, the highwaymen finally made their charge. Patrik waited for the sorceress to cast another blast of fire at them, but instead she stretched out her arms to either side. A pair of iron daggers appeared in her hands as, snarling, she leapt to meet them.

She probably has some kind of cooldown on her Fire Lance, Steve chipped in.

Patrik had no idea what a cooldown was, but watched on in fascinated horror as Thalia closed with the highwaymen, Giovanni just a step behind. Without a weapon of his own, O'Malley remained with his back to the cliff playing his lute, but if the music was magic, it had yet to have any effect.

Patrik squared his shoulders and drew in a breath, preparing to join his companions in battle.

That is, until he actually saw Giovanni and Thalia in action.

As the sorceress met with the bandits, she suddenly sped up. As her form took on a blurry edge in the darkness, her knives flashed out, finding the gaps in her opponents' leather armour to plunge into flesh. At first, Patrik thought she must have put all her stat points into Dexterity—but then that seemed unlikely, given her sorcerous powers. Only as he looked closer did Patrik notice the faint gleam to her silhouette. She had cast some kind of spell on herself to increase her speed.

Men cried out in pain as she passed amongst them, health bars appearing over their heads. The damage dealt wasn't lethal, but her strikes certainly infuriated the men, who made wild swings at her shadow in their attempts to strike back. None landed. The wily woman was already gone, moving on to her next target. She left a trail of distracted and bewildered opponents in her wake.

Which was where Giovanni came in.

He followed in after the sorceress, brute force and skill to her speed and magic. His sword hissed—actually hissed—as it carved through enemy flesh. Screams sounded in the dark as the blade found its mark again and again.

Patrik watched in horror as one man lost an arm. The *thump* the dismembered limb made as it struck the ground seemed shockingly loud. Lying in the dirt, it twitched, as though the muscles didn't quite realise yet that its tendons were no longer attached to a body. Patrik couldn't tear his eyes away —until Giovanni sliced his sword through the belly of another highwayman. The bandit screamed as his entrails tumbled from the open gash. They steamed in the night air, accompanied by the terrible stench of faeces. The man's screams were silenced as Giovanni reversed his blade and drove it through his throat.

Patrik's stomach lurched as the body hit the ground. Dead. The man was dead. Just like that. His health bar hit zero, and he was gone. The sight left a sour taste in Patrik's mouth. What was he doing in this place, with these people? He wasn't a warrior. He'd never even punched a dude, let alone stabbed one.

Amidst the silhouettes of their enemies, Giovanni pressed on. Another bandit fell, while others staggered away from the fight, grievously wounded. Yet their numbers seemed endless, as yet more men emerged from the trees. It was only a matter of time before the slower Giovanni took his first blow.

Already bleeding from a wound left by Thalia, a bandit charged at the swordsman. His sword already locked with another bandit, Giovanni didn't see the danger. Patrik cried out a warning as Giovanni drove his blade through his enemy's eye socket The silent swordsman swung to meet the newcomer— just in time for a bronze longsword to plunge into his chest.

Heart thundering, Patrik took a step towards them, but…it was already too late. Amidst the battle, Giovanni pitched back from the bandit, several inches of bronze sword protruding from his chest. The blade master staggered a second, and Patrik's heart lurched to a stop.

Craaaap.

That was definitely a mortal wound—

Nah, that thing's only bronze. It's just a scratch for your mate there.

Well that was utterly ridiculous. Patrik was about to tell the PQA as much, when roaring, Giovanni straightened and hacked out with his own sword. The blow caught the bandit square in the neck, decapitating him in a single swing. The headless body toppled to the ground with an audible *thump*, at which point Giovanni paused long enough to spit on the corpse.

Then somewhat awkwardly grasping the hilt of the sword in his chest, he tore it out and tossed it aside.

Patrik watched with bewilderment as the man went looking for his next enemy. The blade had left a jagged wound in Giovanni's chest, but upon closer inspection it didn't appear to be any more than a shallow scrape. Even the man's health bar had barely dropped, leaving him well in the green.

Standing on the edge of the battle, Patrik fingered the hilt of his iron sword. He felt stronger, holding it. And yet…still he hesitated. His stomach twisted itself in a knot as he watched another bandit fall screaming, clutching at a severed limb. Despite the blood pumping from the wound, he didn't fall silent until the slightly blurred form of Thalia slid past, a dagger tearing open the man's throat and silencing him once and for all.

There the sorceress paused, chest heaving as she cast angry blue eyes across the battlefield. They narrowed as she found Patrik and his untouched sword.

"Don't tell me you're a coward, Earthling," she snared.

Then she was back at it, silhouette merging with the night, dagger rising and falling, leaving behind a trail of pain and death.

Wait, are you scared? Steve interjected.

I'm not scared. You're scared. Fuck off, Steve.

Come on, I'm the voice in your head, you can talk to me!

Patrik swallowed, watching as Giovanni pressed on with the slaughter. Half a dozen bandits were already dead or grievously wounded. But more continued to emerge from the trees. And still O'Malley played his lute. It sounded like some kind of children's song, like a *Barney the Dinosaur* knockoff track. Wildly inappropriate, considering the grisly scenes playing out before them.

It's just…overwhelming, he said at last. *I've never killed anyone before.*

Tell that to those orphans—

A shout drew Patrik's attention back to the battle. Giovanni had copped another blow, this one substantial enough to drop his health into the orange. Beyond, a sudden stillness came over Thalia. She stood amidst the enemy, daggers extended in each hand, the glint of magic fading from her silhouette.

"Giovanni!" Her voice called over the cries of the wounded.

Dark eyes turned in her direction. Her daggers came up as the first bandit lunged, fending off his attack. Giovanni moved to join her, a deadly shadow in the night. Gathering his courage, Patrik had just resolved to follow, when a voice came from behind him.

"Oh, Patrik my friend!" It was O'Malley, calling out in a normal voice between song lyrics. "Would you mind dealing with this good gentleman?"

Turning, Patrik immediately spotted the source of the bard's disquiet. One of Giovanni's victims had not been entirely put down. His health had fallen into the orange and he was missing an entire arm—but apparently that wasn't enough to stop this man. Blood still spurting from the grievous wound, he staggered towards O'Malley. The man had lost his sword, but now he held a bronze dagger like the one Patrik had been using to cook his…actually, shit, it *was* his dagger. Only one of his chicken drumsticks remained—

the rest had disappeared, no doubt lost to the dirt and trodden underfoot.

An inexplicable rage swept through Patrik. His stomach rumbled and a growl came from deep in his throat. Theft he could accept. Murder and wanton debauchery, fine. Attempting to kill them all for a few trinkets, well, a man had to make a living *somehow* in this insane world.

But *his fucking chicken?*

The sword shook in his hand as he stalked towards the wounded bandit. He hadn't been spotted, and the high-wayman didn't even look up when Patrik swung. His blade struck home in the bandit's ribs with a jarring *thud*, tearing through leather armour and bony flesh. The bandit staggered sideways, reeling as his health bar plummeted into the red.

Then, despite the blood now spurting from missing arm and broken ribs, the bandit turned and stabbed Patrik in the throat.

It hurt. A lot.

Patrik's scream came out more as a gurgle as he reared back from the bastard highwayman. The iron sword tumbled from his hands as he clutched at the dagger still lodged in his flesh. Panic engulfed him, sweeping away reason as he fumbled at the bloody hilt. It was slippery, drenched in his own blood, but finally he tore it loose.

The metallic taste of blood flooded his mouth. He choked and flailed, and felt the dagger slam into something solid. The bandit, he realised belatedly as the man collapsed. It hardly mattered to him just then though. Chest straining, gasping, he struggled to inhale, but it was impossible. His throat was torn—

Air flooded his lungs as he sucked in a breath. Immediately the stars that had been dancing before his eyes faded, leaving Patrik standing once more amongst the shadows of their camp-fire. He blinked, looking from the dagger in his hand—the one that had torn out his own throat—to the dead bandit at his feet.

How the fuck am I alive?

Mate, it was only a bronze dagger and your constitution is at 10. Sure, he got in a good critical hit, but it'll take more than that to finish you off. You should probably use another health potion though, before someone else takes a shot at you.

Patrik stood stupidly for a moment longer, staring at the dagger. The piece of chicken hung by a thread of sinew. Drenched in blood. His own blood. More blood than he could possibly have lost and survived. He should at least have a woozy head.

"Good job, my friend," O'Malley called. He was still playing his lute, though it hadn't done anything to the bandits. Patrik was beginning to think the bard was there for emotional support. "If you wouldn't mind, it looks like there's another one coming."

That shook Patrik from his stupor. Looking up, he saw the bard was right. Across the broken ground, Thalia and Giovanni fought back-to-back, drawing most of the highwaymen to them. But one had broken past and was advancing on their position. His health bar shone green and his copper longsword glinted in the firelight.

Fear galvanised Patrik into action. He tossed aside the copper blade and retrieved his iron short sword, then toggled on the first of his hotlisted health potions. Strength rushed through his body as he felt torn flesh reknit itself. He stepped between the bandit and O'Malley and raised his blade in readiness.

Then he paused, glancing at the body at his feet. A thought came to him as the bandit closed the gap. With a shrug, Patrik pointed at the dead bandit and concentrated. Dark light spilled from his hand to engulf the fallen man. An arm twitched, then a leg. A groan of dead air squeezed from crumpled lungs followed as, moving like a puppet on strings, the dead bandit came to its feet.

Raise Dead [level 6]: You can temporarily revive a person or creature up to [your level + 5]. Raising a creature of a higher level than yourself will endure

an additional cost of 1 mana per level higher. Duration: fifteen minutes. Cost: 10 mana [+1 mana per level higher] [-50 Alignment]

Despite the macabre scene, Patrik found himself smiling. He hadn't used the spell since the Enchanted Forest, but if he really was going to battle his way across this land to Bledross, he needed to use every tool at his disposal. The highwayman was a few levels higher than him, but well within the capabilities—

"What the *fuck?*"

It was the first time any of the highwaymen had spoken since Thalia had fire blasted their leader. Patrik stared at the man who'd been about to try and hack him to pieces with a bronze sword. The bandit looked genuinely horrified to see his former associate back on his feet—albeit in a way that left no doubt he was still dead.

"Eww, Patrik, seriously," O'Malley called from behind. "I thought we talked about reining in your evil urges." Still strumming his lute, the bard looked apologetically at the bandit. "Sorry, he's from Earth."

Whatever response the bandit might have offered, he didn't have a chance to find out, as the zombie highwayman fell on him with bloody dagger in hand. Within minutes, there was a fresh body at Patrik's feet and his undead creature was stumbling towards the fray between Thalia and Giovanni and the others, hopefully to help out.

Patrik stared at the dead man for a long moment, wondering if this counted as the second person he'd killed. He sighed. Raising his hand, he cast Raise Dead again. Now that his Intelligence was at level 10, he had more than enough mana to use the spell a few times. The dead bandit creature climbed to its feet and stumbled off to join the other.

"Seriously, Patrik," O'Malley muttered. "That is messed up." His grizzled face had paled several shades.

"They're trying to kill us, aren't they?" Patrik countered. He was genuinely surprised by the bard's reaction. Were necromancy spells not common here?

"Some things are just not done, my friend," the bard replied, but he made no move to interfere with Patrik's zombies. Instead, he returned his concentration to the strings of his lute. A few minutes later, Patrik finally found out the reason why.

With a final, crackling shout, O'Malley brought the song to an end. The last notes of the lute echoed from the cliffs and faded to silence. And with that silence, there came a stillness. It took a moment for Patrik to realise what exactly had happened.

The highwaymen, every single last one, had frozen.

Wherever they had been, whatever they had been doing. Blade raised to strike, midstride charging towards Patrik and O'Malley, falling over with their health flashing red from a blow of Giovanni's blade, all of them were now fixed in place. A symbol had appeared over each of their heads. It looked like a little starburst. Patrik had a feeling it meant something along the lines of *stunned*.

"Holy shit," he muttered.

"I can only use the song once every forty-eight hours at its current level," O'Malley admitted, sadness in his voice. "And it takes a long time to complete."

"That's…insane," Patrik whispered. "How long does it last?"

"About half an hour for humans, but some creatures can resist or break it early."

Standing amidst the bandits, Giovanni and Thalia took the opportunity to down health potions. Patrik watched their health bars, which had fallen well into the orange, creep back to green. The pair of zombies he'd awoken finished hacking apart their current opponents, then paused, as though confused by the state of their former companions. A few seconds later the ten minutes on his spell ran out and they collapsed back to the ground.

"So what do we do now?" he asked as the pair finished healing.

Turning from the battlefield, O'Malley took a seat on a

boulder and pulled out a piece of Manticore jerky. "Well, that's my part done," he replied, taking a bite. "I'm a pacifist, remember?" His words were somewhat mumbled as he chewed the fiery meat. "I don't kill."

"So what, we just leave them here?"

Patrik's answer came not from O'Malley, but in a squelching *thud* from behind him. He spun in time to see the body of one of the bandits hit the ground. The man's head struck a second after the body, having been cut clean off by a swipe of Giovanni's sword. The pair were moving through the helpless bandits and slaughtering them at their leisure.

"Hey, Earthling," Thalia's voice carried above the sounds of the massacre. "You better get in on this if you want the experience. And killing these scum should help with your negative Alignment. Maybe then I won't want to punch you in the face so much."

Patrik could only stare in open-mouthed horror. Logically, he knew these men had been intent on murdering them all. That if they were not dealt with now, they would soon revert to their normal, murderous selves. And yet…a part of him still screamed that there was something terribly, terribly wrong about killing all these men in cold blood.

In the end, he could only shake his head and look at O'Malley. "And you think *I'm* the evil one?"

CHAPTER 14
THE ETHICS OF MURDER

CONGRATULATIONS! HIGHWAYWOMAN BRITTA [LEVEL 16] HAS been defeated! [+20 Alignment]

Congratulations! Your skill 'Hack and Slash' has increased to level 4!

Congratulations! Your spell 'Raise Dead' has increased to level 7!

Quest Complete: Exterminate the Riffraff. Reward: 200 gold coins. [+100 Alignment]

Ring! Ring! Ring!! Congratulations. You have reached level 17! You have been awarded 3 stat points. You have 6 stat points to assign.

Patrik slumped to his knees, gasping, as the last bandit fell to his sword. His lungs were burning like he'd just run a half-marathon. Funny how much energy you burned killing helpless men. Even with his inhuman strength, after swinging his sword repeatedly for half an hour, his arm felt like it was about to fall off. How did people manage when the other person actually fought back? The entirety of the Hollywood action genre was a lie.

"Finally," Thalia muttered as she wandered over. "I was beginning to think you wanted the bitch to wake up so you could perform some elaborate Earthling mating ritual."

Sucking in a mouthful of air, Patrik finally caught his breath. "Wait, that was a woman?"

He glanced at the corpse, but his final swing had all but cut her head in half. His stomach roiled uneasily and he quickly looked away again. With the leather armour and short-cropped hair, she hadn't *looked* like a woman. Swallowing, he glanced at the field of corpses their night of slaughter had left, and decided it really shouldn't matter.

"Are you Earthlings blind as well as stupid?" Thalia grunted. "Wait, you know *I'm* a woman, right?"

"Really?" Patrik said, feigning surprise. "I hadn't noticed!"

Thalia was not amused. Leaning down, she caught him by the front of his shirt and hauled him to his feet. They stood there a moment, face to face, breath puffing on the cool night air. It was somewhat comical given their height difference. The fiery sorceress was now forced to look up to meet his gaze. Under different circumstances Patrik might have laughed. In this case, he decided to hold his tongue.

"A shame we don't have time for an anatomy lesson," she said at last, then sniffed. "Your Alignment has improved. Good. Now go loot your kills. You're on first watch and the rest of us would like to get some sleep." She made a gesture towards the battlefield then turned away.

Patrik bit back a sharp retort at her retreating backside. Not because it was a nice backside—well, maybe a little—but mostly because he was quickly learning Thalia was not a woman you crossed. She might look the part of a sweet school-teacher, but that fantasy ended the moment she opened her mouth. Her tongue was as sharp as any dagger.

Instead, he turned his gaze back to the battlefield. If you could even call it that. The battle part of the encounter had only lasted a few minutes. The rest…

Patrik hung his head. The rest had been a slaughter. A slaughter that he had participated in. He, Patrik Conroy, had killed men—and women. Not just in the metaphorical sense, like with Monmouth. Not just in the magical sense, in that he'd reanimated corpses and ordered them to kill their former comrades. This was real. This had been his own hands—his own sword cleaving in skulls and smashing through ribs, hacking off limbs.

Each death sat in the pit of his stomach like a concrete brick.

"Bloody hell, Earthling!" A scream from Thalia interrupted his thoughts. "If I have to come over there and loot your corpses myself—"

"I'm going, I'm going," Patrik muttered, climbing to his feet. *Hell, she's worse than Dolores Umbridge.*

Ha! Well, there probably are some centaurs in this forest...

Patrik shook his head. If a centaur showed up, O'Malley would probably sing it to sleep with a lullaby, then butcher it for their next meal. Another eyeball in his soup was the last thing he needed just now. Instead, he staggered across to the last bandit he'd killed. A box popped and he selected the 'loot all' option. It was basically habit by now.

As the text faded, he saw that Thalia was indeed correct. The bandit had been a woman. He swallowed as another brick settled in his stomach. It really shouldn't matter. He was a feminist. Equality and all that. But still…even with the bloody corpses of all his other victims lying about him, this…this felt worse.

And yet…he'd received positive Alignment for her death. For all the highwaymen he'd killed. That was just how things worked here, apparently. Kill someone or something with negative Alignment, and you got positive Alignment—and vice versa.

Patrik had also steadily gained experience, bringing him up two levels, while the stronger Thalia, Giovanni and O'Malley had each gone up one. That, plus the loot he was now collecting, made this an entirely profitable venture.

And they'd been bad people, hadn't they? Thieves preying on the weak, seeking to take by force what others had earned with their own hard work. They were evil—the system of this world said as much…

A system that also claimed *he* was evil.

His stomach churned. Forcing *that* particular thought from his mind, Patrik returned to his task. For an hour after their deaths, a body could only be looted by the person responsible for their deaths. The others had already cleaned up their own kills, leaving naked bodies strewn across the clearing—and making it easy for Patrik to recognise his handful of victims.

There were at least a dozen.

With a heart heavy, he wandered from one to another and repeated the looting process. To his relief, there had only been the one woman amongst his dead, although he spotted a few others here and there. When he was done, he wandered back to his companions, leaving the dead to rest where they lay. Apparently bandits didn't merit a burial in this world.

"Finally," Thalia muttered as he joined them at the camp-fire. The sorceress had already found herself a patch of ground to lie down. "You and O'Malley are keeping first watch. Wake me in three hours."

"What happens—" Patrik started, but he was already too late.

The sorceress began to snore within seconds of closing her eyes. The others might not have their own PQAs, but apparently the sleep system was incorporated to every humanoid species in this world. Letting out a sigh, he settled himself back down on the fallen tree trunk. A chicken drumstick lay in the dirt nearby. Ruined. He sighed and picked it up, then tossed it into the fire.

O'Malley said nothing, only settled himself down on the other side of the fire and began fiddling with his lute. He alone of the three adventurers seemed affected by the deaths of the bandits. The swordsman had disappeared into the trees—probably to check for stragglers—but he soon returned and found his own spot near the fire. His snores immediately joined those of Thalia.

Letting out a sigh, Patrik turned his attention inwards once more. He hadn't paid much attention to what he'd gotten from the bandits, but if he had to sit awake for the next three hours, he might as well do some investigating.

Did we get anything good, Steve? He asked the PQA.

Hmm, let's see, you've got a handful of leather breastplates. They're about as useless as...well, robes that are beyond above your level. Wearing one will give you a +1 Constitution boost, but you'd have to take off the robes.

Patrik thought about it a moment, but in the end the thought of wearing clothing he'd looted from someone he'd *actually* killed—as opposed to the wizard that he'd only *accidentally* killed—was just too much. He could find some better equipment in Anchorpoint.

No? Okay, what else? Oh yes, bronze daggers and swords. Lovely. That'll get you a few coins if you sell them, I suppose. Oh, here's something. You have a few enchanted rings, see:

Sapphire Ring of Strength. A sapphire ring enchanted to improve its user's Strength [+1 Strength]

Sapphire Ring of Constitution. A sapphire ring enchanted to improve its user's Constitution [+1 Constitution]

Sapphire Ring of Dexterity. A sapphire ring enchanted to improve its user's Dexterity [+1 Dexterity]

Pursing his lips, Patrik pulled up his inventory and the rings appeared in his hand. It was the same predicament as the clothing. These had come from men he'd killed. But...at least it wasn't their *clothing*. He guessed. Kind of. It was still...

Just put the damn rings on and stop being a baby.

Patrik grated his teeth. But...the PQA was right. He needed to stop being so squeamish about these things. The rings were a good start. He slipped them onto his fingers without further complaint, and felt an immediately tingling as their magic—or whatever you wanted to call it—took effect.

Anything else?

Hmm, let me see, ahh, just this, I guess?
Silver Amulet. Purpose unknown.

That was strange. There wasn't anything more to the description, so Patrik pulled it from his inventory. The amulet, along with its silver chain, settled in his hand. A closer examination didn't reveal any special characteristics to this particular piece of jewellery. He was about to toss it, when a hidden clasp gave a little *click* and it popped open. Inside he found a portrait of a dark haired woman and a young girl of maybe sixteen. A scrap of paper also fell out. Patrik's heart twisted into a knot when he saw it. he wanted nothing more than to hurl it into the fire. He read it instead, of course.

My dearest Warren.

Oh how I curse Fate for these foul times, which force you to stray so far from my bosom. My lips shall yearn for you on these long nights, and my body burn with desperate longing. I pray you remember that flame as you venture into the harsh world, that the dark deeds you must perform will not corrupt your spirit. Know that all you do, you do for your family. Let not our time apart see your passion dwindle, nor your memory forget the warmth of my hands upon your chest, nor my lips upon your shaft—

Ahhh, should we be reading this?

Patrik's cheeks were already burning, and nodding, he skipped to the end. It was long. Really long. And detailed.

Know that your faithful wife and fairest daughter await your triumphant return to Anchorpoint. We shall never forget the sacrifice you have made for your family.

Forever yours, Ezra.

Another brick settled in Patrik's stomach. Scrunching up the paper, he forced it back into the amulet, which then disappeared into his inventory. It was too much.

Up came the contents of his stomach. Which, unfortunately, was more Manticore. It burned as much coming up as it did going out the other way. Coughing and choking, Patrik slumped to his knees in the mud. He clasped at the dirt, seeking something, anything solid in this insane world.

"Is everything alright, my friend?" O'Malley asked, rising from his boulder and wandering over to join Patrik on the log.

"I told you the Manticore was getting old. Come on, I got a bit of mermaid heart from my share of the loot. I'll cook you up a stew, should sort that nausea in no time."

Jesus, they eat mermaids? His stomach lurched again. This time he tasted acrid bile in the back of his throat. It took an effort of will to force it back down. He offered O'Malley a shaky smile.

"It's not the meat," he croaked, before making a gesture towards the dead highwaymen. "It's just…all of this. I know you think we're evil in my world, but this is the first time I've actually killed someone." He swallowed. "I found…I found a note on one of their bodies. He had a family, a life."

O'Malley stared at him for a long while, a frown on his face. Then he looked across the fire, to where the bodies of the bandits still lay. "I admit, I too am uncomfortable with such death. In an ideal world, I would have offered each of these sorry souls a chance for redemption. To give up their evil ways and leave this forest." He shrugged. "But we do not live in an ideal world, my friend. Had we talked with these men, their friends would have crept up behind and stabbed us in the back. I do not know about you Earthlings, but I prefer to keep the blood inside my body."

Patrik nodded. "Us too."

The giant bard smiled. It was probably meant to be comforting, but on his ferocious face the expression came off almost as a scowl.

"It must be strange, waking up in an entirely new world," O'Malley continued. "Everything you have ever known, just gone. No wonder you lashed out in your first days here. Did you leave anyone behind, back on Earth?"

It was a good question. He hadn't seen his father in years, not since…the new baby. And he and his mother didn't talk much these days, not since Chris…

"I had a girlfriend," he said instead. "Clara. But we broke up a while back. Mutual separation, of course…"

Oh, is that what you call those three months you

spent balling your eyes out on the sofa watching
Friends*?*

"Of course…" O'Malley seemed about as disbelieving as Steve.

Patrik rolled his eyes. "Seriously," he muttered, "why does no one—just, never mind. It was for the best, you know? Different interests and all that. Besides, us young guys gotta spread our wings, right?" He paused, glancing at the sleeping Thalia and Giovanni. They weren't *close*, but they also weren't *not close*. "Are they…?"

He asked the question more to change the subject than out of any real curiosity. So far those two had treated him with just-about-utter contempt. He cared more about the Kardashians' love life than that pair, which was of course to say, not at all.

***Ooooh, I just discovered that show. This is amazing! Do the women of your world regularly form clans to overthrow the male-dominated order—oh, yeah, never mind, just flipped the page onto the feminist movement. That is* dense.**

"Oh Fate no," O'Malley replied as Patrik did his best to ignore the PQA's ramblings. "Thalia gelded the last dude who looked at her the wrong way. Not even Giovanni is that mad. Why do you ask?" He raised an eyebrow. "You don't—"

"God no," Patrik said, whipping his head back and forth. "Just making sure I don't go putting my foot in my mouth, you know?"

"Ahh…" O'Malley trailed off, looking from Patrik's face to his feet. He was still wearing the wizard's slippers—which had actually performed surprisingly well in the forest. "Why…why would you want to put your foot in your mouth, my friend?" the bard continued slowly. "I assure you, it will not taste half as good as a bit of mermaid stew, if you would only wait a moment."

"Oh, yeah, sorry, I didn't mean literally," Patrik said, holding up his hands. "It's just…a saying on Earth. Comes from way back. I think it has something to do with the plagues of Foot and Mouth disease that swept through the cow herds of Europe in the 1900s."

"So…" the bard said when he finished. "Your people…eat these cows on your world, which are prone to this…Foot and Mouth disease?" He blinked. "That would…that would seem to be the definition of insanity, my friend."

Patrik chuckled. "It's pretty rare these days. We've been more preoccupied with people eating bats the last few years."

A look of horror crossed the big man's face. "People on Earth eat *bats?*"

Shaking his head, Patrik gave the bard a pat on the shoulder. "Not anymore, my friend. Not anymore."

Then he turned and wandered away from the fire. Of his three companions, he enjoyed O'Malley's company the most, but…that wasn't really saying much, and just now he needed the space to think. He didn't plan to go far—earlier the bard had been *way* too excited about the monsters that apparently occupied this forest—but he did need to consider which attributes he was going to assign his latest stat points too.

Could I make a suggestion?

I swear if you mention charisma one more time…

It's not about charisma!

Patrik let out long sigh. *Fine, I'm waiting.*

Although…you know what, never mind. Let's not whip a dead centaur. I was going to suggest you improve your Intelligence. Not cause you're stupid or anything. No, definitely not. You make great decisions. But if you can get it to 15, you'll finally be able to use that scroll of yours.

Scroll…

Patrik's eyes widened. He'd almost forgotten the scrolls he'd taken from Tenser! He quickly pulled them up in his inventory.

Scroll of Lightning Bolt [permanent]: Use this spell to learn the spell 'Lightning Bolt'. Requirements: 15 Intelligence.

"So if I increase my intelligence to 15, I'll be able to use this lightning spell? Permanently?"

Yeah, that's the normal way to learn a spell. Still not sure how you managed the whole necromancy thing. You bring some cheat codes over from Earth or something?

Patrik shrugged. "Sounds like a plan."

Scrolling to his attributes, he dumped five points into Intelligence. Then because he wasn't a particularly big fan of how people kept stabbing him, he put the last point into his Constitution. A brief warming sensation spread through his limbs—particularly his head—as he assigned the points.

Next, he pulled open his inventory and found the first magical scroll listed there—

Wait, wait, wait, wrong scroll!

"Huh?" Patrik asked, before realising the PQA was right.

He had two magical scrolls. The other was a single use fireball spell.

Scroll of Inferno [single use]: For emergency situations only. Hurls an enormous fireball at your enemies. Requirements: none. Effect: massive damage

Yeah, that's not something you want to waste on a tree! The PQA tisked. *That's a get out of jail free card if ever I saw one.*

Patrik let out a long breath. He could see Steve's point. Given it didn't even list a particular amount of damage, he assumed it would be enough to take down anything in this Circle. But it could only be used once. He quickly assigned it to his hotlist for use emergency situations, then moved on to the other scroll.

This time the tingling in his body wasn't so much warmth, more a thousand tiny pinpricks simultaneously stabbing into his skin. He would have screamed, but it was over before he'd even fully processed it had begun. A notification from Steve popped up.

Congratulations, you have learned the spell 'Lightning Bolt' [level 1]. Use this spell to cast a lightning bolt. Effect: deals 1 damage per second of spell

charge, for a maximum damage of 30. Overcharging may lead to general discharge. Cost: 1 mana per second

Overcoming the wave of dizziness that went with the attribute boosts and spell knowledge, Patrik came to a tree at the edge of the clearing and leaned back against its trunk. Then he pulled open his stat box.

PATRIK THE CHOSEN ONE   LEVEL 17

PROGRESS TO NEXT LEVEL: 25%

RACE	ALIGNMENT
Human	-1550

HEALTH	MANA
170/170	80/80

STR	CON	INT	CHA	DEX
16(+4)	11(+1)	15	1	10(+1)

Equipped: Iron short sword (+3 STR)
Sapphire Ring of Strength (+1 STR)
Sapphire Ring of Dexterity (+1 DEX)
Sapphire Ring of Constitution (+1 CON)

You have no stat points to assign.

SPELLS [LIMIT: FOUR]

RAISE DEAD	LIGHTNING BOLT
level 7	level 1

SKILLS [UNLIMITED]

HACK and SLASH	ARSON
level 4	level 6

Well, he was making progress. He wasn't sure what that meant in the grand scheme of things, considering his arch nemesis was apparently a Dark Lord capable of commanding entire armies. If the dude ever learned of Patrik's identity, no amount of grinding on backwater highwaymen was going to save him.

But still, despite the philosophical questions and the constant danger and the terrible, *terrible* food, there was… something about this place. About the sensation each time he advanced a level or increased his attributes. Or learned a spell.

He clenched his fingers at the thought, awakening this freshly developed part of his mind—or perhaps it was only a part of his mind he'd never known he possessed. Either way, the affect was immediate, as every hair on his body suddenly stood on end. Little flashes of light burst across his skin before gathering in his fingertips, eventually coalescing into a little ball of lightning. It continued to grow as the seconds passed, and with it the heat of its fire…

Ah, might want to let that go before it pops, mate…
Patrik didn't ask twice. He pointed at a nearby tree.
Boom!
The forest lit up like it was the Fourth of July—only instead of something exploding in the sky, the lightning struck a nearby tree. The subsequent crash was more like a bomb going off that any firework Patrik had ever seen. As the light faded he found himself blinking in the dark, hardly able to see for the stars dancing in his eyes. And the smoke.

When his vision finally cleared, instead of a shattered tree, Patrik found a very, very angry looking Thalia standing before him. Yelping, he scrambled away, only for a tiny fist to catch him by the shirt and haul him back. Sapphire eyes burned behind her thick-framed glasses as she dragged him down to her eye level.

"What. The. Fuck. Was. That?" she snarled. A tiny ball of fire appeared in her hand. Tiny, but very, very hot, Patrik realised as he felt its heat on his face.

"I…what…how…awake!" Patrik stumbled over the words in his panic. He was still trying to work out how she'd woken herself up from the artificially induced sleep, let alone formulate an answer to her question.

"Is that it then?" she roared. "Your dastardly plan was to take us while the fighters slept? Did you think I would really be foolish enough to *actually sleep* in front of an Earthling with only a *goddamn bard* for protection?"

"Wait, wait, arg—" Patrik's words turned into a scream as Thalia's fireball doubled in size. Suddenly, it was no longer just hot. Suddenly, he could actually feel his flesh searing as she held it closer to his cheek.

"Do not play games with me, Earthling." The sorceress's eyes flickered in the light of the flame. Its heat didn't seem to have any effect on her, though it was unclear if that was because it was her own fireball, or some other innate power of the sorceress. "I will end you."

"I…what…no…" Patrik tried to speak, but the words came out garbled. Taking a long breath, he fought through the agony. "I…I just learnt that spell. I didn't mean to actually cast it!"

His eyes darted past her to the fire where he hoped to see O'Malley coming to his rescue…but the bard was sitting calmly on his boulder sipping a bowl of…well, probably his mermaid stew.

"You just learnt a lightning spell?" Thalia hissed, regaining his attention with a vigorous shake. "Just like that?"

"I had a scroll!"

The sorceress's eyes narrowed. "A scroll? What was a little noob like you doing with a magic scroll?"

"Tenser gave it to me!" Patrik gasped. "Before…before he ah…left."

"Is that so?" Thalia leaned in until their noses were practically touching. "Tell me, Patrik the Chosen One. I've been meaning to ask. Why, oh why, would Tenser go through all the trouble of summoning you to this realm, if he was just going to abandon you mere moments later?"

Mate, you're sweating bullets. Chill!

Seriously, not helping, Steve!

"I…you…you know wizards," Patrik stuttered. "They're always wandering off at important moments. Abandoning people in haunted hills or going off to fight a Balrog…"

"Oh yeah, goddamn experience hogs," O'Malley muttered loudly from somewhere over Thalia's shoulder.

Patrik swallowed as Thalia's ocean-blue eyes continued to drill into him. She was so close now that they're lips were practically touching. His mouth was suddenly very dry. Despite O'Malley's earlier warning and the entire situation, he felt an inexplicable urge to kiss her. He was still a man, after all.

"Fine," she snapped, much to his surprise. "But that still doesn't explain how you could use the scroll. If I'm not mistaken, that was a Lightning Bolt. You're telling me your intelligence is already at level 15?"

"Ah…yeah," Patrik replied, confused by her new line of questioning. "I just put my last round of stat points into it."

Thalia said nothing for a long moment, just continued to stare. Why did everyone in this world seem intent on having a staring contest with him?

"What, is that unusual?" he demanded after a full thirty seconds had passed.

"Being a human at level seventeen, your attributes should average out at eleven," Thalia said calmly, as though she hadn't just assaulted him.

Patrik frowned. "Sure, if you assign them all evenly."

"Yes, but your physical attributes have clearly also been advanced, or you would never have kept up today." Her eyes suddenly widened. "Fate, you've been neglecting your Charisma, haven't you!"

"Huh?" Patrik asked, then: "Wait, how do you know that? And so what, anyway, its only Charisma!"

"So…?" The sorceress closed her eyes with a sigh. "So *that's* why I keep having this inexplicable urge to stab you." Shaking her head, she released him. "Gods you're an idiot. It's a good thing you've got that whole bad boy thing going for you."

Lurching back a step after being released so abruptly, Patrik straightened to his full height and made a show of tidying up his shirt. Inwardly, his heart was racing. He could hardly believe she'd actually *bought* all that.

It was a second before he processed what she'd actually said. "Huh?"

Too late. Thalia had already returned to her log by the fire. Seating herself, she took out a book from her inventory. He approached slowly, waiting to see what she would do next. She didn't move, but when he tried to take a seat, her eyes flickered in his direction.

"Get some sleep, idiot," she snapped. "There's still a long walk to reach Anchorpoint tomorrow and I'll not be waiting for you."

"Ah…you kind of have to, with the quest and all."

Thalia did not deign that with a reply, but the glare she gave him from behind her glasses left no doubt that she would sooner leave him dead in a ditch, the reward unclaimed, than put up with another second of his shit.

Patrik gulped. "No waiting. Sleep. Right. Gotcha."

He didn't need telling twice. Curling up behind a log, he lay staring at the fire for a while, his mind drifting as it usually did before sleep. Or how it had back on earth at least. Here… here he supposed there was no need for it, being able to ask Steve to make him sleep at a moment's notice and all. But… strangely, he found he missed those quiet moments. Of lying in his bed, his mind lingering on all the highs and lows of his day.

He missed a lot from home, in fact. What would Clara have thought of this place, if they'd somehow been dragged in here together. And they hadn't broken up. What about his mother? A lump rose in his throat. He missed the warmth of her voice. It had been so cold, these last few years. What would she think of his disappearance? Would she even notice? Or care?

Suddenly the quiet was no longer so peaceful.

Steve?

How long would you like to sleep?

Let's start with three hours—

Everything went black.

CHAPTER 15
MARY HAD A LITTLE LAMB

ANCHORPOINT TURNED OUT TO BE A TINY FISHING VILLAGE nestled beneath the cliffs of a sheltered bay. The ground rose steeply from the shore and terraced villas had been constructed to make the most of the narrow stretch of ground between sea and mountains. In some places the ground was so steep that rather than roads, long stairwells stretched between the houses. The sight would have had Joaquin Phoenix busting out his dance moves.

Hey, I've seen that one! Steve exclaimed. *Ah, let's not go getting any ideas, shall we?*

Patrik rolled his eyes.

The terraced buildings were built from stone and had slate rooftops to keep out the wild ocean weather—both probably quarried from the nearby cliffs. Broad windows looked out towards the north, where waves crashed upon the rocky shore. Further out across the bay were a collection of islands of stark white stone.

Gulls cawed overhead as the fellowship made their way into the village. The road they walked entered from above and switch-backed down the cliffs until it encountered the first of the terraced houses. There the fellowship was met by the swirling wind and sharp scent of brine and rotting fish.

Giovanni took the lead, plunging into the narrow streets

"

with a manner that suggested he knew this place. The route he chose led them between the tall buildings and down damp tunnels carved through the cliffs themselves. The constant *boom* of the waves upon the shore grew steadily louder as they made their way lower in the town.

Only once reached the creaking wooden docks did the silent swordsman finally pause. The others drew up beside him, Patrik puffing gently in the fading light. He really needed to focus on his Constitution and Dexterity next, if he wanted to keep pace with his higher-level companions.

The sun had already dipped behind the clifftops, but out in the harbour it still shone, catching upon the white of the islands and setting them ablaze with the scarlet light. Amidst the swirling waters, Patrik glimpsed the dark sails of a few ships, but most were already docked.

Drawing in a breath of the ocean air, Patrik allowed his mind to drift, carrying him back to the vacation home his family had once owned on the Californian coast. So long ago now, their last visit. He'd just been a kid then, his brother a golden-haired hero, his father a giant of a man they both worshiped. Even his mother smiled in those memories…

"You okay there, Patrik?" O'Malley asked. The bard placed a hand on his shoulder and adopted a concerned expression.

"What…oh, it's nothing," Patrik replied, shaking off the giant of a man. "Just remembering something."

"Ah," O'Malley replied in an unusually sage tone. "I see. Truly, Earth must be a terrible place, to put such a foul expression on your face."

"Actually, I was thinking about my family." He forced a smile. "But never mind that. What are we doing down here?" He made a gesture back the way they'd come. "After seeing what happened in Monmouth, I'd really rather sleep in a *stone* building."

Several buildings stretched along the waterfront, including a tavern and what looked like a general store. Unlike the rest of the town, these constructed of timber and seemed more a part of the wharf than the town.

"Beggars cannot be choosers, my friend," O'Malley chuckled.

"And uncharismatic idiots don't get to make decisions," Thalia added with a scowl in his direction.

O'Malley flashed him an apologetic look as the sorceress stalked off towards the tavern, Giovanni in tow. "Sorry about her," he said when the pair were out of earshot. "Tomorrow is the Thousand Years Festival and every inn of any worth will be packed to the rafters tonight. Believe me, Thalia hates staying in the budget places as well, but…" He spread his hands.

"Isn't she the daughter of some sort of noble?" Patrik queried as they moved towards the inn. "What's she doing scrambling around in the dirt for trinkets with the rest of us?"

"Oh, that's easy! Her parents cut her off. Didn't support the whole Warrior of the Light dream and all that."

Huh. That he could actually kind of understand. His level of respect for the sorceress lifted, if only a little.

As they reached the inn, Patrik finally took in the name and realised belatedly this was the Sailor's Wife—the place Johnny had recommended. He felt a pang of regret for the friendly, one-handed innkeeper.

The guy practically force-fed you centaur stew.

Actually, that was true. Thinking about it that way, Patrik didn't feel *quite* so bad about…well, everything.

The harsh roar of rowdy voices and a badly played guitar spilled from the inn as Thalia pulled open the front door. Within, half a hundred men and women had crammed into the ramshackle building, filling up long tables and crowding what looked to be a dance floor in the corner. Somewhere a single guitarist was strumming the same three cords over and over and trying to sing to his inattentive audience.

As soon as O'Malley heard the music, his face darkened and he stomped across to Thalia. "Oh come on, seriously, you can't seriously expect me to listen to *that* all night?" he grumbled.

"If I have to share a room with one of you three morons, you can put up with some bad music," the sorceress snapped back.

Patrik and O'Malley shared a look. They both decided at the same time to make themselves scarce. The bard wandered off into the crowd muttering something about teaching the guitarist a few lessons, while Patrik's rumbling stomach drew him to the bar—although he wasn't expecting much. The room stank of unwashed bodies and stale beer. All up, it wasn't the most appetising of venues. And that was ignoring the likelihood of their food having a human face.

The setup was similar to Johnny's place, with a long bar and a door behind that lead back to the kitchen. An older woman—presumably the sailor's wife—was busy serving a group of men, who cheered as half a dozen beers were set in front of them. Next in line for her attention was Thalia, and Patrik found himself drifting in the opposite direction, where a patch of space had appeared.

A young woman seemed to be serving the clients at this end, but she did not look up as he approached. Patrik made a quick check of her description as he approached.

Bel the Barmaid [level 13]. The only daughter of a local sailor, Bel was on a fast track to join the Magician's Academy in Bledross until her family fell on hard times. Now instead of setting off for the big city, she is forced to work the bar at her family's tavern, at least until her absent father returns. Good luck with that one, kid.

Bel's eyes stared off into the distance as she leaned against the counter, one finger toying absently with a lock of her hair. She couldn't have been much older than eighteen, though her auburn hair had been tied back in pigtails that gave her a younger, more innocent look. Puberty had clearly been much kinder with her than it had ever been with Patrik. Her golden cheeks were untouched by acne and he'd already noticed her... other assets drawing looks from his fellow patrons.

No one else seemed game to approach though, so smiling, he wandered up and took the stool across from her.

"Happy Thousand Years Festival?" he offered, while inwardly he cursed himself for not requesting information from his PQA when O'Malley had mentioned it earlier. *Steve?*

Information Requested: Thousand Years Festival. This festival marks the coronation of the Dark Lord Malus as the one true leader of the Four Circles.

Patrik winced. Maybe this *wasn't* the sort of festival you wished one another best wishes, if it marked the date the Dark Lord had taken over the place. Luckily for him, the young woman across the bar didn't seem to have heard him.

"Huh?" she whispered. She blinked her emerald eyes and lifted her head as though waking from a daze. "What was that?"

"Oh, I ah, was just wondering what was on the menu tonight?"

"Menu?" A scowl replaced her confusion. "Why don't you ask the stinking humanitarians what happened to our menu." She sniffed and turned her head away from him.

It was a dismissal if ever Patrik had seen one. But her words intrigued him.

"Ah, sorry, I'm new here. What was that about humanitarians?"

"You don't know?" Her youthful face showed surprise, though the anger didn't entirely vanish. "They're a bunch of right bastards, that's what. Think they're so righteous, going around telling people they shouldn't eat things with faces."

"Ah…" Wow, this lot sounded like something Patrik could get behind. But the barmaid wasn't finished yet.

"They've been out there, blockading the harbour for more than a week now. None of the ships can go out for the mermaid harvest." She made a gesture to the packed bar. "Honestly, what do they expect us to eat! We've already eaten what we had in storage and there won't be anything from Bledross for who knows how long. People…people…"

Suddenly the girl's eyes teared up. "People are resorting to cooking…to cooking their *pets*!"

Patrik's heart sank and he glanced towards the door out back. "So what…you've got some dog cooking back there?"

"Dog!" The girl exclaimed, then hiccupped. "Fate, I wish we had dog! Do you have some?" Her eyes welled up again when he shook his head. "No, we don't have any dog. Mum… mum, she says I have to go put down Lamb Chop, but…but I *can't!*"

"Ah, Lamb Chop?" Patrik asked quickly. Surely it couldn't be… "Err, just to be clear, this Lamb Chop is…"

"A sweet little baby sheep!" Bel wailed as she burst into tears. Again. Patrik was beginning to realise why the other patrons avoided this corner.

Still, the perfect opportunity for a *real* meal had just been laid out for him on a silver platter. Trying not to appear overeager, he reached across the bar and laid a hand on Bel's shoulder.

"Bel," he said softly, "such a dark deed should not be yours to carry. Let me be lift this burden from your shoulders."

The young woman's eyes widened at his words and for a moment he thought she was going to cry again. Then the moment passed and her jaw hardened. She gave a curt nod, then straightening, she gestured for him to follow her. His heart began to pound.

Dude, are you really this excited about slaughtering a little girl's pet lamb?

Have you *ever tasted lamb?* He shot back. The girl led him behind the bar and through the kitchen—which was empty but of a sombre-looking man stirring a pot in the corner—then out into a courtyard in the centre of the tavern. *Also, she's hardly a 'little girl'…right?*

Of course not, she has a level. That means she's come of age. And level 13 no less. She's probably seventeen or eighteen, if I had to guess. There was a brief pause. **Of course, what you're really asking is whether she's too young for you—the answer to which**

is of course: yes, Patrik, she is much too young for you.

"I wasn't going to try anything," Patrik muttered. Bel had vanished into another room, leaving him standing in the shadows of the courtyard. Several windows looked down from the second storey. He presumed they belonged to the rooms in which guests such as himself stayed, though just now he couldn't see anyone behind the shutters. "I only wanted to be sure. You know, just in case."

Sure, Patrik. Sure.

Before Patrik could reply, a soft cry came from behind him. He recognised it instantly. It was only with a serious effort of will that he managed to keep the grin off his face as he turned and found Bel leading a lamb across the courtyard. It gave another bleating cry as it danced along behind her, tiny hooves clacking on the stones.

Seriously, Patrik. You're going to kill that? Steve exclaimed. The PQA sounded genuinely upset. *But its...it's so adorable!*

Patrik agreed, of course. He wasn't a monster. Lamb Chop skipped along before the slim form of Bel, the happiest little lamb he could be. Only the most heartless, cruel of souls would contemplate snuffing out that little life. And there was of course also Bel, who was in something of a state as she stopped in front of Patrik. Silently she held out her hand, offering him the leash.

Come on man, you're not really going to do it. Pretend all you like, but you have a heart. We can find another way.

Patrik swallowed. The PQA was right. He'd never really even been on a farm. The only time he'd encountered farm animals were at petting zoos and those birthday parties where a company brings along sheep and bunnies for the kids to torment. He wasn't a murderer.

Was he?

Half an hour later, Bel was curled up in the corner of the bar sobbing to herself and the forlorn-looking chef still looked forlorn—only now he had a pot of water *and* meat bubbling on the stove. Not exactly how Patrik would have cooked it. Actually, it was a bit of a waste, considering the effort he'd gone through to procure it. But the man hadn't exactly seemed pleased to be presented with a platter of freshly carved meat, and in the end it had seemed better to leave him to it than offer any further pointers.

Mate, I can't believe you just did that, Steve said as Patrik returned to the bar for a drink. The PQA's voice barely rose above a whisper. ***I mean, I know everyone from Earth are meant to be monsters, and from what I've read it's pretty much true, but…mate, that was cold. Even for you.***

You heard Bel—people here are starving. he replied. *I did what needed to be done.*

Back in the common room, he found the volume of voices had only grown louder, though the general topic of conversation seemed to be around the delicious scent of cooking meat now drifting from the kitchen.

And do you really think these people are going to be happy when you serve them up a bowl of murdered sheep?

Patrik smiled. "Better than an empty stomach, right?" Spotting O'Malley, Thalia and Giovanni at the bar, he wandered over to join them. "Hey, good news, you three! They were all out of mermaid, but I manage to help them prepare a recipe from my own world."

"They're all out of mermaid?" O'Malley asked, sounding aggrieved.

Giovanni slammed his fists down on the bench, then rose silently and stalked away, disappearing into the crowd.

Thalia raised her eyebrows. "Oh joy," she murmured, before seating herself on a stool and crossing her legs.

Momentarily distracted by the movement of the sorceress's short skirt, Patrik shook his head and made a gesture towards the kitchen.

"It wasn't easy," he said, allowing an edge of pride to creep into his voice, "but judging by everyone's reaction to the smell, I think they're going to enjoy it."

Seriously, you're a monster.

It was another ten minutes before the food began to appear, during which time the excitement of the patrons only grew. There were a lot of hungry people in the room, and the rich aroma that filled the tavern had many a stomach rumbling. In fact, Patrik was beginning to have reservations about giving the chef free reign. He'd yet to find any herbs or spices in this world, but they could have at least roasted the lamb over a flame. It would have taken longer, but the flavour—

His thoughts were interrupted as a cheer filled the tavern. The older woman—Bel's mother, he assumed—had emerged from out back with four bowls of steaming broth. One in each hand and another two balanced in the crooks of her elbows. A wail of grief came from somewhere behind Patrik, followed by a bang as the door to outside slammed closed. Poor Bel.

And yet he still found himself smiling as the bowl was plonked down in front of him. Others were set in front of Thalia and O'Malley, followed by a pause as the innkeeper found Giovanni missing. With a shrug, she handed the remaining bowl to another patron before bustling back into the kitchen for more.

"What's this then?" O'Malley asked. He picked up a fork and prodded at a lump of meat in the bowl.

Patrik was practically salivating at the sight of the broth. The chef had added vegetables that looked like potatoes, carrots and peas—all a bit plain in flavour, unfortunately, but the bits of _real meat_ bobbing amongst the broth were enough to have him leaping for joy. He settled for a grin.

"Why don't you try it?" he told the big bard as he scooped up a piece of meat and shoved it into his mouth. After the incident with the bandits and his precious chicken, he wasn't taking any chances.

It was…nothing special, if he was honest. Really quite plain. The chef had completely blanched the meat, boiling it without any sort of condiments. Not even salt. His heart broke just a little at the waste, but…at least there weren't going to be any human eyeballs bobbing to the surface in this broth. He would take the win.

The others were more hesitant, but under Patrik's watchful eye, O'Malley took a bite. Well, a bite was a bit of an understatement. The innkeeper had given the bard an overly large spoon to fit his enormous hands. Half of O'Malley's bowl disappeared down his gullet in a single scoop. Thalia was more polite, dipping her spoon into the liquid, then lifting it to her lips and blowing, before finally taking a bite. Both chewed politely, but he saw their noses wrinkle at the taste.

"Sorry, the chef did a terrible job," Patrik said, keeping his voice low. "We should have salted it and cooked it over some coals. Roasted lamb is just the best. Dad used to cook it, but mum…"

He trailed off, suddenly aware of a stillness in the bard beside him. O'Malley sat with spoon halfway to his mouth. As he watched, the colour slowly drained from the giant's face. His Adam's Apple bobbed up and down as he swallowed. He slowly lowered his spoon back to his bowl.

"You…" he rasped. "You…"

"O'Malley—" Thalia started to speak.

"You made me eat a sweet little baby!" O'Malley screamed.

Actually screamed. The bard's stool crashed to the floor as he leapt to his feet and started wiping furiously at his tongue, as though that might scrape away the taste. When it clearly didn't help, he burst into tears and ran from the room. With a sigh, Thalia rose and followed him, though not before she flashed Patrik a glare that could have dented steel.

She left behind a silent common room. A *very* silent common room. Somewhere, someone coughed. The guitarist tried to start a song, but with a harsh *shriek*, one of his strings snapped. Cursing, he tossed the instrument aside and reached for his drink.

"Ah," the only other man at the bar to be served so far

finally spoke up. He had a spoonful of broth halfway to his lips. "What…exactly is in this soup?"

"Oh…" *Shit, shit, shit.* He caught the older woman behind the bar flashing him a look that screamed *don't you dare say anything.* He decided lying through his teeth was probably the best policy. "Oh…ah, don't worry, its centaur meat. But only the horse part. You know how things are just now."

"What was that the giant said about babies?"

"Oh, I'm not sure. He's just the sensitive sort." *God fucking damnit O'Malley!* Patrik was really scrambling now. "It was probably…a kid centaur?"

"Oh, yeah, I guess that makes sense." And just like that, the man shrugged and went back to his meal.

Behind him, the guitarist finally got his new string strung and began to play a grating jib about a fisherman and the sea. Slowly the conversation picked up again. The innkeeper watched him for a few more seconds, as though reassuring herself he wouldn't suddenly blurt out the truth, then disappeared out back for more broth.

Eventually the celebrations began to wind down. Patrik signalled the innkeeper for a drink and nodded his thanks when the woman placed a frothing glass of ale in front of him.

"So this Thousand Years Festival," he asked, making conversation since none of his companions had returned. He wasn't even sure which room he was meant to be sleeping in. "Why the celebration, when it's the anniversary of the Dark Lord's coronation?"

"Since when do people need a good excuse to drink?" the woman replied. "Other than that, it also marked the end of some stupid war, although no one can even remember who was fighting—excuse me."

Stepping out from behind the bar, she stomped over to a group that had just entered. Patrik was surprised to see they were little people—

Dwarfs!

Right, dwarfs. He hadn't seen any since Monmouth. Given the late hour, he assumed the innkeeper was sending them on their way. Sure enough, with much grumbling and angry glares, they soon turned around and retreated into the night.

"Sorry about that," the woman said when she returned. "Can't let riffraff like that in. Anyway, where were we? Ah yes, the festival. Fate knows, we needed a good night. Thank you for helping with my daughter—and for not spilling the beans on the secret ingredient."

Patrik smiled. "It's something of a delicacy where I'm from." He paused. "So the 'humanitarians', what's their deal?" Maybe *they* had some decent food amongst them.

The innkeeper's face hardened. "They're vermin," she replied, voice suddenly iron. "Thieves and cutthroats, that's what they are. Driving honest men out of business." She sighed. "But I suppose times are tough for even honest men, nowadays."

"Your husband…"

The woman pursed her lips. "He has found employment… outside of Anchorpoint. In the forest."

"Oh, to the south?" Patrik asked with a smile. "We've just come from there. Is he working in lumber or something?"

"Not lumber," the innkeeper replied, her face closing over. "He's a good man, my Warren. But he's doing what he must. Maybe if the tavern was this full every night…but no, tomorrow we'll be quiet again. And school in Bledross is expensive. We need more…" she trailed off with a shake of her head. "He's a good man. He's doing what he has too. For his family."

Nooo, Steve interjected. ***No, you don't think?***

Patrik could only stare at the woman. He felt as though he'd been punched in the gut. Mouth suddenly parched, he reached for his glass to cover his shock. He gulped down most of the mug without rediscovering the nerve to speak. He did manage to do what he should have done from the beginning, and examine the woman.

Ezra the Sailor's Wife [level 17]. Ezra and her husband, Warren, have been together since they were high school sweethearts. Using the profits from

mermaid fishing, they opened the local tavern in Anchorpoint together and have been slowly accumulating wealth over the last forty years. Things looked bright for the couple and their only daughter, until the humanitarians blockaded the harbour and annihilated half their business overnight. Now both husband and wife have resorted to desperate measures to keep their business afloat. Like slaughtering their daughter's pet lamb and feeding it to their unsuspecting patrons. Or murdering people in the forest. Which are totally comparable, by the way.

Well, shit.

You should really be checking the description of everyone you meet, mate.

There were like fifty people in here earlier!

You managed to read Bel's description.

Patrik's cheeks warmed. Laughter echoed in his thoughts but the PQA mercifully didn't press the point. Even better, by the time he'd finished reading, Ezra had already moved on to serve another patron. He watched her as she moved between clients.

Only now did he notice the resemblance to the woman in the locket. He didn't dare take it out in the bar, but…yes. There were more lines to her face now, more silver streaks in her hair, but this was the same woman. The girl had grown another year or two as well, but there was no doubt in his mind that it had been Bel. He should have recognised her sooner. He just hadn't been looking.

The locket in his inventory belonged to Ezra's husband. A husband that would never return home. A husband that he, Patrik Conroy, had killed. Whose body even now lay rotting in the forest somewhere.

His stomach churned, the concrete bricks of his guilt grinding against one another until he was sure they would tear him apart. He doubled up against the bar and saw stars, while a groan slipped from his lips. Fuck. What had he done? How…

He staggered to his feet. His eyes were burning and he

knew if he looked the woman in the eye, the truth would come tumbling out whether he wanted it to or not. Which…

Thalia was standing behind him. Where had she come from?

"You didn't tell her." The sorceress's words were not a question.

Still reeling from his realisation, Patrik shook his head. "No," he rasped, then his mind began to catch up. "Wait, you knew? Of course you knew. Why didn't *you* tell her?"

"Are you an idiot, Patrik the Chosen One?" Thalia asked slowly. An iron hand settled on his shoulder and drew him away from the bar, leading him towards the stairwell to the upper level. "Or do you just like to hurt people?"

"What!" he spluttered. "No! It's j—"

"Good," the sorceress said smartly. "Then come with me. She's coming back and we are apparently bunking together." She waved over his shoulder as they started up the stairs, apparently to the woman they had recently made a widow. "O'Malley is having a tantrum and has taken my bed in the room with Giovanni."

"Wait, what?" Patrik asked as they reached the landing and stumbled into the upstairs corridor. "We're sleeping in the same room?"

"That's right, Patrik." Thalia replied with a nod. Her eyes glinted in the lantern light. "And you had better not snore."

CHAPTER 16
CHANCE ENCOUNTERS

THE NEXT MORNING PATRIK WOKE EARLY, HAVING THANKFULLY survived the night without being murdered in his sleep by the vengeful sorceress. While he was about ninety five percent sure that Thalia was *really* asleep when he woke—and therefore all but impossible to wake—he still slipped from the room on the tips of his toes and closed the door as softly as possible behind him. No point taking unnecessary risks, right?

Below, he found the common room of the inn surprisingly quiet. Even for the early hour, he'd expected a few locals in for breakfast or travellers to have risen early in preparation for their journeys. He supposed it being the morning after the big festival, most would be sleeping off their night's excesses. Plus, given the innkeepers description last night, he assumed word would have spread about what was *really* in the stew. Or had that been tailored slightly based on his own personal knowledge.

Huh, that's a good question, Steve remarked as they stepped from the front door of the Sailor's Wife onto the docks. The PQA did not elaborate further.

Despite his revelations the night before and the lumpy pile of straw he'd slept on, Patrik felt fully rested. He had to admit, there were *some* things he liked about this world. Back in Seattle, he struggled to sleep most nights Anxiety and all that. But here, not even the weight of a dozen dead men on his conscience could keep him from dreamland.

Actually, now that he thought about it, that was just a little messed up.

Nonsense, they were* bad *dead men, remember?

Patrik sighed, his breath misting on the chill morning air. He and the PQA had spent some time discussing the philosophical dilemma the night before, until Thalia threatened to stab him if he didn't stop twisting and turning. Since she obviously wasn't going to sleep before he did, he'd given up the argument then. Now in the fresh light of day…he found it was a subject he didn't really want to continue.

Fine. So, what are we doing up this early? A spot of baby sheep murdering? Or maybe you'd like to go kick some puppies?

"Don't they eat dogs here?" Patrik asked, his teeth chattering as he walked along the dock. He rubbed his hands together for warmth, but it didn't seem to do much against the ocean breeze.

Sure, yeah okay, but the point stands.

Patrik rolled his eyes as he came to a stop outside the building he'd identified the night before as a General Store. "Fine," he muttered, before allowing a smile to cross his face. "If you must know, we're going shopping."

At that he climbed the wooden steps and pushed open the front door. It was heavy—probably to keep it closed against the winds—but still nothing for his augmented strength. It was another reminder that not *everything* in this world was terrible. He needed to savour the good stuff if he was going to keep his sanity—at least until he found a way home. Only when he was safely back in Seattle could he spare the time for a proper mental breakdown.

"Good day, sir," a cheerful voice greeted Patrik as he approached the counter.

A little man—no, a dwarf—wandered in from out back. He seemed significantly more jovial than any of the others of his…kind…species…race…that Patrik had seen. Following Steve's advice, he quickly pulled up the man's description.

Tilly the Storekeeper [level 18]. Owner of the General Store in Anchorpoint, Tilly has plied her wares to the local fishermen since her parents first opened the business almost a hundred years ago. Now though—

Patrik snapped the description closed. He'd seen enough about destitute families in the last few days. He supposed he should be grateful that Anchorpoint hadn't become a ghost town overnight like Monmouth. Though at least he wasn't responsible for this particular piece of economic strife.

Still, the description had given him one important piece of information. This dwarf was a female. Which…well, let's just say he wouldn't have guessed *that* from looks alone. Or her voice, for that matter. Which, now that he thought about it, had had a distinctly British twang.

"Good morning, Tilly," he said, offering a smile of his own. "I just came in last night. My friends and I don't intend to be in town for long, but I thought you and I might do some business before we depart."

"Well, well, well," the dwarf offered a toothy smile. Definitely British. Also definitely the least lady—actually, he forced the unworthy thought from his mind as Tilly continued. "What goods in particular might interest you, Mr. Chosen One?"

"It's just Patrik, if you please," he replied. "And let's see… health potions, maybe some pants if you have some…weapons, armour…whatever you've got, really?"

"Very good, very good. I'm afraid my options are limited on clothing. And by limited, I mean we really only have rags. The First Circle is a bit of a mess in that department since old Monmouth went under. But let's see, oh you're in luck, I have one health potion." A vial filled with red liquid popped into existence. She set it on the counter and continued speaking. "Now, weapons…got some bronze short swords and oooh, an iron dagger if you're feeling rich, Mr. Chosen One." The items continued to appear in her hand as she listed them. "Armour, just the usual leather cra…aftily created breastplates from the local tanner. No leggings though. Oh I also have an oak short bow and some bronze arrows. Are you interested in archery, sir?"

By now a decent pile of equipment lay on the bench before Patrik. Apparently deciding that was enough for now, the dwarf stepped back and made a gesture for him to take a look. As he stepped closer and concentrated on each of the items, the familiar description boxes popped into existence, though with a few added details.

Bronze Short Sword [property of Tilly the Store-keeper]. A bronze short sword. Good for stabbing things Effects: +1 to Strength. Cost: 100 gold.

Well that wasn't even better than his bronze dagger. Plus he had a bunch of slightly better bronze longswords in his inventory. He moved onto the next item.

Iron Dagger [property of Tilly the Storekeeper]. A dagger made from iron. Do you really need this part? Effect: +2 to Strength. Cost: 1200 gold.

Well that was no better than the bronze longswords he had…

No, but stronger opponents become resistant to weaker grade weapons, remember? Those bronze blades barely hurt you with your Constitution—

I don't know if I would call that 'barely'…

Well, just wait until you find out what it feels like to be stabbed by iron. Maybe you should ask Thalia for a demonstration…

"I'll take the iron dagger," Patrik muttered.

As Tilly put the dagger to the side, he continued with his inspections. The leather breastplates were each as crappy as the ones in his inventory and quite pricy at 500 gold a piece. And even though it wasn't listed, Steve assured him the armour would inhibit his Dexterity. Given dodging painful blows seemed a superior strategy to taking them in his unprotected face, he decided to forgo the armour for now.

Oak Short Bow [property of Tilly the Storekeep-

er]. **A short bow made from oak [*that's the weakest type of wood by the way]*. Effect: +1 to Dexterity. Cost 1000 gold.**

"Damn that's expensive," Patrik muttered.

"Oh, I'm sure I could move a little on the price for a lovely human like you, Mr. Chosen One," Tilly said with a smile.

Patrik's heart almost skipped a beat. A grin briefly appeared on his lips before he forced his face to straighten. He could negotiate! It had been years since his trip backpacking through Thailand and its neighbouring countries, but he'd become quite a deft hand at the ancient art of bartering.

"Is that so, Tilly?" he said, casting another eye over the items.

The only other thing he actually needed from the pile was the health potion. He only had one of those left. A quick examination showed it cost an exorbitant 1000 gold. Which made *no* sense, given Thalia and Giovanni had both downed at least one of the things in the Monmouth quest. The reward for that entire venture had only been 1000 gold.

It's the limited supply here, Steve offered. *In Bledross, given its shared with the Second Circle where health potions are more common, the price will be half that.*

Hardly reassuring if I need this one before we get there, Patrik muttered.

Still, he *did* have plenty of gold. He hadn't visited the stables yet, but a horse couldn't be *that* expensive. Surely. Besides, he could barter. Get these prices down a bit. And he had plenty of loot of his own to sell next.

"Okay Tilly, what can you do for the health potion and the iron dagger?"

"No short bow, Mr. Chosen One?"

He shook his head. He'd already considered it, but Steve was right about one thing. That arrow back in the forest had hardly budged his health. He could just imagine turning a bandit into a pincushion and still having them hacking at him. No, better he focused on his Hack and Slash. Hopefully he would begin to see some improvement as it continued levelling up.

"Very well, how does 2000 even sound to you, my friend?" The dwarf offered with a smile.

Patrik found himself grinning back. "Perfect!" The coins appeared in his hand, these marked with the Roman numeral C for one hundred, and the trade was made.

Congratulations! You have learned the skill Barter! You have proven yourself a [passable] negotiator when trading.

Now Patrik was truly beaming. Finally something he could understand in this bloody world. Something he might even be good at. Opening his inventory, he pulled out one of the leather breastplates and bronze longsword he'd collected from the bandits.

"Don't suppose you'd be willing to offer me a good price for any of these?" he asked. "I've got quite a supply."

"Well now, aren't you full of surprises, Mr. Chosen One?" Tilly replied without missing a beat. "I'm sure I could give you a decent price for those."

To Patrik's disappointment, Tilly started at 25% of what she was charging to sell the same items in her store. That was steep. But after a few minutes discussion—interspersed with a few theatrical displays of indignance on Patrik's part—he had her up to 35%. Still terrible. But at least it was an improvement. Even better, as they shook on the deal and exchanged products, a fresh notification popped up.

Congratulations! Your skill Barter has increased to level 2!

So it was that Patrik left Tilly's store feeling a great deal lighter both in spirit and physically—well, metaphysically, or whatever mystical weight accumulated in the spatial void that was his inventory system. He was even whistling a merry tune. Or attempting too, at least. No doubt O'Malley would find him completely out of tune, but at that moment, Patrik was just happy to forget his troubles.

The sun had topped the cliffs behind the town by then and

he set off along the waterfront, curious to see the ships at the docks. He still wanted to find the stables and hopefully purchase a horse, but for now he was happy to breathe the fresh ocean air. Since crashlanding through that portal, Patrik hadn't had too many moments of quiet to himself.

Hey, is that meant to be Avril Lavigne?

Patrik sighed as the PQA intruded on his thoughts. Not *quite* to himself. Still, it was peaceful here in Anchorpoint. The cliffs loomed in an arc around the cove, shielding the town from the worst of the wind. Now it was light, he could see they weren't as solid as they'd appeared. In fact, much of the stone was pitted and broken, with dark shadows in places that were probably caves. Rockslides would probably be an issue for the buildings beneath them, but the villagers didn't seem overly concerned.

Continuing along the docks, Patrik came to the first of the dozen fishing ships sitting at anchor. Here nets hung drying along the railings and he noticed several of the nearby buildings had been painted with murals depicting mermaids tangled in lines or being savagely stabbed with boathooks. One even had bright red hair and scallops as a bra. Poor Ariel.

The fishermen hunting them all looked very noble in the images. Several were also lounging around the boats. As usual, reality did not quite match the artists' imagination. These men were grizzled and unkempt, their hair matted and faces streaked with grease from the nets. Most were playing cards or dice and drinking from brown bottles wrapped in paper bags. Patrik wrinkled his nose as several approached him.

"Please man, something to keep a man going…" one asked, wrinkled hand outstretched.

"…just until I get my hands on my next mermaid," another pled. "I'll pay you back."

No stranger to the homeless—he'd visited San Francisco, after all—Patrik lowered his eyes and continued along the dock, doing his best not to acknowledge them. Apparently some problems were universal—

"Ay, what kinda shit was that?"

Patrik jumped as a rough hand grabbed him by the shoulder and spun him around. He found himself face to face with a very angry looking sailor.

"You think you're better than us?" Spittle showered Patrik as the sailor screamed right in his face.

He was so shocked he just stood there for a full ten seconds, staring at the man. This…this was not the response he'd expected.

What exactly* were *you expecting?

A normal response! I ignore them, they move onto the next person. Then the next, and the next, until someone finally gives them something.

Normal? Wait, that's normal on Earth? Hold on, wait, I need to read, shit, mate, why is there an entire chapter on homeless dedicated to just *Los Angeles*?

Ignoring the PQA, Patrik realised he should say something to the very violent looking fisherman standing in front of him. "Ah, sorry?" he offered, holding up his hands in a show of appeasement. "I was kinda in a rush." Then he pulled up the man's description.

Jacko the Sailor [level 24]. Blessed by good weather and an ocean ripe with plump mermaid flesh, Jacko once sailed the seven seas with his head held high. Many a mermaid quailed in their warrens upon his approach, hoping they might be the one he spared. Sadly, with a collection of humanitarian protesters blockading the harbour, Jacko and his ilk have been grounded, and the mermaids live to see another day.

How the hell are these guys so strong?

Jacko was the strongest of the three men confronting him, but the others were also in their twenties. Yikes. Suddenly Patrik didn't feel quite so confident standing there alone on the dock.

Huh? Oh, that. You realise you don't just get experience from killing things, right? There's more to the Four Circles than murder. Which, by the way, this

homeless stuff? Wild! You just straight up treat people like animals on Earth, ay?

Ignoring the PQA, Patrik focused on how to deescalate the situation.

"You hear that boys?" Jacko sneered. "He was in a rush! Suppose you're someone important, Mr. Chosen One?"

"No, no, not at all," Patrik replied quickly. He glanced around in search of help, but the only other souls nearby were other sailors. With a sigh he resigned himself to be extorted. "Look, whatever, I'll give you some gold. Is a hundred coins enough?"

Ten coins each marked with an X appeared in his hand as he spoke. The sailors stilled at the sight, their eyes going wide.

There, was that so hard? Steve chimed in. *A bit more generosity and maybe you'd have less homeless on Earth,* and *less billionaires.*

Pretty sure Bill Gates donated like ten billion dollars to charity last year.

"Well that's more like it," Jacko was the first to recover from the shock.

The sailor's eyes took on a greedy glint as he reached for the money. Despite himself, Patrik experienced a flickering of anger. It was most of what he'd just gotten from Tilly. He'd worked hard, negotiating a good price for those items. It irked him to now have these men strong arming him out of the cash. Still, he wasn't going to say anything…

"Just don't spend it all on booze," he muttered as Jacko took the gold.

Ohhhh, fuck you did not just say that.

What—

"What did you just say to me, you little shit?" Jacko snarled.

Coins bounced from the wooden boards at their feet as they dropped from the sailor's fingers. A glint of iron appeared in his hand as a dagger replaced them. Rage shone from the man's eyes as he stepped in close and raised the weapon. Patrik leapt back, his own sword appearing in his hands.

That gave the sailor pause. The fisherman might be a higher level, but Patrik was better armed. And if Jacko had really gained all his experience fishing up helpless mermaids…well, maybe he could bluff his way out of this situation yet.

"That's right," he snarled, gesturing wildly with his blade. "You'd better watch yourself, Jacko, or you might just end up sleeping with the fishes!"

Yeah, get em! Steve exclaimed. ***Beat up these homeless dudes like you never had the guts to do on Earth.***

Patrik braced himself for a fight. He would attack Jacko first. If he could down the ringleader, maybe the others would back off and the fight would end there.

Except, rather than attack, a sharp intake of breath came from the three fishermen.

"How…" The colour had drained from Jacko's face. He exchanged a nervous glance with his men. "Who the fuck told you that?"

"Huh?" This was not what Patrik had expected. Then in an attempt to cover his own confusion, he added. "Ah…" *Shit.* "I'm sure I don't know what you're talking about." There, that was better.

The dagger vanished from Jacko's hands, which he promptly held up to show they were now empty. "We ah, we didn't mean to start anything."

He swallowed visibly, then made a gesture, as if to ask whether he could approach. Patrik nodded, and the sailor leaned in close. He was actually sweating, despite the cool air.

"Look, I don't know where you ah, found out about all that…" He trailed off, eyes flicking towards Patrik before quickly dropping back to the wharf. Spotting the gold coins lying there, the sailor crouched and scooped them up, then thrust them at Patrik. "Here, no harm, no foul, right? Let's all just go our separate ways. No need for anyone to go talking about…things."

Patrik stood there, somewhat dumbfounded, as the sailor practically forced the coins into his hands. Then just like that,

Jacko and his friends were walking away as quick as their swaying gaits could carry them.

Steve…what the hell just happened?

Mate, I'd be damned if I know. But, ah, there is this…

New Quest: The Fishermen of Anchorpoint. The fishermen of Anchorpoint have a secret. One they don't want anyone to find out about. Not even the PQA system knows what they're hiding. But you're onto them. So find out what it is they're hiding. For the good of the Four Circles. Reward: TBC.

Great, that was the last thing he needed—another quest. And one that didn't even know what its own reward was…

…but on the other hand, he'd somehow avoided the mugging. In fact, he was pretty sure Jacko had shoved a few extra coins into the handful he'd passed Patrik. Somehow, *he* had ended up blackmailing *them*. Letting bygones be bygones, Patrik decided he would ignore the fisherman quest and get on with his *actual* task for the day.

Getting himself a horse.

Turning to the nearest street, he started to trudge his way up the increasingly steep brick road.

But he no longer whistled merrily as he walked.

STANDING on the deck of his ship, *The Mermaid's Tits,* Jacko watched the stranger make his way across the wharf and disappear into the warren of stone alleyways that was Anchorpoint. The others in his crew were still muttering about the man and his thinly veiled threats, their voices slurred from drink.

Only Jacko was sober. The slumped shoulders and drunken demeanour he adopted tended to draw better donations from the public. Or at least, those with actual hearts. That man, this Patrik the Chosen One, was different. He carried the stench of darkness about him. And he clearly knew something of the secret his kind had kept for generations.

"Who do you think that guy was, Jacko?" Trawlee, his first mate, asked, joining the captain at the railing.

"I don't know."

"How could he have learned our secrets?" Trawlee pressed.

This time Jacko let the question stand. A cold breeze blew in across the docks, carrying with it the scent of fish and brine. He felt a stirring within, a gentle burning. The ocean meant freedom, meant life to the men around him. No one would take that from them. Not the humanitarians. Nor a stinking landlubber like this Patrik the Chosen One.

"That is the question."

Trawlee smiled. It was a wicked look on the fisherman's scarred face. "And how should we go about finding its answer?"

Jacko sighed. They had all committed evil acts, these last days. Many of his crew were now at risk of falling onto the wrong side of Fate's counter. Pirates. That's what they would become, if they couldn't deal with the blasted humanitarians.

But they couldn't risk the truth getting out. If that happened, they were truly finished.

"Follow him, Trawlee," he said softly. "Find out where he goes."

"And then?"

"And then we'll get our answers."

CHAPTER 17
THE ART OF THE DEAL

It took several hours and a lot of walking for Patrik to finally locate the stables. Like most millennials, he wasn't big on asking for directions—that required speaking to random strangers—and, well, it was kind of fascinating wandering through the town.

Anchorpoint reminded him a lot of Cinque Terre—the five little towns nestled along the Riviera coastline of Italy. His father had taken them for a trip when Patrik had still been in middle school, back when they'd been one big happy family. Patrik couldn't remember much about Italy other than the colourful buildings and the delicious pizza, but his smile returned as he wandered the narrow streets.

The sun had already dropped behind the clifftops by the time he came upon the stables. They weren't exactly centrally located like the General Store—in fact, they were tucked right up against the cliffs at the edge of town. But he'd found the place in the end. Eager to pick out a horse and head back to the inn, he pushed his way through the double doors and strode inside.

"Hello, anyone in here?" he called out.

Long shadows stretched across the stable and Patrik had to blink a few times before his vision adjusted. He really needed that Dark Sight skill that O'Malley had mentioned. As the stars faded, he found himself standing on a floor of packed dirt covered by a generous helping of straw. Horse stalls stood to his left and right, forming a wide corridor leading to another door at the rear of the building.

No one answered his call and Patrik couldn't help but shiver. The place felt abandoned. It was way too soon since Monmouth to be dealing with any more haunted house story-lines. He almost turned around right then and there, but…he'd been looking forward to this. To riding again. Their father had taken them to a farm outside Portland for lessons when he'd been younger. A family activity, he'd said. Patrik hadn't been back for a long, long time now, but every day he spent in this place, fighting for his life, killing…he felt a need to reconnect with that past, to bridge the wasted years…

"Hello, sir, might I help you?"

Patrik spun towards the voice, only to find himself face to face with…nothing?

An audible sigh came from inside his head. **Look down, mate.**

Following the PQA's suggestion, Patrik jumped as he found the dwarf standing beneath him. He clutched at his chest, trying to calm his racing heart.

"Sorry!" he gasped. "Didn't see you down there."

Apparently, that was *not* the right thing to say. A growl rumbled from deep in the dwarf's throat and a massive warhammer materialised in his stumpy fingers.

"Out!" he bellowed.

You know, if you invested in your Charisma, people might stop screaming at you on first sight…

Ignoring the PQA, Patrik took a quick step back from the enraged dwarf and raised his hands in a show of peace.

"My deepest apologies, noble…ah, dwarf!" he cried. Like Tilly, this dwarf also spoke with a British accent, so he tried to adopt his politest tone as he spoke. "I meant no offence."

He tensed, ready to flee in case peace talks failed. The iron warhammer in the dwarfs' fingers was huge—and there was a shimmer about it that suggested it had been enchanted like Giovanni's sword. He still hadn't seen what that actually *meant*, but given the little dude clearly knew his way around a weapon, Patrik wasn't eager to find out.

Thankfully, his words seemed to give the dwarf pause. "Are you mocking my accent, human?" he asked.

"I, ah, no, I would never!" Patrik stuttered. "I only wished to display my everlasting regret for any offence I might have given your ah…noble personage…"

Okay, that time you were definitely mocking his accent.

Another growl rumbled from the dwarf. Patrik swallowed, but to his surprise, the warhammer shimmered and then vanished—presumably back into the man's inventory. Letting out a long breath, he pulled up the dwarf's description box.

George the Dwarven Horse Merchant [level 28]. Don't let his gruff words and warhammer fool you— when it comes to horses, there's no one better in the First Circle than old George. Well, maybe Gorria the Quick, but it's not like *she's* ever around to actually do her job. Unfortunately, being a dwarf, George does not take kindly to comments about his height. Especially from humans. Keep your head about you if you don't want to lose it.

"You speak with a noble twist," George said finally. "My apologies, Lord Chosen One, for the afront upon your person. I did not recognise a fellow man of taste." He leaned his head to the side, as though curious. "Though…you lack a title. Perhaps it has been stripped from you, as part of a noble quest?"

"Ah…" Patrik had no idea where this was going. It was probably best just to go with it. "You would be correct, my good sir…" he trailed off at the end, making his words seem more question than statement.

You are…not good at this 'acting' thing.

Miss Tallow said I showed promise!

And that was…what, tenth grade?

A sharp whinny snapped Patrik back to the present. He looked up in time to see a horse's head appear over the door of a nearby stall. It reached towards the dwarf and snickered. Smiling, George lifted a scarred hand and ran it over the horse's nose. Muscles rippled beneath a sleek grey coat as the creature nickered its pleasure.

"I see you have an appreciation for the equestrian arts, good sir," George said as he turned and found him watching the horse.

Patrik nodded and stepped up beside the dwarf. "May I?"

The dwarf wore a strange expression on his twisted face, but he nodded and Patrik reached out a hand to stroke the horse's neck. As he did so, a fresh description box popped up.

Human's Bane [no level]. This gentle mare once ran wild and free across the southern steeps of the First Circle. That is, until a certain dwarf came and tamed her wild spirit. Now she awaits a noble soul to ride her once more across the wild planes she once called home.

"Human's Bane?" he asked the dwarf. The horse gave a whinny at the mention of its name. One great hoof pawed at the ground.

George chuckled, the sound light despite his earlier threats. "Do not take offence, Lord Chosen One. Surely one of your breeding knows well the lack of couth amongst your fellow man."

"Ah…of course?" Patrik murmured, then deciding it was best to steer the conversation towards more productive subjects, he turned back to the horse. It was snuffling now at his outstretched palm in search of food. "As it so happens, I find myself in need of a mighty steed."

"And you have of course come to the right place, My Lord," the dwarf announced, offering a little bow. "There is no finer horse trader in Anchorpoint!"

"There are no other horse traders in Anchorpoint," Patrik said with a frown.

Actually, now that he thought about it, that seemed strange. There had been mention of a railroad, but Patrik had yet to see any evidence of its existence. As far as he could tell, the First Circle at least was thoroughly stuck in medieval times. Yet so far, horses seemed exceedingly rare.

"You are of course right, Lord Chosen One," George announced as he straightened from his bow. "But fear not. You have treated this humble merchant with respect, and so I could offer naught but the best of value for the noble Human's Bane. I could part with her—and a saddle for my new friend—for a scant fifteen thousand in gold."

It took a full ten seconds for the dwarf's looping, fanciful language to hammer through Patrik's dense head. "Fifteen *thousand*," he exclaimed. Holy shit. That seemed…excessive.

"I assure you, good sir, that you will find no better price in Anchorpoint!"

Obviously, Patrik muttered, but kept the thought internal. *Steve, any pointers here?*

Value in the Four Circles is set by supply and demand. And since he's the only game in town…

Great, trust capitalism to be the one *thing that works the same here as on Earth.*

Fifteen thousand was basically everything he had, even after the last couple of quests and his back and forth with Tilly. The few thousand gold coins he'd have left would be enough to get him to Bledross, but once there…well, he'd be relying on the answers being in Tenser's house. It made the purchase a terrible risk, but he was loathe to leave this place without that horse. He *really* didn't want to spend another three days walking on the open road.

So Patrik decided to go with the third option.

"A generous price indeed, my friend," he said, imitating the horse merchant's earlier bow, "but…I cannot help but feel an obligation to point out old Human's Bane is growing a little long in the teeth. No doubt she was a fearsome steed once, but

I could not possibly take her from your hands for more than ten thousand."

Rising from his bow, Patrik couldn't help but keep the hint of a smile from his lips. This was far from his first rodeo. In Thailand the merchants had often started out with ludicrous prices and sweeping statements as to the fine deal they were offering. It was all part of the game, of course, and just as he had with Tilly, Patrik was more than happy to play—

"You would call me a crook to my face?" The dwarf growled.

His face hardened, and in that instant his appearance changed once more from friendly merchant to hardened warrior. The warhammer did not reappear, though Patrik still took a quick step back.

Did you seriously just try to bluff a level 28 merchant who's only purpose in life these last thirty years has been to buy and sell horses?

"No…no!" he exclaimed, not quite sure whether he was talking to Steve or the dwarf. "I'm sorry! I am new to this realm and still learning your ways!" When the dwarf continued to glare, Patrik began to mumble. "I mean, I have this amazing Dexterity now. And Constitution. I can run for *ages*. Will a horse even help me? Can Human's Bane even run as fast as me? I just don't know!"

Did you seriously just try to barter with this dude again? Steve exclaimed. ***This is not your friendly little dwarf of the General Store, mate!***

Shit. Steve was right. For once. Patrik clamped his jaw shut before he could say anything else that might offend the dwarf. Silence fell, throughout which George continued to glower. At last he gave a little harrumph and waved a hand.

"You make a wonderful point, *sir*," he said the title like it was dirt now. "I suppose you could find out…for a measly seventeen thousand in gold…"

Patrik sighed. "Fi—wait, *what?* You said fifteen!"

"Indeed I did." The dwarf crossed his arms with a grunt. "Now I'm saying eighteen."

"Eight…" Patrik raised a finger, then slowly lowered it.

The dwarf stood poised, waiting. One look into those beady eyes and Patrik knew there would be no negotiation now. Opening his mouth would only push the price higher. Not that it mattered. Eighteen thousand gold was everything he had left. He would be left a pauper, with no safety net to fall back on. His father might have cut off his trust fund, but he'd never been *that* poor.

"Very well," he croaked, defeated.

Shoulders slumped, he turned and started for the door.

"Ha!" the dwarf's taunts chased after him. "Now you truly show your breeding. Only the most common of your foul species would try that negotiating tactic."

Patrik ignored him. It wasn't a tactic. Just when he thought he had this place figured out, it found a new way to bend him over the kitchen table and fuck him.

"Hey, don't you walk away from me! You walk out that door, there ain't no coming back. You can walk the rest of your life for all I care."

Yes, he would have to walk. All the way to Bledross. That was, what, another hundred miles? If he grew any more levels along the way he'd be putting the stat points into Dexterity, that was for sure.

"Fine, fifteen thousand!"

And Constitution. If it made literally being stabbed in the chest hurt less, then presumably it would help with the muscle cramps. Anything to make the journey more bearable—

"Twelve!"

Then there was the food. Walking meant another couple of days on the road. Which meant more of this world's horrible, horrible food. Or perhaps he could make a deal with Ezra, at the Sailor's Wife. Bel might have another pet he could… purchase from them. He would pay well. Afterall, if he couldn't tell Ezra about her dead husband, he could at least try to make their strife a little less.

"Okay fine, eight thousand gold! That's the best I can do."

The words of the dwarf finally cut through Patrik's

thoughts. He froze, one hand on the door. Had he…heard that right? His heart quickened and he drew in a breath.

Steve?

Damn mate, maybe you know what you're doing with this bartering thing after all.

"Deal!" Patrik exclaimed, swinging around and meeting the merchant's gaze from across the room. "So long as it still includes the saddle, stirrups and reins."

The dwarf's face hardened, the wrinkles bunching up as his frown deepened. He muttered a few words beneath his breath, then swore loudly. "Fine!" he growled at last. "You have yourself a deal."

A few minutes later and with much cursing, lude gestures and dark looks from the dwarf, Patrik stood outside wearing a smile as wide as Texas. Human's Bane stood before him, leather saddle set in place, her sleek grey coat glinting in the light of a nearby lantern. Night had fallen while he'd been in the store, and with the sky overcast, it would be a gloomy trip back to the inn. Patrik didn't care. He ran a hand along the mare's neck, earning a little whinny. Maybe things would turn out okay after all—

Somewhere behind him, a door slammed. The sound of metallic scrapping as locks were drawn closed followed. Patrik let out a breath, relieved it was only the grumpy dwarf locking up…

Achievement Unlocked! Swindled. Congratulations, your attempts to barter with a merchant have resulted in an absolutely terrible trade. Like, really, just atrocious. Seriously, what were you thinking? Reward: You have unlearned the skill 'Barter'.

"Wait, what the fuck?" Patrik exclaimed to the empty alley. "Steve, what the hell was that all about! I negotiated the price *down!*"

Ah, to be honest, I have no idea what happened there. I don't even know how you got him to drop the price in the first place!

Patrik opened his mouth to swear at the PQA…then

thought better of it. He had his horse. He could make it to Bledross in a few short days, and from there, home. He'd even paid half the price the merchant had first been asking—meaning he had more than enough gold left over for…eventualities. What did it matter if some nonsense rating system said he'd been swindled?

Letting out a long breath, he forced the smile back to his lips and stepped up to Human's Bane. She gave a little snicker and turned her head to nudge his shoulder. He smiled, remembering horses that had done the same, back on the ranch. She wanted a treat. Sadly his pockets were empty.

"I'll get you something tomorrow before we leave town," he promised, moving to her side. He put a foot into the stirrups and then swung himself into the saddle—

Bang!

Stars flashed across Patrik's vision as he slammed face first into the ground. The impact drove the air from his lungs and left him lying in the bricked street, groaning and gasping for air.

Bludgeoning damage inflicted [-10 health].

"Steve, what the hell was that?" he rasped, pushing himself into a sitting position. His ears were ringing. The horse still stood over him. It gave a little neigh and stomped its foot on the bricked streets. It seemed amused.

"You little…" Patrik muttered, scrambling to his feet and catching the beast by the reins. It must have thrown him, though he hadn't even felt it move.

Ah, Patrik, are you sure you know—

"Of course I know," Patrik snapped, pushing the PQA's voice to the back of his mind.

His good humour had completely evaporated now. It was getting cold and he wanted nothing more than to be back in the inn, sitting by the fire, and talking to Bel…

Again, eighteen…isn't there some kind of half your age plus seven years rule on Earth?

"We're not on Earth though, are we?" Patrik muttered as

he threw himself into the saddle. The horse's novelty was already wearing thin—

Bang!

Bludgeoning damage inflicted [-10 health].

"Are you shitting me!" Patrik screamed, pushing himself up from the cobbles. He glared up at the mare, but this time he knew it hadn't moved. Something funny was going on here. Something very…

"Steve…" he grated through clenched teeth. "I swear to God or Fate or whatever the hell passes for divinity here…this better not be some Four Circles bullshit you didn't tell me about!"

You said you knew how to ride a—oh, damn, yep this one's on me. That's my bad, mate. Should have read the fine print. But you know, who reads that stuff?

Patrik drew in a long, long, long breath to calm his racing heart. It did not help. "What. Fine. Print?" he grated through clenched teeth.

Information Requested: Skill: Horse Riding. Once upon a time, the brutal practice of horse riding was practiced in every corner of the Four Circles. The majestic stallions of the wildlands were captured, their spirit broken. Until finally, the Dark Lord took a stand against the cruel practice. While not outlawed, in his great wisdom, Malus restricted the skill of horse riding to those taught by a teacher of noble heritage. All others in the kingdom were made to forget this most inhumane of skills.

Silence. Patrik exhaled. Slowly.

So, ah, the good news is, I figured out why the system classified your trade as being swindled.

"And. Why. Is that. Steve."

Well, ah, it's like I said about supply and demand. Setting the price. The PQA's voice sounded distinctly uneasy. Maybe Steve was watching all the gruesome ways Patrik was imagining murdering it. *Yeah, um, well, since you can't ride a horse, your demand or need...can you stop that? Okay, yeah, your demand was zero. The merchant must have realised, when you tried to barter and all that...you, you okay there, bud?*

Patrik said nothing. Taking up the reins of his useless, horribly overpriced horse, he set his feet in the direction of the inn. And began to walk.

CHAPTER 18
CORPORAL PUNISHMENT

RAIN BEGAN TO FALL AS PATRIK MADE HIS WAY THROUGH THE narrow alleys of Anchorpoint. By the time he made it back to the Sailor's Wife—leading a *very* uncooperative horse—he was drenched head to toe and squelching with every step he took. Shaking uncontrollably, he led the horse down an alley to the side of the building, which he guessed led to the courtyard around back of the inn.

He found a sad looking Bel seated on a bench tucked out of the rain with a chicken on her lap. She looked up at his appearance, her face darkening, before noticing the horse. Her eyes lit up and she leapt to her feet, sending the chicken squawking from her bosom…

"Oh, did you rescue her just for me!" she exclaimed. "I knew you weren't evil. I just…yesterday…" She lowered her head, some of the excitement bleeding out of her. "I know you only did what you had too," she rasped.

Patrik stared at the woman, thinking of all the ways he could respond. Then he recalled the field of dead bandits, the men he'd killed. He didn't even know which had been her father. Abruptly he thrust out the reins at the girl.

"Brush and feed her," he ordered. "I'm getting a beer. I will be back for her in the morning." With that he strode past the innkeeper's daughter and pushed open the back door.

A wave of warm air billowed out to greet him. He sighed in relief, his mood immediately improving. For a second he lingered. Bel hadn't deserved the harsh words. But…he shuddered as he saw again the bodies. He might not know which was Bel's father, but he recalled their faces, every last one. They would remain etched in his memories until his dying day.

Which knowing this world, would probably not be long in coming.

He found the common room eerily quiet after the last night. Apparently the Thousand Years Festival really was that important. Or maybe everyone had found out what the secret recipe in last night's dinner had been. Sadly, before he could even contemplate a drink and a hot meal, Patrik found himself face to face with Thalia.

A very, very angry looking Thalia. It was practically her resting expression when it came to him by now.

"Where have I been?" he spoke up before she could open her mouth. "What have I been doing? What nefarious deeds have I been planning?" Rolling his eyes, he pushed past the sorceress. "What have you got for us tonight, Ezra?" he called, earning a glance from the proprietor, who was busy polishing glasses. "Please tell me you have leftovers?"

The woman wrinkled her nose. "Thankfully, no," she replied, her eyes flickering over Patrik's shoulder to where Thalia still loomed. "A caravan came in from Furness this morning. Fresh satyr."

Patrik wasn't familiar with the mystical creature. No doubt it was something horrendously inappropriate for people to be eating. Whatever. What did he care? He was done. He ordered a helping, along with a pint of ale. Only when he had the fresh glass of amber alcohol in his hand did he turn to face Thalia again.

She stood glaring up at him, arms crossed. The glint in her eyes matched the storm raging outside. "Speak."

"And say what?" he shot back.

Behind the sorceress, Giovanni reclined against the wall, his fingers tapping against the pommel of his sword. O'Malley sat near the fire, gently strumming his lute. As though noticing Patrik's attention, he began to craft the random notes into a song. He did not sing, but hummed along to the chords. Otherwise the inn was empty.

A soft *whoosh* drew Patrik's attention back to Thalia. Flames danced upon her fingers. He raised an eyebrow.

"You sure you want to cast a fireball in here?" he asked, gesturing at the wooden walls. "I thought we learnt not to play with matches in Monmouth."

The fury in Thalia's eyes only burned brighter, but to his relief the flames died away. He should just answer her questions. He knew he should. But after the day he'd had…her attitude, the way she treated him…it was too much. Picking up his mug, he stepped around her again and crossed to the fire.

"What are you playing?" he asked O'Malley.

"Ah…" the bard looked decidedly uncomfortable as he looked from Patrik to the sorceress. "Ah…just a…new song I'm working on."

"Magic or pleasure?"

"*Enough!*"

Patrik sighed. The jig was up. Best not push things too far or—

Pain blossomed in his back. No, not pain. Pain was an upset stomach from drinking too much coffee. This was…

Piercing damage inflicted [-50 health].

The hell…

Patrik's gaze dropped to his stomach. The point of a dagger was protruding from his robes. He stared at it for a full ten seconds, every one of which the agony redoubled…

"You fucking stabbed me!" he screamed.

Blood burst from his lips as he felt the blade yanked back out. He staggered, grasping at the back of O'Malley's chair as he tasted iron in his mouth. Holy shit. That hurt as bad as the fire had on his first day in this place.

See, that's the iron damage. Nasty stuff. And it's not even that good. Wait until you get to the Second Circle and feel the sting of steel.

Patrik groaned and clutched at his stomach. It felt…fuck, well, it felt as though he'd been stabbed. Rage bubbled up inside him. Despite the agony, he knew this wasn't fatal. Not yet. Teeth clenched he swung on the sorceress—

"Shall I do it again?" she sneered, gesturing with the bloody knife. "Or are you ready to start talking?"

Patrik's mouth was already loaded with his first profanity, but…at the sight of the dagger, he quickly reconsidered. Sure, he could survive another stab wound or two…but just because he *could* didn't mean he *wanted* too. Maybe peace *was* the better option.

"Ah, yeah, let's umm, yes, what's up, Thalia?" He forced a smile to his lips. "What did you want to talk about?"

Thalia growled. Actually growled. Then she lowered her dagger until it pressed against his abdomen.

"Oh right, right! Where have I been all day? How could I have forgotten." The words tumbled from Patrik's mouth as he began to babble. "I ah, I've been purchasing supplies for the journey. Don't want to be a burden, you know? And I explored the town a little. Oh, and I bought a horse." He trailed off. Thalia was still glowering at him, but there wasn't really much more to say.

Finally the sorceress exhaled. He thought that might have been the first breath she'd taken since he'd stepped into the inn.

"Why in the Four Circles would you buy a horse?"

"Wait, you bought a horse?" The music cut off as O'Malley looked around. "Oh, oh, is this to make up for last night? Can I pat him—or is it a her? Horses can be hers, can't they, Thalia? Ah I'm so excited, where is she!"

"Ah…sure O'Malley…Bel is taking care of her out back—"

"Woohoo!" The bard leapt to his feet and raced out the door without a backward glance.

But Thalia remained, Giovanni her ever-present shadow. "You didn't buy a horse to cheer up O'Malley," she said matter-of-factly.

"Obviously," Patrik muttered.

"You didn't know only nobles could ride, did you?" she asked, one eyebrow arching above the rim of her glasses. "Don't you have a Personal Quest System to tell you these things?"

Patrik grunted. "You'd think so, wouldn't you?"

Hey let's not make it 'pile on Steve hour', thank you very much.

Patrik was about to reply, when Thalia's haughty attitude suddenly reminded him of something. She came from a noble family. "Wait, can't you—"

"I never learnt to ride a horse," she said with a sniff. "By Fate, I cannot understand why anyone would wish to partake in such a barbaric practice."

"Because my legs hurt," Patrik said. "Because we ran for twenty-four hours straight and I was *tired*. Because I figured I deserved a break. Because I wanted just one good damn thing to happen to me in this god forsaken world. Guess I should have known better."

Thalia weathered his complaints without so much as changing her expression. When he finished, she crossed her arms. "Does everyone on Earth moan as much as you, or did we just luck out?"

That was it. "At least I still feel *something*, you pompous bitch!" he all but screamed. Fists clenched, he loomed over the sorceress. "Killing all those people back in the forest, it didn't even touch you! Even when you found out they had families, friends, you didn't blink. And you call me the monster."

He clamped his mouth shut before he could say anything more. It was already too much. He glared down at the diminutive sorceress, expecting at any moment to be disembowelled. Again.

"The men we killed were the monsters," Thalia said at last, as though that were the end of the debate. "That's why we killed them, remember? Why we all got positive Alignment for putting them in the ground. Why you no longer reek so much of evil?"

"They were *desperate* men," Patrik said through clenched teeth. "That doesn't make them monsters. Had we rode into that forest and offered them work and pay and food, who knows how many might have followed us."

"They were highwaymen. They would not have changed."

Patrik opened his mouth to reply, then paused. Closing his eyes, he exhaled before opening them again. "Just like I can't change, Thalia?" he asked softly.

The glint in the woman's eyes shifted, if only slightly. "That...has yet to be decided, Earthling."

She was lying and they both knew it. Thalia didn't believe he could change. And she was probably right. He had gone along with their slaughter of the highwaymen, but...could he go through that again? All in the name of grinding for Alignment. Or protecting the realm or whatever they wanted to call it?

"Um, excuse me?"

Both Patrik and Thalia jumped at the interruption. Spinning around, Patrik was surprised to find Ezra standing nearby, a plate of pasta covered in some kind of vomit-coloured meat sauce in her hands. The innkeeper's eyes were wide, her lip trembling as she stared at them. Patrik's gut churned in sudden premonition.

"Excuse...excuse me," Ezra said again when neither of them responded. "But...what were you talking about? Something about bandits...in the forest?"

"None of your business, wench," Thalia snapped, making a little wave to dismiss her.

The gesture sparked something inside Patrik. Thalia didn't care. That was it, wasn't it? For all her preaching, for all her show of being a good person, her dreams of becoming a Warrior of the Light—whatever that was—Thalia didn't care about the people around her. 'Good' or 'Bad', they were all just tools on her path to advancement.

Mate, just think about this...

It was too much. All of it. The cinderblocks in his stomach ground together until he felt he was about to hurl...

"None of her business?" he cried. "It's none of her business that her husband is dead? That Bel's father isn't coming home?" He bit back the words, then drew a breath and looked the innkeeper in the eyes. "I'm sorry, Ezra. Warren is dead. We killed him." He shuddered, then flicking to his inventory he summoned the silver locket. He held out his hand as it appeared in his palm. "*I* killed him."

Somehow, the silence permeating the inn grew deeper. It sat upon the room, upon Patrik, like a lead weight. But with the words, the bricks in his stomach had vanished, dissolved with his admission. With his confession.

Ezra, on the other hand, did not look so well. The colour drained from her face, leaving her pale as a ghost. Well, not an actual ghost. But very, very sickly looking. She stood frozen, lips parted as though about to speak, but no words came out. One hand was stretched out towards them, and without speaking Patrik placed the locket between her fingers.

"I'm so sorry," he whispered.

A spasm crossed the woman's face. Her eyes fell slowly to the locket. Patrik braced himself for the screams, for the accusations. But for the longest time, Ezra said nothing, only stared at the open locket in her hand. The picture tucked inside.

Then a tear slid down her cheek, and a dull keening began in the back of her throat. Patrik stared, horrified, as it turned to a terrible wailing, before the woman threw back her head and howled. He flinched back from her, but there was no need. Tears now pouring down her cheeks, Ezra fled. The howls continued as she disappeared into the kitchen, becoming distant and muffled, until with the bang of a slamming door, silence returned to the *Sailor's Wife*.

A very, *very*, uncomfortable silence.

Patrik glanced at Thalia and Giovanni, then decided it was best he kept his eyes on the ground. They did *not* look happy. Well, too bad. It had been a cruel message to deliver, but someone had to do it. Better they know the truth.

Grunting, Giovanni pushed himself off the wall. He

paused long enough for his gaze to linger on Patrik, before giving a shrug and sweeping across the room to the stairs.

His departure left Patrik alone in the common room with Thalia.

"Ah, look," he began as he turned and raised his hands.

"Do you enjoy hurting good people?" Thalia interrupted. Her soft blue eyes watched him from behind the heavy glasses. "Does it give you a kick or something? Or is it just your nature?"

Patrik stood, dumbstruck. "Seriously?" he said at last. "Her husband, the father of her child, is dead! You don't think she had the right to know?"

Narrowing her eyes, the sorceress took another step. Mere inches separated them now. Uncomfortably aware of the knife still in Thalia's hand, Patrik longed to flee, but dared not show his back just then. Instead, he steeled himself to meet her gaze —and just for a moment, he thought he saw something in those sapphire eyes. Something other than disdain. Then it was gone.

"So it's really just your nature then," she murmured, giving the slightest shake of her head. "I wonder, what was Tenser the Great thinking, bringing someone from your world here."

A lump lodged in Patrik's throat. Thalia was so close he could feel the warmth of her breath on his cheek. Still he refused to submit. He dipped his head, the better to meet her glare with one of his own.

"I'm sure I don't have a clue," he hissed.

"No," Thalia replied. "I'm sure you don't. I suppose we'll have to ask the old wizard ourselves, when we meet him in Bledross."

This time it took all of Patrik's strength not to look away. "I suppose we will," he said instead, licking his lips.

The words died between them and still neither looked away, as though their disagreement had become a tableau that each refused to break. Silence stretched over the tavern, leaving only the creaking of the shutters and the distant rumbling of thunder, the whisper of rainfall upon the thatched roof—

Ahem, hate to interrupt, but...

What is it, Steve? Patrik snarled.

The sorceress's eyes flickered, her pupils dilating as she watched him. A gleam of sweat sprung up on her brow and a rosy tint appeared on her cheeks. For a second it looked as though—

Achievement Unlocked! Sticks and Stones are for losers. Congratulations! You have inflected critical damage to another soul with words alone. Truly, your dark deeds are the stuff of legend. [-500 alignment] Reward: you have learned the skill Vicious Mockery [level 1]. Words cut deeper than swords—or at least yours do. Insults may now damage or stun your enemies.

"What the..." Patrik trailed off, glancing at the door through which Ezra had vanished. What exactly did this notification mean. It sounded...ominous.

"You lost Alignment again."

He jerked as Thalia spoke, his head whipping around. It was a moment before her meaning sank in. He quickly pulled up his stats.

PATRIK THE CHOSEN ONE — LEVEL 17

PROGRESS TO NEXT LEVEL: 65%

RACE
Human

ALIGNMENT
-2050

HEALTH
170/170

MANA
80/80

STR	CON	INT	CHA	DEX
16(+4)	11(+1)	15	1	10(+1)

Equipped: Iron short sword (+3 STR)
Sapphire Ring of Strength (+1 STR)
Sapphire Ring of Dexterity (+1 DEX)
Sapphire Ring of Constitution (+1 CON)

You have no stat points to assign.

SPELLS [LIMIT: FOUR]

RAISE DEAD
level 7

LIGHTNING BOLT
level 1

SKILLS [UNLIMITED]

HACK AND SLASH
level 4

ARSON
level 6

VICIOUS MOCKERY
level 1

"Yep, that seems about right," Patrik muttered as he closed his stat box. But he had bigger problems than his negative alignment just now. Like the very angry level 27 sorceress standing in front of him.

"You really can't help it, can you?" she asked at last. Her voice was surprisingly hoarse, like she'd swallowed gravel.

The question flared what little remained of Patrik's indignant anger. "What do *you* think?" he snapped.

What else was he meant to say? That he'd done what *he* thought was right? Not what some ill-conceived, messed up system of morality created by a Dark Lord said was right?

Thalia drew in a breath. "I think you're coming with me."

He opened his mouth to reply, but Thalia made a gesture and spoke a word, and Patrik found himself no longer in control of his own bodily functions. He stood frozen in place, unable to move or run or even scream. It was...disconcerting.

Turning, the sorceress moved towards the stairs. Heart pounding, Patrik watched her go, hoping against hope this was only a warning. Surely she couldn't find *too* much fault in him for such an innocuous exchange…

At the foot of the stairs, Thalia glanced back. A frown creased her forehead. "I said *Come.*"

If the paralysis had been disconcerting, the sensation of his own legs beginning to move on their own accord was outright terrifying.

Thalia was terrifying.

She had his own legs perp walk him across the empty common room. He wanted to scream, but not even his tongue would obey him. Not that there was anyone in the inn to hear him.

She led him up the stairs and along the corridor towards the quarters they had shared the night before. His legs moved in robotic fashion, striding after his gaoler with short, even steps, even as Patrik's mind raced.

Shit, shit, shit, Steve, is she, ah, is she going to kill me? Probably not, right? She's meant to be a good person, killing one of her own fellowship, that's gotta be on the evil side of the counter in any world, right? Right???

Ah, mate, I don't know what to tell ya, but that… ah, that negative Alignment of yours means she'll probably actually get some more positive points if she, you know, knocks you off.

You've got to be—

Patrik bit back his words as a door slammed shut. They had arrived in their room. Thalia stood blocking the door, one hand pressed firmly against the wooden panels. Head bowed, her breathing came in short, sharp inhalations, as though she were working herself up to something. Mentally gritting his teeth, Patrik strained to tear free of her spell and regain control of his body, but there was no escape—

Patrik suddenly found he could move on his own accord again.

"What the hell!" he cried, leaping back from her and almost tripping over a chair.

Stumbling, he righted himself and cast a quick glance around, in case Giovanni was waiting in the shadows. The lantern had been shuttered, but the room appeared unchanged from the night before—a small table, a couple of chairs, and a pair of unmade twin beds. Rain lashed at the thin glass of the only window, and outside lightning flashed.

He swung back to the sorceress, hovering over the button to summon his sword. Patrik had no misgivings about his chances in a fight with the powerful sorceress, but maybe if he could stun her…

"Seriously, what's going on here?" Patrik asked, trying to keep his voice calm. Thalia hadn't moved from the doorway, so he held up his hands. "I'm not a threat, remember? I can barely tie my own shoelaces without falling over myself!"

Still Thalia said nothing, though she trembled. He saw it. Her whole body began to shake with some pent-up emotion.

Fuck, fuck, fuck…

Yeah, this isn't looking good, mate…

Suggestions?

Run?

She's standing in front of the only door!

"Look, let's…since this obviously isn't working out, let's just go our own ways, shall we?" Patrik tried again. "Call it a day on the whole fellowship thing?"

Another tremor. Darkness coalesced in the sorceress's fingers. An object materialised. A leather whip.

"Oh fuck no."

All thought of fighting fled Patrik's mind. Spinning, he took a step towards the window, ready to launch himself through the glass. He wasn't sure what fall damage looked like in this place, but, well a broken bone or two was preferable to being lashed to death.

But he didn't make it a second step.

"*Wait.*"

Another command. Again, Patrik found himself frozen in

place. He stood, heart racing, one foot raised and hand outstretched to punch his way through the glass. A tremor shook him. He wanted to close his eyes, to seek some tiny scrap of peace before the agony began, but even that was denied to him—

The spell released Patrik so suddenly he slumped to the floor, unprepared to take his own weight. But the shock of the magic's departure lasted only a moment. Thalia's mana must be running low—that spell couldn't come cheap. He was about to launch himself back to his feet, when a loud *thump* came from behind him, followed by a moan.

The sounds raised goosebumps on Patrik's neck. He yearned to hurl himself through the glass to safety, but… against his better judgement, he looked back at Thalia…

…and found the sorceress inexplicably on her knees, head bowed and arms bound behind her back by a pair of black metal handcuffs. The whip now lay discarded on the floor before her. For one long, *extremely* uncomfortable moment, Patrik thought someone had broken into the room while he'd been looking the other way and taken her captive.

Then the sorceress raised her head, and those soft blue eyes looked up at him from behind the thick framed glasses.

"Punish me, daddy," she rasped. "I've been a bad, bad girl."

What the fuuuuck?

Mate, for once, I'm just as confused as you.

Thankfully for everyone involved in this hellish scene, Patrik and the sorceress were saved from further embarrassment by an unexpected visitor.

A visitor who arrived by way of smashing through the outside window and barrelling into the room with the force of a small boulder.

Still in shock from everything that had happened in the last thirty seconds, Patrik didn't even react as the dark cloaked figure came to its feet. He barely even moved when the club materialised in the newcomer's hand. Even as the club swung for his face, he was still trying to process—

Crack!

Bludgeoning damage inflicted [-20 health]
Warning: you have been stunned by a heavy blow.
You will lose consciousness—

Everything went black.

CHAPTER 19
MAN EATING MERMAIDS

--FOR ONE HOUR.

"Arg…"

Patrik snapped awake with a jerk that would have sent him tumbling from his bed…except that he wasn't *in* his bed. Or any bed, for that matter. He wasn't even horizontal. Tight bands pressed against his chest, binding him to…a tree? No, that didn't seem right. Was the ground moving? It was so hard to tell. He tried to orientate himself through the pounding in his head, but his mind was mush.

Stifling a groan, he forced his eyes to open. Lights danced across his vision, before resolving into the gentle flickering of a nearby lantern. All else was dark. He tried to move and found he was indeed tied to *something*. The gentle groan of shifting wood came as the ground rocked beneath him. It confirmed his worries.

He was on a boat.

Technically, I believe you're on a ship.

"St…" he tried to speak, but found his mouth stuffed with something resembling cotton balls. He choked, trying to dislodge it, but a scrap of fabric kept him from spitting it out.

Steve, he tried mentally instead, *why the* hell *am I on a ship?*

How should I know? We're occupying the same body, remember? I'm just better at using it.

Yeah, you'd think you'd be more useful.

Hey, that hurts, mate. That hurts.

Gritting his teeth, he forced himself to concentrate on his surroundings. The lantern had been dimmed, but as his eyes adjusted, he saw the PQA had been right. There was a railing a few yards from him. And he…he had been bound to the mast. There was no sign of Thalia, but as he hung from his bonds, Patrik caught the gentle hiss of nearby voices. He strained to hear what his captives were saying.

"…did the right thing?"

"The right thing?" That voice was strangely familiar. The laughter that followed even more so. "The right thing would have been to leave the bitch where you found her, Trawlee."

"But she'd seen me, Jacko!"

Patrik inhaled sharply at the name. Jacko was the fisherman from the wharf! What the hell were these guys doing, breaking into random inns and kidnapping people?

Just throwing out a wild guess here, but it might have something to do with that quest you got?

"And?" Jacko spoke again before he could respond to the PQA. The fisherman's voice was cold now. "That was *your* problem, Trawlee. Bringing her here made it *all* our problem. Hell, you know how low our Alignment has sunk. And you kidnap a goddamn *Warrior of the Light?*"

Patrik's heart sped up. If Thalia was onboard, they might just stand a chance.

"Oh, come on, she was no Warrior of the Light," the unseen Trawlee muttered.

"She was damn well close enough!" Jacko cried. "Just kidnapping her and bringing her aboard lost us all a thousand Alignment. Imagine if we'd killed her? We'd have all been condemned as pirates. I don't know about you, Trawlee, but I prefer my neck *without* a noose around it."

"Geeze calm down, captain," Trawlee shot back. "It all turned out alright in the end, didn't it? Those chains that sick bastard had her in were quality stuff. She won't be going anywhere before they find her."

Shit, what the hell had they done with Thalia?

"Yeah I suppose," Jacko rumbled his agreement. "Which brings us to our little guest. Bout time we found out what he knows, I reckon."

Patrik cursed—or tried to curse—as footsteps approached across the wooden deck. The silhouettes of two men appeared in the light of the lantern, followed by several others. Now Patrik really began to panic. He twisted and strained against his bindings, but the ropes held tight. He needed a knife or something—

Wait…

He had a knife! And a sword! And plenty of other crap in his inventory. The sword would be too big to manoeuvre into place to cut the rope, but the iron dagger he'd purchased from Tilly would be perfect.

Thank God for magic, he thought as he willed his inventory open—

Warning: Your hands are currently constrained. Inventory items are unavailable.

Wait, what?

Ah, well, you see…

Steve, Patrik snarled. *What the hell do my hands have to do with a magical storage system?*

Sorry mate, I don't make the rules.

Patrik drew in a breath. There was no time to argue senseless rules. If he couldn't use his weapons, maybe…

Warning: Your hands are currently constrained. Magical spells are unavailable.

Are you sh—

"Patrik the Chosen One," a voice interrupted. He flinched, looking up to find the shabbily dressed fishing captain standing in front of him. "Do you know why we have brought you here?"

"Mnfo, twu fuoking bystierd." The words didn't exactly come out as Patrik intended, what with the gag and all, but hopefully Jacko would take their meaning.

The sailor chuckled, the sound cold in the flickering light.

He tore the gag from Patrik's mouth and tossed it aside. Then clenching his hand into a fist, he slammed a right cross into Patrik's face.

Lights burst across his vision. He bit back a cry as messages flashed, reading out damage that he struggled to read. The metallic taste of blood filled his mouth. At least he could spit it out now the gag had been removed. Baring his teeth, he straightened against the mast and met the fisherman's eyes.

"What did you do with my friend?"

"Oh, that was your friend, was it?" The man sneered. "Hate to see what a man like you does to his enemies then." He laughed. "You don't have to worry about finishing whatever sick business you had with the sorceress. We left her outside a goblin dungeon. They'll deal with her. Sooner or later."

Goblins. Patrik swallowed. That did *not* sound good. Much as he disliked the woman, in the end she hadn't *actually* tried to kill him. She didn't deserve to die.

"Now, Patrik," Jacko continued, leaning in close so they were face to face. "If we're done with the pleasantries, it's time you told me how you learned our secret."

This again. Gods, what had he said back on the docks that had gotten these men so excited?

"Seriously, Jacko," he swore. "I have no idea what this secret of yours is. I was bluffing."

"Oh yeah?" the sailor asked, scratching at his beard. "Didn't seem like a bluff on the docks, did it boys? Bastard knew right where to poke. Sleeping with the fishes?" He snorted, and an iron dagger appeared in his hands. He rested the point against Patrik's shoulder. "Come now, let's be civilised about this."

Eyes on the dagger, Patrik nodded quickly, though he was still as lost as a rat in a maze. A maze made out of jagged glass...

You are not great at metaphors.

Pretty sure that was a simile...

Pain needled his shoulder as the captain began to press the knife into Patrik's flesh, while the rest of his crew looked on.

"Wait, wait, ow! Wait!" Patrik cried, and the blade paused. "Okay, so, sleeping with the fishes, right?" he rambled. "So, you…ah, have some bodies buried out here—ah, *fuck!*" Jacko had rammed the dagger into his shoulder to the hilt. "What the hell do you want from me!" he cried.

"The truth," Jacko growled. Blood sprayed the fisherman's shirt as he yanked back the blade. "The—"

"Captain!" A voice called. It was Trawlee. "We've arrived. No sign of the humanitarians—yet."

"Good." A grim smile crossed Jacko's face as he took a step back. "Last chance, Mr. Chosen One. Tell us where you learned the truth, and we'll give you a clean death."

"A clean death?" Patrik spluttered. What the hell was this guy's problem? What had he ever done to them, except forgotten to give them some spare change? Rage bubbled up in his chest as he glared at the ring of soldiers. "Seriously? Fuck you, you ugly bastards! I'd rather see you all starve to death than let you go back to slaughtering those poor mermaids—"

He might have said more, but at that moment the captain drove the point of his dagger deep into Patrik's stomach, and suddenly he had more important things to think about. Like the blood bubbling from his lips, or the warning lights flashing at the edges of his vision.

"So you're one of those humanitarian bastards," Jacko muttered as he stepped back. "That's too bad. The mermaids will not show you mercy, for all your supposed kindness. They're going to kill you *slow*. No safety precautions today. You'll be begging us to pull you out before the end. Then we'll have those names from you. Come on, lad." Leaning in close, he waved the bloody dagger in front of Patrik's face. "Why not save yourself the pain and just tell us now."

His abdomen wrapped in agony, vision blurring, Patrik looked into Jacko's merciless eyes and knew there was only one option. He spat a mouthful of blood into the man's face.

Thankfully, the fisherman didn't react by stabbing him

again. Instead, he stepped back and pulled a cloth from his inventory to wipe himself clean. As he did so, he made a gesture in Patrik's direction. Several men responded instantly. Leaping forward, they cut Patrik lose from the mast—though his hands and wrists remained bound—and dragged him towards the railing. Only at the last minute did Patrik realise what they intended.

"Wait—" he began.

Too late. Suddenly he was airborne—though only for a moment. Tumbling head over heel, Patrik struck the water with a splash. He kicked and twisted, struggling to reach the surface, but with his hands still tied behind his back, he made no progress. The silence of the icy depths swallowed him up, the currents carrying him deeper.

Hands. Hands grasped at his legs and arms, clutching him, clawing at him. He tried to scream, but only bubbles emerged. Still he could see nothing, hear nothing. All he knew was the feel of those icy fingers as they locked about his flesh. Then… then a rushing of water around him, as though he were suddenly moving at speed…

Patrik gasped as he burst through the surface, sucking in great mouthfuls of air. Stars danced before his eyes as oxygen filled his lungs. They were moving, racing towards something, carrying him towards…

Land!

Relief surged through Patrik as his legs bumped against rock. Still his unseen rescuers held him, carrying him up from the waters, up onto solid rock, then sand. Patrik coughed and spluttered as finally he collapsed onto the soft ground, safe from the surging waves. His vision flickered, exhaustion drawing him into darkness. He lay there a long time, shivering, dipping in and out of consciousness.

Eventually a strange warmth wrapped around him and he felt the cold recede. At the edge of awareness, he sighed, welcoming the warmth like the embrace of a lover. Time slipped away, and he imagined himself back in his bed in Portland, Clara's arms around him…

__Wake up!__

Memories came rushing back to Patrik as he snapped awake. Clara was gone. His world was gone. And he was alone on an icy shoreline…

__Er, not quite alone mate.__

That was ominous. Completely alert now, Patrik realised the arms embracing him in his dream…hadn't actually been part of the dream.

A Man Eating Mermaid had him in its deadly embrace.

__Now, just keep calm—__

"ARG!" Screaming, Patrik lurched away from the creature.

Unfortunately, he'd forgotten that his hands were still bound, and while he managed to jerk himself into a sitting position, he promptly fell flat on his face into the sand.

"Arg…" he groaned.

Darkness pressed in as he struggled to roll further from the creature, but it had already disappeared into the gloom. Heart pounding, he struggled to his knees. In the distance he glimpsed the glow of a lantern. The ship. Shadows shifted around him, the crunch of sand rising above the gentle lapping of waves against the shore. He swallowed.

Light flared amidst the black as a dozen lanterns were unshuttered. The hulking shape of the ship loomed above the tiny island upon which Patrik found himself. Sailors gathered at the railings, their faces lit by the brilliant glow. They jeered as they saw him, shaking their fists and shouting profanities.

"What the…"

Patrik trailed off as he finally took note of his surroundings. It hadn't just been one mermaid. Emerald tails flapped upon the rocks and sand as the creatures dragged themselves onto the shore. Others had already gathered nearby. A dozen eyes watched him with unmistakeable hunger.

The mermaids hadn't rescued him.

They had brought him here for their supper.

A lump lodged in Patrik's throat. He stared at his captors and they stared back…though he had to admit, it took an effort of will to…to keep his eyes…on…their…faces…

Ah, are you…okay?

I'm not…not okay? he replied.

Yep, he was surrounded by mermaids alright. There wasn't a merman in sight. Except…unlike the delightful tales of the *Little Mermaid*…these creatures weren't exactly…bashful. Nope, no clam shells or scallops or whatever covered Ariel in the next movie. Patrik had just woken up on a beach surrounded by a dozen absolutely stunning, half-naked women.

Well, if you ignored the part where they each had an enormous fish tails instead of legs.

Also, didn't the fishermen say the mermaids would torture you to death? Steve chipped in with his usual habit of looking on the negative side of things.

Patrik swallowed. Right. He'd momentarily forgotten about that. Wonder why. He quickly examined the nearest of the creatures.

Man Eating Mermaid [Level 18]. Found only in waters of the Mermaid Isles, these creatures are considered a delicacy in many parts of the Four Circles. However, since they spend much of their life-cycle deep beneath the surface of the ocean, little is known of their biology. Only that they are perilous creatures. Few who enter their waters ever return, and those that do are left as remnants of their former selves, their bodies withered, their voices rendered mute.

"Addaday?"

Patrik flinched as one of the creatures spoke. It shuffled towards him, its, ah, skin, glistening in the lantern light. He tried to scramble back, but they had him surrounded on all sides. Shit. This…this role reversal wasn't his idea of a good time. He needed something to cut these ropes.

His heart quickened as his fingers encountered a sliver of shell. It would have to do. He clutched at it with a desperation he usually reserved for coffee early in the morning, and struggled to bring it to bear on the rope. He could only hope it was sharp enough. Or that his augmented Strength would make up the difference.

Behind you!

Patrik rolled at the PQA's warning as a mermaid flopped onto the sand where he'd been lying.

"Addaday?" It cried, stretching out a hand.

He scrambled backwards, but the others were close now. A hand scrabbled at his robes. Unfortunately, being magically enhanced they did not rip, and he found himself being dragged across the sand towards the creature. Desperate, he lashed out with his boot. The blow caught the mermaid in the face. Giving a mournful cry, she released him and lurched back.

Two more soon took her place.

"Addaday? Addaday? Addaday?"

The voices were all around him now and Patrik was alone. The rope refused to give, no matter how hard he sawed at the twisted fibres. Error messages flashed across his vision as he tried again and again to open his inventory or cast his lightning spell. Nothing worked.

"Addaday? Addaday? Addaday?"

God, what were they saying? Their voices sounded human enough, but they clearly didn't speak English…though, there *was* a familiarity to the word they kept repeating. Strange as that might seem…

Mate, don't you have more pressing concerns just now? Like, I dunno, escaping from a pack of Man Eating Mermaids?

Man eating. That…that struck…something. He froze, staring at the nearest creatures. Her…it…her, damnit, which was it? *Her*, he decided, looking into the creature's eyes. They were wide, their sapphire depths conveying an…innocence that belied her deadly name. Dragging herself forward another foot, she paused, her still-wet skin glistening in the lantern light.

Blood pounded in Patrik's ears as he watched the creature push herself up by her arms. The action left her…screw it, his eyes flickered down, taking in a pair of breasts covered in sand. He swallowed. Maybe this wouldn't be such a bad way to go after all…

"Addaday?"

Okay, that was definitely ringing a bell. He shook himself, looking back at the mermaid's face. She swayed back and forth, sapphire eyes watching him with an intensity that made him shudder. Slowly, she stretched out a hand. When this time Patrik did not react, she grasped a fold of his robes and gave a gentle tug.

"Addaday?" she said again. Patrik said nothing, and releasing his robe, she reached for his hand instead. He allowed her to take it—with a surprising tenderness —and lift it to her…breast. "Uckfay emay?"

That…that new phrase. Patrik knew that phrase. He hadn't heard it used in years, not since he and his brother had been children and trying to swear in front of their parents. They'd read about this secret language on the internet. One no adult could ever crack.

Pig Latin.

"Addaday?" the mermaid said again.

And suddenly all the pieces of the puzzle clicked into place.

CHAPTER 20
THE FISHERMEN OF ANCHORPOINT

STANDING ON THE SANDY SHORE, PATRIK WATCHED THE rowboats make their slow way across the channel towards his little island. The storm from earlier had eased, and now the violet glow of sunrise lit the distant horizon. Even so, the fishermen still relied on their lanterns to guide them through the dark waters. He wondered what they thought, seeing him standing here in one piece, untouched by their 'Man Eating Mermaids.'

A little shudder ran down his spine. He glanced at the creatures. Mermaids surrounded him on all sides, still muttering in their little voices to one another. Repeating that word in their strange language, almost like it was a prayer.

Are you sure that's a language? Steve interjected. **Seriously, still sounds like gibberish to me.**

Patrik exhaled. Oh, it was a language alright. And the word the mermaids were whispering...

"Addaday?"

Dadda?

Jesus, he'd encountered some bizarre and disturbing things in the Four Circles, but this...

I'm sure there is a logical explanation...

Where are the mermen, Steve? he shot back. *Where are the mermen?*

They don't exist!

Patrik sighed. They'd had this argument several times while he waited for the fishermen to come and investigate what was happening. They couldn't just leave him standing here. Not with the things he knew…

The things you suspect. No way you're right. No. Way.

Glancing at his half-naked companions, Patrik wished he was wrong. But…he wasn't. He knew it. The fishermen knew it. Hell, he was pretty sure even Steve knew it at this point. The PQA was just being stubborn.

How do they reproduce, Steve? he repeated. *If mermen do not exist, how do they reproduce?*

Steve had no answer. The PQA already checked its 'database'. It was a secret. Just like the mermaid description claimed. Just like the quest notification had said. A secret the world wanted uncovered.

He turned back to the approaching boats. The boats packed with fishermen. It looked like Jacko had brought most of his crew, leaving only two aboard the fishing ship. These were the only ones in the world who knew the secrets of the Man Eating Mermaids.

An appropriate name, as it turned out. Though…not in the way most people probably assumed. His stomach churned.

Are you going to throw up again?

Patrik closed his eyes. The gentle lapping of waves rose above the whispers of the mermaids, and for just a moment he could pretend he was someplace else. On a beach in California, maybe, in the late autumn. Enjoying one last morning on the sands before they returned to Portland—

The sound of a keel scrapping against sand snapped Patrik back to the present. Opening his eyes, he watched the fishermen step from their boats. They didn't seem overly concerned to find themselves surrounded by Man Eating Mermaids. But then, why would they? These creatures…they weren't a threat to these men.

Only prey.

Jacko led his fishermen up the shore, a perplexed expression twisting his weathered face. He couldn't understand why Patrik had not been…consumed. Patrik clenched his fists and imagined his iron sword tearing through the man's throat. Here at last was an evil he wouldn't mind putting an end too.

But…no. Jacko had a small army at his back, and while they weren't all as strong as their captain, they were more than enough to take care of Patrik. So letting out a long breath, he forced an easy expression to his lips.

"You look confused, captain," Patrik called as the man drew to a stop several yards from where he stood.

Jacko nodded slowly. His beady eyes flickered to the mermaids that surrounded Patrik. "They do not usually…stop once they begin on their victim."

"I imagine not," Patrik grimaced. "You know, in my… universe we have many legends of mermaids. Some are uplifting stories of red-haired princesses who dream of the world above the sea. But others…others are older, darker. They speak of monsters who would lure unwary sailors into the water, to use and discard at their will."

"Ah…" Jacko replied, "so this is…how you learned of our secret?"

"No, Jacko," Patrik said with a shake of his head. "I had no idea what your secret was until they told me." He gestured to the mermaids. "Turns out they're quite talkative, once you get to know them a little. Maybe you should try it sometime."

The frown the captain had been wearing deepened. "Talk? They don't talk. They are dumb, unintelligent creatures, incapable of complex thought."

Patrik nodded sagely. "I have known men to say the same of women in my world." His jaw hardened. "Doesn't make it true."

"You're…you're mad, aren't you?" Jacko replied after a long moment. "That's why they didn't touch you." He grunted. "Probably for the best, wouldn't want that taint amongst the breeding stock." An iron scimitar appeared in his hands as he glanced at his men. "Come on then, lads. We'd best be quick, before those humanitarians discover us here. Trawlee, Flanders, help me deal with madman. The rest of you can whet ya whistle. We'll cull a few at the end for the market."

A rumble of agreement came from the sailors as two of their number joined the captain in confronting Patrik. While the others…

Ewww! Ew, ew, ew! No, that is…I mean, they have fish tails instead of…I mean* how…*you know what, I really don't want to know.

Patrik grimaced. "Me neither," he muttered. "Let's just hope…"

"Dadda!"

A stillness came over the sandy shore as the high-pitched voice rose over the crashing of the waves. Another soon joined in, and another and another, until all the mermaids were crying out in unison. It was the same word they had been calling before, when they had pulled Patrik from the ocean. Only, now he had spent the past couple of hours painstakingly teaching them to translate it. They'd only managed the one word, but…

Patrik watched with grim satisfaction as the fishermen turned to stare at the mermaids. One by one, the colour drained from their faces. Some opened their mouths as though to speak, while others staggered back from the creatures, a slow horror dawning behind their eyes.

"Dadda. Dadda. *Dadda!*"

The mermaids advanced on them, hopping through the sand on their long tails. They wouldn't harm the men, unfortunately. At least, not intentionally. But in their collective shock, not one of the fishermen were paying attention to Patrik now.

They were too busy staring at their horde of illegitimate daughters.

Yeah, ah, but can *we* kill them?

"Not today, Steve," he muttered. Their shock wouldn't last long if Patrik started butchering them. This wasn't one of O'Malley's spells. He needed to be gone before one of these assholes remembered why the mermaids suddenly knew how to say 'Dadda'.

Quietly, he slipped away from the distracted fishermen, down to the shoreline where they had left the rowboats. With no one watching, he pushed the boat into the water and took up the oars. It took him a few tries to orientate the boat in the right direction, but eventually he got it right. He didn't have a lot of experience with rowing, but his enhanced Strength mostly made up for his lack.

Unfortunately, he was barely fifty yards from the shore before the fishermen noticed his absence.

Patrik swore as Jacko and the other men piled into the remaining boats. The chase was on. "Steve, any ideas?"

Well, considering rowing a boat is literally part of these guys job description, and until a few weeks ago you were basically a college dropout...I'd rate your chances of escaping about 10%.

"I. Did. Not. Drop. Out," Patrik panted each word between strokes. Even with his augmented Strength, rowing was hard. *And that was not helpful.*

Sorry, little short on ideas.

Patrik was just coming up to the ship. An idea came to him as he spotted the rope ladder hanging over the side. He dug in one of his oars and his boat turned ponderously towards the larger vessel.

Ah, chances of escape falling. You barely know how to row—how are you going to pilot something that large?

Shit. The PQA was right. He was no Jack Sparrow. But the other rowboats were coming on fast now. His distraction had not lasted as long as he'd hoped. No time for another change of course. Maybe if...

The keel of his boat bumped against the fishing ship. No more time to think. Abandoning his oars, Patrik leapt for the rope ladder. Still unsure of his plan, he went up hand over foot, before swinging over the railings to land on the deck—

Look out!

Patrik threw himself to the side at the PQA's warning, just in time to avoid a wild swing of a bronze cutlass. His impact with the wooden boards drove the breath from his lungs, but there was no time for pain. He summoned his iron blade in time to block a second wing from the enemy.

Clang!

The blades came together with a clash of sparks and—

Congratulations! Your skill 'Hack and Slash' has increased to level 5! You are now [adequate] with edged weapons.

Surging to his feet, Patrik's sword hissed out to meet the enemy's next attack. This time as the blades came together, he gave a flick of his wrist that sent the point of his iron sword twisting around to strike beneath his foe's cross-guard. A scream echoed across the water as the sailor who'd been left to guard the ship staggered away, clutching at the bloody stump that had been his right hand.

Patrik followed in without hesitation, his blade aimed low to take the man in the groin. It seemed appropriate—and more importantly, the area wasn't covered by his leather breastplate. The blade struck home and the already orange bar above the sailor's head vanished.

Heart racing, Patrik paused a moment to stare at the dead man at his feet. Where…where the hell had *that* come from?

Your Hack and Skill hit level 5. Every five levels of a skill or spell mark a new level of proficiency.

"That's…" He was going to say ridiculous, but, well…

Footsteps came from behind him. Patrik spun to find the second sailor left to guard the ship approaching, a bronze hatchet clutched in one trembling hand. His eyes kept flicking to the body of the first man. They had probably been friends or something. Well, at that particular moment, Patrik didn't care. These people had kidnapped him, tortured him, tried to feed him to Man Eating Mermaids…well, that last part might not have been as bad as it sounded.

But then they'd tried to kill him.

Now, good or evil, negative Alignment or positive, they could all die for all he cared.

Swallowing his terror, the axeman bared his teeth and came at Patrik in a rush. His iron sword came up, catching the hatchet by the wooden haft and slicing through in a single blow. The bronze axe head went soaring out over the waters, leaving the sailor holding a useless piece of wood.

Patrik didn't give him the chance to run. His sword arced up, hacking through the man's neck. It didn't quite make it all the way through this time. Blood sprayed across the wooden boards as he yanked back the blade. The sailor staggered, the ruined hatchet falling from his fingers as he clutched at the terrible wound. He must have had decent Constitution, because while his health had plummeted into the red, he didn't die. At least, not until the second blow from Patrik's sword.

Silence fell over the ship as the second body hit the floor. But it was only a momentary respite. Patrik stood amongst the gore, blood still dripping from his blade, his breath coming in long, measured gasps. Despite his newfound skill, he felt no elation. Maybe that would come later.

Or maybe not, he found himself thinking as his eyes lingered on the dead sailors.

Ah, hate to interrupt the melancholic thoughts, but we have less than 60 seconds until Jacko and the rest of the mermaid fuckers arrive.

Patrik exhaled. "Okay," he said, casting his eyes around the fishing ship. The sails had been furled and he had no idea how to get them up. Without them the vessel would be going nowhere fast. "Think, Patrik."

Or…you could just do what you normally do?

"And what's that, Steve?" Patrik asked distractedly. There were fishing nets hanging over the side. Maybe he could use those…

Burn things.

"That is not…" he began to reply, then trailed off.

Fire. That…that wasn't a bad idea. If he lit a fire on the ship, Jacko and the sailors would have to put it out before they could come after him. They couldn't afford to lose the ship, after all. It was their only source of income. An incredibly messed up, disturbing source of income, but income all the same…

He began to pull the last spools of spider silk from his inventory. He'd been saving them for toilet paper, but he would just have to do without for a few days. Well, he hoped it would only be a few days. Within seconds the ship was covered in the sticky white silk he'd collected from the Enchanted Forest.

Pulling out his flint, Patrik was moving towards the rope ladder when he heard voices below. His stomach twisted. A glance over the side confirmed his worst suspicions. Jacko and his friends had arrived.

"Shit," he muttered, head whipping one way, then another in search of an exit. Nothing.

"Patrik the Chosen One!" Jacko bellowed from below. "Did you think your cheap parlour tricks would fool us? For countless generations our fathers have fished these waters, living in harmony with the sea."

So basically, they've been hunting—

"Don't need a play by play here, Steve," Patrik snapped, as below the captain continued his monologue.

"You will not turn us aside from our ancient traditions. Now come, humanitarian, and surrender. You cannot fight us all."

"Well he's right there," Patrik muttered.

He crossed to the other side of the ship and looked out towards the coast. They were at least a mile away from the mainland. Could he swim that far? He heard the scrambling of boots against wood from behind him and turned as the first of the sailors scrambled over the side. It was Trawlee, the first mate. He was practically Jacko's shadow. The man himself wouldn't be far behind.

Patrik was out of time. Making a split-second decision, he leapt up to the railing and balanced there a second, poised as Trawlee screamed and drew a cutlass. Patrik clenched his fist. There was no time left now for playing with flint. Lightning crackled as it gathered between his fingers. He counted down the seconds as Trawlee paused, eyeing the blue light shining between Patrik's fingers. But the first mate wasn't his intended target. As the count approached thirty, Patrik threw out his hand.

Boom!

Thunder roared, so loud Patrik felt his ears go *pop*, and a brilliant flash seared his eyes. Already turning away, Patrik didn't see if his lightning hit its mark. Instead, he hurled himself over the side of the ship and tumbled down, down into the murky depths. The icy waters closed over his head, but this time he was ready, his hands unbounded. He clawed his way back towards the light and burst through the surface to suck in great lungfuls of air.

Only then did he risk a glance back.

Above, Jacko, Trawlee and several others from the crew stood at the railings. But they wasted only a second to shake their fists in his direction. Probably because, behind them, a thick column of smoke rose from the deck of the ship.

Yes! Patrik exalted.

His lightning had lit the spider silk on fire. It looked like the stuff was really going up too. Jacko and his crew would have a fight on their hands if they were going to save their only source of income from going up in smoke. Hopefully that would give Patrik plenty of time to cross the open waters back to the mainland.

Though…he had to admit, this was going to be much worse than walking. His boots and robes were already water laden. Although…

He grinned as clothes and shoes disappeared, leaving him floating naked in the ocean. Well, small miracles. Turning from the smoking ship, he set his sights on the distant shore and began an easy forward crawl stroke. Before his college years, Patrik had spent some time in the swimming pool, going to swim meets and even competing in a few local championships. It was going to be a long haul, but he would make it—

Congratulations! Trawlee the Sailor [level 20] has

been defeated! [-20 Alignment]

Congratulations! Flanders the Sailor [level 16] has been defeated! [-20 Alignment]

Congratulations! Jacko the Sailor [level 24] has been defeated! [-20 Alignment]

Coughing and spluttering, Patrik came to a stop in the water as the messages continued to flash across his vision. There were *a lot* of them. They continued, one after another, until…

Achievement Unlocked: Serial Killer. Wow, mate, come on. What'd those good sailors ever do to you? You've accumulated fifty kills of positively aligned individuals. Reward: 500 gold coins. [-500 Alignment Points]

Quest Complete: The Fishermen of Anchorpoint. Congratulations, you discovered the secret of the fishermen of Anchorpoint—and sent their ship to the bottom of the ocean. Unmolested by their natural predators, the Man Eating Mermaids are finally free to laugh and love and spread. Their population may now expand beyond the Mermaid Isles. Reward: 1000 gold coins

Congratulations! Your spell 'Lightning Bolt' has increased to level 2…3!

Congratulations! Your skill 'Arson' has increased to level 7!

Ring! Ring! Ring!! Congratulations. You have reached level 18, 19, 20! You have been awarded 9 stat points. You have 9 stat points to assign.

Treading in the water, Patrik stared at the notifications. How in the hell…sure, the spider silk burnt well, and he'd lit it with lightning, but…surely Jacko and his crew could have put out the fire easily enough. Turning, he looked back the way he'd come…

Patrik swallowed. He'd made it maybe fifty yards from where the ship had sat at anchor. Now…it had been replaced by a blazing pillar of flame. The fire he'd lit had spread from the water line right to the tips of the mast. It had only been, what, two minutes? How had it spread so fast? And why hadn't Jacko and his crew abandoned the ship?

Your Arson skill, Steve offered.

"My what?" Patrik asked, still staring at the blazing ship.

Remember after you burned Monmouth to the ground, you gained the Arson skill. It was level 6. That means any fire you set will burn hotter, faster, and bigger ***than any natural flame.***

"Well that's…something," Patrik muttered.

He fell silent then. They both did. They watched as the ship sank lower and lower in the water. Steam hissed and spat where the flames met the sea, but still the inferno burned, spewing smoke high into the morning sky.

And burned, and burned, and burned.

Until there was nothing left.

And still Patrik lingered.

So it was that the humanitarians found him there, treading water not far from the first of the Mermaid Isles. He did not resist as they dragged him, naked, aboard their vessel, though when the cold breeze blew across the deck he did resummon his wizard's robes. Apparently the mystical void of his inventory did nothing to dry them though. He shuddered as the soggy material settled against his skin.

The crew drew back from him then, watching him with suspicion. They seemed to be waiting for something. Or someone. Patrik took the chance to cast a glance over their numbers. Most had levels in the high teens, though a few were level 20 like himself. None were actually marked as 'humanitarians', which seemed strange to him.

A commotion drew Patrik's attention back to those closest in the crowd. A man had pushed his way to the front of the crowd. He looked vaguely familiar. Upon seeing Patrik, a look of amazement broke across his face and he fell to his knees, bowing his head in apparent reverence.

"Oh Chosen One!" he cried. "Thank Fate, you have returned to us! Please, this humble servant begs you offer him your wisdom once more, that your followers might better oppose the vile works of the Dark Lord!"

Patrik could only stand and stare at the man. "Ah…"

Oh, hey, look at that! It's the guy from the tavern in Monmouth!

FAR TO THE SOUTH, in the ruins of Solime, the demon prince Rhian looked upon the fruits of his conquest. Five hundred former soldiers of the light knelt before him, ready to swear fresh vows of allegiance—

"My prince!"

Rhian grimaced as the little voice carried to him. Men and women looked around as the orc threaded its way through their ranks. Rhian fought to keep the exasperation from his face as the servant approached.

"Garfunkel," he greeted the orc in a cold tone, "I am currently occupied."

The orc drew to a stop before the demon prince, breath coming in ragged gasps. It looked around, only now seeming to realise its audience. Eyes widening, the orc turned back to Rhian and fell to its knees.

"Forgiveness, my prince!" it cried. "But this news could not wait!"

"I will be the judge of that," Rhian said.

The orc bowed further. "Of course, my prince," it paused to draw in another breath. "I have been investigating the disappearance of the elven princess, as you commanded. During my travels, I stumbled upon a great disturbance. The town of Monmouth has been utterly destroyed, my prince!"

A frown creased Rhian's brow. "I…see," he murmured. Raising a hand to his chin, he turned from the creature. Another blow to the forces of light? Truly, the scales were out of balance. Was this some ploy of Fate, some thread in her never-ending narrative of good versus evil? Or was something else at play here?

"And what of the Warrior of the Light?" he asked.

"Apologies, but I have found no sign of the elven princess, my prince. Only…" the orc trailed off.

"Yes?"

The orc swallowed visibly. "Monmouth is not the only town affected. There is another. Not yet destroyed, but…unbalanced."

"Which town?"

"Anchorpoint, my prince."

Rhian pursed his lips. "Then perhaps our answer is there." He drew himself up. "Garfunkel, prepare the teleportation circle, I will go there myself—"

"Oh, oh, oh, are you going on a fieldtrip?"

Despite his audience—or perhaps because of it—Rhian cringed as a young woman came racing across the square.

"Oooh, can I come, brother?" she exclaimed. Coming to a stop in front of him, she bounced from one foot to another in excitement. "I promise I won't get in the way!"

Gritting his teeth, Rhian glared at his sister. "No, Dolzeroth, you may not," he snapped. His heart twinged as her face fell, but he steeled himself against her wheedling. "You would only prove a liability. We cannot afford your…eccentricities with a rogue elven princess roaming our Circle."

"Oh." The demon princess stilled, her shoulders slumping. "Okay."

Rhian was already regretting the harsh words as his sister wandered away, but that did not detract from their truth. Something was at hand in the First Circle, something unwitnessed for decades. The scales were shifting beneath their feet, and while so far they seemed aligned with the forces of darkness, they could swing back just as violently. And he did *not* want to be the one to tell father something had happened to his youngest daughter.

Shaking himself, he turned back to his orcish servant.

"Garfunkel, ready an escort," he said grimly. "On the morrow, we take the teleportation circle to Anchorpoint."

CHAPTER 21

NECESSARY HEROICS

PATRIK THE CHOSEN ONE　　　　LEVEL **20**

PROGRESS TO NEXT LEVEL: 45%

RACE	ALIGNMENT
Human	-2960

HEALTH	MANA
200/200	95/95

STR	CON	INT	CHA	DEX
16(+4)	14(+1)	18	1	10(+1)

*Equipped: Iron short sword (+3 STR)
   Sapphire Ring of Strength (+1 STR)
   Sapphire Ring of Dexterity (+1 DEX)
   Sapphire Ring of Constitution (+1 CON)*

You have no stat points to assign.

SPELLS [LIMIT: FOUR]

RAISE DEAD	LIGHTNING BOLT
level 7	level 3

SKILLS [UNLIMITED]

HACK AND SLASH	ARSON	VICIOUS MOCKERY
level 5	level 7	level 1

Well, he had made...progress. If you could call slaughtering bandits and fishermen progress. He'd split his latest stat points between Intelligence, Dexterity and Constitution—and experienced the familiar rush of blood to his brain. Such a strange sensation, like feeling his mind change up a gear. There was no extra bulk to his muscles this time, but he *did* feel lighter on his feet. And more...sturdy somehow? Was this what it felt like to be nearing peak human?

Closing the stats menu, Patrik looked across the bow of the humanitarian ship. They were already approaching Anchorpoint. He'd asked Larry—who he'd apparently inspired to start the entire humanitarian movement during their brief encounter in Monmouth—to drop him off at the port. Thankfully the man seemed entirely devoted to the 'Path of the Chosen One', whatever that meant. He had obeyed without question.

Unthankfully, the man himself kept hovering at Patrik's shoulder, listening intently for any nugget of wisdom he might inadvertently let slip. After the kerfuffle with Monmouth and the bandits and now the fishermen, Patrik was trying his best to keep his mouth firmly closed. So it was with enormous relief when the ship finally touched up against the docks, allowing him to climb over the railings and return to solid ground.

Footsteps on the gangplank served to remind him that Larry and his crew would not be so easily perturbed. He turned as they followed him onto the docks. There were more than twenty humanitarians on this ship alone, a number that had apparently been growing every day, buoyed by refugees from Monmouth and discontents from across the First Circle.

Looking at the motley crew, and the earnest face of Larry, Patrik stifled a sigh. As though afraid he'd caused some displeasure in their messiah, the humanitarian leader fell to his knees. The others followed suit, a ripple spreading through the crowd as one by one they bowed down.

"Please, oh mighty Patrik!" Larry cried without looking up. "I beseech thee one final time for your guidance, that we might better follow the Path of the Chosen One!"

Patrik couldn't help it. He rolled his eyes. Seriously, this place…but, fine. If he was going to make a difference, he could think of worse things than protecting the subhuman species of this world. In fact…

"Continue as you have been doing," he commanded, attempting to adopt a god-like tone. "Protect the weak against those who would seek to do them harm."

With that he turned and walked away.

There, how could that possibly go wrong?

Yes, because issuing ultimatums to humanity never *leads* in unintended consequences.

I hear your sarcasm, Steve, Patrik muttered. *What do you want from me?*

The PQA didn't immediately reply, and when Steve did finally speak, his tone seemed…muted. **Honestly, I don't know, mate.** An audible sigh whispered through Patrik's thoughts, accompanied by an idle turning of pages. **Maybe your Earthen culture has corrupted me. But I can't help but feel…you were right. Maybe there are some problems with this world. I'm still not convinced those mermaids were speaking a real language though.**

Approaching their inn, Patrik was about to reply, when he noticed the sign outside the building: *The Bandit's Daughter.* "What the hell?" he muttered.

His conversation with Steve forgotten, he stomped up the steps and pushed his way through the swinging doors. Inside he was greeted by the familiar gloom—and the sight of the young Bel standing behind the counter. He paused at the sight of her, and so caught the confusing mess of emotions that crossed her face when she saw him. Surprise, rage, hatred— before she finally settled on a the most patently false smile Patrik had seen since crash landing in this world.

"Mr. Chosen One," she said cordially. "I had not expected to see you again after your rather…atypical departure. Your horse has been duly cared for. However, I would kindly ask that you settle the bill for the damages to your room before we discuss any further business."

"Ah…" Patrik could only stare at the young woman. She seemed all grown up compared with the Bel of yesterday. "Sure…how much would that be?"

"Two thousand gold for the broken window and furniture."

Ouch. But he wasn't going to argue. He nodded and drew the amount from his inventory, before wandering over to place it on the counter. "Sorry about that. So, ah, where is your mother?"

The young woman said nothing, only swept the gold from the table and flashed him a final glare, before turning and disappearing into the kitchen. Patrik was left staring after her, not entirely sure whether he was meant to follow and collect Human's Bane, or wait here for something…

"Patrik?"

Patrik startled as a voice came from behind. He turned to find…

"O'Malley! Giovanni!" he cried, surprised to find them standing directly behind him. "What are you doing here?" He'd thought the pair would be out looking for himself and Thalia.

They looked equally as surprised to find him in the Bandit's Daughter. Giovanni was the first to recover. Of course, he didn't speak, but in his usual silent way, he managed to get the message across by grabbing Patrik by the front of his shirt and heaving him into the air. A dagger appeared in the swordsman's hand.

"Ahh…" Despite his every instinct screaming at him to fight, Patrik forced himself not to react as cold iron touched his throat. "Nice to see you too, Giovanni?"

"Patrik," O'Malley said, sounding unusually serious for the jovial bard. "We followed your trail to the goblin cave. What have you done with Thalia?"

"My trail?" Patrik gasped. He frowned. "You mean the fishermen! They were the ones who kidnapped us."

"The fishermen?" O'Malley asked. "What have the fish-ermen got to do with any of this?"

"It's kinda a long story—" Patrik started. He broke off when Giovanni gave him a violent shake. "Okay, okay! Just… put me down and I'll explain!"

A growl rumbled from the swordsman's throat. The pair shared a glance, then somewhat reluctantly Giovanni set Patrik back on his feet. He made a brief show of straightening his still-damp robes, before launching into his tale of violence, incest and explosions. He left nothing out. By the end, even O'Malley looked a little pale.

"So the mermaids…"

Giovanni grunted. Turning, he began to pace back and forth across the inn. The pair seemed…conflicted. It was clear he'd placed them in somewhat of an ethical bind. Had Patrik done the right thing, killing the fishermen? They had still been positively Aligned when they'd died, so in a very clear sense burning their ship had been an evil deed. On the other hand… well, there was a reason they'd been keeping the mating rituals of the mermaids a secret.

Still, at that moment, their little fellowship had other concerns. "Wait, so what about Thalia?" Patrik asked finally. "You said you followed her to a goblin cave?"

Giovanni nodded.

"Yes," O'Malley spoke on the swordsman's behalf. "The creatures obviously found her and carried her into the depths before we arrived."

"Why didn't you go after her?"

O'Malley blinked. "It's a goblin cave. We were offered a bounty of 5000 gold to clear it of enemies. We couldn't have attempted a quest that difficult *with* Thalia, let alone without her."

Good thing you never told them how much your quest to Bledross is worth.

Patrik ignored the PQA. "But…she's your friend, isn't she?" he asked, confused by the pair's attitude.

"Of course," O'Malley replied, his voice mournful. "But it's suicide, Patrik."

"But…you're heroes. Isn't impossible odds kind of in the job description?"

A frown furrowed the bard's forehead. "She is likely already dead, Patrik," he said slowly, as though talking to a simpleton. "Only a fool would go in there…"

Patrik stood staring at the two men for a long, long minute. This…*fuck*, every time he thought he had a handle on this place. Hell, it wasn't like he'd expected them to come save *him*. Well, it would have been nice. O'Malley was the closest person he had to a friend in this place—***Hey, what about me***—but Thalia…she was their actual companion. And they hadn't even *tried* to rescue her.

Somehow, the bricks were back. Their weight sat in his stomach, twisting, grinding, churning. This place…

Emptying his lungs in a long exhalation, Patrik turned his back on O'Malley and Giovanni.

You know…you don't have to go.

I know, Steve, He pushed open the doors to the inn and stepped back into the sunlight. No hint remained of last night's storm now, though the air still carried a briskness.

If your positions were reversed, she wouldn't do the same for you.

You're probably right.

He pulled up his map. The details had been filling in everywhere he'd been so far in the First Circle. He spotted the goblin cave immediately. It was less than a mile from the town. Setting his sights in the direction of the cave, he began to run. Silence passed between man and PQA for a time, filled only by the rhythmic pounding of boots against stone.

I mean, you did almost have that fling, Steve spoke again as they left the sleepy seaside town, ***but risking your life for a bit of tail…going a bit far, don't you think?***

You know that's not what this is, Steve, Patrik replied.

He was moving along the shoreline now. The cave wasn't far from the ocean. The sailors must have loaded them both onto the ship and then come here to deposit Thalia at the entrance to the cave, before taking him out to the islands.

A sigh came from his own thoughts. *I know,* Steve murmured. *I just...like the bard said, she's probably dead already. Why are we risking our lives to help her?*

We?

I'm in here too, you know.

Patrik slowed at that. Despite the PQA's insistence it was embedded in his brain, Patrik had come to think of it as some distant force, a voice projected into his head. Or a brain worm. Neither of which really begged him to ask the question...

"What happens to you if I die?"

That's...classified.

"Convenient."

Not...really.

Patrik grimaced, but realised he would get no further on that particular point. He returned to the PQA's original question instead. "I don't really know why I'm doing this. I know we probably won't survive..."

Probably? Oh it's a little worse than probably. I calculate a 1% chance of success.

"Calculations that are based off...what exactly?"

Fate knows. Another pause. *You know she hates you, right? That one day she's likely going to try and kill you?*

"I know."

Then...why?

Patrik sighed. "Because she's in this mess because of me, because she tried to help me. Even if it was in her own demented way."

He came to a stop. Ahead, a shadow marred the stark stone of the seaside cliffs. The goblin cave.

New Quest: Clear the Goblin Cave. For years, this goblin enclave has been neglected by local adventurers, allowing its numbers to grow. Now a practical army of wart-faced monsters wait below, ready to

slaughter anyone who dares trespass in their territory. Reward: 5000 gold [Bonus: Rescue the Sorceress. Thalia the Sorceress has been taken captive by a horde of goblins. Who knows what torments she has suffered in the depths of their lair? Of course, one thing we do know is that anyone who follows her is likely to suffer the same fate. But don't let that deter you. Venture down into the shadows and rescue the sorceress. Bonus: 1000 gold].

Patrik let out a long breath as the text faded. He had arrived.

Patrik…are you sure you want to do this?

He grimaced. "No."

But…you're going in there anyway?

Patrik found himself smiling. "It's like you said: _To be a good person, you have to do good things._"

And with that, he stepped into the darkness of the cave.

CHAPTER 22
YOUR MOMMA

PATRIK'S HEART RACED AS HE STUMBLED IN THE DARKNESS, FEET tripping on the uneven floor. He could hardly see two inches before his face. Damn, he should have grabbed a torch from Tilly before coming in here. Idiot. But there was no time to turn back now. Every moment that passed was another moment of agony and torture for Thalia. If she wasn't already dead.

I mean, chances aren't great, mate...

Pushing aside the disembodied voice, Patrik toiled on. And as he walked…he noticed the darkness was no longer quite so impenetrable. He started to see the faint outlines of the undulating walls, rather than crashing into them, and saw the twisted shapes that hung from the low ceiling. *Stalagmites*, he realised as he ducked under one of the low hanging spikes.

I think its stalactites.

Huh?

Aren't the ones on the ceiling stalactites?

I'm pretty sure—wait, how is this relevant right now?

Sorry, just trying to lighten the mood.

Shaking his head, Patrik continued into the depths. It was definitely growing brighter now, though he'd yet to spot a source of light. Or goblins, for that matter. Strange. Based on Steve and O'Malley's warnings, he'd expected to be wading through blood to get this far. Where were all the goblins? Sure, there was an undeniable stench to the place, a general reek of unwashed bodies reminiscent of his old college dorm.

But no monsters. At least, not yet.

Let's not look a gift horse in the mouth, shall we?

That…too soon, Steve. Too soon.

The cave itself twisted and turned, but thankfully Patrik had yet to come across any branches or intersections. Just now they were spiralling downward towards gods only knew what—

A pair of shadows stepped into Patrik's path, sending his heart rate spiking. Letting out a very…manly yelp, he scrambled backwards. Squinting, he tried to sift the shadows from the darkness, and found himself staring at…well, at two of the ugliest faces he'd ever seen.

Their skin was a mottled green and split by great crags seeping yellow pus. Hideous warts covered the twisted noses and yellow slitted eyes practically glowed in the gloom of the cave. Their arms were long and scraggly and seemingly double jointed, since each creature's legs twisted in opposite directions. Rusted iron chainmail vests covered their torsos, while leather caps served as protection for their mishappen skulls.

Goblin Foot Soldier [level 13]. These nasty little buggers aren't the strongest enemy a brave adventurer can face in the First Circle, but what they lack in ability they more than make up for in pent up rage and overwhelming numbers. You ever seen that scene in the first Hobbit? Yeah, I didn't like those movies either. But believe me, you don't want to piss these bastards off.

Thankfully, the pair turned out to be just as surprised as Patrik to find a human wandering their tunnel. They stumbled to a stop and exchanged wild glances before their faces twisted with anger. Weapons appeared in their hands, one a bronze battle axe, the other a scimitar. And they began to scream.

"Atwhay ethay ellhay areyay ouyay oingday inyay erehay?

Patrik froze. "What the hell? These guys speak Pig Latin as well?"

An audible sigh came from his head. ***This again? Come on, mate, this is no time for jokes.***

It's true!

Fine, then tell them we come in peace.

Ah, okay, let me think—

Steve fell silent, but unfortunately the pair of goblins had other ideas. Screaming in their ridiculous language, they slammed into Patrik with the force of…well, they were each seven levels lower than him and wielding bronze weaponry. Scimitar and battle axe struck him in the shoulder and knee, opening only shallow gashes and barely ruffling the wizard's robes. His health did drop, but only some twenty points, barely ten percent of what he had now.

"Huh," he muttered. "That bronze stuff really is crap."

I thought you said you could speak their language… Steve remarked as Patrik's iron sword appeared in his hand.

"I said I *recognised* their language," Patrik grated as his blade lanced out, skewering the brains of the scimitar wielder. Its health plummeted, but didn't zero out until he yanked his weapon back, tearing more flesh and causing more damage. "It's *Pig Latin*. It's just English, but you take the first consonant and move it to the end, then add 'ay'."

That's…stupid.

"Obviously!" Patrik sidestepped another swing from the battle axe. The blade hissed as it fell, but he was already far from its path. Damn, his increased Dexterity was becoming useful as well. Why would *anyone* ever bother with a stat like Charisma when you had the power of gods on the table? "I haven't used it since my brother and I were kids. I'm hardly going to know, *I come in peace*, off the top of my head, am I?"

His sword lashed out, decapitating the second goblin. He drew to a stop, puffing…lightly. Man, that was a nice change. He found himself grinning at he looked at his fallen enemies. He looted them out of habit. This…this wasn't so bad. What the hell were O'Malley and Giovanni so worried about? These guys were pipsqueaks.

At that moment, three more goblins wandered around the bend, saw him, screamed, drew weapons, and charged.

Patrik grimaced. At least he was training his Hack and Slash skill…

…actually, if these things *did* speak a language, there was another skill he should *really* try out. You know, just to make sure he was utilising his full arsenal of attacks. Now, if he could just get the translation right…

"Ahem," he cleared his throat as the three goblins charged, before continuing in Pig Latin: "Shit you guys are hideous."

He wasn't sure whether the skill would work, especially since it was more observation than insult. These things truly were hideous. One had a hideous wart-like abscess on its neck, while acne just *covered* the face of another. The third was missing an eye, and the empty socket was weeping pus.

Regardless, at his words the three goblins stumbled to a halt. Their faces registered shock as health bars appeared above their heads. Each lost a slither of their green, so damage was taken. It just wasn't an awful lot.

Congratulations! Your skill, Vicious Mockery, has increased to level 2.

"I suppose that's something." Still, unless his enemies decided to stand around all day while he insulted them, he wouldn't be killing anything with this ability. At least, not for the immediate future.

Then again…

"What," he called again, focusing on acne face, "did your mother drop you in a vat of acid when you were little?" he asked. "Oh wait, no, I bet you didn't *have* a mother. One look at that face and she probably ran screaming in the other direction!"

This was apparently a much better joke, as the target of his abuse paled to a sickly green and its health dropped a larger chunk. But that was all the time Patrik had for games. Screaming something in Pig Latin he didn't have a chance to translate, pimple face hurled itself at him with scimitar extended.

"Ymay othermay ovedlay emay!".

The combination of Patrik's enhanced Dexterity and Hack and Slash skill allowed him to easily evade the blow, then launch a counterattack. Sparks flew as his sword smashed the bronze scimitar from the goblin's hand. Even then, the creature did not relent. Still screaming what Patrik suspected were profanities, it threw a punch, a dagger appearing in its fist. Only bronze, thankfully, but this attack slipped past Patrik's guard.

He cursed as the blade sank into his flesh. It stung no worse than an ant bite, but he was beginning to see the danger of these creatures. Individually they were no threat to him, but collectively it was a different matter. He only had two health potions in his inventory. He needed to be careful with his health.

Launching another attack at pimple face, he separated the creatures head from its shoulders, then leapt back and clenched his fist. Lightning crackled, its glow lighting up the cavern. The two remaining goblins shrieked and covered their slitted eyes. Huh. So they didn't like bright light. That was useful to know.

As the energy in his fist gathered to breaking point, Patrik threw out his hand. An explosion rocked the cave—or at least, a roar of thunder equal to any explosion. Light so bright even Patrik had to cover his eyes filled the cave, followed almost immediately by the smell of cooking meat. Shit, how strong were his spells becoming?

Blinking to clear his vision, he immediately discovered the answer: not very. The two remaining goblins stood unmoved, their yellow eyes blinking rapidly as the gloom returned. The lightning had at least struck both targets, leaving both with nasty looking burn marks across their faces and torso. But their health bars had only moved down by about a third.

Patrik sighed. Typical. He glanced at the body at his feet. Raise Dead was not his favourite spell. It cost him Alignment every time he used it, but…well at this stage he had mana to burn. So…

…dark light flowed from his hand as he pointed at the dead

goblin. A groan rasped from its empty lungs as it twisted, fingers clasping at the hilt of its fallen scimitar. In jerking, unnatural movements, pimple face climbed back to its feet.

"Right then," Patrik muttered, pointing his blade at the two remaining goblins. "Let's have at em."

The undead goblin screamed its agreement and lurched towards its former companions—both of whom looked absolutely horrified.

"Atwhay ethay uckfay, Artymay!" The one-eyed goblin screamed as the undead creature stabbed it in the chest.

The definitely-mortal-blow wasn't enough to kill one-eye, so as the battle ensued between the two, Patrik made a move on the last goblin. Wart-neck screamed as he approached, swinging its hatchet wildly at empty air, as though that might fend him off. Patrik took the opportunity to slip in another insult. The mother jokes seemed to be pretty effective, so…

"Your momma hates you. She told me so last night when we made love."

Fate, you're terrible ***at this, you know?***

The goblin didn't seem to think so. Like before, it froze as a chunk vanished from its health bar, dropping it well into the orange. Considering how much other effects hurt when he lost health, Patrik wondered what that *actually* felt like.

Congratulations! Your spell, Vicious Mockery, has increased to level 3.

Nice, this could actually prove useful. Nearby, the undead goblin and one-eye had torn one another apart in their rage. Time to finish this. Leaping forward, Patrik swung his blade and helpfully lanced wart-neck's boil. And also halfway decapitated it. With its health already low, wart-neck fell to the ground dead beside its companions.

Silence returned to the cavern…

…except, it wasn't quite silent now. A whisper echoed up the tunnel, a distant cry, almost like…a woman screaming.

Patrik's heart quickened. Could it be Thalia? Was the sorceress *actually* still alive? If so, it didn't sound like she was having a very pleasant time. Pausing only long enough to loot his fresh kills, he set off down the tunnel at a jog. As the minutes passed and he moved deeper and deeper into the tunnel, the sounds grew louder. Someone *was* screaming. A woman. But she wasn't alone. A low, distant buzz of voices accompanied her cries, almost as though—

Still moving at an easy jog—which was probably more like a fifteen mile an hour sprint with his current abilities—Patrik didn't have time to stop when the tunnel suddenly opened into an enormous cavern. And so he found himself quite literally barrelling into the middle of what could only be described as a goblin rave.

A goblin rave with *a lot* of goblins. Not just dozens. Hundreds of them. If not thousands. It was difficult to tell in the poorly lit cavern, which had to be at least the size of a football field. Every inch of which was packed with heaving, sweaty goblin bodies.

All of which promptly turned towards the commotion at the entrance, and so saw the singular human stumble into their midst.

Patrik only had a second to take in his predicament. The walls of the cavern rose at least fifty feet around him, ending in a ceiling riddled with cracks. Torches burned in brackets, though only enough to give the place the atmosphere of a cheap underground club. The only exits appeared to be the one he'd entered through, and another cave on the opposite side of the cavern—though the goblins seemed to be avoiding that area.

Elsewhere…they partied with abandon. That was the other sound he'd been hearing. Goblins singing in that terrible language of theirs, and dancing, and swinging weapons around their heads like they were karaoke microphones. He even spotted some on one another's shoulders, while others crammed into the corners doing a very different kind of horizontal dance.

All of which seemed to be in celebration of the enormous fire pit that had been set up in the centre of the chaos. Well, the fire pit, or more accurately, the screaming woman that had been strung up over the flames.

"Holy shit."

That was all Patrik had time to say before he turned tail and fled back the way he'd come. A hundred screaming goblins were quick to give chase.

"Shit, shit, shit, Steve, what the hell was that!"

He couldn't keep the image of the sorceress strung up over the fire out of his mind. She was still bound hand and foot—he was pretty sure with the same bonds she'd used on herself the night before—but the goblins had strapped her to a pole and hung it horizontally over the flames. It was high enough above the pit that she wasn't directly in the fire, but that didn't mean she wasn't burning. Just burning *very slowly*. They even had a goblin standing at the edge of the fire slowly turning a handle that rotated the pole. Presumably so their meal would be cooked on all sides.

Oh, goblins are all about their communal eating. Grab a human, put 'em on the spitroast, throw a rave for all their mates. Everyone has a good time.

"They're cooking her *alive*, Steve!"

Yeah...they say it's got something to do with the taste—

"For fucks sake, this is what happens when you normalise cannibalism!" Patrik panted.

They're a different species, Patrik. It's hardly cannibalism.

Patrik had no response to that. The goblins had momentarily fallen behind, but there were way too many to fight. And he couldn't leave, not now he'd seen Thalia. Seen her being *fucking cooked alive*. But what could he do? If they caught him, he would only end up joining her over the fire. He did *not* want to be cooked alive. He needed a plan, something that—

Ahem.

"Yes, Steve, I understand it's not *actually* cannibalism, but—"

It's not that.

"What then?" Patrik gasped. Despite his increased Dexterity and Constitution, running up hill in the shadows was taking its toll.

Well, it's just, I might have a plan for you.

"Okay…"

You're not going to like it.

"Just spit it out, Steve."

Well, you remember when we left the Enchanted Forest?

"Yeah?"

Well…did I mention you're not going to like this?

CHAPTER 23
GOBLIN RAVE

PATRIK STOOD IN THE DARKNESS, LISTENING AS THE SCREAMS and hooting of the goblins finally grew loud enough to hear over the pounding of blood in his ears. His mouth was dry, his throat parched with terror. There were too many. Way, way, *way* too many.

This better work, Steve!

It'll work, mate. It'll work.

The first of the goblins barrelled around the bend in the corner. No time to run now. Others followed just a step behind, weapons raised, putrid faces screaming for his blood. Well, not blood. His flesh, really. But only once it'd been cooked nice and tender…

Cries of confusion echoed from the narrow ceiling as the pack stumbled to a halt. Glowing yellow eyes stared at him in confusion. He had to act quick. Throwing out his hand, Patrik pointed up the tunnel towards the distant exit and screamed the words he'd been desperately practicing in his head the last thirty seconds.

"Ehay entway atthay ayway!" *He went that way!*

There was a second of hesitation from the goblins as they stared at him. Then with a united scream, they lifted their weapons once more and charged past, up towards the distant light of day.

Patrik stared as rank upon disordered rank of goblins swept past him. Hundreds. There were definitely hundreds of the little fuckers. More than enough to tear him to a thousand pieces—or drag him back to the fire to cook as a side dish.

But not one of the many, many goblins seemed to notice their quarry standing idly by the wayside, waiting for them all to go by. Until finally, Patrik found himself alone once more in the tunnel.

"I can't believe that worked," he muttered.

I told you, they're just dumb animals. There was a 95% chance of success. Better odds than any plan you've had.

Patrik shook his head. The goblin armour was way too small for him, so its chest plate dug into his flesh. Even the leather cap was a struggle to fit on his head. It kind of just perched on top of his skull, held there by the straps. It certainly wouldn't be offering any defensive capabilities. And the battle axe was heavy and unwieldy in his hands.

In short, he looked like a complete idiot. The fact every piece of equipment absolutely reeked of BO only made matters worse. But…he couldn't argue with results. Somehow, his Hitman style disguise had actually worked. The goblins had believed Patrik was one of them.

"Seriously, my skin isn't even green," Patrik muttered as he set off down the tunnel towards the chamber.

He found the large cavern considerably emptier than his last, brief, visit, though there were still at least a hundred goblins present. Two were waiting near the entrance. One held a scimitar, the other a spiked club. Apparently, the creatures had decided to set a guard now.

Drawing in a breath, Patrik decided to trust in his disguise, and marched right up to them. Despite the ruckus caused by his prior appearance, the pair seemed relaxed. Patrik supposed if he had a hundred friends out hunting a single enemy, he wouldn't be too anxious about guard duty either. Even so, the goblins still swung around at his approach.

"Eetingsgray, otherbray," the one with the scimitar called. "Owhay oesgay ethay unthay?"

Greetings, brother. Patrik quickly translated. *How goes the hunt?*

He formulated a reply: "Eway avehay ethay umanhay orneredcay, utbay miay ungryhay, osay iyay eciddedday otay eturnray." *We have the human cornered, but I'm hungry, so I decided to return.*

Seriously, that is literal gibberish.

The goblin guards exchanged glances. He swallowed. Maybe he shouldn't have tried such a complicated sentence. But finally the pair lowered their weapons. The one with the scimitar made a screechy noise Patrik interpreted as laughter.

"Ayyay, eway areyay ungryhay ootay. Ityay isyay onglay incesay eway uppedsay onyay umanhay eshflay." This took Patrik a moment to translate, but he thought he had it with: *Ay, we are hungry too. It is long since we supped on human flesh.*

Letting out a long breath through the crushing breastplate, Patrik smiled. Then another scream echoed from the firepit. His relief evaporated like summer rain.

"Oundssay ikelay ethay umanhay isyay almostyay oneday," he said, his tone growing darker. *Sounds like the human is almost done*

"Almost," the creature replied. Patrik was getting the hang of the language and this time he was able to translate as it spoke. A silence fell between them for a moment, but the goblin with the scimitar continued to stare at Patrik, almost as though… "If you do not mind my saying, brother," it said suddenly, "you must be the strangest looking goblin I have ever met…" The creature left the statement dangling, as though to indicate a question.

Shit. Patrik's bubbling fear almost boiled over into a full-blown panic. This was it, the moment it all unravelled.

"My ah…mother…" he said, resisting the urge to switch to his iron sword. It was difficult enough just to translate his words to Pig Latin, let alone come up with an explanation for his appearance on the fly. "She…ah…it shames me to admit, but she had an affair with a human."

Horror and disgust showed on the twisted faces of the goblins. "By the Dark Lord…" the one with the scimitar whispered. It seemed to be the talkative one. "That is…disturbing. But…ah…I suppose a goblin should not suffer for the crimes of their sires."

"Of course," the one with the club added quickly. They exchanged a nervous glance, as though ashamed they'd been caught expressing inappropriate thoughts. "Come, brother, enjoy the feast. The chef has prepared the human with a marinade of sweet apple and cinnamon. You know how bland they can be without the proper seasoning."

Another blood curdling scream punctuated the goblin's words, though Thalia's voice sounded hoarse now. She couldn't be far from her limit. Patrik's stomach churned, but he managed to nod his thanks and walk calmly between the pair.

Then he was amongst the horde. He immediately realised that calling this a rave had been understating it. Half their number might be off on a wild goose chase, but the rest apparently were not perturbed by the absence. Everywhere he looked, already intoxicated goblins were sculling horns of fowl smelling liquor. And they were getting rowdy, dancing and singing to the out of tune music that was playing from…somewhere.

Basically, if he closed his eyes, the entire event could easily be mistaken for a college frat party. Except instead of 'alpha' males and plastic sorority girls, this party was filled with hideous creatures that would hack him to pieces if they learned what he really was. So, you know, maybe not *that* similar after all.

But Patrik had a mission. He waded into the press of bodies, making for the centre as quickly as he could without appearing suspicious. Thalia's screams were pitiful by now, not really screams at all. Just long, drawn out moans. He shuddered, imagining the pain she was suffering, and picked up the pace.

As he neared the pit the crowd thinned a little, and the

stench of the goblins gave way to a richer scent, almost like a chicken roasting on the barbeque…

Eww, mate, what the hell? All that complaining about eating mermaids and centaurs, and you're salivating over literal human meat?

Patrik's stomach lurched. He'd realised it at the same moment as Steve. He had to struggle just to keep from retching. Ahead the crowd parted. Patrik forced himself forward, only just stopping himself at the edge of the pit. Even from there, he could feel the heat of the fire from below. The hairs on his neck tingled. Hadn't O'Malley told him he wouldn't burn when his Constitution got high enough?

A quick look over the side solved that question. The fire was purple. The goblins had obviously enchanted it to affect individuals of higher Constitution.

Up until then, Patrik had avoided taking a closer look at Thalia. He forced himself to do so now, and almost lost his breakfast. Figuratively speaking. He hadn't stopped long enough for breakfast. Idiot. Although…he was kind of glad he had nothing left to throw up now.

Thalia…was not in great shape. The flames had burnt away most of her clothing. Beneath, her skin was burnt and blackened, even bubbling in places as the heat seared deep into her flesh. Her eyes were clenched tightly closed against the heat, but there was no masking her agony. He couldn't understand how she had endured this long. If not for the health bar —deep into the red by now—he wouldn't have believed it possible to survive such wounds. Even in this insane world.

Whatever their differences, Patrik knew he had to help her. Most of the goblins in the chamber were thoroughly intoxicated from whatever they'd been drinking, but from the corner of his eye he could see a steady stream of creatures returning from the tunnel. Apparently his pursuers had given up. Every moment he delayed, the odds of his being discovered increased. But at this moment, only one goblin seemed to be paying any attention to Thalia.

Frederick the Goblin Chef [level 20]. Unlike your

regular goblin foot soldier, Frederick grew up with a dream. A dream to be the very best chef in the land, goblin or otherwise, and win the annual Monster Chef competition. But every year, his dreams were foiled by a prominent bartender in Monmouth. Every year, that is, until now. With his competition out of the running, Frederick is ready to make his mark. One taste of his sweet apple cinnamon human, and the Four Circles will be changed forever.

Great, of course it had to be stronger than the others. He drew in a breath.

Here goes nothing.

Straightening his shoulders, Patrik wandered over to the creature manning the spit and waved a greeting.

"I think…she's had enough," he said in disjointed Pig Latin.

The goblin chef frowned, then to Patrik's absolute horror he leaned out with a bronze knife and stabbed Thalia in the leg. Her moans briefly rose to a scream as she thrashed against her bonds. Ignoring the sorceress's agony, the goblin withdrew his knife and licked the blood from the blade. Only then did the creature shake its head.

"It's still raw!" The goblin spat in their weird language. "Sorry, brother. You will have to wait a little longer. Perfection takes time!"

Patrik started to reply, then noticed the goblin was still leaning over the pit. He smiled grimly. This was his chance.

"I said she's had enough," he said again, and then doing his best impression of Leonidas of Sparta, he lurched forward and kicked the goblin chef in the back.

The goblin screamed as it toppled into the pit. A *whoosh* came from the purple flames as they swallowed him up, followed by another high-pitched scream. Stepping back from the edge, Patrik pointed at the fire, feigning shock.

"Oh no, he fell!" he cried. "Quick, get water!"

It was at this point that everything fell apart. It had *seemed* like a good plan. Push the chef into the fire, creating a distraction where everyone tried to help him, during which the human sacrifice would just happen to disappear. And it would have worked too, except…

"I did not!" The chef's agonised voice carried up from the pit. Despite its clothes being completely aflame and his plummeting health, the chef was still able to scramble at the sides of the pit, trying to climb out. "You pushed me…aaarg!"

"It's true, sir," Another of the goblins nearby remarked. "You pushed him in. I saw you."

"Did he insult your mother?" someone else asked.

"I bet he just wants all the food to himself!" a goblin with a club that looked suspiciously like the one from the entrance called out. "Bloody halfling."

"Wait, were you following me?" Patrik blurted out.

The creature just glowered at him with its slitted eyes.

Ah, lets focus less on the racial discrimination, more on the horde of goblins you've just pissed off, shall we?

"I mean, it was not I who wished to steal the food, but him!" He gestured dramatically at the goblin in the pit, who had finally stopped scrambling at the sides and succumbed to the flames.

Unfortunately, Patrik's acting was apparently far inferior to his costume design.

"Bullshit," a goblin with a scimitar shot back. The other guard from the entrance.

"Ahhhh…" Patrik hesitated. An ever-increasing number of goblins were turning in his direction.

I think the jig is up, mate. Unless…oh, is this the part of the heist where everything seems to be going wrong, but is actually all part of your cunning plan?

Steve, this is not Ocean's Eleven.

Damn. So we're really fucked then?

It would appear that way…

Backed up against the pit, Patrik looked from the flames to the goblin horde. This wasn't looking good. Still propped over the flames, Thalia gave another moan. He wasn't even sure if she was conscious at this point. He honestly hoped not. Her blackened skin was beginning to crack, revealing the still-pink flesh beneath.

A lump lodged in Patrik's throat. Thalia was dying, of that there was no doubt. And doing so in absolute agony. His heart sank as he stared at the sorceress. Another brick settled in his stomach. He knew what he had to do. There was no escaping this place. Not for him. Certainly not for Thalia.

Patrik clenched his fists. Drawing in a breath, he faced the sorceress. He would make it quick. Her health was so low, it wouldn't take much. A full powered Lightning Bolt, just to be sure, and her suffering would be over. Energy crackled between his fingers as he cast the spell. The goblins didn't seem to notice. They were still watching him though, as if expecting him to make a move for the food.

"I'm sorry, Thalia," Patrik whispered as he raised his hand. "You deserved better than this…"

He trailed off as a faint noise whispered across the cavern. A note of pure, unaltered, joyous music.

It was the sweetest sound Patrik had ever heard.

He froze in place as the crowd of goblins parted to look towards the entrance.

And there they were. Two figures stood alone in the shadow of the tunnel. One a giant, hulking brute of a man with a lute cradled to his chest. The other slim and muscular and deadly.

O'Malley and Giovanni had arrived.

Hope swelled in Patrik's chest as O'Malley strummed his lute and began to sing…

Ah, Patrik, don't forget—

Boom!

At that moment, the Lightning Bolt he'd been charging hit its thirty second threshold and exploded.

Right in his fucking hand.

CHAPTER 24
HUMAN MATING RITUALS

Hoooly crap that hurt. It was like he'd come full circle to his first day in this universe and just shoved his level 1 hand into the fire. He couldn't even look at it. All he knew was: one, he was an *idiot*. And two, he'd just shaved off an impressive chunk of his already dwindling health.

> ***I did try to warn you…***

So as the confused goblins looked from the pair of humans to the 'goblin' that had just half-exploded itself, he cycled to his hotlist and activated a potion. Warmth immediately flooded through his body, smothering his various aches and pains and snuffing out the burning in his hand.

One left.

No time to linger on that grim thought. His companions might have arrived, but there was still a cavern full of goblins to deal with. Those nearest him still flicked suspicious glances in his direction, but the arrival of two humans had apparently diverted the majority of the horde's attentions. It would take a few more minutes for O'Malley to finish his hit number. They needed a distraction.

> ***Also the sorceress is literally cooking alive, right?***

Oh shit, right…

Actually, that gave Patrik an idea. As the first strums of O'Malley's song vibrated through the chamber—which apparently had some *amazing* acoustics—Patrik stumbled sideways. Arms windmilling and crying out in dramatic fashion, he crashed into the stand that held Thalia's spitroast across the pit.

"Onaaaaaay!" he cried as the metal support tumbled over. A collective gasp came from the goblins closest to the pit, but Patrik's hand had already whipped out to catch the falling pole holding Thalia, keeping her from falling into the fire.

"Quick!" he screamed in Pig Latin, gesturing wildly at the support on the other side. "Grab it, before it burns!"

That got a reaction. No fewer than ten goblins rushed to grab the other end of the pole. In the rush, one was even knocked screaming into the fire. Patrik was pretty sure it was old spiked-club. Good riddance, the racist bastard. The others didn't seem overly bothered by his lost. The three who arrived first grabbed their end and together with Patrik lifted Thalia clear of the pit.

Hanging limp from her bonds, Thalia hadn't moved through any of this. Only when they set her down did she give a low moan to confirm her alive status. Of course, it also let the goblins know she still lived—and they were none too happy about it.

"Hey, it's not even fully cooked!"

"Practically raw. Some of us don't like our meat rare, you know."

"Good enough, I say," another muttered, raising its scimitar.

"Wait!" Patrik cried, holding out a hand towards the crea-ture. He recognised it as the second guard from the entrance.

Much to his surprise, the creature actually froze. Indecision played across its face as it looked from Patrik to the human, as though to ask: *why?* Patrik didn't really have an answer. All he knew was that he needed to stall.

"Umm…" he started, struggling for something, *anything*.

The sweet tones of O'Malley's lute carried across the cavern. He couldn't get a good look at his companions through the circle of goblins, but so far his antics had at least split their attention. The other creatures seemed to be locked in a staring contest with Giovanni, who stalked back and forth in front of the bard, naked sword in hand.

"Ah, wait, I…ah…think the human is singing you a love song!" He regretted the words as soon as they'd left his mouth.

Wait, what? Steve exclaimed.

The goblin was just as confused. "What?" it asked, scimitar still poised above Thalia.

"Ah, yeah…" Shit he had to go with it now. "You know how I'm half-human, right?" he said, ploughing on with the tale. "Well, when my human father…seduced my mother…he um, did it with a song! Yeah, a song just like this! It, ah, it means the human has come here to profess his love!"

The goblin with the scimitar stared at Patrik as though he'd completely lost his mind. Then another, one with an enormous growth coming out of its lips, spoke up.

"Wait, why would it be in love with Vladimir?" It interrupted. "I bet the human is really here because of me!"

Patrik blinked.

"You, Augustus?" the goblin with the scimitar—apparently called Vladimir—shot back. "How could it possibly love you? I heard your mother put out her own eyes rather than look at that ugly face of yours."

"You keep my mother's name out of your fucking mouth!" Leaping forward, Augustus slapped Vladimir across the face.

"Ah…"

"No, it's got to be me!" another of the creatures cried. This one was larger than the others and carried a wicked looking battle axe. "See how it has eyes only for my lovely figure."

The hell is going on here?

"Screw you, Yohanas!" Vladimir gave the new challenger a shove, sending it tumbling backwards.

"You're all wrong, it's me!" yet another decided to get involved.

Suddenly all was pandemonium as the chamber descended into a violent mosh pit. Goblins pushed and shoved one another, their drunken voices slurring in Pig Latin as each lay claim to the human lover who had come here to seduce them. Patrik could only watch on, half in horror, half in delight that his ridiculous ploy had somehow worked.

Seriously, that is…just, wow.

You said it, Steve.

Patrik held his position over Thalia as the fight began to wrap up—the scimitar wielding Vladimir coming out on top. Thankfully, by then O'Malley was just coming to the end of his song, and with a final, haunting note, the familiar stillness came over the cave.

Letting out a long breath, Patrik sank to his knees beside the sorceress and took in the chaos around him. O'Malley's spell had frozen every goblin in the cavern. Some had finally drawn swords and launched themselves at Giovanni, while others had been in the middle of stripping down to their birthday suits in an apparent effort to impress the bard. Still others at the edges of the chaos had ignored the arrival of the humans altogether and were busy getting busy with one another.

All in all, it was a hideous tableau. But somehow they'd done it. He was alive. And so was Thalia. Though considering her condition, she might wish she weren't at that moment. No matter. Once freed of her bonds, she could take a health potion and be good as new. With that in mind, Patrik summoned his iron dagger and was about to cut through the sleek black handcuffs, when a voice bellowed from across the cave.

"Ah, that's weird. One didn't freeze…" Heavy footsteps approached. "Hey there, little guy. Would you mind taking your hands from our companion?" O'Malley wore a cheerful expression on his face as his shadow fell across Patrik. "Otherwise, my friend here is going to gut you like a mermaid." The bard hesitated, before adding: "Well, truth be told, he's going to gut you anyway. Sorry about that. But I suppose he'll, ahh, gut you slowly if you do not step aside."

Giovanni, who had followed the giant, grunted his agreement.

Patrik just stared at the pair. "O'Malley, what the hell are you talking about?"

"Holy crap!" The bard screamed and leapt backwards. "That goblin can talk!"

Even the normally stoic Giovanni had a momentary lapse during which he looked absolutely shocked—though of course he still did not speak. The pair stood there and stared, dumbstruck, at Patrik. He stifled a sigh. Surely this was a joke. Or had the pair both banged their heads on the ceiling on the way in?

"Come on guys, cut the crap," he said, rising to his feet and gesturing at Thalia. "Help me with her."

"Ah…" O'Malley shuffled his feet. "I am sorry, little goblin, but we cannot let you eat our companion," he said, then paused before continuing: "Though if you don't mind my asking, what…exactly did you do to her? Those…smells…is that apple? And what is that other—"

"Ewww, O'Malley that's gross. Also stop being an idiot. It's me, Patrik."

"Patrik?" O'Malley frowned. "No, no, little goblin. Patrik wears these weird wizard's robes that are a size too big. You probably already met him. Did you eat him? Oh, I hope not. Such a bright soul. I mean, a little evil, but he was really trying to do better. I had this whole story to tell him about my parents being barbarians, and how they wanted me to be a barbarian as well, but how I changed my destiny instead…"

Patrik sighed. This was getting them nowhere. Popping open his inventory, he switched the goblin armour for his wizard's robes and breathed a sigh of relief. That breastplate had been really cutting off his circulation. And the robes were *really* comfortable.

The reaction of his companions was about what he might have expected. Not logically, of course. Just now that he was a resident of an entirely insane universe.

"Patrik!" O'Malley exclaimed, his face lightning up with joy. "Where did you come from!"

Giovanni didn't seem quite so happy. His eyes narrowed and his jaw hardened.

"Goddamnit, O'Malley, I was in disguise," Patrik sighed, then frowned as he remembered their conversation back at the inn. "Wait, what *are* you two doing here? You said only an idiot would accept this quest. Something about it being suicide…"

The pair exchanged a glance, before O'Malley shrugged. "I…cannot say I know why we followed you, Patrik," he said, his tone unusually dour. "Only…something just seemed wrong…about leaving her down here, you know?"

The reply surprised Patrik and he found himself smiling. He reached up and patted the bard on the shoulder, the same way O'Malley had the day they'd met.

"Well what do you know," he said. "Maybe we'll make an Earthling out of you yet, O'Malley."

"If you three…are quite done…with your girly little reunion," a voice like sandpaper came from the floor. "Would you mind getting these fucking handcuffs off me?"

Great. Looked like Thalia was awake. Patrik found himself suddenly regretting all the effort he'd put into rescuing the sorceress.

I did warn you.

Ignoring the disembodied voice, Patrik crouched and used his iron dagger to slice through the cuffs binding Thalia's hands. A second later, a deep, luminescent light appeared beneath her skin. Her flesh began to mend before their eyes, charred skin brightening to fleshy pink, the gushing cracks closing, even her hair regrowing to shoulder length. Patrik could only shake his head. He doubted he would ever tire of watching the effects of a health potion take hold.

As the last of the burns faded from Thalia's body, bright red silk robes appeared around her, along with a fresh pair of glasses. The familiar blue backpack—which didn't seem to have any actual use—even appeared on her back. Apparently she had a spare for everything. She cast a quick look around the chamber as she stood, before her gaze settled on Patrik.

"So you're alive," she said bluntly.

"I think what you mean to say is: 'thanks for saving me, Patrik.'" he replied with a scowl.

The sorceress gave a little snort. "As insolent as ever, I see." Her eyes narrowed. "And more evil by half, unless I am sorely mistaken. What innocent souls have you sent screaming to the void this time?"

Patrik couldn't believe it. After everything he'd risked, the odds he'd battled against to reach her, to do the right thing, and here Thalia was still judging him, still looking down her nose—figuratively, since he stood a good foot over her—at him. It was…it was too much.

"You know what—" he began, but Thalia had already turned her attention to their companions.

"And what the hell were you two thinking, coming in here?" she snapped.

"Oh, ah, umm," O'Malley obfuscated, his eyes falling to the ground. Beside him, the silent swordsman glowered, but not even he dared to meet Thalia's glare.

"Well?" Thalia growled. "Did you suddenly develop a death wish while I was absent?"

The giant flinched at the accusation, his head seeming to shrink into his shoulders. But to his credit, he managed a complete sentence this time. "You were in trouble!" His voice hardly rose above a defiant murmur.

"I see," the sorceress's voice was low now, dangerous. Her eyes did not leave the bard as she stepped in close. "It was the Earthling, wasn't it?"

"I…" the bard hung his head. "I don't know…I guess, maybe?"

"Geeze O'Malley, way to sell a guy down the river," Patrik muttered.

"I warned you this would happen, O'Malley" Thalia growled. "That he would corrupt you. But *oh no*, the pacifist had to try and *redeem* him. To make him *good.*" She rolled her eyes. "Honestly, O'Malley, you're so hopelessly naïve, it's a wonder the fae haven't lured you into the woods and eaten you yet." Teeth bared, she turned on Giovanni. "And *you!* What, just because he knows your father, you lose all perspective? What were you *thinking*—"

"Enough!" That was it. Patrik couldn't listen to the woman a second longer. He placed himself between the sorceress and the two men. "Leave O'Malley and Giovanni out of this. They were only doing what they felt was right. Seriously, what is your problem?"

The sorceress glared at him for a long moment before exhaling. "What is my problem?" she whispered. "Well, for one, your Charisma is so low that every time I look at you it takes every fibre of my being not to punch you in the face." She drew in a deep breath. "And two, is that good people seem to have a habit of dying—or disappearing—around you, Patrik."

"Oh." He swallowed. She…kind of had him there.

Shaking her head, the sorceress seemed to dismiss her own rage with a flick of her hand. Her soft blue eyes turned to the goblins, which still stood petrified all across the cavern.

"No matter," she muttered. "Fellowship…arrangements can be discussed later. For now, we have a job to do." A pair of familiar iron daggers appeared in her hands as she moved towards the nearest creatures.

Patrik sighed and was about to summon his own weapon when he noticed the goblin Thalia was approaching. It was one of the guards from the entrance, the one with the scimitar that had tried to be accepting of Patrik's supposed half-blood status. The one that had fought hardest to win O'Malley's heart. Seeing it standing there, eyes wide, scimitar still raised in triumph, helpless as the sorceress bore down on it…

Goddamnit, this wasn't right, killing like this. People or monsters, slaughtering them in cold blood, while they stood frozen by a spell, unable to even beg for their lives…

"Wait!" he cried.

Ah, Patrik, what are you doing?

It was a good question. Patrik didn't have an answer.

"Wait for what, Earthling?"

"They're not evil!" The words blurted out before he could stop them.

Thalia stopped and looked at him. "Two minutes ago they were literally cooking me alive."

Good point. "Ah…what I mean to say is, they're not just mindless beasts. They can talk and love and…well the ah… chef…he was following a recipe and everything."

Thalia stared at him for a full minute before clearing her throat. "Are you…seriously trying to convince me to spare these goblins because—let me get this straight—one of them smeared me with apple sauce before *literally cooking me alive?*"

"Well, when you put it like that…" Patrik muttered.

Thankfully, O'Malley came to his rescue. "Wait, did you say they could *talk?*" The bard's eyes were wide as his voice dropped to a whisper. "That they could *love?*"

"Yes!" Patrik exclaimed. Seizing on the narrative, he darted past Thalia and approached the goblin with the scimitar. "In fact, this creature is in love with *you,* O'Malley."

"Oh you've got to be kidding me." Thalia facepalmed. Literally.

"*Wait!*" This time it was O'Malley who spoke up. "I would…like to hear him out." He turned to Patrik. "You can truly understand them?"

Lips pursed, he nodded.

"Then prove it."

So saying, he pointed his lute in the direction of the goblin and played a few chords. As the last note struck, the creature with the scimitar sagged, shoulders slumping as its muscles were freed of the musical spell. Its head whipped around, eyes wide with panic. Patrik spoke quickly before it decided to attack.

"Do not move," he said, switching back to Pig Latin. "My friends here will not hesitate to kill you."

The creature started. Its yellowed eyes glared at Patrik before widening in recognition. "Brother," it cried. "Why have you betrayed us?"

Patrik sighed. "I was never your brother," he replied. "I

deceived you in order to rescue my…companion." He gestured towards Thalia as he spoke.

The goblin pursed its warty lips. "Loyalty amongst humans," it said slowly. "Never would I have suspected it from such a murderous race."

"Ah…sure." He didn't point out whom had been cooking whom. Instead, he turned to the others. "You see?"

The three humans stared back at him.

"What kind of nonsense was that?" the sorceress muttered.

"Sorry, Thalia," O'Malley replied with a sigh. "He must have hit his head or something. You can go ahead and kill it."

"Ah…"

Mate, I told you that wasn't a real language.

Thalia rolled her eyes. "Giovanni, would you like to do the honours?"

Grunting, Giovanni drew his sword.

"Wait, it's really a language, I swear!" Patrik held out his hands to stall the swordsman.

"Patrik, it's okay." Suddenly O'Malley was at his side. A giant hand descended on his shoulder, holding him in place. "You have a concussion, but we're going to get you the treatment you need."

"I…" Patrik trailed off as he looked into the bard's gentle face and realised nothing he said would convince O'Malley of the truth.

"They're going to kill me, aren't they?" the goblin murmured. Its slitted eyes were fixed on Giovanni's shining blade.

A lump lodged in Patrik's throat. "Yes," he said. "I'm sorry."

"Tell me," it continued, and he saw now its eyes were on O'Malley. "Did the human ever truly love me?"

Patrik swallowed. "No."

The goblin nodded, bowing its head. "So be it."

Too late, Patrik realised the goblin's intention. Of course, it was no threat to any of them. Individually. But it knew that. For rather than attack, an enormous horn carved from bone appeared in its hand. Raising it to its lips, the goblin blew long and hard.

Whoooorl!

Fuck. Patrik cringed as the last echoes of the horn died away, waiting for the united screams of the goblin horde to descend on them. That was what the horn was for, wasn't it? To break the spell over the others? How *this particular* creature just *happened* to have a horn that could free its friends from O'Malley's music, Patrik couldn't say. But since everything in this world seemed to be against him, that was surely where this was going…

Thwack!

The goblin's head made a sickly sound as it struck the ground, separated from its shoulders by Giovanni's enchanted sword. It rolled in a slow circle, leaving a sticky trail of blood on the stone floor, before finally coming to rest against Patrik's foot. He could only stand and stare at it, waiting for the other coin to drop.

Silence.

His skin crawling, Patrik drew in a long breath and forced himself to look at the ring of goblins.

The horde stared back, eyes unblinking. Not one moved an inch.

Patrik exhaled with relief. "Oh thank—"

Thud.

The ground shook and the words died in his throat.

"What the hell was that?"

The others didn't seem to have an answer. They stared back at him. Well, O'Malley and Giovanni stared. Thalia glared.

Steve? he tried the PQA.

Sorry, mate, I got nothing.

Thud.

The ground shook again, sending ripples through the pool of blood at Patrik's feet. He swallowed. That…that seemed ominously like the scene from—

Hey it's like that Jurassic Park movie!

"Oh *fuck*—" Patrik began.

Crack!

Stones flew in all directions as something *huge* burst from the cave on the other side of the cavern. Shit, Patrik had forgotten that was even there. A hideous face emerged from the shadows, beady eyes blinking in the dim light. It was followed by an enormous, hulking body. Standing at least twenty feet tall on its hind legs, the creature towered over the chamber. Hundreds of scars covered its leathery skin and long arms hung at its side, one meaty fist clutched around the haft of a massive club spiked with…

***Wow, those are actual swords in its club. That fucker is* big.**

No kidding, Steve.

Another tremor shook the cavern as the monstrous creature took a lumbering step, the club dragging behind it. Patrik hardly dared to examine the thing, but…

Tony the Cave Troll [level 29]. Oh boy, the goblins of Anchorpoint have been hiding this bad boy for a while. Locked in an enchanted sleep to prevent it from levelling out of the First Circle, this cave troll is the goblin version of a nuclear deterrent. Kill one goblin? Not a problem. Kill a dozen? Their tribe will hunt you down and cook you alive. But still mostly no problem. Threaten to wipe out their entire community? Well, now you have a troll problem. And they get 10 stat points per level increase. In case you can't do the mental math, that adds up to a case of your being *royally* fucked.

"Ah poop," Patrik groaned. "They have a cave troll."

The troll roared.

The sound rang through the chamber, echoing, reverberating until it seemed even Patrik's body shook with its power. He clamped his hands over his ears to block out the sound, but it made little difference. Clenching his teeth, he persevered until silence finally returned…

Warning! An ally's spell has been negated by

enemy's Roar of Rage. All enemies in the vicinity are no longer charmed.

Warning! Enemy's Roar of Rage has changed the status of all enemies in your vicinity. All enemies in your vicinity are now inflicted with Rage. Effects: +5 Strength, -5 Intelligence.

A fresh roar went up from around the cavern, this time as every goblin present simultaneously tore free from O'Malley's spell. Swords and daggers and clubs materialised in the hands of the creatures as a thousand slitted eyes turned on the four companions.

"Well fuck…"

CHAPTER 25
THEY HAVE A CAVE TROLL

THRUMMMMM!

A terrible, screeching note reverberated from the ceiling as O'Malley slammed a fist against his lute. Light flashed from the instrument, brilliant and burning as it swept outwards until it encompassed the four companions. A stillness fell as the screams of the goblins and the roar of the troll were abruptly cut off.

Patrik blinked, unsure whether to trust what his eyes were telling him. A crystal bowl had sprung up from nowhere, effectively cutting them off from their enemies. Outside, the goblins froze, staring in bewilderment. Then understanding dawned in their yellowed eyes and they began to pound on the barrier with their little weapons.

"Huh, just like The Simpsons Movie," Patrik muttered as he turned from the barrier to O'Malley. What other spells did the bard have tucked up his sleeve?

A dull *boom* penetrated the dome as the troll swung its club. Patrik flinched. Thankfully the blow did not penetrate, but a thousand tiny fractures sprang up around the impact site.

"It won't last long," O'Malley announced, sounding overly cheerful. "And that was my only use for the day." *Boom.* "So ah, what's the plan?" He trailed off, looking to Thalia.

The sorceress wasted a second to glower at Patrik. He had

the good sense to keep his mouth shut. Yet another *boom* echoed through the dome as the troll continued its assault. Cracks now radiated throughout the crystal barrier. It wouldn't be long before it fell. When it did, the goblins would overwhelm them with sheer numbers.

If the troll didn't flatten them first.

"Did someone say something about a plan?" Patrik asked, also looking at Thalia.

Thalia rolled her eyes. "Oh fine," she muttered. "Giovani, I'm going to need you to take care of the troll. They have a natural immunity to my magic, but when the barrier goes down, I'll cast Hasten on you. It should give you a fighting chance. Think you can handle it?"

Giovanni grunted and offered a short nod.

"Good." Thalia turned to the bard. "I'm going to be vulnerable without that speed, so we're going to need your strongest healing ballad. Can I trust you not to fuck it up?"

"You got it Thalia!" O'Malley began to strum his lute and Patrik felt an immediate tingling in the little scrapes he'd picked up pulling Thalia from the fire.

Then Thalia turned her sapphire eyes on him. "Well, Earthling? Are you with us this time, or are you going to try and hug the goblins into submission?"

Patrik supposed he deserved that. Grimacing, he summoned the iron short sword. "I'll fight," he said. "What do you want me to do?"

"Kill." Was all the sorceress said, before the world turned to chaos.

With a final blow from the troll, the dome shattered into a thousand pieces.

O'Malley began to sing.

Screaming, Thalia threw out her hands. Dark globes of light appeared in each, then went whizzing across the cavern to strike Giovanni.

For a second, two swordsmen seemed to stand where one had been a second before.

Then he vanished.

Standing dumbfounded in the centre of it all, Patrik watched in horror as a hundred goblins rushed towards them. He needed to lift his sword and fight, but he just kept staring at the spot where Giovanni had vanished. The swordsman had betrayed them, fled. Without him, the troll stood unopposed, its terrible club poised to strike—

Crack!

His head jerked up as an explosion of force rocked the cavern. Except...that wasn't an explosion. It was Giovanni. The swordsman had reappeared before the troll, his enchanted blade arcing up to meet the descending club. The force of the impact roared like thunder across the cavern, followed by the screech of breaking rock as the troll's weapon was deflected into the ground.

The creature answered with a bellow of anger. Gripping the club in two hands, it swung again at Giovanni, moving with shocking speed for its size...

...but the swordsman had already vanished again—only to reappear behind the monster's back. The troll bellowed in pain as his sword tore into its calf.

Shit. Giovanni hadn't abandoned them after all. Surrounded by that strange light cast by Thalia, he was just... moving faster than Patrik's mind could process. Like Goku versus Vegeta.

The PQA snorted. ***More like a mosquito buzzing at King Kong's ankles.***

Patrik grimaced. Steve had a point. He'd seen Giovanni decapitate bandits with a single swing of his blades, but the troll's health had hardly budged from full despite several attacks. That thing wasn't going down quickly.

Which meant he'd better get on with his own job.

He braced himself as the goblin wave crashed upon them like a tsunami, raising his sword to fend off the first attack...

...and screamed as three bronze blades of varying shapes stabbed him. One in the chest. Another in the neck. He stopped paying attention at that point. Pain swamped him, though not as bad as when Thalia had stabbed him. They were only bronze weapons, after all. He twisted to tear the weapons from his flesh, lashed out with his iron sword at the nearest goblin, then checked his health. It was already creeping back up, fed by the notes of O'Malley's song.

Well that's useful.

He and Thalia had taken up position on either side of O'Malley. Now he made it a priority to keep the creatures at arm's length from the bard. Without his music the enraged horde would cut them down in seconds, but with it…

…well they probably still didn't stand a chance.

"Come on you ugly bastards!" he bellowed to keep the fear from claiming him. He spoke again in Pig Latin so the goblins would understand. "Your mother showed more spirit in the bedroom when I fucked her last night!"

A groan came from behind him as O'Malley's song faltered. "Thalia, he's lost it again."

Patrik ignored the bard as the front row of goblins staggered, slivers of green disappearing from their health. He used the opportunity to go on the offensive, his blade arcing out to catch one goblin, then a second, off-guard. Both lost arms and most of their health, though neither went down.

Cursing, Patrik leapt back and clenched a fist. Before either could escape, he threw out his hand. Lightning arced from his fingers. It was only a weakly charged bolt, but more than enough to finish the pair as it leapt between them. Several others were also caught up in the blue fire, though these it only enraged further.

He glanced at the bodies on the floor. The others wouldn't like it, but…

He cast Raise Dead on the pair of bodies.

Groans came from the pair as they stumbled to their feet and turned to attack their former companions. But this time, enraged, the goblins showed no hesitation in falling on the pair of undead and tearing them to pieces.

Damnit, he'd hoped to gather enough of the undead warriors to push back the tide of goblins, but like the goblins themselves, the creatures were weak individually. He'd have to stick to the Lightning Bolt spell and his other skills. Maybe he could start setting the goblins on fire somehow.

Another wave of the hideous creatures surged forward, weapons stabbing for Patrik's flesh. Trusting in O'Malley's spell, he didn't even bother deflecting the attacks. Instead, he hacked at the goblins, shearing through bone and slicing off limbs with each swing of his iron blade.

Within seconds Patrik was drenched head to foot in goblin blood, but still he waded into the horde, throwing out offhand insults and Lightning Bolts as he fought to keep his enemies off-balance. His mana bottomed out and he drained his only mana potion without hesitation. Expensive or not, he couldn't take it with him if he died. Tireless, he retreated only occasionally to give O'Malley's music a chance to catch up with his healing.

Behind him, Thalia battled with controlled fury. Fire lit her daggers as she cast her fire spell on the weapons, fuelling additional damage to her strikes. Despite the weakness of the goblins, they did not fall to single blows from the sorceress, but rather succumbed in groups over several minutes as she wore them down. In fact, most died screaming in agony from their burns, something Patrik couldn't help but think was by design, after what the woman had suffered.

Even so, the absence of Giovanni and her Haste spell was telling. Patrik assumed most of her stat assignments had been to Intelligence, Dexterity, and Constitution, with some Charisma—for some reason—on the side. Her part in combat was to use her speed and magic to distract and harass the enemy, while the swordsman dealt the real damage. It had been a devastating combination against the highwaymen.

Here, forced to defend the bard and deprived of her movement spell, Thalia was rendered vulnerable. Patrik tried his best to fill the absence left by the swordsman, but he was proving to be a poor substitute. There were just too many of the enemy, and not enough swords on their side. He tried casting the Raise Dead spell again, but the results were no different. And his mana was running low again already.

Minutes stretched out as the fellowship fought their desperate battle, goblin after goblin falling to their blades. For a time, Patrik lost himself in the melee, in the thunder of blood in his ears, the pounding of adrenaline in his veins. He'd never been a fighter, never had any desire to partake in boxing or martial arts or anything more strenuous than a swim race. But now, in the heat of battle and freed of any philosophical questions, he found himself awash in a kind of ecstasy, in the rush of testing himself against the hatred of the world—

Thalia's Haste spell ran out.

Giovanni staggered as his overworked legs suddenly became like lead—just in time to catch a blow by the troll's club directly in the chest. The impact tore his health in half and sent him hurtling across the chamber. To his good fortune, he landed directly amongst his companions. Less to Thalia and Patrik's good fortune, his fall was broken by the hulking figure of O'Malley.

And as the bard's music fell silent, so too did the healing magic of his song.

Whelp, we're fucked.

Patrik looked around. The goblins, despite their best efforts, were still everywhere. Giovanni was down, half his chest torn open by one of the spikes on the troll's club. O'Malley lay beside him, unconscious. Only Thalia still stood. She was battling like a maniac to keep from being overrun— but even she was fading without the bard's magic.

Then there was the troll. Its battle with Giovanni had carried it to the other side of the cavern, but now it approached. One thumping footstep after another.

"Any ideas?" he asked, deflecting a goblin blade before decapitating its owner.

Well…just the one. Use that Scroll of Inferno you've got tucked away to burn a path through the goblins and make a run for it.

Patrik stilled. Yes, that could work, except…

"I don't think the others are going to be able to run, Steve," he whispered.

Even as he watched, a goblin snuck up on Thalia and sank its teeth into her calf—having apparently remembered she was their designated meal for the day. A slash of her dagger killed the creature, but she limped away from the encounter. He assumed she had no more health potions, as her health was already well into the orange. Patrik still had one, but…

I didn't say anything about the others, mate, the PQA's voice was unusually solemn.

Patrik swallowed. "Right."

He glanced at the exit. A hundred goblins separated him from the tunnel, but…he could make it. If the scroll was as powerful as the PQA claimed, it would carve a path through the goblins. He could down the health potion and make a break for it with a fresh burst of energy…

…and leave the others to certain death.

Good people seem to have a habit of dying—or disappearing—around you, Patrik.

He shivered as the words of the sorceress echoed in his mind. Shit, Thalia had been right. If he hadn't insisted on coming down here, on trying to save her, O'Malley and Giovanni would have never been drawn into this mess.

They were going to die because of him.

He couldn't let that happen. Not again. Not after Chris…

He turned towards the troll.

Wait, what the hell are you doing? Didn't you hear the bloody sorceress? It's resistant to magic!

"You're saying it won't hurt it?"

Well no. It'll hurt the big bastard. Might even get its health into the red, if you're lucky. But it won't die. Then you're out of options. There ain't no plan C this time.

"Okay, Steve," Patrik whispered.

His eyes didn't leave the troll. Stepping over the unconscious swordsman, he pulled up his hotlist and found the Scroll of Inferno.

Please, mate, the PQA's voice was a whisper now. **I'd**

rather not die again. I just got a lava lamp set up in here.

"I thought a PQA couldn't die."

ERROR: Information not found.

Patrik let out a long breath. He could worry about the mortality of the disembodied voice living in his head later. If he survived. He continued towards the troll. It had seen him now. Mouth stretched wide, it roared in rage. A wave of putrid air swept over Patrik as he stared into the maw of death. He gagged, vision blurred with tears. By God, or Fate, or whatever force ruled this cursed land, that was foul.

It was time to end this. Breathing through his mouth—since taste is the weakest of the senses—he set the troll in his sights. The Scroll of Inferno hung before his eyes. One click was all it would take—

Crack!

Overhead, the ceiling exploded into a thousand pieces as a column of pure, blinding light descended into the chamber. It slammed into the troll, scorching its leathery skin and hurling it backwards. Thunder rumbled from the walls as the beast screamed.

The light flickered and began to fade. A silhouette appeared amidst the white, drifting down to alight on the cavern floor. Patrik squinted, trying to make out the person within the column. Who could it be?

"Holy shit!" O'Malley staggered to his feet, shaking his head and clutching his lute to his chest. "What the hell is a Deus Ex Machina doing here?"

"A what?"

The bard frowned. "A Deus Ex Machina. You know, an elven warrior? Bastards are always arriving at the last moment to steal all the experience for themselves."

CHAPTER 26
MERITH OF IRLEGROTH

MERITH, ELVEN PRINCESS AND HEIR TO THE THRONE OF Irlegroth, had been preparing for battle when Tenser the Great's summons had found her. This was no surprise. Ever the dutiful daughter, most of her time in the First Circle had been spent fighting or preparing to fight the forces of darkness. Lead by the demon prince Rhian—youngest son of the Dark Lord Malus—armies of orcs and goblins and the occasional troll were a constant threat on the southern border. She had even crossed blades with the demon prince himself on any number of occasions, though of course their encounters always ended in stalemate.

Such was the way of things in the Four Circles. A delicate balance hung between the forces of good and evil. It had been that way for centuries, especially here, in the First Circle. Every year, an army of some vile creature or another would descend from the mountains to fall upon Tunstead or Solime or Furness or Tergaron. And every year the forces of good would muster against them.

Decade after decade, good men and women gave their lives for the cause, while those lucky few who survived levelled up and advanced to the Second Circle.

So it was that the status quo was maintained.

And if not…well, the Dark Lord would look poorly upon any who tried to shift that balance.

For ten long, tedious years, this had been Merith's life. Ever since reaching elven maturity in her sixtieth year, she had led the battle against the forces of darkness. Unlike other races, as an elf she had begun her journey to power with an expanded suite of six magical spell slots. That alone made her a powerful operator in the First Circle, where magic was limited. Once the ten stat points she received per level were added, her kind became an unstoppable force against all but the most powerful of First Circle inhabitants.

Counted against this was their slow rate of advancement. In her ten years in the First Circle, Merith had watched many human warriors come and go. None would ever be her match, and yet still the speed of their advancement carried them onwards to greater battles in the Second Circle. And all the while she remained, locked in never ending battle with the Demon Prince Rhian.

She wondered at times whether Rhian felt the same tedium. If he too longed for the day he crossed the threshold to level 30 and could leave behind this meatgrinder of a circle for brighter pastures.

Only one thing had kept the young elf from losing her mind these past ten years. One dark, forbidden secret.

Her liaisons with Kabir the Bright, the human prince of Bledross. Their love had been a rare joy in an otherwise dull decade of endless war. If only their affair had not been so fleeting. The young human had taken only three years to advance to the limits of the First Circle. A year ago, they had bid one another farewell in secret, and promised to meet again in the Second Circle.

For that next year, every day, every hour, every minute had seemed an eternity for the young Merith as she crept towards the ever-distant level 30 that would finally free her from this place.

So it was with mixed emotions that Tenser's summons found her on the day she was to finally advance. Yet she had sensed the urgency in the wizard's message, cast magically across the long miles.

Merith of Irlegroth, the time has come. I have found a secret weapon against the Dark Lord's power, a Chosen One who can twist the threads of Fate. But he must have help. I cannot protect him in this Circle —but you can, Princess of the Elves. Look for me in the Enchanted Forest, and together we will herald a new dawn for the forces of good.

Merith had been loath to abandon the coming battle. Over the past days, her forces had been steadily pushing the orc horde back towards the mountains. And she was so close now to passing the threshold to level 30, to liberation…

But Tenser's words had ignited something deep within her. The part that railed against the Dark Lord's so-called 'equilibrium'. The piece of her that yearned to be unleashed, to tear through the enemy forces with reckless abandon and banish them forever from the promised lands.

So she had withdrawn, vanishing from Solime and riding for the Enchanted Forest as swiftly as her horse would carry her. But within a day, the beast pulled up lame. The commoners of these lands, forbidden from riding, had no use for horses and so lacked workers who could have healed the beast.

She had traversed the remaining distance by foot. Arriving late, she had stumbled upon a scene of devastation. The town of Monmouth, razed. Tenser the Great slain, his body abandoned in the woods. The irreplaceable Giant Silk Spiders, wiped out.

Horrified, Merith had searched for some connection to Malus or his demonic prince, but there was no trace of their evil fingerprints about this calamity. A stench of dark magic hung over the town, but nothing so powerful to suggest demonic interference.

Finally, she had come upon a trail leading towards the coast and followed it into the forest. There she encountered more death, though now the victims were those of negative

Alignment. Bandits and highwaymen had been slaughtered, the forest cleansed of their dark infection.

Her confusion greater than ever, the elven princes continued on the trail, tracking her quarry at last to the seaside town of Anchorpoint.

Only there did she finally hear whispers of the man called Patrik. Enemy of the Dark Lord. The Chosen One.

But again she arrived too late. The villagers claimed he had left just that morning with his companions, determined to eradicate the occupants of a nearby goblin cave. Few had high hopes for their return.

So it was that Merith found herself venturing into the darkness in the forlorn hope of saving Tenser's Chosen One before the goblins tore him to pieces. She had not expected to arrive in time, but knew the effort had to be made.

And yet…she was not so deep into the cave before she sensed the disturbance below, a tremor as something evil woke.

A Champion of the Dark had appeared.

There was no time to spare. No human could stand against a Champion. Not in this Circle, where only the most powerful counted amongst their rank. So Merith cast her spell of last resort—Transcendent Light. Carving through rock and stone, she arrived in the underground chamber as a beam of enormous power.

Her heightened senses assessed the situation in a fraction of a second. Battle raged in the centre of the cavern, a handful of humans against an untold number of goblins.

And in the centre of it all, the troll.

Merith acted instantly. Directing her spell against the enemy Champion, she hurled it back from the Chosen One and his allies.

And the battle was engaged.

Merith of Irlegroth [level 29]. Elven Princess of Irlegroth, Merith has led the forces of good in the First

Circle for nigh a decade. Her exploits are legendary and her prowess with magic and the blade unmatched. You definitely want to stay on this chick's good side.

"Well, not all the experience of course," O'Malley continued. "We should get a decent share for holding it off all that time. And given we were about to die and all, I suppose it's not such a bad thing she showed up. This time."

Patrik was hardly listening to the bard. He watched, mouth agog, as cave troll and elven princess came together with a *boom* that shook the ground beneath their feet. Blazing light still lit the elf, setting her elegantly crafted armour aflame. The iron plate mail covered her from head to foot, but she didn't move like she was weighed down at all.

In fact, her movements had already become a blur, though the elven princess showed no sign of the magic that had accelerated Giovanni to such awesome speeds. If she had dumped all her stat points into Dexterity, Merith didn't show it, as she blocked a swing of the troll's club with an enormous two-handed blade. Before he could even blink, the elf reversed her swing and struck a blow against the troll that had it lurching backwards across the cave. A dozen goblins were trampled under its massive feet before it recovered.

Standing nearby, Thalia grunted. "Bloody elves and their bonus stats."

"Elves get ten stat points for each level they gain," O'Malley elaborated. "And there's the extra spells on top of that."

Patrik nodded his understanding, then cast a glance at their other foes. The goblins had backed off for now, apparently waiting for the battle between the two titans to be decided before making their next move.

Letting out a long breath, he turned his attention back to the epic battle. "Then…we're saved?"

"It would seem that way," Thalia muttered. She didn't seem overly thrilled about it.

"Oh come on, Thalia!" O'Malley exclaimed. "It's not often you get to see a Warrior of the Light in action!"

The sorceress scowled. Crossing her arms, she blew a whisp of hair from her face and glowered in the general direction of the fight.

Leaning in close, the bard said to Patrik: "Don't mind her. She wants to be a Warrior of the Light as well, but us humans don't really become strong enough until the Second Circle."

"Such a shame…" Patrik murmured sarcastically. "Can't think of anyone more deserving…"

Another explosion rocked the cavern as the elven blade met the troll's club. Energies rippled outwards, darkness and light clashing above the heads of the two combatants before fading. The elven princess leapt back from her foe and grinned. Her health had fallen a little, but remained solidly in the green, while the troll's bar was steadily falling through the orange. A voice rang from within the elven helmet.

"Surrender now, my wee friend, and I'll let you die quick."

The troll roared back something unintelligible. Or, well nothing that sounded like words to Patrik, at least. Maybe they really were unintelligible creatures. You know, unlike the goblins or mermaids or god only knew what else that people here claimed were unintelligent.

It didn't have to be intelligible for the elven princess to understand the answer.

"Oh fine," she replied. "We'd best get this over with then."

And the battle was resumed.

Ten terrifying, explosive, epic minutes later, the cave troll gave a final roar of defiance. It had gotten in a few good blows, finally dropping the elf's health into orange. But only a sliver remained of its own health. Raising its enormous club high, it made one final, desperate attempt to crush the powerhouse of a creature before it.

But the elven princess would not be caught off-guard this late in the game.

Her shining blade arced up to meet the club. With a terrible *crack*, it sheared through wood and iron, tearing the troll's weapon in two before sweeping on to bury itself in the heart of the vile creature. A last, desperate moan whispered from the troll as it slumped to its knees, its health bar vanishing…

Quest Complete: Clear the Goblin Cave. Congratulations! The Champion of Darkness employed by the goblins has been defeated and the rest of the clan is now fleeing for their lives. Reward: 5000 gold. [+500 Alignment] [Bonus: Rescue the Sorceress. Congratulations! Thalia the Sorceress has been successfully rescued from the goblin cave. Reward: 1000 gold [+200 Alignment]]

Congratulations! Your skill 'Hack and Slash' has increased to level 6!

Congratulations! Your skill 'Vicious Mockery' has increased to level 4!

Congratulations! Your spell 'Lightning Bolt' has increased to level 4!

Congratulations! Your spell 'Raise Dead' has increased to level 8!

Ring! Ring! Ring!! Congratulations. You have reached level 21, 22, 23! You have been awarded 9 stat points. You have 9 stat points to assign.

Wow, that was a lot of—

Thwack!

Blinded by the stat boxes, Patrik didn't see the broken half of the troll's club as it tumbled through the air. At least, not in time to avoid it turning him from fascinated bystander to collateral damage as it slammed into him with the force of a charging rhinoceros.

Ah, shit, mate. Did not see that coming…

Oh god. Suddenly everything hurt. Really, really bad. This was no iron dagger in the guts. It felt like he'd been stabbed a dozen times—and the blades were still inside. A weight was pressing down on him, robbing him of breath, but his supernatural Strength had abandoned him. All was darkness, except…

You know, that was a pretty accurate metaphor,

mate, there was a desperate edge to Steve's voice. ***A rhino's charge contains 345...***

A spark of white appeared, growing slowly, pressing back the black, and a voice whispered to him, as though from a distance...

Sorry, little bro. Not your time...

Patrik screamed as the weight vanished and the blades were torn from his chest. Red exploded across his vision, a flashing, brilliant red that came from his plunging health bar...

A flood of energy swept into him, bringing with it a wonderful warmth, pushing back the agony. He gasped, his body jerking upright. It was like someone had just given him a shot of adrenaline. Heart racing, he looked at his health. It remained in the red, but the downwards momentum had been halted.

Blood still pounding in his ears, Patrik finally sucked in a breath. Air rushed into his lungs. It tasted like a cold IPA after a long day of study. He blinked, his vision returning, and found himself looking up into the face of his saviour...

"What the hell?"

Patrik blurted out the words before he could stop himself. He also couldn't stop himself from staring. The elven princess stood over him, hand still outstretched and glowing from the healing spell she had cast on him. She had removed her helm now and, well, she was not what he'd expected. Certainly not after witnessing her defeat an unstoppable troll and set a horde of goblins fleeing. Curly silver hair spilled down around her iron-plated shoulders, and a warm smile lit up her face.

Her very, very wrinkled face.

Seriously. It was like the spirit of Betty White—bless her memory—had come to his rescue. In a full suit of plate mail armour. And with a blazing sword of light.

"Ahhhhh..." he continued, searching for something—anything—to say.

The old woman smiled. "I am Merith of Irlegroth. And I have been looking for you, Patrik the Chosen One. Tenser the Great pled for me to join him in the Enchanted Forest, but alas my steed was injured and I was delayed. I have been tracking you ever since. Thank the Forbidden Gods that I arrived in time."

"Ahhh…" Still nothing. Shit. "Ahhh, did you say you could ride a horse?" Yeah. That was something. Focus on that. Not the fact the supposed "princess" looked to be about a hundred. "Could you teach me?"

What the hell, Steve? I thought you said she was a princess!

She is a princess. She's also seventy years old, mate. What were you expecting?

The elven princess smiled, and her cheeks broke into a thousand wrinkled lines. It was all very…grandmotherly.

"Of course, Patrik. You are the Chosen One. I will teach you to ride, and so much more."

Under different circumstances, Patrik would have been incredibly excited by that news. But staring at the old lady who'd just saved his life, all he could think was…

She's an elf, Steve. Doesn't that mean…

…they live a very, very long time. Yeah. Her parents are like, a five hundred years old.

Wait, wait, wait, so they live forever but, what, they just keep aging?

Exactly! Well, not quite forever. They can die. And I assume they're pretty much just big white prunes by the time they hit a thousand.

That's insane.

No one escapes the grips of time, Patrik.

Right…

He swallowed. By now the elf's smile had been replaced by a frown. Well, this wasn't *quite* the strangest thing Patrik had encountered in the Four Circles…today. Best get on with things. Forcing a smile, he reached up and took her offered hand. She hoisted him to his feet without any apparent effort.

At which point, Patrik's body reminded him that her healing magic had only staved off death. His health remained well and truly in the red. Agony enfolded him in its by-now-familiar arms, his vision turning red. Gasping, he doubled over.

"Are you alright, Chosen One?" Merith asked, her face

wrinkling somehow even more with concern. And age. Mostly it was just the age.

"Yes," he gasped. Putting on a brave face, he forced himself to straighten. "Just…give me a moment…I'll be better once I heal…"

Barely able to see through the stars in his eyes, Patrik pulled open his hotlist and clicked.

Wait—

Whooosh!

CHAPTER 27
I DON'T NEED ANY OF YOU

WHOOOOSH!

Heat washed across Patrik's face, followed by a muffled *boom*. He staggered, aghast, as a *tidal wave* of fire exploded from his hands. Red hot and terrible, it engulfed the elven princess —and half the chamber. Boiling flames filled the cavern with their roaring, all-consuming brilliance.

But even above that roar, you could hear the screams.

Awful, awful screams.

They echoed from the walls, one long, drawn out wail of agony, of unbearable pain. Amongst the inferno, the silhouette of the princess could be seen, limbs thrashing wildly to some unknown dance. She must have had some incredible Constitution or a lifesaving power, for surely the flames would have killed even a being as powerful as Merith instantly. Which was unfortunate for the elven princess, as this spell was no ordinary fireball. It was more like napalm, for even as the heat died down, the flames clung to her body like glue. Burning. Consuming.

Patrik watched, helpless, as the elven princess fell to the floor. Her clothes were gone, her flesh blackened and melting, and still she screamed.

And screamed.

And screamed.

Until a final, horrible silence fell across the dark chamber.

Achievement Unlocked! Giant Slayer II. Congratulations! Wow, did you really go out and kill *another* combatant who exceeded the level requirements of your current circle? Look at the balls on you. Reward: 1000 gold.

Achievement Unlocked! Princess Slayer. Congratulations! You've gone full dark side and killed an elven princess. There's bound to be untold consequences for this action. Probably gone and started a race war or something. But what do you care? You're evil! Oh, I should probably mention the elven king has been notified of his daughter's death. Good luck, champ. Reward: 5000 gold [-1000 Alignment].

Achievement Unlocked: Serial Killer. Mate, you killed another of your friends? Seriously, who are the dumbasses that still trust you at this point? I mean, given your track record, this is really on them now, isn't it? Reward: 500 gold. [-1000 Alignment Points]

Ring! Ring! Ring!! Congratulations. You have reached level 24...27! You have been awarded 12 stat points. You have 21 stat points to assign.

Patrik stared in open-mouthed horror at the scorched ground in front of him—and the still body of the elven princess. The princess that had just saved his life. That had saved all of them. Words...words did not begin...

Maaaaaaaaate...

"Don't..." Patrik whispered.

As the heat died away, he felt again the agony of his wounds and instinctively activated the health potion he'd meant to use earlier. Its healing warmth washed away the pain. If only it could do the same for his conscience.

Yeah, but seriously, mate...

Patrik closed his eyes. "I know."

Footsteps approached. His eyes snapped open. His companions, thankfully, had been standing behind him when…when he'd misfired. Drawing in a breath, he turned to explain—

Slap!

He reeled back as Thalia struck him across the face. Strangely, it didn't hurt, but the shock still left him standing there clutching at his cheek. He gaped at the diminutive sorceress, unable to form a response.

"Do you have any idea how much Alignment you just cost me?" she hissed. Her eyes were bright, her teeth bared, her pupils dilated. "I knew we should have killed you when we had the chance."

"Please, let me explain, I didn't mean—"

"To kill a Warrior of the Light?" Thalia snorted. "Sure, you just hid a scroll of incredible power, biding your time, waiting for the right moment—only to use it by accident, right?"

"Ah…" Patrik scratched his head. "Kind of?"

The sorceress rolled her eyes. "Sure, and I fart candy and rainbows." Hands on her hips, she glared up at him. "I knew you couldn't change."

"I…" He bowed his head. "I'm sorry." What more could he say?

"Earthlings," Thalia muttered. She swallowed, tongue darting out to lick her lips. "Arg, I just want you to take me behind that boulder over there and have your way with me, bad boy…" She trailed off, then suddenly raised her fist. Patrik flinched, but this time, the sorceress slapped herself across the face. "No!" she snapped. "Bad girl!" She glared at him. "Goodbye, Patrik the Chosen One. I hope you get what's coming to you."

Drawing herself up, the diminutive sorceress gave him one last glare, then stalked across to the tunnel entrance and disappeared into the darkness. There was no sign of the goblins, having apparently all fled when the troll died.

Patrik stared after the sorceress, somewhat shocked she hadn't tried to kill him.

With all that fighting and the troll and I think they

even got some of the credit for the elven princess, since you were technically fighting together... Steve trailed off. *She's level thirty now. They all are. None of them can touch you in this Circle.*

The next set of footsteps to approach were Giovanni's. The silent swordsman paused before Patrik, hard eyes glinting in the dim light. Patrik swallowed, unable to meet his gaze.

"My father is dead, isn't he?"

Patrik flinched. The words were so sudden, so softly spoken and unexpected...he knew he could not lie. Not this time.

"Yes," he said, "it was—" He tried to explain, but the swordsman cut him off.

"—an accident," Giovanni surmised. His lips drew into a thin line, but otherwise his face showed no emotion. "Lot of fatal accidents happen around you, don't they, Earthling?"

Man has a point.

Patrik's mouth was suddenly parched. Again, he had no answer.

Giovanni nodded. "Let it be known," he rasped, "that I swear a new vow of silence. When next I speak, your corpse shall lie at my feet, Earthling."

Yeah, that seems about right.

Patrik held his silence as the swordsman walked away, eyes fixed to the floor.

He didn't want to face his last accuser. The only one who had believed in him, to have treated him like a person.

Heavy boots crunched in the rubble.

Drawing in a breath, he lifted his head to look O'Malley in the eye.

But the bard walked straight past, his gaze fixed deliberately on his departing companions. Patrik's heart lodged in his throat. He tried and failed to call the giant bard back, to explain. Lute clutched in one hand, his powerful body taut with anger, O'Malley strode towards the exit.

"O'Malley," Patrik rasped, finally finding his voice as the man stepped into the shadows. "O'Malley, wait, please, let me explain."

The bard's stride faltered. Patrik stared at the man's massive back, watched his head dip slightly. For the briefest of seconds, he thought his friend might listen, might be willing to forgive…

"No, Patrik," the bard said, casting a glance over his shoulder. "No, not this time."

Attention: You have been booted from the fellowship of Thalia the Sorceress. Feats and experience will no longer be shared.

Something ignited inside Patrik as he watched the bard turn away. A spark of anger. No, more than that. Rage. Rage at this place, at everything he had suffered since being dragged through that cursed portal.

"Go on then!" he screamed after his departing companions. "Leave! That's what everyone does anyway!"

O'Malley did not look back. Patrik watched as the giant bard disappeared into the shadows of the tunnel.

Then he was alone.

"I don't need you," he whispered, anger vanishing as quickly as it had come. "I don't need anyone."

Silence.

Don't worry, mate, you still got me! Steve chirped up, then after a long pause: ***Also, since you seem to be forgetting…***

Would you like to loot the body of Merith of Irlegroth?

Patrick closed his eyes. "Seriously?"

What? I'm just saying, the chick is dead. No point leaving all that precious, precious loot on her corpse for the goblins to find.

"Whatever," he whispered weakly. "Do it."

Oooh, holy crap, mate, check out some of this stuff, wow, is that really…

Patrik tuned out the PQA with an effort of will. Items flashed across his menu, but he ignored them as well. Sinking to his knees, he hung his head. His eyes burned. There was no one to see him now. The tears started as a trickle, then became a fountain as the dam burst. He sobbed. Proper, heaving sobs that shook his entire body. A good, kindly old woman was dead. Because of him.

And now he was alone. His friends had abandoned him. He couldn't even blame them. What else could they have done?

Patrik's head jerked up abruptly. What was that? He glared at the empty chamber through blurry eyes. That sound…it was so out of place, it took him longer than it should have to identify it. Applause. Someone was *clapping*.

"What the hell?"

He pushed himself to his feet, searching the cave for the source, and glimpsed someone watching him from the hole in the ceiling.

"*Who* the hell…"

Laughter rained down from above as his observer realised they'd been spotted. A flash of…darkness, somehow, followed. Then a dark-cloaked figure was alighting on the ground in front of him. Long robes swirled about the newcomer as they straightened, before reaching up to throw off their hood…

"Ahhh!" Crying out, Patrik scrambled back.

It was a *demon*. Just his goddamn luck. Sure, it took the form of a shapely young woman who barely came up to Patrik's shoulders, but what did size matter in this world? There was certainly no mistaking the creature's demonic presence. Two scarlet horns sprouted from her forehead and the eyes that watched him were pure, unadulterated darkness. Then there was her skin, which was a very unnatural pink. Already dreading what he would read, Patrik pulled up the creature's description.

Dolzeroth the Destroyer [level 28]. The youngest child of the Dark Lord and demonic princess of the First Circle, Dolzeroth is kind of the black sheep of the family. Much as she tries, poor old Dolzeroth has never been able to match the dark deeds of her brothers. Inevitably, her attempts at evil go awry, or worse, end up helping others. She lives for the day when one

of her dastardly schemes finally makes her father proud.

Well that didn't sound good.

"Ah, look, Dolzeroth—"

"Dolly," the creature interrupted.

"Right, Dolly…wait, what?"

"Yeah!" The demon bobbed her head up and down. "It's kinda my nickname!"

"Ah…"

"I know, I know." She wrinkled her nose. "Rhian is always telling me it's not very demonic." Her eyes brightened. "But I like it! And I read in a book that you should celebrate the things that bring you joy."

"Sure…"

Dolly—or the demon, or Dolzeroth, whatever she was exactly—ignored him. Instead she began whistling a merry little tune and she skipped over to the blackened patch of ground his spell had left. Stretching out a foot, she gently nudged the body of Merith with her toes—then leapt back as though afraid of being bitten. Or smote, or whatever bad things an elf could do to a demon.

Nothing happened. Obviously. Merith was basically a lump of charcoal in human shape by this point. Which seemed to give Dolly no end of delight.

"Oh, that's so neat!" she exclaimed, bouncing up and down and clapping her hands. "You actually did it! So cool. So evil! You really have to show me how!"

"Ahhhh…" *Steve?*

Seriously, I have no idea what the hell is going on here, mate.

Helpful as usual, Patrik muttered.

He stared as the creature in the young woman's body finally settled down. Could this really be…a demon of pure darkness? A daughter of the Dark Lord, sworn to unleash death and destruction upon this world? If that was the case, why hadn't she tried to tear him apart already?

"Like, can I get your autograph or something?" the demon

continued. "I bet you're going places. Like, it'll be worth a fortune in a few years, I just know it!"

"Okay, seriously, am I being punk'd right now?"

Mate, even in your world, the audience is way too young to get that reference.

"I don't care—*holy shit!*"

A *tail* had just risen over the creature's shoulder. A gods-honest-truth, devil style arrow-head tail that swayed back and forth like a snake. The young woman—demon—paid it no attention.

"You…you have a tail," he stuttered, somewhat stupidly.

Very stupidly.

Fuck off, Steve.

"Yeah! Cool, isn't it?" Dolly's tail rose higher and seemed to give a little wave. Then she sighed, her lips twisting into a pout. "But its inherited, so Daddy says I haven't really *earned* it yet."

"I…ah, I'm sure that's not true." Patrik said quickly, deciding it best to keep the demon princess in a good mood. God, he was *not* cut out for this. The stress was eating him alive. He ran a hand through his hair—

And froze. His hand had encountered something…something that should *not* have been there.

There was a lump, just above his hair line. Which was definitely not receding. Two lumps, actually, he realised as he encountered another. What the hell was this? Cysts? Some form of growth? *Cancer?* His heart began to palpitate. Had the portal, or the crazy magic infecting his body, done something to his cells? Was that really the reason he had a voice in his head? Was this *all* just a manifestation of some induced psychosis…

Geeze, carried away much? Chill out. They're just your horns.

Patrik blinked. "My…horns?"

"Wait, you have horns? *No way!*" Dolly interrupted. Before the PQA could reply—or Patrik could avoid her—she bounded forward, grabbed him by the head, and forcibly pulled him down so she could inspect his skull. "*You do!*" she exclaimed. "That's so amazing. I mean, not as good as *mine*, but again, inherited."

Patrik stumbled as the demon released him just as abruptly as she'd grabbed him. His hands went to his head again. He prodded one of the lumps with a finger. It was hard. There was definitely bone beneath the skin.

Horns.

For some reason, that did nothing to ease his panic.

"Seriously, Steve, why the *fuck* are horns growing out of my forehead?"

It's, ah…you know waaay back in Monmouth when we talked about your Alignment, and it…affecting your appearance?

"Yes," Patrik grated through clenched teeth.

Well, yeah, so it would appear your Alignment is so ah…bad that, well you're beginning to manifest demon horns!

"Why the…" Patrik drew in a breath. "You know what, Steve?"

Fuck me?

"Yeah, fuck you, buddy." He sighed. He would worry about the horns later. Somehow, he had bigger concerns just now than horns growing out of his head. He shouldn't really be surprised by now.

"So, Dolzeroth—"

"Dolly," the demonic daughter of the Dark Lord corrected.

Patrik just stared at her for a moment. Then he drew in a deep breath. "Okay, *Dolly*, umm…" He decided to come right out and just say it. "Are you here to kill me then?" She'd no doubt read his description about slaying the Dark Lord, so it served to reason…

"What? No silly!" Dolly exclaimed. "Why would you think that?"

"Ah, I dunno, because your father is the freakin' *Dark Lord?*" Patrik exclaimed.

"Oh, don't worry about *that*," the demon said, waving a

hand. "He doesn't know I'm here. My brother told me I couldn't come, but I said to myself, now, if I really want to learn how to be evil, *that* dude sounds like he knows how to be evil, maybe he can teach me. So I snuck out, and here I am!"

"Your…brother?" Patrik asked after a long pause.

"Yeah!" Dolly bounced up and down again. "*He's* the one you really need to worry about. Rhian commands the forces of darkness in the First Circle. Usually he only really fights Merith, but not anymore!" She looked at the elf's body and giggled. "I suppose he's going to be pretty upset though. About you destroying the balance in his territory and all." The smile faded from her face. "Yeah, he's going to be *really* pissed actually."

"Great," Patrik muttered. "That's just great. How does he know about me?"

The demon girl shrugged. "Something about a trail of death and destruction?" She waved a hand. "Who really cares? What *I* want to know is your fiendish plan to deal with him!"

"Ah, what?"

"The cunning trap you've laid for Rhian!" Dolly said the words like they were a statement of fact. "You know, for when he arrives in a few minutes?"

"*What?*"

"Yeah! I probably shouldn't let him see me, but when you're done, I'd really like to talk some more about your evil feats. Seriously, I don't think anyone has caused this much of a stir in the First Circle for *at least* a century!" She sighed somewhat dramatically. "But anyway, I'll see you after…" She started to turn away.

"*Wait!*" Patrik snatched at the demon girl's hand. "Please, just wait a second…I need…a moment…to think…"

His breaths came in short gasps as he fought the onset of panic. And failed. He was halfway to a full-on panic attack when the demon put a hand on his shoulder.

"Are you okay?" She asked, a frown twisting her scarlet face.

"Not…really…" he panted.

If the past few weeks had taught Patrik anything, it was that he was *not* cut out for this. But he could wallow in self-pity later. Right now, certain death was approaching and his only hope was to convince a demonic princess to help him. He didn't like his odds.

"Dolly," he said, struggling to keep his voice steady, "I don't suppose…your brothers have a secret weakness?" Sometimes the boss in a video game had flaws you could exploit. He remembered that much at least.

"Nope," she replied happily. "Daddy makes sure we're all perfect in every way. Well, except me." Her face fell. "I'm his greatest disappointment."

That was something. He seized it with both hands. "Well, maybe we can poke your father in the eye today."

"Oh, that wouldn't be a good idea. His eyes shoot fire."

"Sorry, that's just an expression from my world. What I meant to say was, if you help me, we can show your father—and your brother—that you're not entirely useless."

Dolly's lips pursed in thought. "What did you have in mind?"

"Well if we were to escape together…"

"Hmm, that doesn't sound very evil to me."

"No, the evil part would come later," Patrik said quickly. "In fact, after we thwart your brother, I swear to teach you all I know about the art of being evil." *Which is nothing…* he added silently.

You sure about this, mate?

Patrik ignored the PQA.

"Ooh yes, yes, please!" Dolly exclaimed. She clasped Patrik by the arms and spun him around. "Oh, yes, this is the happiest day of my life! How do we start? Taking candy from babies? It's harder than it looks, you know. They're just so cute. And their mothers get grumpy and start hitting you with their purses."

"Ah…maybe we should discuss your lessons a little later?" Patrik said, glancing at the exits. "We need to get out of here first. Which way is your brother coming from?"

Dolly snorted. "Oh, don't worry about that. We've still got a minute or two."

"*A minute?*"

Wrinkling her nose, Dolly sighed. "Oh fine. I can see you're not going to be able to concentrate until we're 'safe'." She made air quotes with her fingers for the word 'safe'. "So where do you want to go?"

"Go? I just want to get out of here!"

"Yes, yes, yes, but it's best if the spell has a destination. Once I used it a few drinks into a bender and ended up five hundred miles away, in the middle of a desert. Believe me, you do *not* want to be hungover in the middle of the desert. And since I can only use the long distance function once a month, we may as well make the most out of it."

Patrik stared at the demon. He hadn't made sense of a single word of her rant.

She has a teleportation spell, idiot.

"Ahh…" He had to think fast. "Well, I'm meant to be going to the house of Tenser the Great in Bledross—"

"Done!" the demon exclaimed, grabbing him in a hug.

Blip.

Patrik's world abruptly turned on its head.

EPILOGUE
GOING HOME

Boom!

The world went insane. For a few, spinning, swirling, rainbow-coloured seconds. Then they were smashing back through the fabric of the world and crash landing in the middle of an old-timey living room. On top of the dining room table, to be exact, which promptly collapsed beneath the combined weight of a thirty-year-old community college student and the demonic daughter of the Dark Lord.

Quest Complete: Journey to Bledross. Congratulations! You have successfully delivered the [Unidentified Ring] to the House of Tenser the Great in Bledross. Reward: 5000 gold coins.

Warning: You have entered the Second Circle without reaching the level requirements. Individuals up to level 60 may now engage you in combat.

Coughing and spluttering, Patrik waved away the notification. He'd seen on the map that Bledross bordered the Second Circle, but hadn't realised Tensor's house would actually be *inside* of it. Or that he could cross the threshold between the Circles without reaching level thirty. He supposed it made sense. A kind of 'enter at your own risk' rule.

Hopefully it wouldn't matter. All things going well, this would be his last stop in the Four Circles. Next up, home!

He was just pushing himself to his feet when the aftereffects of being teleported several hundred miles in the blink of the eye caught up with him. The room spun. Groaning, he bent in two and squeezed his eyes shut, trying to stave off the dizziness. It didn't really help. Before he could stop himself, the remnants of last night's dinner were on the floor.

"Ewww, gross, you got it on my tail!"

Drums began to pound against Patrik's skull as he forced his eyes to open. The demonic princess had crash landed alongside him but was now scrambling to her feet to escape the vomit pooling on the broken table. Her tail whipped back and forward, sending goblets of…

"Arg!" he scrambled back as several drops got him in the face.

"Well no kidding," Dolly exclaimed. "By daddy, that's the last time I'm teleporting you, Mr. Chosen One!" Taking her tail in her hands, she held it up to her nose and smelt it. She made a face. "Seriously, that was *not* part of our deal."

Patrik shook his head as the last of the dizziness faded. "That was…something."

Rising carefully to his feet, he cast his eyes over the room in which they'd landed. He wasn't sure *what* he'd expected from a wizard's house. It wasn't like the movies ever focused on Gandalf's home life. But this…this definitely wasn't it. This living room's décor reminded Patrik more of his grandfather's cottage before they'd moved him into the retirement village than the home of an all-powerful wizard. There were velvet sofas and intricately carved chairs and faded paintings of scenic lakes and corn fields. The carpet was so worn it probably should have been replaced a decade ago. It even *smelt* like his grandfather's house. Which was to say, like old man.

That Tenser dude was like three hundred years old. It's a wonder the funk hasn't taken on a life of its own.

Patrik was nodding his agreement when he glimpsed movement out of the corner of his eye. He swung around in time to see a pale figure step through a doorway from another room he hadn't yet noticed. He blinked. The newcomer looked exactly like Tenser. Well, not quite. His robes were purple instead of blue and on closer inspection there was more black in this man's hair and beard than grey. Even so, the resemblance to the all-powerful wizard was unmistakable.

The man lifted a hand to his mouth and yawned as he wandered into the room. He didn't seem to have noticed his guests—his eyes were on a large book in his hands. It gave Patrik an opportunity to examine him.

Destiny the Not-So-Great [Level 55]. The only legitimate son of Tenser the Great, Destiny doesn't exactly live up to the family motto. That's a polite way of saying he's a good-for-nothing coward and a slacker, who hasn't done an honest day of work in his entire life. This is what happens when you spoil your kids rotten, folks.

Patrik barely got past the man's title. Level 55? Shit, that was almost at the limits of *this* Circle. Ridiculous name or not, 'Destiny' was exactly who Patrik needed to bail him out of this mess.

"Help!" he cried, leaping from the wreckage of the table. Best to put some distance between himself and the demonic princess. "Help, it's a demon, get her!"

Wow, dick move, mate.

She wanted lessons on how to be bad, he shot back.

Unfortunately, the purple robed wizard did not react in the manner he'd hoped. Instead of summoning cleaning fire or some arcane power to dispose of Dolly, he yelped at just the sight of them and hurled himself down behind one of the sofas.

"Please!" His feeble cry came from behind the piece of furniture. "I'll do whatever you say, just don't hurt me."

"Ah…" *He's level 55, why the hell is he whimpering?*

Some people never grow a backbone, however powerful they become.

Patrik glanced at Dolly, expecting the worst, but the demon only sighed.

"Damnit, see, I never would have thought of that!" she said in a forlorn voice. Wandering around the sofa, she leaned over and inspected the wizard, who was still whimpering on the floor. "Trying to stab me in the back the second you had what you wanted? Brilliant! I have so much to learn."

The wizard glanced up at her, yelped, and scooted backwards until he reached the corner of the room. "Please!" he cried again. "Please, don't call your father down on me, I swear I never knew anything about dad's plan to destroy the Dark Lord!"

That got Patrik's attention. He walked over to join Dolly. "We never said anything about the Dark Lord," he reasoned, "but I *am* interested in Tenser and his plans." Head between his hands, Destiny didn't reply, only continued to whimper and plead from the floor, until finally Patrik rolled his eyes. "Oh come on man, pull yourself together. We're not here to hurt you."

The snivelling trailed off. Eventually. The wizard lifted his head. "You're not?" He looked from Patrik to the demon. "But you're evil!"

"That's not…" Patrik bit back the words. He could spend the rest of his days arguing the ethics of this world with his Portland classmates when he finally got home. Just now he needed to cut to the point. "Look, I'm afraid I have some bad news for you, Destiny. Your father is dead."

"What?" the man blinked. "But…that's impossible!"

"Impossible or not, it happened. I was there. And with his dying breath he gave me a quest to bring this here. I guess to you?" As he spoke, Patrik drew out the unidentified ring he'd carried since that fateful day in the forest. As it settled in his fingers, he held it out for the cowardly wizard.

Excitement bloomed in Destiny's eyes at the sight of it. "Hey, my Invisibility Ring!" He practically snatched it from Patrik's fingers. "I thought I'd lost it!" He frowned. "Oh wait, this is a new one. Dad must have gotten me a replacement!" His lips turned downward. "He was always thoughtful like that."

"Ah…wait, that's it? That's all it was? An invisibility ring? Why…" He trailed off.

He knew why. All this time he'd been hoping his Dark Lord situation might have a Frodo takes the ring to Mordor type solution. But of course nothing was ever that easy. Life never was. Tenser had mentioned the ring and protecting destiny, and well, here a Destiny was.

"Okaaay," Dolly interrupted. "You gave him the ring, now can we go?"

The demonic princess had grown bored with their conversation and wandered off. Approaching a shelf in the corner, she paused to inspect its contents. It displayed the figurines of dozens of different monsters. Apparently the demon was not impressed, as with a snort she continued her lap around the room. As she walked away, her tail came up and swept across the shelf. The figurines tumbled to the ground and smashed into a thousand pieces.

"Hey, those were mine!" the wizard whined at the same time the demon gave a little whoop of joy.

"Hey, Patrik, that actually worked!" she exclaimed, bouncing back across the room to where they stood. "I bet if we burned this entire house down it'd be *great* for our negative Alignment!"

Patrik ignored her. Moving to the sofa, he sank into the cushions. It was way too soft. Or maybe it was just old. He didn't care. His mind was still on the ring. If it wasn't the magical McGuffin that would allow him to defeat the Dark Lord, then he *really* needed to get out of this world.

"My father brought you here, didn't he?" Destiny said, moving to stand in front of him. "Sorry, I just read your description."

Patrik nodded. "From Earth."

The wizard lost another shade of colour from his already pale face. "Right," he said. "Then in that case, this must be for you." He held out a silver disk. "Father left it here when he left. Said that if someone…strange came looking for him before he returned that I should give it to them."

Patrik reached out a hand to accept the disk. As soon as his fingers touched the metal surface, light sprang up around it. Swirling outwards, it rippled and expanded, changing until it formed a ghostly projection of an old man. Tenser—or at least some kind of magical memory of the old wizard.

"Greetings, Chosen One," the old man's voice was clear despite the flickering nature of the display. "If you are listening to this recording, then it is likely I have perished on my quest to free the Four Circles from the Dark Lord's reign." The wizard paused, and his wrinkled face took on a thoughtful expression. "Strange, to think it might end while my life's work remains uncomplete."

"Still, if you are here, Chosen One, then all is not lost. Fate plays her games, but you are the one piece of the puzzle she cannot foresee. A force of chaos in a land governed by laws and regulations that have resisted all efforts to change the status quo. I can only hope it will be enough."

Patrik grated his teeth. "Screw your hope, you old bastard, how do I get home?" He knew it was just a recording, but couldn't keep his frustration from seeping through.

"I know you made a great sacrifice in coming to this land, Chosen One. I thank you for that, and hope that you can grow to love this world as if it were your own." The wizard paused to draw breath. "For alas, there is no way to reverse the spell that drew you across the boundaries between universes. It was with heavy heart that I set myself on this path. Perhaps that was the doom of me. No matter. I will not apologise, for I knew full well the consequences of my actions. Though I would gift you this house as small compensation. My son can move to the villa in Blowtown."

"Oh come on, dad..." Destiny muttered. "Blowtown sucks!"

Patrik hardly heard him. The eyes of the dead wizard seemed to be watching him.

"I cannot know the nature of the one I have summoned," Tenser continued, "whether you will run towards or from this challenge. Nor can I guide you, for even my powers cannot resist the whispers of Fate for long. I can only wish you good luck on the journey I have set you on."

The image flickered and died as the last words whispered through the room. Patrik sat on the sofa and stared at the space the hologram had occupied. He…he was stuck in this place. In this awful, terrible world that tried to kill him at least once a day. Forever.

"You've got to be shitting me," he whispered.

What was he going to do now? The ring was a bust. Tenser's house had led nowhere. His companions had all turned against him. And now there was no way home.

Hey, you still got me, buddy!

"And me!" Dolly exclaimed. "Come on, let's burn this place down! And then I read this story about this supervillain dude that stole the moon, we can totally do that!"

Looking up into the demonic face of Dolly, something just…snapped. "Are you stupid?" he asked softly.

"Huh?" A frown touched the demon's horny forehead.

"I asked if you were stupid," Patrik repeated. Rising from the sofa, he loomed over the little demon. "Seriously? Did you *really* think I was going to help you? *You?* The daughter of the guy trying to kill me?" He snorted. "No wonder he thinks you're a failure."

Dolly's mouth parted as though to respond, but the words did not come out. Her lips trembled and her big black eyes shimmered with unspilt tears. The words hung between them for the longest moment, before abruptly she turned and fled the room.

Well, that was tactful, Steve remarked.

"I don't care," he muttered, slumping back into his sofa.

"Ah…" Destiny still stood nearby, twiddling his thumbs. "So…ah, you're going to kill the Dark Lord?"

"That's why your father brought me here, isn't it?" Now it was the wizard's turn to shuffle uncomfortably beneath Patrik's gaze. "Against my will, of course." He snorted. "So why the *hell* would I do anything that old man wanted?" Lying back, he lifted his feet and rested them on the coffee table. His shoes were covered in mud from the cave and left streaks on the wood.

He didn't care.

"Okay…" the wizard started, "so, then you *do* want the house? Just checking, cause you know, it's really quite a trek to—"

"Get out," Patrik cut him off.

"What, now?" Destiny exclaimed. "Come on, let's just think about this a minute. I have things to pack and the sun's going down—"

"*I said get out, you piece of cow turd!*" Patrik bellowed.

He came to his feet as the cowardly wizard reeled back from him. Destiny's health bar appeared above his head as Patrik's Vicious Mockery ability struck. It barely took a sliver from the level 55's health, but he still yelped like he'd been bitten.

"Okay, okay, I'm going! Geeze, you said you weren't going to hurt me."

Whipping his robes around him, the wizard spun in a circle and promptly vanished.

And then Patrik was finally alone. Completely and utterly—

Ahem, still here, mate.

"Fuck off, Steve," he whispered.

There was silence for so long Patrik thought the PQA had finally listened to him.

Mate, I've tried to help you, I really have.

Patrik didn't dignify that with a reply.

You know what, screw you man. You might hate this world, but its only given back what you gave it. Another pause in which Patrik refused to speak. **Fine, be that way. I wasn't going to mention it, being a nice PQA and all, but you realise you left your stupid horse in Anchorpoint, right? It's now two hundred miles away through monster infested swampland.**

"Just. Leave. Me. Alone."

And the PQA did.

Patrik breathed in the silence. Maybe he would just wait here. One of his enemies would find him eventually. Finish him off. What else could he do? Tenser had summoned him to this place, but the wizard had never had a *real* plan. Patrik was just a massive gamble that had gone terribly wrong from the start. Exhaling, he pulled up his stat box.

PATRIK THE CHOSEN ONE   LEVEL **27**

PROGRESS TO NEXT LEVEL: 95%

RACE   **ALIGNMENT**
Human   -5230

HEALTH   **MANA**
270/270   95/95

STR   **CON**   **INT**   **CHA**   **DEX**
16(+4)   14(+1)   18   1   13(+1)

*Equipped: Iron short sword (+3 STR)
Sapphire Ring of Strength (+1 STR)
Sapphire Ring of Dexterity (+1 DEX)
Sapphire Ring of Constitution (+1 CON)*

You have 21 stat points to assign.

SPELLS [LIMIT: FOUR]

RAISE DEAD   **LIGHTNING BOLT**
level 8   level 4

SKILLS [UNLIMITED]

HACK AND **SLASH**   **ARSON**   **VICIOUS MOCKERY**
level 6   level 7   level 4

That was it. The extent of his time in this world. Everything he had achieved, held in a dozen little boxes and numbers. Everyone and everything else had betrayed him, turned against him. Or he'd driven them away.

An hour passed before boredom finally urged Patrik to move. Rising, he crossed the living room and stepped out the front door. He may as well explore some of Bledross before a demon prince or his ex-companions or whatever else was hunting him came and killed him.

In the entrance though, he paused. Soft sounds came from the open front door. Hesitantly, he approached, fingers clenched in preparation to summon his sword. But there was no need.

Outside, stone steps led down to a bricked road. Dolly sat on the bottom step, knees pulled up to her chest, tail swishing back and forth behind her. The demon's head was buried in her hands, but that couldn't completely muffle her sobs.

Patrik's heart twisted in his chest. He stood for a long while in the doorway, watching her. Dolly might be a demon, but… who was he to judge? Hell, she was about the only person in this world who hadn't judged him at first glance. And she had brought him here to Bledross, where so many others had failed, or obfuscated, or betrayed him. In return, all she'd asked for was a little advice.

"Hey," he said, walking down the steps and seating himself alongside the demonic princess. "I thought you left."

"Oh," Dolly hiccupped as she looked up and saw him. "Sorry, I didn't…I'll just get going then."

She started to rise. Patrik caught her hand and drew her back down. A frown crossed her scarlet face, but she said nothing as she settled on the step. Finding her pure black eyes unnerving, Patrik fixed his gaze on the ground. They stayed that way for a while.

"I don't know if I can help you," he said at last.

"But you're so—"

"Evil, I know," he held up a hand. "Believe me, it's not deliberate."

"Oh…"

"So I don't know if I can teach you to be evil," he continued, "but back in the goblin cave, you said something about celebrating the things that bring you joy." He let out a long breath. "Well, maybe we should focus on that instead. What do you think?"

He risked a glance at the demon and found her dark eyes

staring off into the distance. There was a little twist to her lips, as though she were deep in thought. Following her gaze, Patrik found himself looking out over the city of Bledross. It was far larger than Anchorpoint or Monmouth, and built across a cluster of hills. Tenser's house had been built near the top of one of the hills, while on the tallest, an enormous citadel loomed over the city. The setting sun turned its curtain walls a brilliant red.

"Okay," Dolly had stopped crying now. She looked at Patrik and smiled. "But I still want to be evil!"

"Oh don't worry." Patrik found himself chuckling. "Knowing my luck, that won't be a problem. I just didn't want to over promise."

The demon held out her hand. "Deal then?"

"Deal."

EXTRA HEAVY FORESHADOWING

Two hundred miles from Bledross, in the backroom of the Bandit's Daughter, Bel the Innkeeper sat beside the bed of her mother and wept. Her heart ached with the weight of her loss, with the pain of her grief. First had been Lamb Chop, the sweetest little sheep that had ever lived. That had been bad enough, but then had come word of her father's death. Cut down by adventurers in the forests outside of Monmouth, killed for the crime of providing for his family. And now...now...

A tear streaked Bel's cheek as she squeezed her mother's hand. There was no response. She just lay in her bed, eyes firmly closed, just as she had every day since receiving the letter. The doctor had come by a few times, but his visits only confirmed what Bel already knew. Overwhelmed with grief, her mother had gone to sleep.

No one knew how long she might have set the system. But she was already beginning to waste away, the skin sagging against her face, her hair turning slowly white. She would not survive much longer.

A sob tore from Bel. Then she would be all alone. It wasn't fair. Why had this happened? She'd had a future once, dreams of studying at the Magician's Academy, of traveling the Four Circles, of seeing the world.

Instead, her life had been plagued by one terrible fortune after another. What had she ever done in her life that Fate would weave her a life of such horrors?

"Why, nothing at all, child."

Bel started as a voice spoke from behind her. She swung around, trying to identify the speaker, but her lantern barely lit the room beyond her mother's bed.

"Who's there?" she demanded.

A chill spread down her spine as a young girl stepped from the shadows. "Had events unfolded as ordained," the girl continued, "you would now be in Bledross, a student of the academy, with a bright future ahead of you."

"I…what…" Bel trailed off as the girl crossed the room to join her at her mother's bedside.

"And your parents…" the girl sighed. "And your parents would still be here in Anchorpoint, happy and in love." She blinked and turned two emerald eyes on Bel.

Bel found herself trembling beneath that gaze. "Who… who are you?"

"You know who I am, child."

"Fate," she said the word like a talisman, and the young girl nodded. "Why…why are you here?"

A sigh came from the young girl—the goddess. She looked back at the comatose body of Bel's mother, but whatever hope the young innkeeper might have had was immediately crushed.

"I cannot bring back your parents," Fate whispered. "Nor restore the fortune I had planned for you." She paused. "But I can offer you something else."

"What?" Bel breathed.

"Vengeance."

As Fate spoke the word, the door creaked open. Bel turned to see an enormous shape step into the room. It was followed by two others. Her heart palpitated. Only as they stepped into the lanternlight did Bel realise she knew them. The bard, the sorceress, and the swordsman who had stayed at the inn a few days past.

"A force of chaos has entered our world," the goddess

continued. "I cannot act against him directly. But of all he has touched in this world, the threads of your four fates have been twisted beyond recognition." A smile spread across the young girl's face. "So will you be my weapons against the chaos?"

There was a pause, a second's hesitation.

Then four voices spoke in unison.

"We will."

OKAY OKAY OKAY, you want serious? Let's be serious with my next book, <u>Darkstrider</u>, and if you realized this was a satire and enjoyed it don't forget to leave a review ;-)

AFTERWORD

So that was me, giving it my all in a brand new genre. And trying to be funny. Hopefully successfully. But you, my dear reader, will be the judge of that. And your court will of course be the court of public opinion, which is to say, the book's Amazon review page. That's right, this is the part where I ask for your review. Pretty please with a cherry on top! Okay thank you :-D

And if you DID enjoy this book, well it's my first LITRPG story with hopefully many many more to come. But if you can't wait (and I strongly encourage you not to), you'd be most welcome to check out some of my other stuff. I would recommend starting with either Oathbreaker or Reborn. They're two of my favourite and both series are finished.

ACKNOWLEDGMENTS

I would first like to give a big shout out to Benjamin Kerei for being the one to introduce me to LITRPG and convincing me to give it a go myself, and giving me tips and pointers along the way to finishing this novel. His book, Oh, Great! I was Reincarnated as a Farmer, is such an amazing read and a must read for any fans of the genre (though I'm sure you've probably already read it!).

My other recommendations would include Dungeon Crawler Carl (love those books!) and Will Wight's Cradle series (although I guess that's technically progression fantasy).

Finally, I couldn't have managed this book without all the memes and DnD references and comments from those members of the Gamelit Society and LITRPG Books groups over on Facebook. They're a must to join for any fans of the genre.

JOIN THE FAN CLUB

So if you've enjoyed this book and want to keep in touch, I have a weekly newsletter I send out with updates on my upcoming projects, along with any sales or specials I'm running. **You'll also get a couple of books and a short story for free just by joining.**

FOLLOW AARON HODGES

https://aaronhodgesauthor.com/newsletter

NEW YORK TIMES BESTSELLING AUTHOR
AARON HODGES
DARK STRIDER
THE BLADES OF HEAVEN AND HELL

CHAPTER 1

DARKNESS.

Absolute black. A never-ending emptiness stretching out to eternity. It should have been terrifying. Horrifying, to know he was a part of it, that the infinite had swallowed him up, made him a part of the nothingness that was the universe.

But there was no terror in this place. No fear, or anger, or love. Emotion had no place in the dark. At least, not at first.

Not until something broke the perfect void. A light. A spark.

With it came the fear. An unspoken, unknown terror for what it represented. Life. And more than that. An awareness. A consciousness that probed the dark, seeking, searching for something amidst the black. Something that did not belong.

Him.

He felt himself separate from the void. Expelled for his own conscious thought. For his fear. Suddenly he was exposed, adrift in the infinite, alone.

Except...

...he was not alone.

Error. System failure. Breach imminent!

Boom!

Mikael Heaton's first sense of awareness was of burning. A fiery heat and energy, sizzling, crackling, *condensing*, as though his own physical self were being dragged from some unexplainable ether and shoved back together piece by piece. It was the most unpleasant awakening he could have possibly imagined.

The next thing he noticed was the warm stone beneath him, pressed against his cheek. Not hot enough to burn, but still hot enough to suggest it had just been licked by flame. Already it was beginning to cool.

Then it was the cold. Icy air flowed over him, raising goosebumps across his naked body and leaving him trembling. Shivering. *Cold.* He did not like it. Blinking, he struggled to get his bearings, to find the source of the sensation.

Instead, brilliant light pierced his eyes, drilling a pair of agonising circles deep into his skull. So bright, as though he had not used his eyes in a very long time. Instinctively, he scrunched them closed again, though that hardly helped with the pounding. He felt as though someone had struck him in the head.

His ears were ringing as well, as though he'd just been playing Beethoven's ninth symphony several notches of volume too high through his…

He paused as the thought met…emptiness. There was a gap in his memory. What…what had been that image in his head? It was already gone, floating away like a child's stream of bubbles in the noonday sunlight.

His skin crawled as he lay back against the cooling stone. He drew in a breath and his nose twitched, tingling as he smelt burning ash. And beneath that, something less pleasant, like… the stench of a boys' changing room.

Confusion claimed Mikael. He drew in his next breath through clenched teeth. His stomach churned, as though something inside him yearned to escape. He forced it back down. Another breath. His heart slowed a fraction, panic retreating as his mind took hold.

He needed to open his eyes. To figure out where he was. And…and what else he was missing?

Pull yourself together, Mikael.

Light. Bright, though it cut less this time. It still felt like fists were crashing against his skull, but he could cope. Just. With a groan, he commanded his body to move. It took time, as though the connections in his mind had somehow forgotten how this went. His fingers twitched. Then an arm. Finally, with a groan, Mikael pushed himself to his knees.

By now his head was truly pounding, his stomach churning. A thought came to him, along with the image of a hideous green beast.

Better out than in…

He needed no further encouragement. His stomach convulsed as he hurled acidic bile onto the smooth rock beneath him. He was crouched in a strange indentation in the stone, and a distant part of his mind found itself thinking how it had been formed. The way the rock dipped where he lay, crystal veins twisted into ripples, almost as though it had been heated to melting point and flowed together…

Shaking himself, he dismissed the idle thoughts. The strange memory had provided sage advice and he found himself feeling slightly improved. Physically at least. His mental discomfort only increased as he tried to recall how he had come to be lying in a stone indentation in a…was he in a cave? How…

There was nothing.

It was with rising panic that Mikael scanned his memories and found his mind completely, entirely blank. No memory. Not a single recollection of a life lived. There was only… knowledge? Like for some reason, he knew the layers of rock in the cave wall had been formed over millions of years of heat and pressure.

But he could not remember a single face, not his mother or father, not even the goddamn barista at his local cafe. Which… okay, apparently, he only had *some* knowledge. For while he could remember the words, his mind pulled a blank as to what exactly a barista *was*.

Letting out a long breath, he tried to calm himself. His head hurt, so he must have hit it on something. This was obviously some kind of amnesia—which his ever-so-helpful mind told him was a disease of the brain. He needed to be methodical about this. There must be some clues about how he'd arrived here. Now that his eyes had adjusted, he found that the cave was gloomy, though he could see the distant light of day around a bend in the stone.

Mikael was just readying himself to look around, when he glanced down and was struck by a realisation.

He was naked.

Naked.

That was wrong. Just as he knew his name, something instinctual inside him *screamed* that that was wrong. He needed clothes, though the little voice of intuition didn't offer a reason. Because he was cold? That seemed logical. What other reason would there be to cover himself?

Certainly his body did not seem anything to be ashamed of. Small, with a beige tint to his skin—which the helpful part of his mind informed meant he probably spent time outdoors. His arms were skinny, but his legs seemed to have plenty of spring in them, and the digit between his legs…

Warmth flushed his cheeks and he felt a strange sensation of discomfort. Embarrassment. Ah, so it *was* about more than just warmth. Strange. Without the context of his own memories, it seemed a somewhat pointless convention.

Though it was obviously not as bizarre as a naked man sitting alone in a cave, with no memory of how he had come to be there, who he was, or what manner of world might exist beyond the walls of this stone tomb.

Solutions, not problems, Mikael.

He focused on the first of his problems. Clothes. The last of the uneasiness in his body had left him now, though there was still a sense of clumsiness as he began moving about the cave, like his body didn't quite fit with what his mind remembered.

Thankfully, the cave didn't appear to hold any immediate danger. His eyes struggled in the gloom, but it was clear from a cursory glance that someone had been living here until recently, because their belongings remained. Leather-wrapped bedrolls were scattered across the stone floor and several pieces of clothing had been draped on wooden stakes set in the ground around an empty firepit.

Following instinct, he crossed to the circle of stones and tentatively pressed a finger into the ashes. Cold. So they'd been gone some time. Though not long enough for the stench of their unwashed bodies to dissipate.

His bare foot nudged a discarded dagger as he stepped away from the pit. He paused to pick it up. The blade was tarnished and speckled with rust, the leather strapping on the hilt crumbling. He let it fall. It would probably break the second he used it as a weapon and he'd already spied several more promising items. Another dagger, several swords, a rusty hatchet…

Mikael paused, already halfway across the cavern to the first of the swords. Why had his mind leapt to seeking out a weapon? What manner of man had death on his thoughts upon first waking in a strange cave?

An intelligent one.

He supposed it was not the worst reflex. Considering the strangeness of the situation, it wouldn't hurt to be armed. Still, clothes first. Those on offer were plentiful, but whoever had been living here obviously had not believed in hygiene. Even the pieces staked out around the dead fire stunk something fierce.

Do they not have soap in this place?

Still, beggars could not be choosers, so he settled on a pair of black leggings with only one hole in the knee and a brown button up shirt he thought had probably been white once. Neither smelt particularly pleasant, but Mikael tried to keep his mind on other thoughts. He outright refused to even look at the undergarments. He had some standards, apparently.

The coarse fabric chafed against his skin as he pulled on each item of clothing, but despite the unpleasantness of the situation, he felt better covered. Less vulnerable. And more prepared to face the world outside.

He considered the weapons again, settling on the hatchet and the best of the knives. It had no sheath, but after spotting some rope in the corner, he cut a piece from the tangle and looped it around his waist. He was just tucking the knife into his makeshift belt, when he spied something that set the hairs on the back of his neck tingling.

Beneath the rope and other discarded belongings in the pile he'd been rummaging through, the floor changed from stone to dirt. Dirt that appeared to have been disturbed recently. He knelt, his mind patiently putting the pieces together as to why he found this interesting.

Hidden treasure.

Hmm. The image of a chest overflowing with gold and silver and gemstones sprang into his mind—accompanied with a man wearing a sable fedora hat and holding a whip. Interesting. There was no spade to dig in the earth so he used the dagger instead. In the end there was no chest, but he did pull a cloth bag from the dirt that chimed when he tossed it in his hands.

It was heavy, too. When he pulled open the drawstrings, he saw the gold coins inside and frowned. That was…wrong. And yet…a tingle of excitement raised the hairs on his arms. This was…money? Not like he was used too. But it was something that could be used to purchase things. Like better clothes, and underwear that had not been worn by another man.

Mikael collected a worn-out pack from amongst the discarded belongings and tossed the coin purse inside, followed by a spare set of clothes and a leather skin he thought could be filled with water. He also added whatever scraps of food he found, though that was little more than a few stale biscuits and some type of dried meat.

Finally satisfied with his work, Mikael set his hands on his hips and cast a final glance over the cave. All in all, it was a fortunate place for him to have ended up, given his situation. It had supplied everything he might need in the unknown world beyond the stone walls. Or so he hoped.

He wondered what had become of its original occupants, why they had left. They had certainly lived a rough existence, judging by what remained here. There was a remoteness about this place, a sense of living off scraps, far from the comforts of society.

Well, everything but the gold pointed to that at least. The gold coins…did suggest some sort of connection to society. He'd only paused to examine one quickly, but they seemed to be stamped with the face of some lord or king. Given the way they'd been hidden, they were obviously valuable. So why had the occupants not spent their money on better clothing or tools or even weapons…

Outlaws.

Mikael's hackles stood on end as the answer came to him. That was it, wasn't it? He was standing in the hideout of some kind of criminal outfit. A pressure rose in his chest, a sudden sense of urgency. He needed to leave. Because what if the thieves *hadn't* abandoned this place? What if they were just out on a raid, and were returning even now? He doubted that men prepared to exist off scraps and live in a cave would be particularly charitable to his situation. Especially not when they found out he had robbed them.

He considered replacing the gold, but no, that was just his panicked brain ticking into overdrive. The ashes of the fire were cold. No one had been here for some time. In all probability, these men had been caught by the authorities and locked away. Though…that still left the question around why *Mikael* was here. Was he one of them? No, that didn't seem right either.

Closing his eyes, Mikael focused on the pounding of his heart, the whisper of breath in his lungs, on that chill breeze blowing through the cave. Slowly, he calmed, and his mind began to work again. Nothing had changed. He had his supplies. All he had to do was leave out the front door. The thugs might return at some point, but by then he would be long gone.

A smile came to his lips, and opening his eyes, Mikael made for the cave exit. Despite his newfound calm, he was eager to be away. The chances of the bandits returning at this moment might be low, but it wouldn't hurt to be gone anyway. No point pressing his luck.

Hefting the pack on one shoulder and leaning the hatchet against the other, Mikael wandered out into warm sunlight. His eyes took a moment to adjust, but when his vision cleared he found himself at the top of a small rise leading down to a forest of pine and beech. He could not say how he knew those names, only that the spikey needles and purpled leaves and rich scents on the air matched with what was in his mind.

Turning, he appraised the mouth of the cave. It emerged from a massive cliff-face and was little wider than a crevice. From farther down the slope it would probably appear as no more than a shadow on the granite rock. Its disguise, however, was somewhat ruined by the trail of flattened grass leading up the slope to the opening. The outlaw group hadn't been particularly cautious about concealing their hideout.

A grievous error, Mikael thought, given the location of the cave. Sheer cliffs rose behind it and curved away on either side to create a half-circle formation. A good place for a last stand. Theoretically. Of course, if you were *really* being hunted by the law, it would surely be better to pick a camp with an escape route. As it was, if the cops ever found this place, they could have set up in the trees below and starved the bandits out. There was a small stream tumbling down the cliffs nearby, so they would have water, but eventually the outlaws would be forced to either surrender or launch a suicidal charge across the open ground.

A frown came to Mikael's face as he considered all this. Strange, that those ideas came so readily. But he could consider his unknown origins at a later date. For now, it was time to leave this place, before—

He froze as the whisper of voices came from the trees.

A moment later, a group of shaggy looking men stalked from the trees below.

CHAPTER 2

BJORN CRESWELL, LEADER OF THE MIGHTY CURSED SONS, WAS feeling exceedingly pleased with himself as he strode the narrow path through the forest. Many of his men had doubted him when he'd led them into the Highlands and away from the rich trade routes and gilded cities of the Gurrian Empire. Sure, people liked to gossip about the hidden riches in these lands, but no one actually *believed* it. The uncultured clans hardly knew the value of gold over a clod of dirt, after all.

But Bjorn's foresight was far beyond the simple minds of most men. Sure, the roads of the Empire might flow with riches. For a time, the merchant caravans around Skarta had kept his company's bellies full and their purses heavy. But those riches had come with an infamy that could catch up with an incautious man. The local governor might be the snot-nosed brat of some noble back in the capital, but even the most incompetent of leaders would eventually be forced to do *something* about a gang of thieves wreaking havoc on his trade routes. The last merchant they'd robbed had even had Pathfinders as guards. Only a few Copper rankers, enough to deter ordinary thieves. Bjorn had laughed as he cut them down. The fear on their faces as they realised their own mortality had been a joy to behold.

But Bjorn was no fool. It had been time to quit while he

was ahead. The Highlands might lack physical wealth, but an innovative thinker like himself could find treasure anywhere. Demand from the flesh markets of Skarta for slaves was practically insatiable, and there just happened to be a ready source of bodies nearby—if one had the strength to take them. Some amongst his men had grumbled when they'd learned of their new occupation, but their complaints would soon quiet when they reaped the rewards of Bjorn's brilliance. And if not…

…well, given the pitiful fight put up by the village they had raided, he could afford to shed some deadweight. The place hadn't even had a palisade wall! With most of the villagers out in the fields, the Cursed Sons had strolled into town in full daylight and taken what they wished. Most of those remaining in the town had hidden rather than fight.

And the few who *had* chosen to fight, well, they were fortunate that Bjorn wanted prisoners instead of bodies. Their first captive had been a middle aged man who'd come at one of them with a dagger. He'd been easily disarmed and knocked unconscious by a few of Bjorn's men. While that had been happening, a red-headed boy tried to intervene. Unfortunately for the kid, he was so scrawny it had only taken a backhanded slap from Bjorn to knock him on his ass. But the cry as he fell had drawn yet more attention.

The next to attack had actually surprised Bjorn. A woman —the village blacksmith he guessed by her ash-streaked clothing—had stepped from a building with a hammer in each hand. All rippling muscle and with a face that could have been chiselled from stone, she had demanded they release her son without so much as a hint of fear.

Bjorn might have laughed in her face, but his infallible instincts had screamed a warning instead. Just in time, as she launched herself at him with an impossible burst of speed. Had he reacted a second slower, she would have caved in his skull, Bronze rank or not. Instead, he ignited his *Movement Surge* ability to match her own and turned to grab her by the wrist, at which point his superior strength was enough to disarm her.

Even so, she'd continued to struggle until Bjorn knocked her out cold with a blow to the back of the head.

Only then had he activated his *Aura Sense* to confirm his suspicions. The woman was a Steel ranker. Incredible. Almost as good as uncovering a chest of gold in the basement of a whorehouse. Steel-ranked slaves—especially women—were practically unheard of in the Empire. She would fetch a fine price in Skarta.

The rest of the raid *almost* went off without a hiccup. Two more young men who made an inconvenience of themselves were added to their prisoners, thankfully larger than the first. They'd been just wrapping up when Bjorn caught the whiff of smoke. Enraged that someone had disobeyed his order to start no fires, he was just starting towards the source of the smell when one of his men came stumbling from a doorway— completely wreathed in flames.

Bjorn stood there, gaping, as the man fell, still burning. A moment later, a woman emerged from the same doorway, a fistful of flame in one hand. There was no need to use his *Aura Sense* to confirm this one was a Pathfinder. She was younger than the last, and prettier too with that dark hair and honey-coloured skin—or at least, she would have been, if not for the burn scar that marked her chin.

Before anyone could react, the young woman flung out her fist and sent a column of flame swirling into another of his Cursed Sons. A terrible scream tore from the man's throat as the fire swallowed him. He thrashed about for a second, but there was no escaping mana-fuelled flame. Not unless the caster herself ran short of power.

Which happened just a few seconds later, as the Pathfinder threw out her hand for another attack. The flames burst from her like before, but this time they guttered out before reaching their intended victim.

There was a pause, as the Cursed Sons and the woman stood there in the middle of the street watching each other. She was bathed in sweat and swaying on her feet. Bjorn hesitated before activating his *Movement Surge* ability again. It would drain him, but while the woman looked to be a spent force, there was no point taking risks. He had smashed her from her feet before she had a chance to raise a hand in her defence.

So it was that Bjorn Cresswell and his Cursed Sons had found themselves leaving the Highland village in possession of not just one, but *two* Steel ranked Pathfinders. He was going to make a fortune in Skarta. Truly, the Elohim had smiled upon his latest venture.

Not that his prisoners agreed.

"*Stinking b—*"

The curse broke off with a muffled *thud* as somebody hit the ground. Bjorn sighed and turned. He'd had the Pathfinders bound and set two of his men to guard each. That should have been plenty. So why did he now find one of his men on the ground nursing a swelling cheek, while the other struggled to hold the older woman still?

"By the Elohim, you'll pay for that!" His man snarled as he surged to his feet. A knife appeared in his hands.

"*Enough!*" Bjorn bellowed.

Allowing his anger to show, Bjorn strode to where his guards stood with the older woman. The one who'd been struck was amongst his inner circle, Edrin something-or-rather. A coldhearted killer that Skarta's watch had been hunting before Bjorn invited him into the Cursed Sons. The other was Lunden Marcs. The man was a former soldier who had escaped from his recently conquered nation, Ressi. Cowardly, without question, but when Bjorn gave him a command, he could usually trust it to be followed.

"What's going on here?" he demanded of the pair.

"Boss!" Seeing Bjorn towering over him snapped Edrin from his murderous rage. Fumbling with the knife, he struggled to place it back in its sheath. "Sorry, wasn't really gonna hurt her, I swear, just trying to frighten her!"

Bjorn said nothing, allowing the man to squirm beneath his gaze, before turning to Lunden.

"Marcs?"

"Edrin was getting handsy," Lunden said with a shrug. He offered nothing more.

Bjorn's frown deepened. He didn't like the glint he saw in the man's eyes. But he could deal with that later. For now, he needed to make sure his precious cargo reached their hideout in one piece.

He turned to the woman standing between the two men. She was no beauty, that was for sure. Her features were plain and wrinkles were beginning to show at the edges of her eyes. Well past forty, he guessed, and a mother at that. It would detract from her price on the stands. Still, her fiery eyes did not dip as he glowered down at her.

"Are you not afraid, woman?"

She lifted her chin to meet his gaze. "What do I have to fear from a dead man?"

That surprised him. Here she was, surrounded by powerful men, confronted by a Pathfinder more powerful than she could even imagine, and she dared to threaten him? He was beginning to see why Edrin had lost his temper.

"You had your shot, woman," he chuckled. "Did you not learn your lesson from our earlier exchange?"

"I saw the fear in your eyes when Isabel was burning your men alive." Then she laughed in his face.

There was a shrill edge to the laughter, as she was unable to conceal her terror, but still she laughed, mocking him with that wild grin. He clenched his fists, towering over the woman. Despite her muscular bulk, he could crush her in an instant. Wrap his mighty hands around that tiny throat and squeezed until the laughter stopped.

Instead, he drew a breath and turned to Edrin. "Bring me the child."

The man smiled. It was a chilling sight. "Yes, sir!" he said, turning on his heel and retreating down the line of stopped men in search of the other prisoners—even as the woman cried out in panic. Clasping his hands behind his back, Bjorn ignored the woman's wailing.

"Sir," Lunden Marcs interrupted his contemplation, "are you sure that's a good idea?"

He turned his terrible eyes on the Ressian man and watched him shrink. "If I wanted your opinion, Marcs, I would ask for it," he said coldly. He stared at the man, then turned his back. "Go fetch the other one. If I'm giving lessons, they should both get to watch."

There was a moment's silence as Lunden lingered, followed by the sullen trudged of footsteps as he went in search of the other Pathfinder. Bjorn grimaced. The man was becoming a problem. If a coward like Lunden could find the guts to speak out against this new venture, others might as well. He snorted. Weaklings, all of them. They could not see the wood for the trees. That was why the strong ruled and men like Lunden followed.

It wasn't long before Edrin and Lunden returned, the first dragging the redheaded boy they'd found with the blacksmith. The boy was small and gangly and clearly their least valuable captive. But he meant something to the woman. Lunden lead the darkhaired woman with a gentle hand.

"Fiachson!" the first woman shouted as she saw the boy. She tried to go to him, but Bjorn caught her by the arm and dragged her back.

The boy's head jerked up at the name. "Mom, help—" His cry was cut off as Edrin cuffed him in the back of the head. He tumbled to the turf in front of Bjorn.

Bjorn stood there, silent as the boy struggled to his hands and knees. It was somewhat surprising that he did not begin to snivel and cry. He really was a scrawny little runt, making his age impossible to determine. Somewhere between thirteen and twenty. Honestly, Bjorn would have left him in the village but for his mother.

"I am Bjorn Cresswell, famed outlaw of Gurrian Empire." He paused, looking from one woman to the other, offering them a chance to react. If either had heard the name, their faces did not show it. Pursing his lips, he went on. "From this day forth you are my slaves. The property of Bjorn Cresswell."

When Bjorn spoke this time, he stepped closer, until he stood face-to-face with the blacksmith. Close enough to see the whites of her eyes. Then reaching down, he grasped her son by the arm and hauled him to his feet. The kid struggled, of course, but he was like a dove in Bjorn's powerful Bronze rank grip.

"Now, Bjorn Creswell would never wish any harm to his property," he continued. "You have great value in your present condition." Calmly, he drew the dagger from his belt. The boy froze in his struggles when he saw the steel. Bjorn could feel him trembling, but his eyes never left those of the women. "But Bjorn Cresswell will not tolerate disobedience from his property."

He lowered the blade until the point pressed against the boy's chest.

"Do we have an understanding?"

Silence. Bjorn allowed not a hint of emotion to cross his face. Not anger. Not doubt. Not even amusement. There was a fine balance to these threats. He didn't actually want to kill the boy. That would remove his bargaining piece and enrage his mother to the point of hysterics. But he also couldn't back down. So he needed the woman to break. Already the other Pathfinder was trembling, though it was difficult to tell with her whether from fear or anger. She could be trouble too. Best to crack down on that behaviour here and now.

"Or…"

The kid cried out as the point of Bjorn's knife bit through the thick cloth of his shirt. Just a cut, but it was enough.

"*Stop!*"

Bjorn grinned as the first woman's shoulders slumped and her head fell. Victory.

"Bjorn Cresswell prefers his property on their knees when they speak."

This time there was no resistance. Tears shone in the woman's eyes as she slumped to the ground. The dark haired one followed, reluctantly. "Please…" she rasped. "Don't hurt him. Fiachson never hurt a soul."

Bjorn let the tension build a few moments longer, making sure the pair knew their place. The fate of the two women belonged to him now. Satisfied, he tossed the boy to Edrin.

"Take him back to the others," he grunted.

Tears had spilt down the cheeks of the mother and her short hair was a tangled mess. The plain clothes were of fine enough quality, but they were basically rags beside the riches that could be found in the Empire. He would dress her in scarlet silks to match her eyes when they presented her to the auctioneers. Hopefully that would hide the plainness of her looks.

"Lunden, take the mother back as well. I'm done looking at her."

The man obeyed reluctantly and Daniyal turned his attention to the second Pathfinder. The caster with the fire mana powers. Her hands were bound but that would not be enough to stop her magic. Thankfully, while her abilities were clearly powerful, at Steel rank she could only draw enough mana to use them a couple of times without exhausting herself. It would take another day before she recovered enough to use them again, judging by how close she'd come to collapsing back in the village. By then they would be in Skarta and up for bid in the flesh markets. This one he would put in armour and give a sword. The gladiator pits were always in search of decent fighters.

"He'll come for us, you know."

His thoughts were interrupted by the softly spoken words. Probably too soft for mortal ears to catch. But…he stepped forward, his presence towering over her.

"What did you say?"

The dark-haired young woman glared at him but did not speak. There was still defiance in her eyes. That would change. His hand snapped out, catching her by the chin with rough fingers. She tried to flinch away, but he would not release her. He forced her to meet his gaze.

"I asked what you said."

Snarling, the woman tore herself loose from him. "The

Darkstrider will come for you," she spat. "I hope he guts you like the pig you are."

Silence fell amongst the trees. Bjorn cursed silently. He couldn't let an insult like that stand. The eyes of his men were all around, watching him, waiting for a response. Blood would have to be shed now, or others might question whether he had the strength to lead, whether someone else deserved the mantle. He was not afraid of the challenge, of course. He could crush any man in single combat. But a dagger in the night? No, better they understood the consequences of defiance.

He was just about to call Edrin back with the boy, when something tugged at his senses. Not his physical ones, but those deeper, connected with his abilities as a Pathfinder. He had just opened his *Aura Sense* when the wave of power swept over him.

A gasp hissed from his throat, a rare loss of composure for the legendary outlaw. He would have cursed himself for the slip, if his heart hadn't been pounding like it had his first time with a whore. That power…there was someone else in the forest, though his senses were not fine enough to figure out who or what it might be.

All he could tell was the direction.

The surge of power had come from their hideout.

The same hideout where he had stashed his hard-earned gold from the last five years of banditry.

"Men!" he cried, rage igniting within him. Nostrils flaring, eyes wild, he swung on his followers, the rebellious prisoner and her empty threats forgotten. "Men, to arms! The enemy is at our camp!"

CHAPTER 3

Jaxon Daniyal was angry. Actually, furious would be more appropriate. Furious that he had not sensed the raiders until it was too late. That he had allowed himself to be lulled by the long peace. That he had neglected to watch over his people, and now they suffered.

His long legs ate up the miles as he strode across the broken hills, scanning the way ahead. There was a boot print. There, a gouge in the dirt where a man had slipped. If the raiders were attempting to hide their trail, they were doing a poor job of it. For that he was thankful.

It had been a lightning raid, the hooded men thundering down from the hills while most of the clan were in the fields harvesting the last crops of the season. Those who'd been in the village had fled into the nearby forests or gone for help, leaving the rogues to plunder what they could.

Unfortunately, Sarton was a poor village with little wealth to speak of. They were a long way from the eastern mines or the greater Highland cities like Furness or Pine Harbour. What did have came from what they could grow. Cattle and grain were not exactly something raiders could carry away on their backs.

People, however…

The leather of Jaxon's bracers squinched as he clenched his

fists. Had the bandits planned to take prisoners from the beginning, or was it an afterthought when they discovered how meagre the loot from the village would be?

At least the raid had been bloodless. Taldar the stonemason had confronted the men when they first arrived and taken a blow to the head, but given they'd bothered to carry him away, Jaxon hoped he was fine. Maisiwan, the village blacksmith, had also put up a fight, along with several of the younger villagers who had rushed in to help. In the end though, only Jaxon's own apprentice, Isabel, had made a mark on the raiders. Two burnt corpses lay on the street where the bandits had abandoned them. Ultimately her resistance had been futile though, as she too had been taken.

Blood pounded in Jaxon's skull as he struggled to contain his rage. He had mentored Isabel since returning to the Highlands five years ago, when he'd found the then teenager sneaking in his backdoor, allegedly on a dare. If anything had happened to her…

He started to pick up the pace, before allowing caution to reign him in. Anger would blind him to the danger presented by these men. It did not take a scholar to guess what the outlaws planned to do with their captives. Slaves. The practice had been outlawed in the Highlands for generations, but there were no such prohibitions in the Gurrian Empire, and the border was only ten leagues to the south. The raiders would likely try to dispose of their new "wares" in the frontier city of Skarta.

Traveling on foot meant they still had another day's journey to reach the city. Plenty of time for Jaxon Daniyal to catch up with them.

Releasing a breath he had not realised he'd been holding, Jaxon focused his mind to the pursuit. He could see no sign of his quarry ahead.

Pathfinder Ability *Aura Sense* Activated.

Colours overlaid his vision, but even with his *Aura Sense* ability, the way ahead remained empty. But it was only a matter of time. The bandits were likely trying to put as much distance between themselves and any pursuers as possible before resting, but they would slow when night approached. Unless…

Unless they had a Pathfinder amongst them.

Jaxon's fingers twitched. Pathfinders were humans who could draw mana from the land and use their own aura to influence the world around them. Humans like himself. In the Highlands, the title was considered a sacred responsibility. Those beginning their journey started at Copper rank and advanced through training and dedication to their chosen path. Jaxon had become a warrior, using his talents to protect all the clans of the Highlands. In his years of service, fighting off Detian raiders and hunting down murderers, the people had come to know him as the Darkstrider.

But those were the days of his youth, before he'd travelled to the lands in the south and fought beneath the banner of the Gurrian Empire, learning their ways. Before he had sullied his name and returned in shame to his homeland.

His stomach twisted and he strained his *Aura Sense*, seeking his quarry. A Copper ranker or two were unlikely to bother him. Their numbers might—the villagers claimed there were at least thirty—but only if he met them on open ground. Jaxon was no fool. He would find their camp and wait until they slept before freeing the prisoners.

Another hour passed in pursuit before the tracks left by the bandits abruptly changed direction. Until now, they had kept to the low valleys, where the trail made their passage easy. That was logical. It would not matter if they were spotted by the occasional farmer. Denether, highking of the Highlands, tried to keep the roads patrolled, but without a formal army or any pressing threats, it was difficult to maintain them. Days might pass before a force could be mustered. The outlaws would reach the safety of Skarta long before then.

Now, however, the bandits had changed tact, leaving the valley and heading into the heavily forested hills. It was suspicious, to say the least, and he carefully extended his senses towards the trees some hundred feet away. These were young trees at the edge of the forest, tiny in comparison to the mighty oaks and firs that towered over remote parts of the Highlands. The lush soils and warmer climate here in the valley provided for a dense undergrowth of ferns and saplings, making it difficult to see anything beyond the wall of vegetation.

But they made no difference for a Pathfinder with the *Aura Sense* ability.

The world shifted as Jaxon focused fully on the shimmering auras cast by every living thing. At first, all he could see was the verdant green of the forest. But slowly the image resolved, different shades of emerald and olive and lime emerging from the mix. Little pinpricks of reds and oranges and yellows followed—wild animals burrowing in the ground or asleep at their perches. These too he allowed to fade, until…

…there, at last, a large blue and a second purple aura. Two men in the trees. Their energies swirled as he watched them. They were excited. No doubt they had noticed him standing on the trail. Unfortunately for the pair, neither aura had the tell-tale markings of an Essence that would mark them as Pathfinders.

Letting his *Aura Sense* drop, it took Jaxon another few seconds to spot the men now that he knew where they were. His eyes were sharpened by the first ability he'd gained as a Pathfinder—*Enforced Body*. The ability improved every aspect of his body, from his senses to agility to his strength. It was a significant advantage over any mortal who faced him—and at his rank, he had five other abilities to fall back on.

A flash of movement revealed a leather clad man, perched halfway up a tree in the fork between two branches. A second was crouched nearby. An archer and a swordsman to finish him off. He could sense no others.

He strained further and caught a flickering of…*something*. Too faint and distant to be sure, but he thought it might be Isabel or Maisiwan. Both were Pathfinders themselves, Steel-ranked with powerful auras, and respectable warriors in their own right. Their powers were probably why the raiders had targeted them—Pathfinders went for a premium in the flesh markets of Skarta.

His anger building again, Jaxon's attention turned to the bandits in his path. Their auras were flickering, growing nervous. They were waiting to see what he would do. A grim smile touched his lips as he loosened the greatsword strapped across his shoulder. It was the favoured weapon of his people— the Malesie—and while unwieldy in the hands of some, amidst the warriors of the Highlands it was a powerful asset. Few enemies could withstand the charge of a hundred Malesie wielding the enormous blades.

Certain the greatsword would not catch in its scabbard, Jaxon started towards the trees. There was no movement now, but the spike in the pair's auras was immediate. The shimmering blues and purples shifted suddenly to the orange of excitement.

An arrow flashed from the trees, but Jaxon was already moving and the shaft slammed into the earth where he had stood a moment before. Still racing towards the treeline, he drew the greatsword, sunlight rippling from the polished steel. The first bandit rose from his hiding place. Wielding a longsword typically favoured by the soldiers of the Empire, he bellowed a war cry and leapt to meet Jaxon.

Watchful for another arrow from the bowman, the Pathfinder wasted no time. The swordsman had the high ground, but Jaxon planted his feet as the man closed on him and swung his greatsword in a deadly arc. His assailant was ready for this and slowed his charge, evading the blow, before leaping forward to make a strike of his own.

Just as Jaxon had expected. Teeth clenched, muscles wrenching, he put all the power of his *Enforced Body* into reversing the swing of the enormous weapon. An impossible feat for most humans. Jaxon Daniyal made it look easy.

His opponent never saw the blow that killed him. One second, his blade was raised to strike at Jaxon's unprotected chest. The next, the greatsword was carving through his skull.

Blood and brains sprayed across the grassy hill. The body made an audible *thud* as it hit the ground.

Jaxon never broke his stride as he continued past the dead man. His eyes were fixed on the spot where the archer had been, his muscles still tensed, waiting for the next arrow to slash from the shadows. He was fast—faster than these men, certainly—but a shaft fired from a longbow could still strike down a Pathfinder if they were caught unawares. He was not immortal.

He was a few yards from the treeline when the attack came. There was a *hiss* as the arrow flashed for his face, but Jaxon twisted at the last moment and it missed—just. Apparently expecting this, the bandit followed, exploding from the bushes with a sabre now in hand, the blade already raised to strike. With anyone else, the speed of his attack might have succeeded.

As it was, Jaxon was caught in a poor position, unable to bring his sword around in time to deflect the blow. Instead, he surged forward, hand snapping out to catch the bandit by his sword arm. Shock registered in the man's eyes, a second before Jaxon delivered a crunching headbutt to his face. The blow staggered him and the sabre slipped from his fingers. In one fluid movement, Jaxon swept the blade from the air, reversed it, and drove it through his enemy's throat.

The man dropped without a sound. Jaxon let the sabre fall alongside him. A quick sweep of his *Aura Sense* into the forest confirmed there were no others. These two had clearly been left to ambush anyone that followed, while the rest of the raiders made their escape. Sheathing his sword, Jaxon entered the trees.

Shadows swallowed him up, though the senses of his *Enforced Body* had little trouble piercing the gloom. Not that tracking this quarry was a particularly odious task. A blind man could have picked up the trail of torn earth and broken branches they'd left behind.

Still, aware that he'd lost ground in the ambush, Jaxon settled into an easy jog. The pursuit continued, as he occasionally extended his *Aura Sense* to check for his prey. Each time he did, he felt more of his enemy, and more of their prisoners. Slowly he built a picture of his quarry. Until finally, he knew without doubt the power he was sensing was not Maisiwan or Isabel.

The raiders had a Pathfinder of their own. And this was no Copper or Iron ranker. They weren't even Steel. A Bronze rank aura pulsed through the forest, twisted and broken, reflecting a soul as dark as any Jaxon had crossed in his fifty three years.

Grimacing, he decided it was time for haste. He would need to take the Bronze ranker unawares, cutting him down before the other raiders could join the fight.

Jaxon had just started to run when a fresh surge of energy crackled through the forest. He froze, his gaze sweeping the undergrowth. It was a moment before he realised the source of the disturbance was not even close.

What in the name of the Satana was that? Every nerve in his body was tingling like he'd been struck by an electrical mana attack.

Hesitantly, he reached out again with his *Aura Sense*. There was a disturbance in the land. That much was clear. The little creatures of the forest were gone, fleeing the source of the awakened power. Even the *trees* seemed to have quieted, their aura becoming flat and muted. The land was silent.

For the first time since setting off from the village, fear touched Jaxon Daniyal.

CHAPTER 4

BJORN'S GOOD MOOD EVAPORATED ENTIRELY AS HE APPROACHED the hideout. He was panting only slightly despite the three-mile dash through the forest, but even that was surprising for someone as strong as him. It was this cursed land. Unseen roots tripped him as he ran and thorny branches had lashed and torn at his flesh. His fine silk tunic was entirely ruined. He didn't remember the trail being so harsh on the way down. Why had he chosen a cave so far from the damn village?

Over-vigilance. It was his greatest flaw. He had not wanted them to be discovered by the savages that roamed these mountains. He was regretting it now. Gods, he hated this forest. And those looming peaks above. First thing he would do after the slave markets would be to move the camp.

He paused before the treeline, waiting for the rest of his men to catch up. Even though he'd moved at a slower pace for his own *Enforced Body*, some had fallen behind. He eyed the stragglers. Weakness. How he loathed it. Long ago, on the day his father died, Bjorn had sworn himself a vow. That he would never bow to the weak.

Not like his father.

How he'd loathed the man! John Tally. Even his name had been weak. Built like a bull, he'd spent his days labouring in the mud of his farm, struggling to etch a living from the barren soils. And for what? So the merchant guilds could swindle him out of half his earnings, while the taxmen took the rest. By the Elohim, the man lacked a spine! He could have picked up those snivelling tax collectors and snapped them like twigs. Instead, he'd begged them for time, pleaded for leniency.

He hadn't even fought when Bjorn's mother up and vanished one cold spring night, taking all the man's savings with her. No, instead the weak bastard had sobbed for a week, then went back to work tilling the soils. As though she had not ruined them!

Bjorn cared little about the woman herself. She had been cold and distant his entire life. He just wished he'd had the idea himself, instead of enduring with his father in the endless slog of the farm.

Thankfully, fate had intervened to free Bjorn from his own stupidity. He should have walked away long before then, of course, but for some reason he had faltered whenever he thought to leave. That had been so long ago now, he hardly remembered why. Fear? Nah. Even as a youth, Bjorn had feared nothing!

He certainly had not feared the Wargwolf that found them in the field that day. Ah, the memory of his father's terror still brought a smile to Bjorn's face. Monstrous entities like Warg-wolves were not uncommon in the Empire. Commoners were told to report them to the local sergeant, who would then send out a regiment to deal with the threat.

Of course, that assumed the commoner first survived the encounter. And that day, well, there had been little time to think as the creature stalked from the trees.

A terrible beast it had been. On all fours it was taller than most men. Talons pawed at the earth, making light work of the tilling the pair had taken hours to complete. Huge jaws stretched wide as it let out a roar. To this day, Bjorn could recall the tremor that had ran down his spine at the sight. Not of fear, of course. Just, something else.

Then his father had spoken. "Stay calm, son. Withdraw slowly. Do not turn your back."

The words cut through Bjorn's thoughts like a sickle. How they had enraged him! Here they were, facing certain death, and rather than stand like men and fight, John Tally wanted to run.

Bjorn had known then what he must do.

"It has already seen us, Father," he said calmly, even as the beast took another padding step towards them.

"It's okay, son. We're going to get out of this."

"I know, Father," he had replied. "I have a plan."

Fearful eyes had turned to him then, and Bjorn had seen the spark of hope in their crystal depths. "What is it, son?"

"I'm going to run."

"We'll never outrun it—"

Steel flashed as Bjorn swung the plough he had been using to turn the dirt. His father did not move, though Bjorn thought he saw the understanding dawn in the man's eyes. There was a sharp *crack* of breaking bone, followed by a *thump* as his father collapsed. The Wargwolf's head snapped around as a scream tore from his father's throat.

"I don't have to outrun the beast," Bjorn sneered, even as the beast stalked towards them, drawn by his father's screams and the scent of fresh blood. "I just have to outrun you."

Then he had retreated, leaving his father writhing in pain on the hard, unyielding ground as the nightmarish creature stalked towards him.

Ah, what a day that had been.

That was the day Bjorn Cresswell had been born, when he had learned that strong men took what they wanted and cared not for what the weak desired. The weak were dispensable.

Speaking of which, he scowled as the last of his men stumbled into view, the prisoners shepherded between them. The two women had handled the journey better than half his men, who were red-faced as they drew up around Bjorn. The other prisoners brought up the rear, bruised and puffing from struggle through the forest with their hands bound.

Unwilling to delay any longer, Bjorn turned and marched through the trees. He could still sense the trembling of energies from ahead, though he was no closer to identifying their source. Another Pathfinder kicking around his lair was the most likely explanation. But this power felt different. And it was already fading, though it still seemed to originate inside his cave.

Ahead, the trees gave way to the broken ground leading up to their hideout. Bjorn grimaced. It was no palace, though that would come. It was said that a man with a pound of gold could live like a king on some of the recently acquired land in Ressi. Only a year had passed since the war with the rogue kingdom had officially ended, and fresh capital was required to invest in the new province.

Bjorn chuckled. Maybe he would ask Marcs for tips. A mansion on the coast of Ressi, far from the Gurrian capital and those who might recognise him, a man couldn't hope for much better. Perhaps after a few more raids like today…

…but those dreams were for the future. Today, there was the small problem of the rat who dared tread in his territory.

A slope dotted by boulders led up to the mouth of the cave. The perfect killing ground should their lair ever come under attack. A cold breeze blew across the clearing, setting the knee-high grass to swaying. A faint trail led up to a shadow in the cliffs that was their secret hideout.

And there, seated calm as day on a boulder outside, was a man.

Bjorn cast out his *Aura Sense* to take a measure of the intruder. The last pulses of the earlier power had subsided and when his senses brushed against the man, he felt…nothing. No aura of a Pathfinder. No sharp force pushing back. Not even a flicker. As far as Bjorn could tell, the man was entirely normal.

And yet there he sat, alone with a smile on his face, looking down at them as a king would his subjects. His only weapon was a simple hatchet, which, as Bjorn and his men watched, he calmly began to sharpen with a whetstone.

"So the bandits return." His voice carried down to them, absent of fear. There was a strange twang to his accent, one Bjorn did not recognise. With his bronzed complexion, he was no clansman. Putting aside the whetstone, the stranger tested his thumb against the edge. Apparently satisfied, he hefted the axe and rose. Golden eyes picked out Bjorn from amongst the Cursed Sons and their prisoners. "I take it you have come to surrender?"

There was a moment's silence.

Bjorn should have laughed at the man's arrogance, should have marched up the hill and cut his head from his shoulders. But something in the stranger's tone caused him to hesitate. Something in those golden eyes. What in the blazes was he hiding?

The quiet in the clearing broke as men began to murmur and cast glances in his direction. Bjorn ground his teeth, acutely aware he tred on dangerous ground. He could not afford to show weakness. But neither could he go recklessly charging at this unknown man on the hillside. He cast his gaze over the intruder anew, seeking some hint of his true power.

Nothing about his appearance suggested a threat. His arms were thin, his shoulders wiry and narrow, as though unused to physical toil. Even the way he gripped the axe seemed slightly off, his hands positioned too wide to deliver any power behind a blow. Bjorn would have guessed him a bookkeeper or merchant if he'd glimpsed the man in the street.

But no bookkeeper would dare to stand there and threaten the mighty Bjorn Cresswell.

His mind raced. There were Pathfinders who dedicated years of their life to mastery of the soul. It was said they could conceal their aura from even the most powerful of *Aura Senses*. This must be such an adept. Caution was warranted.

"I am Bjorn Cresswell, Scrouge of the Empire, King of the Crossroads. Women tremble in fear when they hear my name—"

"I bet, a face like that?" On the hillside, the man chuckled as he swung his axe back and forth like a club. "Did your mother drop you on your head when you were a baby? Or was she just as ugly as you?"

"Why, you little sh—" Bjorn snarled as he drew his sword.

"Ah, ah, ah!"

Bjorn froze as the stranger's axe suddenly swung in his direction. Despite the distance, he tensed, expecting some manner of mana-based attack. Instead, his foe only flashed that same maddening smile.

"Atta boy." He gestured with the axe at the trees. "Now, as you've probably surmised, I have you and your men surrounded. So if you don't want to be…" There was a pause, as though the stranger was searching for a word. "…skewered with arrows, then I suggest you go ahead and release the prisoners you've got there. Looks as though they can't wait to get away from you. Probably the body odour. Seriously, did no one ever teach you boys how to bathe?"

Bjorn blinked. It took a few moments for him to piece together the words through the strange accent. His hands tightened around the hilt of his sword until the leather grip creaked. Blood pounded in his temples as he glowered at the man. It took every inch of Bjorn's control not to hurl himself up the slope and hack the man to pieces, Pathfinder or no.

Instead, his gaze shifted to the trees. Archers? He tried to cast his *Aura Sense* through the forest, but such was his rage he struggled to detect anything but the pounding of blood in his temples. A snarl rumbled from his throat as he turned back to his foe. He stood there casually, axe leaning against his shoulder, as though he had not a care in the world.

"Bjorn," Lunden Marcs spoke beneath his breath from where he stood nearby. "Maybe we should do as he says."

Coward. Bjorn should have taken his head weeks ago. It would have to wait now, though. Ignoring the Ressian man, he kept his eyes fixed to his foe.

"Who are you?"

"My name is Mikael Heaton."

"Why are you here?"

"A man of your repute, Bjorn, I think you know."

Bjorn pursed his lips. "The governor sent you to hunt me down." His eyes flickered to the trees. How many would there be? With his reputation, it could be as much as a full Force of eighty men. "Should have known the bastard would come after me and my gold." He laughed then, and his mirth thundered from the cliffs. "Too bad I've hidden it where you'll never find it—"

"What, you mean this gold?" The stranger kicked the pack that lay at his side, which toppled over with a clang of metal. Sunlight reflected off the coins that spilled from the top. "Took me all of two minutes to find it. You need to work on your hide-and-seek skills."

Bjorn ignored the gibe, unable to tear his eyes from the sack. Years of toil and hard work, of bloody battle and careful secreting away of the riches they took. His hands began to shake.

"So you see," the stranger was saying, "you have no leverage here, my friend…hey, what are you doing?"

The words were barely audible above the pounding of Bjorn's rage. His vision flickered from yellow to red. He could feel his *Movement Surge* ability within, screaming to be unleashed. It was the first ability he had earned, that day he had struck down his father and left him to the Wargwolf's mercy…

"…I told you, stay where you are…"

Other voices rose above that of his foe. Lunden Marcs and the others, begging him to stop. Cowards, all of them. With his *Movement Surge*, he could be upon the arrogant fool in a heartbeat. He would cut the man's head from his shoulders. Then they would see how brave the archers in the trees proved.

"…last warning, stay back…that's it, men, *fire!*" the man screamed.

Bjorn tensed, energy crackling as he activated his *Movement Surge* and spun, ready to pluck the bolt from the air. But no arrows slashed for his throat, nor for any of his men. In fact, not a single shaft was loosed.

"What the…"

A crunching of stones came from above. He turned to find the man bolting across the hillside, arms pumping, boots scrambling for purchase. He was…fleeing? What in the name of the Elohim? Bjorn stared in bewilderment after his foe, struggling to process what he was seeing.

Until he noticed the pack slung across the man's back.

The pack that contained his gold.

There was no hesitation this time, no need to use his abilities. Fiery anger burned in Bjorn's chest, propelling him after his prey. For he knew now this was not a Pathfinder, but a cowardly trickster, a thief who sought to take from Bjorn his hard-earned riches.

Despite the man's head start, he closed the distance between them in a handful of strides. The thief must have heard Bjorn's approach, for at the last moment he spun and swung the hatchet.

Bjorn batted it aside like a cat would a mouse that had crept into its house.

He loomed over the thief, enjoying the look of terror in the golden eyes now, the way he cowered.

A terrible grin crossed his lips. "What was that you were saying about my mother?"

READ on in <u>Darkstrider</u>

ALSO BY AARON HODGES

The Sword of Light

Book 1: Stormwielder

Book 2: Firestorm

Book 3: Soul Blade

The Legend of the Gods

Book 1: Oathbreaker

Book 2: Shield of Winter

Book 3: Dawn of War

The Knights of Alana

Book 1: Daughter of Fate

Book 2: Queen of Vengeance

Book 3: Crown of Chaos

The Evolution Gene

Book 1: Reborn

Book 2: Havoc

Book 3: Carnage

Descendants of the Fall

Book 1: Warbringer

Book 2: Wrath of the Forgotten

Book 3: Age of Gods

Book 4: Dreams of Fury

The Alfurian Chronicles

Book 1: Defiant

Book 2: Guardian

Book 3: Conquest

The Swords of Heaven and Hell

Book 1: Darkstrider

The Four Circles

Book 1: Help! My Wizard Mentor Had A Heart Attack And Now I'm
Being Chased By A Horde Of Giant Spiders!

The Untamed Isles

The Path Awakens